FATAL FLAW

ALSO BY WILLIAM LASHNER

Veritas
Hostile Witness

FATAL FLAW

William Lashner

wm

WILLIAM MORROW

An Imprint of HarperCollins*Publishers*

This is a work of fiction. The characters, incidents, and dialogues are products of the author's imagination and are not to be construed as real. Any resemblance to actual persons, living or dead, is entirely coincidental.

Grateful acknowledgment is made for permission to reprint the following copyrighted materials:

Brief excerpts from "Totem," "Lady Lazarus," "Ariel," and "Daddy" from *The Collected Poems of Sylvia Plath*, edited by Ted Hughes, copyright © 1960, 1965, 1971, 1981 by the Estate of Sylvia Plath. Editorial material copyright © 1981 by Ted Hughes. Reprinted by permission of HarperCollins Publishers Inc.

HarperCollins books may be purchased for educational, business, or sales promotional use. For information please write: Special Markets Department, HarperCollins Publishers Inc., 10 East 53rd Street, New York, NY 10022.

FIRST EDITION

Designed by Jo Anne Metsch

Printed on acid-free paper

Library of Congress Cataloging-in-Publication Data
Lashner, William.
Fatal flaw / William Lashner.— 1st ed.
p. cm.
ISBN 0-06-050816-7 (acid-free paper)
1. Trials (Murder)—Fiction. 2. Philadelphia (Pa.)—
Fiction. I. Title.
PS3562.A75249 F38 2003
813'.54—dc21   2002067158

03 04 05 06 07 JTC/RRD 10 9 8 7 6 5 4 3 2 1

For my mother

PART ONE

OF
BLOOD
AND
JASMINE

GUY FORREST was sitting on the cement steps outside the house when I arrived. His head was hidden in his hands. Rain fell in streams from his shoulders, his knees, tumbled off the roof of his brow. He was slumped naked in the rain, and beside his feet lay the gun.

From his nakedness and the diagonal despair of his posture, I suspected the worst.

"What did you do?" I shouted at him over the thrumming rain.

He didn't answer, he didn't move.

I prodded him with my foot. He collapsed onto his side.

"Guy, you bastard. What the hell did you do?"

His voice rose from the tangled limbs like the whimperings of a beaten dog. "I loved her. I loved her. I loved her."

Then I no longer suspected, then I knew.

I leaned over and lifted the gun by the trigger guard. No telling what more damage he could do with it. Careful to leave no prints, I placed it in my outside raincoat pocket. The door to the house was thrown open. I slipped around his heaving body and stepped inside.

Later on, in the press, the house would be described as a Main Line love nest, but that raises images of a Stanford White–inspired palace of debauchery—red silk sheets and velvet wallpaper, a satin swing hanging from the rafters—but nothing could be further from the truth. It was a modest old stone house in a crowded Philadelphia suburb, just over City Line Avenue. The walls were bare, the furnishings sparse. A cheap table stood in the dining room to the left of the entrance, a television lay quiet before a threadbare couch in the living room to the right. There was a Jacuzzi in the bathroom, true, but in the furnishings there was a sense of biding time, of making do until real life with real furniture began. In the bedroom, up the stairs, I knew there to be a single bureau bought at some discount build-it-yourself place, a desk with stacks of bills, a fold-up chair, a mattress on the floor.

A mattress on the floor.

Well, maybe the press had it right after all, maybe it was a love nest, and maybe the mattress on the floor was the giveaway. For what would true lovers need with fine furnishings and fancy wallpaper? What would true lovers need with upholstered divans, with Klimts on the wall, with a grand piano in the formal living room? What would true lovers need with a hand-carved mahogany bed supporting a canopy of blue silk hanging over all like the surface of the heavens? Such luxury is only for those needing more in their lives than love. True lovers would require only a mattress on the floor to cast their spells one upon the other and enjoin the world to slip away. Until the world refused.

The mattress on the floor. That's where I would find her.

Rain dripped off my coat like tears as I climbed the stairway. My hand crept along the smooth banister. Around the landing, up another half flight. As I rose ever closer, my step slowed. A complex scent pressed itself upon me like a smothering pillow. I could detect the sharpness of cordite and something sweet beneath that, a memory scent from my college days touched now with jasmine, and then something else, something lower than the cordite and the sweetness, something coppery and sour, something desolate. A few steps higher and then to the left, to the master bedroom.

The door was open, the bedroom light was on, the mattress on the floor was visible from the hallway outside. And on it she lay, her frail, pale body twisted strangely among the clotted sheets.

There was no need to check a pulse or place a mirror over her mouth. I had seen dead before and she qualified. Her legs were covered by the dark blue comforter, but it was pulled down far enough to reveal her cream silk teddy, shamelessly raised above her naked belly. Crimson spotted the blanched white of her skin. The teddy was stained red at the heart.

I stood there for longer than I now can remember. The sight of her unnatural posture, the colliding scents of gunpowder and pot, of blood and jasmine, the brutal mark of violence on her chest, all of it, the very configuration of her death overwhelmed me. I was lost in the vision, swallowed whole by time. I can't tell you exactly what was flailing through my mind because it is lost to me now, just as I was lost to the moment, but when I recovered enough to function a decision had been made. A decision had been made. I'm not sure how, but I know why, I surely know why. A decision had been made, a decision I have never regretted, an implacable decision, yet pure and right, a decision had been made, and for the rest of my involvement in that death and its grisly aftermath that decision guided my every step, my every step, starting with the first.

I took a deep breath and entered the bedroom. I squatted, leaned over the mattress, touched her jaw. It was still slightly warm, but the joint now was not perfectly slack. The skin at the bottom of her arm had turned a purplish red. I pressed a finger into the skin; it whitened for an instant before the color returned. It had been about an hour, I calculated. Still squatting, I leaned farther forward and stared closely at her face.

Her name was Hailey Prouix. Black hair, blue eyes, long-necked and pale-skinned, she was thirty years old and lovely as a siren. While still alive she had peered out at the world with a wary detachment. She had seen too much to take anything at face value, her manner said as clear as words, she had been hurt too much to expect anything other than blows. She wore sharp, dark-rimmed glasses that were all business, but her mouth curved so achingly you couldn't look at it without wanting to take it in your own. And her stare, her stare, containing as it did both warning and dare, could weaken knees.

To gaze at Hailey Prouix was to have your throat tighten with the wanting, and not just sexual wanting, though that of course was part of it, but something else, something even more powerful. There is inevitably, I suppose, a gap between all we ever wanted and all we ever will have, and that gap can be a source of bitter regret. But sometimes there is a glimpse of hope that the gap might be narrowed, might even be obliterated by one brilliant leap. In Hailey Prouix's detached beauty, and the silent dare to break through her barriers, there was a glimpse of that hope. That her detachment might prove absolute and her barriers inexorable was no matter. To take her and hold her, to squeeze her arms, to kiss her, to win her and make her yours seemed to offer a chance to conquer life itself. Oh, yes, she was as lovely as a siren, and like a siren, she had drawn Guy Forrest from his wife and two children, from his high-powered lawyer's job, from his finely appointed mini-mansion deep in the suburbs, onto the mattress on the floor of her small stone house just over the city line. And now, I suppose, as was inevitable from the first, he had crashed upon the shoals.

Before I pulled away from the corpse, I gently took hold of the bottom edge of her teddy and tugged it down to cover the exposed dark triangle.

On a crate by the mattress, along with her glasses, an alarm clock, a lamp, and a couple of books, sat two phones, a small red cellular thing and an old-style, corded phone. If anyone saw me arrive at the house, I didn't want there to be too much of a time discrepancy between when I entered and when 911 logged the call, so I picked up the handset of the line-locked phone, dialed 911, and reported the murder. Then I went to work.

I'm a criminal lawyer. People like Guy Forrest, in the depths of the deepest troubles of their lives, call me in to clean up their messes. It is what I do, it is my calling, and I'm damn good at it. I reach my hand into the mess, rummage around, and pull out evidence. That's what I work with, evidence. I accept what evidence I must, discredit what I can, hide what I might, create what I need, and from this universe of evidence I build a story. Sometimes the story is true, more often not, but truth is never the standard. Better the credible lie than the implausible truth. The story need only be persuasive enough to clean up the mess. But I don't always win, thank God. Some messes are too big to be cleaned, some stains can never be rubbed out, some crimes call out for more than a story. And some victims deserve nothing less than the truth.

If this house had been in the city proper, I'd have had plenty of time to rummage around the crime scene and do what I needed to do. But this house wasn't in Philadelphia County, it was in Montgomery County, the suburbs. There is crime in the suburbs, sure, but of a different quality and quantity than in the city. City cops are overworked, their attentions stretched taut, not so in the suburbs. Out here a murder call trumps shoplifting at the mall. The call was already out, the cars would arrive in minutes, in seconds.

First thing I did was grab the cellular phone off the crate and dump it into my pocket. I was glad it was there in the open, it would have been the first and most crucial thing I searched for. Then I took a quick look around.

In the bathroom, soapy water still filled the Jacuzzi tub, gray and wide, with its water jets now quiet. A Sony CD Walkman and a large pair of Koss headphones sat on the rim, along with a small plastic bag of weed, a pack of papers inside. I left the Walkman and the headphones but stuffed the weed into my pocket with the gun. I didn't need the cops taking Guy in now on some drug misdemeanor—there were things he and I needed first to talk about. I took out a handkerchief, covered my hand with it, and opened the medicine cabinet. I ignored the cosmetics and over-the-counter remedies and went right to the little plastic bottles. Valium prescribed to Hailey Prouix. Seconal prescribed to Hailey Prouix. Nembutal prescribed to Hailey Prouix. The whole Marilyn Monroe attitude-adjustment kit. And then something else. Viagra prescribed to Guy Forrest.

Well, that, at least, was a cheery sight.

Back in the bedroom I started opening drawers, looking for something, anything. Not much in the bureau other than clothes, cufflinks—Guy was a fancy dresser when he was dressed—loose change, condoms. I picked up one of the foil packages. Lambskin. Fifteen bucks a sheath. It pissed me off just looking at it. Under the clothes in the middle drawer was an envelope filled with cash. New hundreds. Two thousand, three thousand. I counted it quickly and put it back.

The top drawer of the desk held stamps, pens, business cards, golf tees, loose change, nothing. One by one I checked the side drawers. File cards, batteries, Post-it notes, bent paper clips, an old driver's license, knicks and knacks, the unexceptional detritus of a now expired life. Who designed these things? Who manufactured them, sold them, bought them, kept them well beyond any useful purposes? I didn't know, all I knew was that there was some great underground industrial complex filling every desk and kitchen drawer in the world with this stuff. I picked up the license and examined it.

It was Hailey's. It had expired eighteen months ago. The picture didn't really look like her, she was scowling, her hair was flat, the glasses were less than flattering. Hailey Prouix was glamorous and cosmopolitan, this woman in this picture looked anything but. Still, I took it anyway, put it in my pocket as a keepsake.

And then, in one of the drawers, I spotted a little paper box filled with change, staples, a staple remover, paper clips, keys.

Keys.

Car keys, house keys, old file-cabinet keys. I used the handkerchief to shield my fingers as I rummaged. I was tempted to take them all, willy-nilly, there was no telling what secrets lay behind their locks, but I had to leave something for the suburban detectives. So I took only one, slipped it in with the license before closing the drawer.

As I searched, I tried not to think of the body on the bed. When I remember back, I am amazed that I could still move with such alacrity, still make snap determinations, no matter how warped. I wasn't thinking so clearly—if I had been I might have taken the money. I might have taken the condom because, well, because it was lambskin. I might have checked those file cards more closely. But even so, what I took proved to be valuable and I am stunned at my level of functioning. If it all sounds so calm and deliberate, so bloody cold-blooded, then that is only in the voice of the remembering, for I assure you my knees were shaking uncontrollably as I moved about that room, my eyes were tearing, my stomach was roiling upon itself from the scent of her blood, her perfume, the sickly sweet smell of smoked marihuana. A decision had been made, and that had calmed me some, but I was still only an inch away from vomiting all across the floor. The Forensic Science Unit technician would have been so pleased as she took her DNA samples.

But then it was time. They would be here any second, and it would be so much better for everyone if I was outside with Guy. At the head of the stairs I took one last look at Hailey Prouix, wiped at my eyes, climbed slowly down.

From the hallway closet, I removed Guy's black raincoat. He was still collapsed on the steps, naked, drenched. I gently placed the raincoat over his body and squatted beside him, like I had squatted beside Hailey. It was strangely peaceful on that suburban street, leafy and quiet except for the stutter of the dying rain and Guy's weeping. The world smelled fresh and full of spring. I stayed silent for a moment, let the rain cleanse the bitter scent from my eyes.

"Why?" I said finally, in a voice just soft enough to rise above the quiet roar of the rain.

No response. He just lay there, sobbing.

"Why did you kill her, Guy?"

Still no response.

I slapped the side of his head. "Tell me."

"I didn't," he said through his sobs. "I loved her. I gave up. Everything. For her. And now. Now."

I stayed silent, let my emotions cool.

"I gave up," he said. "Everything."

"I know you did, Guy." I reached down and petted his hair. "I know you did."

"I swear. I didn't. I didn't."

"Okay. I'll believe you for now."

"Oh, God. What? What am I? What?"

"Shhhhhh. You'll be all right, Guy. I'll do what I can. The police are going to come. They are already on the way. Do not talk to them. Do not say anything to the police until we can talk first. I'll do what I can."

"I loved her."

"I know."

"Victor. God. I loved her. So much."

"I know you did, Guy. I know you did. That was the problem."

I was still petting his hair when came the cars with their sirens and their flashing lights, and the three of us, Guy and Hailey and I, were no longer alone.

GUY FORREST was sitting now at the dining room table, his head in his hands. A cop had brought down some clothes for him, and rain was no longer streaming from the angles of his body, but his head was still in his hands. His head was in his hands and his lower jaw was trembling, as if struggling to say something, anything. But I maintained a hand on his shoulder and made sure he kept it all to himself. That's what defense attorneys do. We're there to make sure our clients don't do anything stupid after they've done something worse than stupid.

With my hand on his shoulder, Guy wasn't talking, and maybe he wasn't thinking either. Maybe he couldn't acknowledge the realities of his world now that Hailey Prouix was dead. Love can do that to you. It can send you soaring higher than falcons, it can rip you open from your sternum to your spleen, it can send you running. That's what Guy was doing now, at the dining room table with his head in hands and his jaw trembling. I wouldn't let him do anything stupid like talk to the cops, so instead, in his mind, he was running, but he wasn't going to get very far.

He was a handsome man, Guy Forrest, wavy dark hair, swarthy good looks, a five o'clock shadow that emphasized his classic bone structure. He worked out regularly, always had, even when we were law students together, but even so, there was something weak about him. His chin was too sharp, his gaze too wavering. Looking at Guy, you had the sense you were looking at a Hollywood facade of what a man should look like, perfect on the outside, but one stiff breeze would blow him down. And now he had been beset by a hurricane.

It had grown crowded in and about that little house. Someone upstairs was taking pictures. Someone upstairs was dusting for fingerprints and swabbing for blood. Someone outside in the rain was examining the windows and flower beds for signs of forced entry. Someone in the neighborhood was going door to door, asking questions. Television vans, alerted by the scanner, were on the street in force. The noose was already tightening around Guy Forrest's neck, and there was precious little I could do about it.

The coroner's van sat on the street by the house's front entrance, its motor running, its lights flashing. The attendants were in the front seat reading the *Daily News,* drinking coffee, waiting for the okay to take the body away. We were in the dining room, drinking nothing, but also waiting to be allowed to leave. I had already given as much information about Hailey Prouix's next of kin as I could extract from Guy, the name of and an address for her sister, and had packed for Guy a small gym bag with a change of clothes. Twice I had tried to exit the house with him, twice I had been politely ordered to remain until Guy could speak to the detectives. Except Guy wouldn't be speaking to the detectives.

"Mr. Carl, is it?" said a tall, good-looking young woman in jacket and pants who entered the room. Her hair was cut short, her nose freckled. With her broad shoulders and confident smirk, she carried the athletic air of a field-hockey coach and referred to her notepad as if it were a playbook.

"That's right," I said.

"And Mr. Forrest?"

Guy raised his head, looked at the woman, said nothing. His eyes were impressively red-rimmed, the eyes of the seriously bereaved. Or, considering what I had found in the bathroom, maybe the eyes of someone who was about to ask you to bust open another sack of Doritos, dude.

"As you can understand," I said, "it's been a very difficult evening for us all."

"Of course," said the young woman. "I'm County Detective Stone. With me is County Detective Breger."

She gestured at the man standing behind her, whose attention was turned away from us as he examined the edges of the dining room carpet. He was a good three decades older than she, with a sad face and plaid jacket. His shoulders were thick and rounded, his posture slumped, he was a great hunch of a man. There was something soft about Breger, something tired, as if he had grown comfortable in a routine that was being shattered by his younger, more enthusiastic partner.

"I am sorry for your loss, Mr. Forrest," said Detective Breger even as he continued his inspection of the room. "I have been doing this now for thirty-six years, and it is still a tough thing to see."

Guy tried to get a thank-you past his quivering jaw and failed.

"Miss Prouix was what to you, Mr. Forrest?" asked Stone. "Your girlfriend?"

"His fiancée," I said.

"Fiancée?" said Breger. "Oh, hell. That is a tough one. When was the wedding supposed to be?"

"As soon as Mr. Forrest's divorce came through," I said.

Stone shot me a look. "Mr. Carl, you're a friend? An adviser? What?"

"I am a friend of Mr. Forrest's, but I am also a lawyer. Mr. Forrest called me when he found Miss Prouix on the bed."

"So you're here now as what?"

"A friend," I said. "But a friend who knows that when a man is in shock over the death of a loved one, maybe it's not the best time to be talking to the police."

"It is if the goal is to get the bastard who did this before the trail grows cold. We have questions for Mr. Forrest."

"I don't think he'd be much help in his current condition."

"Seems to me you're acting more like a lawyer than a friend."

"For the moment, yes, that's how I'm going to handle it."

"Is that what he wants?" said Stone, nodding her head at Guy.

"That's what he wants."

"What about our questions?"

"I'll answer what I can," I said.

Stone looked at Breger, Breger shrugged. This is normally when the cops get angry and indignant, this is normally when it all turns adversarial. This is when Stone starts threatening and Breger holds her back and the whole madcap mad-cop routine plays itself out. I knew it was coming, anxious as I was to get Guy out of that house I was steeled for the onslaught of police craft, but instead of putting on a snarl, Stone smiled. "We appreciate your help. Having you here to assist us will make things easier. At some point we will need to ask Mr. Forrest some questions."

"Mr. Forrest is still in something of a daze. Could your questioning of him wait until tomorrow?"

"If that's what you think best," said Breger, his gaze now scanning the ceiling.

"I do."

"Of course you do," said Breger. "Mr. Forrest is going through an ordeal. His fiancée is dead in their bed, a bullet wound in her chest. Any of us would be in shock. You want him to be able to pull himself together before he speaks to us."

"How's tomorrow morning?" said Stone as she handed me her card.

"I think that would be all right. I'll let you know in the morning if his condition makes it impossible. I was going to take Mr. Forrest to my apartment for the night."

"Good idea," said Breger, who had stepped over to a window and was closely examining the sill. "Mr. Forrest looks like he could use a stiff drink or two."

"He knows not to leave the area," said Stone.

"I'll make sure of it. I'll bring him to you myself tomorrow morning."

"Along with his new attorney," said Stone.

Stone smiled at me. I smiled back. This was something completely new. They were playing good-cop, good-cop. I supposed that's how they did it in the suburbs.

"So now," I said, "if we could be excused, I'd like to let Mr. Forrest get some sleep."

"If it is any consolation, Mr. Forrest," said Breger, looking straight at Guy now, "we are going to do our best to get the bastard who did this. We will put all our resources into digging out the truth and, believe us, dig it out we will. We will not rest until the killer is found and tried and convicted. We will not rest until the killer is rotting away in the penitentiary. I want you to know that, Mr. Forrest, and I hope it gives you some comfort."

"Yes, well, thank you for that, Detective Breger," I said. "Now, if we could be excused."

"Can you just give us a moment, Mr. Carl?" said Stone.

The two detectives stepped out of the dining room. I patted Guy on the shoulder and followed.

"Can you tell us what you know?" said Stone, who was taking the lead in the questioning while Breger examined some paperwork.

"I was home, sleeping through the baseball game, when Guy called."

"What did he say?"

"I can't tell you. Depending on the circumstances, it might be a privileged communication."

"You mean if he was calling you as a lawyer," said Breger, "instead of as a friend."

"That's right. But he didn't say much. He wasn't really coherent. He sounded out of his head, confused."

"Stoned?"

"With grief, maybe. I didn't know what to do. I told him to stay calm, that I'd be right over."

"What number did he call?"

"My home number." I gave it to them. "When I arrived, he was sitting on the steps waiting for me."

"In the rain?"

"Yes. Sobbing. And he was naked. I ran upstairs and found her on the mattress. I used the upstairs phone to call 911. Then I took a black raincoat from the hall closet, went back out with Guy, covered him as best I could. I waited out there with him."

"When you were up in the room, did you see a gun or shells or anything?"

"No."

"Did you smell anything, anything funny?"

"Other than the gunpowder and the smell of the blood? No."

"It must have been a shock for him to see her dead like that," said Breger.

"I suppose so."

"Why, then, do you think he called a lawyer?" asked Breger, his head still in the file. "Of all the people he could call when he saw what he saw, why do you think he called a lawyer? I don't think I would call a lawyer. A doctor, the police, my mother maybe, but not a lawyer."

"He burned a lot of bridges when he left his family and his job to move in with Hailey. We had stayed in contact. He had introduced me to Hailey months ago. Maybe there was no one else for him to call."

"You say Guy left his wife for her?" asked Stone. "What is the wife's name?"

"Leila," I said. "Leila Forrest. They weren't yet divorced."

"Do you have an address?"

I gave it to her.

"That's Berwyn."

"Yes it is."

"Nice place, Berwyn. Any idea who might have wanted to kill Ms. Prouix other than this Leila Forrest?"

"I never said Leila wanted to kill her. And I don't know of anyone else."

"What was she like, the victim?"

"I don't know, Hailey was . . . special. Sweet, in her own way. Pretty. A nice girl. This thing is just tragic."

"Any problems between Mr. Forrest and Ms. Prouix?"

"They were in love, madly in love. Sick in love. Anything else?"

"You want to get him out of here, don't you?" said Breger. "You want to take him someplace where the body of his fiancée isn't lying dead on a mattress upstairs."

"Exactly."

"Good idea. We'll see you and Mr. Forrest tomorrow. Is nine too early?"

"It's going to be a tough night," I said. "Let's shoot for ten."

Breger and Stone glanced at each other. Maybe it was my unfortunate choice of verb.

"Ten it is," said Stone. "You didn't by any chance have an umbrella or something?"

"No, why?"

"Thank you for your help," said Breger, his gaze back in the file. "See you tomorrow at ten."

I left the two of them huddling in quiet conversation and went back to Guy in the dining room. I spoke to him softly. I helped him stand. I helped him put on the raincoat. I took hold of his gym bag. Gripping his arm, I helped him toward the door before Detective Breger dropped his meaty hand on Guy's shoulder.

"Mr. Carl," he said, while looking not at me but at Guy, "we won't ask Mr. Forrest any questions, because you asked us not to, but could we perform one small test, just for our peace of mind?"

"I'm not sure that's such a good idea," I said.

"Just one test," said Breger. "It won't take but a minute. Just a precaution really. Shirley, come here please. Shirley is one of our best Forensic Unit technicians. Shirley, could you do what you have to do with Mr. Forrest's hands?"

"I really should get him out. Why don't we leave this for tomorrow?"

"This won't take but a minute," said Breger. "The strips are already prepared, which makes it go really quickly. And it could really help us move the investigation forward."

"Hold out your hands, Mr. Forrest," said Stone in a quiet but commanding voice that left no possibility of refusal. Guy did as he was told.

Shirley took wide strips of clear adhesive and pressed them on the back of each of Guy's hands, concentrating on the web of flesh between the thumb and the forefinger. With a flourish she ripped the strips off, one at a time, and carefully put them on a fresh backing. Then she did the same to each palm.

"What do you think?" said Breger.

"His hands seem too clean," said Shirley. "How long was he out in the rain?"

Breger turned to me and raised an eyebrow.

"Could have been twenty minutes," I said, "could have been more."

"Doubtful there would be anything left," said Shirley, "but you never know."

"Okay, thank you," said Breger. "We appreciate your cooperation, Mr. Carl. See you tomorrow."

I grabbed hold of Guy's arm and tried to rush him out of the house before they could think of some other hoop through which they wanted him to jump. We were just about to step outside when I heard Breger say, "Oh, Mr. Carl."

I stopped, breathed deep, turned.

He was bent on one knee, examining the carpet to the left of the doorway. Without looking up, he said, "It's a little nasty out there tonight. Be sure to drive carefully."

Suburban cops.

If this had been just a few blocks over, on the city side of City Line Avenue, it wouldn't have gone down with such sweet understanding. The city cops would have put Guy in custody right smack away. They would have seen him as the obvious suspect, as the only suspect, actually. And the fact that he had called a lawyer before an ambulance would have been for them absolute proof of his guilt. Next day I'd be standing next to Guy in the crummy little courtroom in the Roundhouse as he was arraigned for first-degree murder. The DA would have noted the crime was a capital one, the judge would have denied bail, and Guy would have spent the next year growing sallow in jail as he waited for his trial. And with him in jail, what good could I accomplish? With him in jail, how could I ask what I needed to ask, learn what I needed to learn?

A decision had been made and I needed Guy out of jail, even for just a few days, a few hours, to carry it through. It is why I scoured the crime scene like I did, why I took the reefer and didn't tell them about the gun. Even so, I didn't think it would be enough, even so even the greenest city cop would have taken him in. But see, we weren't on the city side of City Line Avenue, we were on the other side, the suburban side, where the police were ever helpful and ever polite. Despite the little incident with the gunpowder test, the suburban cops maintained their form and sent Guy and his lawyer off into the night with a kindly admonition to drive carefully.

"Thank you, Detective Breger," I said, feeling the weight of the gun pull down at my raincoat pocket, "you've been most kind." And I meant every word of it.

3

I CARED for him as best I could.

Like a Secret Service agent, I took for myself the blows of lights and flashes from the cameramen and photographers waiting predatorily outside the house. The reporters had already ferreted out the details of the crime, knew the name of the victim, the name of her fiancé. "Mr. Forrest, any comment about what happened to Miss Prouix?" "Mr. Forrest, who killed Hailey?" "Guy, can you tell us how you feel?" "Are you devastated?" "Show us some tears." "Why did you do it, Guy?" "Was there a stripper involved, like the other one?" "If you have nothing to hide, why won't you talk to us?" "Hey, Guy." "Yo, Guy." "Over here." I deflected their questions with a smile and a few brief words about the tragedy. I strategically kept myself between Guy and the camera lenses while pulling him to my car. Speed and silence, I had learned, were the best weapons against the media, giving them nothing of interest to show their sensation-starved audience. But then again I've always found it hard to turn down free publicity—one of the very few things money can't buy. So even as I pulled Guy to my car, I forced a smile and gave a little speech and handed out my business cards to make sure in the early editions they spelled Carl with a "C."

As I drove off, the cameras and their lights were staring at us through the car windows like alien eyes.

The rain had tapered off somewhat, now it was only spitting on the windshield as we drove through the glum night. Guy tried to tell me in the car what had happened and I wouldn't let him. I wouldn't let him. His face was green from the dashboard light as we drove past the dark, rotting porches of West Philly. I suggested he lie back in the passenger seat and close his eyes. I didn't want him to talk about it just then. The time would come that night, but not just then. I checked the rearview mirror to make sure no reporters were following and spotted nothing.

The street outside my building was dark and wet. I helped him up the stairs to my apartment and sat him on the couch. I turned the lights out except for the lamp by his head, which bathed his trembling body in a narrow cone of light. I gave him a beer. He tried again to tell me what had happened but I shushed him quiet.

I let him sit alone on the couch while I changed the sheets of my bed, the pillowcases, laid out a fresh towel for him, a new toothbrush still in its wrapping, an old pair of flannel pajamas in case he wanted to be cozy. Atop my bureau I placed the gym bag with his change of clothes.

On the table, by my bed, lay a book I had just started rereading, a potboiler to take my mind off the trials of my day. I had bought it for a buck from a street vendor. The story started with a murder, it ended with a confession, there was a cunning investigator, a lecherous old cardsharp, a prostitute with a heart of gold. I stared at the volume, the blue binding and lurid gold letters of the title. *Crime and Punishment.* The words seemed just then like a moral compulsion. I considered for a moment putting it away so as not to trouble my guest and then thought better of it, placing a bookmark in the final page before the epilogue and setting the book beside the reading lamp next to the bed. Before I left the room I switched on the lamp.

With the bedroom taken care of, I stood in the shadows and watched Guy as he finished his beer. I went to the fridge and got him another. I pulled a chair close to the couch, but not close enough to be within the cone of light, and sat down. Once more he tried to speak, and once more I wouldn't let him. The silence acted as a comforter, blanketing us both in calm. My raincoat, still wet, pocket bulging, was draped over the back of a chair. I glanced at it every so often and then looked back at my friend, my friend, as he slumped on the couch.

I cared for him as best I could and I waited until he couldn't help himself and when he started again to say something, this time I let him.

"What am I going to do?"

I didn't answer. He had a sharp voice, the words seemed to gallop out of his mouth with a certainty that turned every question rhetorical. Guy had never been one for self-doubt and it was hard for him to play the role of the confused and humbled man, even if that was exactly what he had become.

"I loved her so much," he said. "She was everything to me. What am I going to do?" The words, which could have been full of pathos coming out of another man, were now like the words of a business executive analyzing a deal that had gone south and asking his lawyer for advice.

"I don't know."

"Why? Tell me why? Why? I don't understand."

"What don't you understand, Guy?" I said, leaning forward. "She's dead. She's been murdered. And you're the one who killed her."

He looked up at me, a puzzled horror creasing his face. "I didn't. I couldn't. You're wrong. What are you thinking? Victor, no. I didn't."

"That's how it looks."

"I don't care how it looks. I didn't do it. You need to make them believe it. She's gone, my life is ruined, and I didn't do it. How can I make it right?"

"See a priest."

"I need a lawyer. You'll be my lawyer. That's what you do, isn't it? Make terrible things right again."

He stared at me for a long moment, his face straining for an expression of pained sincerity, which might have worked except for the raw fear leaking out his eyes.

I leaned back. "Not me. You need someone else. I'll recommend somebody good. Goldberg, maybe, or Howard. He's at Talbott, Kittredge, so he's expensive, but whoever you get, it's going to cost. A case like this will absolutely go to trial, and a trial is going to cost."

"I don't care. What's money? Money's not a problem."

"No?" I said, surprised and interested at the same time. Guy had left his wife and left his job and in so doing seemed to have left all his money behind.

"No. Not at all." He shook his head and a shiver ran through him. "What happened? I don't understand. Who did this to me?"

"To you?"

"Who did this?"

"You tell me."

"I don't know."

"Tell me what you do know."

"I got home from work late. Hailey was in bed already, asleep. I greeted her, tried to kiss her. She wouldn't get up. Instead she murmured something back and pulled the comforter over her, and that was it, the last we spoke. I filled the Jacuzzi, climbed in, put on the headphones, jacked the Walkman loud, turned the timer to start the jets, lay back in the tub."

"What about the reefer?"

"It was already out, so I rolled myself a joint. We used to smoke some, together. Everything was like we were kids again. I might have fallen asleep in the tub, I don't know. The music was loud, the Jacuzzi also, and I don't know if I heard anything, but I did startle awake for some reason. Maybe just something in the music. I took off the headphones, turned off the whirlpool, called out for Hailey. Nothing. I put in some more hot water, lay back, listened to the rest of the disc. When it was over, I got out, dried off, brushed my teeth. That's when I found her."

I tried not to react too strongly, tried to keep it simple, conversational. "What were you listening to?"

"A Louis Armstrong thing."

"What happened when you saw her?"

"I panicked, I went crazy. I looked around, and there, on the floor, I found the gun."

"Had you ever seen the gun before?"

"Yes. Of course. It's mine."

"Yours? Guy, what the hell were you doing with a gun?"

"You think it was easy what I did, leaving everything for Hailey? You think it just went smoothly? My wife went nuts, and her father. Her father, Jesus, he's a scary bastard, a heart of stone. There were threats, Victor, some shady private eye giving me the number. You'll never know what I went through for love, never. I was scared. I had a gun before, when I was out west, and knew how to use it. So I bought one, kept in the closet downstairs. Never touched it, never even took it to a shooting range to bone up. But when I found her dead, there it was, on the floor. I picked it up. It stank of gunpowder. I thought the guy who used it might still be in the house. I went downstairs looking for him. Nothing. I threw open the door. Nothing. I ran back upstairs and saw her there, still, and I fell apart. When I was able to crawl, I crawled to the side table, picked up the phone, and called you."

"Why me?"

"I don't know. It was the first thing I thought about. Hailey had mentioned something."

"Hailey?" I fought to keep the startle out of my voice.

"A couple days ago she had asked me a strange question. Who I would call if I was in serious trouble. I said I didn't know, hadn't really thought about it. She asked about you and I told her, yeah, Victor would be a good one to call. Aren't all your clients in trouble when they call?"

"That's right."

"So I had it in my mind to get you."

"Why not the police? Why not an ambulance?"

"She was dead, an ambulance wasn't going to help. Victor, I didn't know what I was doing. I was in trouble and I called you. You were the only one I could count on, the only who would understand."

I stared at him.

"You're all I have left."

If I was all Guy had left, he was totally bereft.

"Okay," I said. "That's enough. I don't want to hear any more. Why don't we go to bed, get some rest. Tomorrow we'll get you an attorney, and together you'll figure out what to tell the police. I set you up with a towel and new sheets."

"I'll sleep on the couch."

"No, you need your sleep. I'll stay out here."

"Victor, how much trouble am I really in?"

"More than you could imagine."

"It's hard to believe it could be worse than I imagine." Pause. "Hailey's gone. And I didn't do anything. It's not fair."

"Fairness has nothing to do with it. They found her murdered on your shared bed. From what I could tell, there were no signs of forced entry. They'll check fingerprints, but my guess is they'll discover yours and Hailey's, that's it. By now they've found the money in the bureau, so they'll rule out robbery. And then they'll dig into your lives and find a motive. Had you been fighting?"

"No. God, no, we were in love."

"No trouble in the relationship?"

He looked away as he said no.

"They'll find a motive, Guy. There's always a motive between a man and a woman: jealousy, passion, heat-of-the-moment anger. It doesn't take much to convince a jury that one lover killed another. How were you and Hailey really?"

"Fine. Great."

"Tell me the truth."

"We were great."

"Was there anyone else?"

"No. I had given up everything for her. We had been planning our future together just the other night. We were going to Costa Rica for two weeks. Why would I screw around with anyone else? Everything was rosy."

I stared at him. He stared back.

"Rosy," I said.

"That's right. And then this nightmare. That's what it is, a nightmare. And it's only just beginning, isn't it? Jesus."

"Let's get some sleep."

"What am I going to say to them tomorrow?"

"You're either going to tell the truth or you're going to say nothing. Those are the options."

"Which one am I going to follow?"

"It's not up to me," I said. "We'll get you a lawyer tomorrow, and the two of you will figure it out."

I helped him up off the couch, took him into the bedroom.

"Thanks, Victor," he said as I stood in the doorway. "Thanks for everything."

I nodded and closed the bedroom door behind me. Then I sat in the living room, outside the cone of light, and waited. The toilet flushed, the faucet turned on and off, the toothbrush scrubbed, the faucet turned on and off once again. I wondered if he would glance at the page in the novel I had left marked for him, but the light under the crack disappeared too quickly for that. I waited a while longer and then, when I heard no sound for a quarter of an hour, I stood and went to my raincoat, still hanging over the chair.

I took out the portable phone, the expired license, and the key and placed them in a kitchen drawer. I took out the marihuana and ran it, wad by wad, through the garbage disposal until there was nothing left of it. Then, with my handkerchief, I lifted the gun out of the raincoat pocket.

I lifted the gun out of the raincoat pocket.

The gun.

I took it to the kitchen, wiped the trigger guard where my fingers had touched it when I picked it off the step, and dropped it into a plastic sandwich bag.

It was a revolver, thick and silvery, a King Cobra .357 Magnum, so said the markings on the barrel. It felt heavy, solid. It felt just then like a serious instrument of justice. Even in its plastic sheath it was a comfort in my hand.

I brought the bagged gun with me back to the couch. I turned off the light, lay down with my head on the armrest, placed the gun on my lap. I had never much liked guns before, never even wanted to fire one, but, I had to admit, it gave one options. I lay down on my couch with the gun and tried to figure what to do about my old friend Guy Forrest. What to do about Guy. Because, you see, I had listened very carefully to everything he had to say about Hailey Prouix and her murder, listened to his whole sad story, and, at the end, I knew, beyond a reasonable doubt, beyond any doubt at all, that dear old Guy was lying.

GUY FORREST and I attended law school together. Two kids from poor, dysfunctional families looking to reinvent themselves, we took to each other right away. I used to crack wise to him about everyone else in the class, laughing at all their elevated aspirations even when my aspirations were just as inflated, only more so, and he would smile tolerantly. I was in law school because I saw it as a way to make some real money in the future, something that had always been denied my father. Guy saw it as a lifeline out of a misspent youth. Through college and beyond he had lived wild; drugs, women, a scam out west that had gone bad, the details of which he never quite laid out for me but which had left him with a tattooed skull on his left breast and a crushing desire to go straighter than straight. To that end he strangled his wild inclinations with a grim seriousness that he thought appropriate for his new profession and never let go of his grip.

Guy worked harder than I did, he had a true grinder's mentality—we all made outlines; he outlined his outlines—but I was the sharper student. In our first year, when they try to teach you a new way to think, I adapted pretty quickly, but Guy had troubles. He found it impossible to pull out the crucial differences in fact patterns that distinguished one case from another. Something in the way his brain worked made it difficult for him to prioritize. I think one reason Guy hung with me was that I could see order in what to him was a blizzard of meaninglessness. I hung with Guy because, in the bars where the law students scarfed wings and sucked beers, he was a chick magnet and I hoped to the catch the runoff.

Guy actually ended with better grades than mine, hard work does pay, but neither of us did well enough to guarantee our careers. At Harvard, middling grades will get you a freshly minted job at some hotshot Wall Street firm. Where we went to law school, middling grades leave you scrambling to find any kind of work. I applied to the best firms in the city, was rejected by each and every one, and was forced to hang my own shingle. I asked Guy if he wanted in on my fledgling enterprise but he turned me down, so I partnered instead with a sharp night-school graduate in a similar predicament, Beth Derringer. Guy was determined to find a respectable job, and he did, at a nasty little sweatshop called Dawson, Cricket and Peale.

Dawson, Cricket was one of the defense factories that burned out scores of young lawyers as it churned each year through thousands of cases representing insurance companies against a myriad of both worthy and unworthy claims. At Dawson, Cricket you were on the side of the doctor against the patient butchered by incompetence, on the side of the insurance company against the sick and the injured, on the side of money. It was not a place for lawyers with much social consciousness or joie de vivre. Up and out was their motto, and most of the young associates were sent packing after their youthful enthusiasm was torched by the brutal workloads and less-than-thrilling pay, but not Guy. The usual tenure for young lawyers at Dawson, Cricket and Peale was eighteen months; Guy stayed for eight years and was teetering on the verge of partnership. It helped that his billable hours were far and away the most at the firm. It also helped that he met, wooed, impregnated, and married Leila Peale, daughter of one of the firm's founding partners. Guy had seen what he wanted, reached out to grab hold, and there it was, seemingly within his grasp.

Then he left it all, the job, the family, the wife, the life, left it all to shack up with Hailey Prouix.

Ain't love grand?

Oh, it was love. Probably not at first sight, at first sight it was probably lust, Hailey had that effect, that mouth, the way it twitched into a smile, God, but lust surely turned into love for Guy Forrest. Lust will make a fool of any man, but it is only love that can truly ruin him.

What are we looking at when we are looking at love? Eskimos have like six billion different words for snow because they understand snow. Don't ever try to snow an Eskimo. But for six billion different permutations of emotional attachment we have just one word. Why? Because we don't have a clue.

Guy said he loved Hailey Prouix, and he did, I had no doubt, but where on the emotional matrix his particular brand of love fell, I couldn't for certain have told you. Was it selfless and devotional? Not likely. Was it platonic? Viagra, lambskin condoms, the way Hailey could turn even the most innocuous remark into something blatantly erotic, please. Was it a romantic dream, a mutual commingling of souls to last through all eternity? I guessed not. Was it a false projection of all his hopes and aspirations on a person ill equipped, no matter how lovely, to make those hopes and aspirations come true? There lay my bet. Whenever we look in our lover's eyes, we see a reflection of the person we hope to become and that, I believed, was what Guy fell in love with. It wasn't pure narcissism, the reflection in her eyes was different from the reflection in his morning mirror. The mirror showed a man trapped by the dreary burdens of a certain kind of success, Hailey showed to him all the freedom for which his soul pined. To Guy Forrest, Hailey was more than a woman, more than a lover—she was a way out.

He despised his work at Dawson, Cricket and Peale. Only his perverse desire to make partner there outweighed his hatred for the place. He was tired of his wife. She was a warm, funny woman who talked too much of too many things about which he didn't care. They seemed to be a good match on the surface, his seriousness countered by her light touch, but he had never shared her interests in literature and culture and had lost whatever sexual desire he might have felt for her from the start. Night after night, lying awake by her side as she clutched him close, he felt the trap growing ever

tighter. His house was too large and took too much work to maintain, his children were draining and unresponsive.

Most of us have those moments when nothing seems right and
we are in desperate need of a savior. Some suck it up and soldier on,
some take up painting, some take up golf, some actually make dras-
tic changes in their lives, more consult a chiropractor. But the truly
lost among us often see their savior in someone else, someone like
Hailey Prouix. When Guy gazed into Hailey's lovely blues, he saw
not a woman with her own desperate needs and complex motivations, a woman with impenetrable barriers forged in a past that
haunted her right through to her death, but instead the reflection of
a man suddenly free of the shackles he himself had forged about his
limbs, someone who could smoke reefer in the bathtub, listen to
Louis Armstrong sing "Mack the Knife," make sweaty love on a
mattress on the floor. Someone who lived like he had a tattoo of a
skull on his breast.

And Hailey Prouix, what did she see when she looked into the
dark, handsome eyes of Guy Forrest? Her soul mate? Her future?
Or a terrible, terrible mistake? I'll take door number three, Monty.

Was I guessing? Yes, of course, but not as wildly as you may
imagine. Guy confided in me during the storm of his relationship
with Hailey. We were at that age when most of our contemporaries
are either married or contemplating such and therefore not recep-
tive to the strangled yearnings of a man breaking free through infi-
delity. But I was alone, and lonely, and for some reason Guy
mistakenly thought I was vastly interested. And as for how Hailey
Prouix felt about it all, well, she had told me herself, the very afternoon before the evening of her death, told me that she and Guy
were good as through.

She is looking into a mirror, fixing her makeup, painting her lips
with the shocking red she favors. Her heels, stockings, her gray
checked skirt are all in place, but her white blouse is unbuttoned
and untucked as she stands before my mirror. I lie in the bed, arms
behind my head, and watch her left breast as it slides and bounces
ever so slightly while she works. And it is there, then, while she
stands in my bathroom and makes up her face, that she tells me she
is going to finally, unequivocally, end it with Guy.

She has told me this before and each time after has backed away for some reason she wouldn't explain, but this time I sense is different. She has been tense now for days, ever since she came back from a business trip, tense and angry and more lost than usual, but this day she bursts into my apartment as if the weight of a hundred pasts has been lifted off her shoulders, and she makes love with a joy that hasn't been there before. Ever.

She is a woman in perpetual trouble, it was obvious from the first, it is much of what draws me to her, she is a woman in perpetual trouble, but this day she seems less in trouble than before. This day there is from her the rarest of things, an unironical smile. And forgive me, but I feel as if I have helped, as if I have been a source of succor in her time of need. For weeks now I have been urging her to take control of her life. Things are not preordained, I have told her. Your life is full of choices, not imperatives, I have told her. I have given her the existentialist creed. It isn't missionary work, there isn't much missionary involved in what we do on stolen afternoons, but certainly all along I have seen a pain in her that I feel compelled to salve. She is a woman in perpetual trouble, and I want to help, and if her taking control of her life meant I would take Guy's place upon the mattress on the floor, all the better.

What are we looking at when we are looking at love? What did I see when I looked into my lover's eyes? Was I deluding myself to believe I saw Hailey Prouix clear? Was I no different from Guy, falsely projecting my hopes and aspirations upon that trim, lithe body? Guy was looking for a savior, I suppose I was looking for someone I could save. Were we, both of us, fools? I couldn't know then that the answers, brutal as they were, would come after me with a vengeance, answers that haunt me to this day, as they haunt also Guy. No, this I could not know, but there was one thing I believed I could know, one thing of which I was then absolutely certain.

Lying on my couch with that gun on my lap while Guy Forrest lay asleep in my bed just a doorway away, I closed my eyes and I could see her, standing at the mirror with her shirt open, telling me of her determination to be free at last from Guy, from her past. And I could see her press her lips one upon the other to set the lipstick and dab at it with a tissue folded thin. And I could see her turn to look at me and toss her hair and smile that dazzling, strangely sincere smile. And she comes right over to the bed and sits down and tells me how happy she is that she knows it now will be over in the right way. In the right way, whatever that means. I reach out and with my fingertips brush that lovely breast, the breast that just a few minutes before I had suckled while she writhed and bucked above me, with my fingertips I brush that lovely breast and feel the softness, the firmness, feel the soft pulse of her blood beneath the white of her skin. And I tell her, with a trill of laughter to belie the seriousness, that I love her. But I do, in all seriousness, love her, of that I am certain, of that I hold no doubt. Maybe it is twisted and wrong. Maybe it is based on my perception of her needs and my abilities, perceptions that were, both of them, spectacularly misjudged. Maybe it is, by the very misconceptions at its core, doomed to fall apart at the slightest touch, like a spider's web. Still, there it is. And even though she doesn't make the rote response, even though she scrupulously avoids that word with me, always, I believe in my naïveté that she does, that she does. And my fingertips still move softly upon the surface of her breast, back and forth, up and down, circling her taut nipple. And she takes her own hand and presses my fingers into her breast, presses them hard, and as she does she arches her neck ever so slightly, but enough for me to know, for me to be certain. And I could still feel her hand over my hand, her breast pressed beneath my fingers, the jaggy beat of her heart, still feel it even as I awoke, startled, my erection tenting my suit pants just above where lay the gun.

It was time. I was ready. I waited for my erection to subside, and then I stood, taking hold of the gun as best I could, still as it was in its plastic bag. I took a step and then another toward the bedroom door. What was it Lenin had said about truth coming from the barrel of a gun? Well, maybe it wasn't Lenin who said it, and maybe he wasn't talking about truth, but you get the idea.

Guy had lied when he said everything was fine between him and Hailey, and if Guy was lying about that one crucial point, isn't it likely that he was lying about everything? And if he was lying about everything, then he had killed her. He had killed her. She had told him that she was leaving, and he had reacted as she should have expected him to react, like a man about to lose his savior, like a man driven to the edge, with nothing to lose but his desperation, and he had killed her.

Guy's decision had been made, and so had mine. His decision was to kill my love dead. My decision was to act as a perfect instrument of justice, to rely not on the tribunals of law whose imperfections I knew all too well, but to take matters into my own hands, to discover the truth and be certain it was served. I made my living spinning the lies that allowed desperate people to escape the just consequences of their unjust acts, but over the dead body of my lover a decision had been made, an implacable decision yet pure and right, a decision had been made that no lie would allow the killer of Hailey Prouix to escape the hard consequences of that heinous act. No lie, under no circumstances, whatever the price to be later paid.

He was asleep in my bed, in the sheets I had changed just so he wouldn't recognize her scent upon the pillow. He was asleep in my bed, but not for long.

I held the gun, still in its bag, in my right hand and stepped toward the doorway. The gun had the heft of a grand jury subpoena, the precision of a syringe filled with sodium pentothal. It would serve as an intricate and powerful truth-finding machine. In the confused and frightening moments after he was awakened, he'd be most vulnerable to the truth. I had more questions to ask my old school chum, and the sight of the gun in my hand, that gun, his gun, the sight of the gun in my hand would compel his confession.

I grabbed hold of the knob. Slowly, silently, I turned the knob and opened the door.

In the indifferent light from the street I could see the bed, the sheets, a strange lump in the middle. It didn't look right, he didn't look right.

Without taking my gaze off the bed I grappled for the switch.

A harsh yellow light flooded the room, and then I could see what had happened. Then I could see.

The book was spilled disdainfully on the floor, the drawers had been ransacked, the gym bag was missing, and that lying bastard, that lying bastard, he was gone.

THE BEDROOM window was closed. I shoved it open and scanned the street, slick and black, still wet though the rain had stopped. Nothing. It was three flights down, a fierce jump with nothing to grab on to except the spindly branches of a struggling urban maple. The desperate leap to the sagging tree was not Guy's way, though until tonight I would have said that murder, too, was not Guy's way.

I performed a quick search of the room. I opened the closet, checked the bathroom, threw back the shower curtain. No Guy. He had disappeared from my grasp like a phantom.

How had he gotten away without my knowing? I couldn't figure it until I remembered my remembrances of Hailey Prouix, a reverie that had faded into a dream. I ran back into the living room.

The chain latch of my front door, the chain I fastened each night out of habit, was hanging loose.

The chain latch was undone, as were my plans. I'd had him exactly where I wanted, and then I let him slip away while I was asleep. Damn it. Now he was on the loose, now he was fleeing to freedom. I shucked on my raincoat, stuffed the plastic bag with its gun into the pocket, grabbed my key, and headed out after him.

He could have gone anywhere, I thought at first, but as I sat in the driver's seat of my car and considered each possibility, I realized that wasn't true. He couldn't go back to his wife. He couldn't go to the offices of Dawson, Cricket and Peale. He couldn't go to the police. His parents were dead, his brother lived in California, his friends had all sided with Leila. Where once the world had been open to him, now his options were completely limited. Who would still embrace him and take him in? Who had his love for Hailey not betrayed? I thought it through, went over one possibility and the next and the next until, suddenly, his destination became clear.

He was going to her, to Hailey.

The old saw holds that criminals always return to the scene of the crime and like most old saws, this one contains a portion of truth. Arsonists are often in the crowds surrounding the blazes they set; police routinely videotape the funerals of the murdered dead to see if they can spot a killer paying his final disrespects. A criminal, by definition, is defined by his crime, and which of us doesn't return again and again to the crucial moment of our lives, where we married, where our children gamboled, where we spent an eventide of abandon that fuels still the fantasies that warm our cold, lonely nights. Guy Forrest had a family, a profession, a circle of accomplishment, but if you asked him about his depths, he would have said simply he was a man in love. If you asked me, I would have told you he was a murderer. Both the lover and the murderer were created in that house, in that bedroom, on that mattress on the floor. He was going back, he couldn't not. And I was going, too.

The bloody night was on its way out, the darkness already cracked from the force of dawn. I must have slept longer than I had imagined. I must have been dead asleep. I drove as fast as I dared with a gun in my pocket. I wondered if Guy had seen the King Cobra on my lap as he skulked out of the apartment. Probably not, probably too busy skulking. He hadn't turned on the lights, he hadn't wanted to wake me. He had stayed as far from me as possible as he made his way out of the bedroom and through my apartment door. Who could have imagined he had developed the honed survival instincts of a cockroach?

I drove west on Walnut to Sixty-ninth Street, took a right, heading to Haverford Avenue. It was a familiar route, I had driven this way before on the nights when Guy was out of town. Is it cheating to cheat on a cheating bastard? I had felt bad about it at the first when we made our initial assignation, but it hadn't lasted, the guilt, it hadn't lasted past the first time I tasted Hailey Prouix's tongue. Maybe Guy's guilt over cheating on his wife had died the same sweet death. There were more cars on the road than I expected, the early shift heading into work, the occasional cab. That's what he had caught, a cab. Maybe he even phoned for one from my bedroom before leaving.

"Where to?" had said the cabby.

"To the scene of the crime," had said Guy.

I passed a cop car going the opposite direction, and I ducked. I ducked. I had never been afraid of the police before. Working with them or against them had always been simply part of my job, there had never been the fear that I felt now. But then again never before did I have a gun in my pocket. I was not a gun person. Or a cat person. The only time I ever before wanted a gun was to kill a cat. But here I was, heading out in the rain with a gun in my pocket and my quarry on the loose and I was ducking in my car when the police drove past. It was a strange, hard feeling, all of it. And I liked it. I liked it. It's the only kind of feeling you want after you see your lover dead on a mattress on the floor.

Out Haverford Avenue, across City Line, into the twisting suburban streets, old trees leaning over the roadbeds, calm homes still asleep to the rising morn. Down this short road, left at that stop sign, right at the next, up the hill and to the left, and there it was, dark and solitary.

There was no yellow tape. I thought there would be yellow tape. There was no yellow tape, there were no police cars, there was no police presence whatsoever. In the city the place would have been swaddled in yellow caution tape like a newborn in its blanket. But this was the suburbs, no reason to make a spectacle for the neighbors, no reason to place property values at risk. The sight filled me with anger. They were going to screw it up, they were going to let him off. It was up to me. All along I had known it was, all of it, up to me.

I parked across the street and waited. The lights were off. I didn't know if he hadn't yet gotten to the house or if he was already inside, doing whatever he was doing in the darkness. I parked across the street and waited. There was no rush. If he wasn't yet at the house, he would be, and if he was, which I suspected, he wouldn't be there long. He would do whatever he felt compelled to do and then he would leave, he would run, he would take the keys from the desk drawer and head straight for one of the cars, his or Hailey's, parked out front. Hailey had driven a new Saab convertible. Guy drove a new black Beemer. Both cars were on the street, waiting for his great escape, and so was I.

Waiting. Waiting. And then waiting no more.

He came out from the back, his shoulders hunched, his black coat turning him almost invisible, his head swiveling this way and that as he checked the empty road for watchers. He carried a large, hard-shell suitcase. He was making for the BMW.

I climbed out of my car and stuck my hand in my raincoat pocket so that it gripped the hard hunk of metal. Then I headed off to intercept.

"Guy," I called out.

He looked up at me, startled, before setting his shoulders in a posture of determination and continuing to the car.

"Guy," I called out again, shuffling as quickly as I could toward him. "What are you doing? Where are you going?"

"Don't try to stop me, Victor. I'm getting out of here."

"Why?"

By now he had just about reached his car and I had just about reached him. As he tried to stick his key in the slot, I pulled at his arm. Keytus interruptus. He stared up at me with an unfathomable fear.

"They're going to kill me," he said. "You told me that yourself."

"No, I did not."

"In so many words, yes, you did. They're going to arrest me and throw me in jail and kill me. I'm not going to sit around and let them. I didn't do anything."

"And this is going to convince them of that? Come back with me to my apartment."

"Forget it."

"You can't run, Guy."

"Watch me," he said as he pulled his arm from my grasp and slid the key into the lock. I tried to grab him again. He swung at me with his suitcase, I raised my hand in defense. The suitcase banged into my shoulder. I fell back hard onto my side. The butt of the gun dug into my hip.

He slammed the door, locked himself inside, started the engine.

I spun onto my back, tightened my grip on the gun.

Suddenly another car, boxy and brown, just missed running over me as it pulled alongside Guy's Beemer and stopped dead, blocking him in.

Guy slammed on his horn, but the brown car didn't move.

Guy tried to pull forward, hopping the curve and riding on the sidewalk, around a parked car, and back onto the street to get away, but another car, boxy and black, pulled up suddenly and blocked him in again.

From out of the black car jumped Detective Stone, who quickly drew her gun and aimed it at Guy.

Detective Breger calmly exited his vehicle, ambled over to Guy's BMW, and peered in the window. He gestured for Guy to open the lock. As he patiently waited, first one, then two, then three police cruisers appeared on the street, their flashing lights painting acres of aluminum siding red and blue.

I rose from the ground, my hand out of my raincoat pocket. Breger calmly motioned me away, and I stepped back.

Guy did nothing, did nothing, and then, finally, he electronically unlocked his car. Breger opened the passenger door and leaned inside.

"Going somewhere, Mr. Forrest?"

Guy tried to say something, but Stone, gun still drawn, swung open the other door and cut him off. "Step out of the vehicle, please."

Guy began again to speak.

"Step out of the vehicle, please," repeated Stone.

Guy slowly climbed out, looking at me helplessly for a moment before Stone holstered her gun and jammed him roughly up against the Beemer's side, cuffing his hands behind him.

"You are under arrest for the murder of Hailey Prouix," said Stone when the cuffs were in place. She spun him around and began to read him his rights.

"I'm a lawyer," said Guy halfway through.

"Good," said Stone. "That means there won't be any misunderstandings." She continued.

I walked over to Detective Breger, who, with surgical gloves in place, was rifling through the contents of Guy's suitcase.

"What are you doing?" I said.

"Search incident to arrest," said Breger without looking up from the suitcase. "*Chimel* v. *California*."

"I know the damn cite. How'd you know he was here?"

"Where do you think you are, Mr. Carl? A woman is found shot dead in her bed, all the doors locked, the windows, no evidence of a break-in, no evidence of a robbery. You think we let the only other person in the house walk without a tail? Stone was following from the moment you left here. Saw him sneak out of your building, grab a cab, take it here, where I had been waiting all night just in case, hoping he would do exactly what he did."

"Well, aren't you the clever pair."

"Clothes," he said as he continued his search through the suitcase, "toothbrush, a prescription of"—he held the bottle away from his face and squinted at the label—"Viagra. Anticipating some fun, was he? And what is this? An envelope filled with cash. It's not the three thousand, we already logged that, and it was much slimmer. Whoa. Ten, twenty, maybe fifty, sixty. Our Mr. Forrest had plans. Oh, and look, how sweet, his passport."

"Is that what you were hoping to find?"

"It is what I was expecting to find. The coroner called in a preliminary report. Said Miss Prouix was beaten before she was killed. Her left eye was bruised."

I fought to keep my emotions in check, I bit the inside of my cheek and fought to bat not an eyelash as I heard about the bruise. I stood stone-still and watched as Breger kept searching the suitcase and then, disappointed, started in on the car, the glove compartment, the back seat, the trunk. Finding nothing, he called over to Stone, "You pat him down?"

"Only a wallet," said Stone, leaning against the side of the car into which she had deposited Guy.

"What are you missing?" I managed to get out.

"The gun. We still have not found the gun. I figure the gun is the final rail in your buddy's prison cell."

"Is that what you figure?"

I didn't wait for an answer, I simply turned and walked toward one of the police cars with its lights still flashing. Guy was sitting forward in the back seat, his mouth tight, his fists clenched behind his back. He looked at me angrily when I came over, and I looked away, hoping to hide what it truly was I felt about him.

"I didn't do it," he said through clenched teeth. "Victor, I swear I didn't do it."

"Don't talk," I advised him while surveying the scene, purposely avoiding his gaze.

"I loved her, you know I loved her. How could I have killed her? Victor, I swear I didn't do it."

"What did I just tell you? Don't say anything to anybody, especially when you're sitting in a police car. Don't talk to the cop driving you to the station, don't talk to the cop processing you for admittance, and for heaven's sake don't talk to whatever greaseball they happen to stick you with in the lockup. Do you understand?"

"Will they let me out today?"

"Do you understand what I said?"

"Yes. I understand. I was in the same damn Criminal Law class as you, Victor. Will they let me out of jail today?"

"You were running away. You had sixty thousand dollars and a passport. They're going to charge you with murder. No judge, even a suburban judge, is going to grant you bail. You're in till your trial."

"I am so cooked."

"Yes you are."

"Will you represent me?"

I turned to stare at him.

"I'm desperate," he said. "I need someone I trust. At least for now. I need someone who understands. Victor, I'm begging you. Will you represent me?"

It didn't take me a moment to make up my mind, it didn't take me a moment to run through the implications and make up my mind. "Yes. I'll represent you."

He gave me a wan smile.

I returned it along with a chuck on the shoulder. "Now there's something I need to do, all right? So do as I say, and I'll see you at the arraignment."

I waited as one of the uniforms shut the car door and another climbed behind the wheel. With the lights still on, they drove Guy away, into the dying night. I suppressed a smile and headed over to Breger, who was continuing to search through the Beemer.

"You might want to know, Detective, that Guy Forrest just asked me to represent him on more than a temporary basis, and I agreed."

"Bully. You get a retainer?"

"I was hoping it was in that envelope you found."

"That envelope, along with its contents, is evidence. Evidence, as you well know, stays in our custody all the way through appeal."

"Too bad," I said as I reached into my pocket. "It would have looked nice in piles on my desk. Still, we'll see what the judge has to say about it. But I have something for you. I can't tell you how I got this, attorney-client privilege now in full force and effect, but I believe I'm obligated as an officer of the court to turn it over, as it may be material to your investigation."

I pulled my hand out of my coat pocket and offered what was in its grasp to Detective Breger. The detective's eyes bulged.

"Is that . . . ?"

"You have tests to identify it, don't you?"

"Yes. Of course."

"Well, then."

He took the bag with the gun and hefted it in his hand, and something suddenly went out of me, something ugly and hard. It was as if a brutal rod of steel had been extracted from my spine.

"I might have been rude back there," said Breger, still gazing at the gun.

"Are you trying to apologize for your manner, Detective?"

"I want you to know that I am sorry if I was rude. I should not have been rude. You're a guy just trying to do your job. It has been noted that you went after him when you discovered he sneaked out of your place. It has been noted that you tried to stop him from running and he knocked you down with his suitcase. It has now been noted that you turned over what might prove to be the murder weapon. The law says you need to turn it over, I know, but still, nine out of ten would have buried it. So all of that has been noted, and I am sorry if I was rude back there."

"Okay," I said.

He nodded and, without saying another word, headed off to show his shiny new prize to his partner.

I stayed at the scene until all the police, car by car, had left, until the dawn had fully broken through and the morning stretched and twittered and came alive. I thought about what had happened that night, what I had lost, what I had just done, what I had just set about to do. I felt my weary sadness turn to determination. I was glad the gun was gone. It was all wrong for me, a gun, like boxing gloves on a poet. But that didn't mean it was over, that didn't mean I was through.

How can you defend a man you know is guilty?

No matter where I was, at a bar or a ball game, whenever my profession was discovered, the inevitable question was raised. And never yet had I found an adequate answer.

Oh, I knew the Constitution, I could cite the Sixth Amendment backward and forward, the case law, too, but still the question always gave me pause. Where in the Constitution did it provide that every participant in a criminal trial was duty bound to seek the ends of justice with the sole exception of the attorney for the defense? Where in the Constitution did it say that assistance of counsel meant assistance in escaping the just consequences of your merciless crime? I had been asked the question dozens of times, and now, here, with my lover dead on a mattress on the floor, I finally had my answer: I can't, I won't. And it wasn't enough to refuse the case, let someone else do the dirty work. This was no time to punt. A decision had been made to discover the truth and be certain it was served. A decision had been made, and I would follow it through. I had discovered the truth that very night, in my apartment when Guy lied so shamelessly and later, on the street, when he whacked me with his suitcase as he was about to make good his escape from justice. The second part, I was sure, would be a snap.

Yes indeed, I'd represent that son of a bitch. What better way to keep my pledge? What better way to remember Hailey Prouix?

SHE SITS across from me, leaning away from me, arms crossed, legs crossed. She leans away from me, but her bright red lips are curved and challenging. She raises her cigarette to her mouth. Her blue eyes, framed dramatically by the dark rails of her glasses, squint from the smoke. Her narrowed gaze rakes across my face, down my throat. I look at her and forget to breathe.

"Victor," says Guy Forrest, sitting beside her at the table, "I'd like to you to meet Hailey Prouix."

"So pleased," I say, and I am.

We are in a Spanish restaurant on Twelfth Street, modern, cruelly lit, cold stone tables for the hot paella. You want comfort, stay in bed. Guy had called and asked me to meet him, and here I am, forgetting to breathe, and I feel a love surging inside me. Love, not for her, because she is nothing yet but possibilities, instead love for my dear friend Guy, who thought well enough of me to introduce me to her, to set up this setup. Was ever a friend dearer?

But they are sitting side by side. That should have been my clue.

We order drinks, we chat. I smile and do my best to be charming. I am jolly, I am self-deprecating, I am wry. Oh, am I wry. Guy tells me Hailey is also a lawyer. I make a joke. He tells Hailey that he and I went to law school together. She asks what kind of law I do.

"Mostly criminal defense, but I also pursue the intentional torts that flow out of crime. Fraud, assault, the occasional wrongful death."

"Lucrative?"

"Sometimes, sometimes not, but it keeps me busy. Though not as busy as they keep Guy at Dawson, Cricket. How's the sweatshop, Guy?"

"Fine, I suppose, but I'm not going to be there much longer."

I stare at him blankly. I hadn't heard through the legal grapevine that he had been in trouble at his firm.

"I'm taking a page from your book," says Guy. "I'm going to try it on my own."

"You're six months from partnership."

"I want something new."

"What does Leila say?"

"She doesn't have a say," he says as he puts an arm around Hailey. "I'm leaving her, too."

Ah, so there it is. My charming smile freezes on my face, the love I had felt for a loyal friend withers. This isn't a setup, this is an announcement. I turn my head to look at her. Her lovely lips are pursed, as if she were examining me for some reason, as if there were something she might want from me. She smashes out her cigarette and excuses herself. Guy scrambles to stand as she slides out of her seat, and we both watch while she walks down the aisle. She walks as if she knows what she is doing, as if she has been walking near all her life.

"You look happy," I say to Guy, even though he suddenly looks positively miserable.

"Oh, I am. Like I've never been before."

"Where are you going to live?"

"She has a small house. Nothing fancy. A sofa, a table, a mattress on the floor."

"A mattress on the floor?"

He gives a boyish half grin that makes me want to smash him in the face. He reads my expression, and the grin dies. "You don't approve," he says.

"It's not up to me to approve or disapprove, is it? I'm only trying to understand what you're doing."

"I've decided to change my life."

I snap my fingers. "Just like that."

"I don't have a choice. I love her, Victor. What else is there to understand? I'm sick in love with her."

And just then he looks it, sick in love, as if love were an illness that he has caught, an exotic virus that was biding its time in the nuclei of his cells until it burst forth to ravage him.

"Well, that's great, Guy," I say, "just great. I'm glad for you. Really."

I take a sip of my Sea Breeze and I am suffused with the bitter aftertaste of disappointment. But is it with Guy, with what he is going to do to his wife and his children and the image I had held of his happy, happy family, or is it because he hasn't brought her to this restaurant for me?

When she returns, the conversation is awkward, charmless, wryless. There is no longer flirtation in the air. Guy talks, I listen, Hailey smokes. But at the end, as we part and say our good-byes, in a moment while Guy looks away, I am staring once again at her lips when they silently mouth "Call me," and I do.

WE MEET for a drink after work. Nothing secret or surreptitious, we are in the open, in a public place, the bar of a famous restaurant where Guy could march in at any time, but he won't. Even so, he is with us, as real a presence as the man with the toupee and the flowered tie sitting two stools down. Hailey drinks an Absolut martini, I drink my usual Sea Breeze. The man with the toupee drinks Scotch. Hailey's eyes are bluer than I remember, her lips freshly lacquered and in constant motion, hovering uneasily just beneath a smile. I can't take my eyes off them, they are devouring.

"I have a client that might be facing criminal charges," she says. "I wondered if you wanted to handle the case."

"So this is a business meeting."

"What did you think it was?" Her words are accusatory, but her smile is anything but. It feels like a seduction, but I wonder who is seducing whom.

"I thought we were going to talk about Guy," I say.

"No we weren't."

"You're going to destroy him, aren't you?"

"And that would concern you?"

"He's my friend."

"And that's why you're here, having a drink with me, because he's your friend?"

"You phrase questions like a psychiatrist, not a lawyer."

"Objection noted. Answer the question."

"There you go. Fine deposition form."

"You're not here having a drink with me because Guy is your friend, are you, Mr. Carl?"

"No."

"Good. At least that's settled."

"Is it so easy?"

"Yes, yes it is."

And she is right.

WE COURT like Victorians, slowly, chastely. The strange omnipresence of Guy is our chaperon. He is always there, the guy with the afro, the guy in the tweed suit, the guy cross-dressing who thinks we can't tell. He is always there, and his presence lets us pretend that we want only to be friends. Merely friends. That is all. Isn't it obvious?

There are more drinks in the twilight. She crosses her legs and we bump knees. Just the thought of her turns me blue, but she won't let me kiss her. She says that nothing can ever happen, that she is devoted to Guy. Her admonitions allow me to assuage any guilt that our meetings are other than innocent, but when she crosses her legs, we bump knees.

On nights when Guy is busy, we have dinner. She orders fish but barely eats a thing. She drinks more than she ought and smokes when she drinks. Mostly what we do is talk. We talk of incidental things, our cases, our tastes in movies. She is not one for weepy chick flicks. She likes action-adventure, she likes explosions. Arnold. John Woo. She has a longing for Sylvester Stallone.

"Whatever happened to him?" I ask.

"He tried to get serious."

"Is that fatal?"

"Always."

"You've never been serious?" I say.

"I didn't say that. But whenever I've been serious, I've been seriously bad."

"You exaggerate."

"No, no I don't."

"Tell me about it, tell me the worst."

"Are you a priest? I could only tell a priest."

"I didn't know you were religious."

"I'm not, and that's why. So I never have to tell."

"It's not that bad, I'm sure."

"That's sweet of you. Or dim of you. One or the other. Which is it?"

"Sweet?"

"Too bad. There is nothing more appealing sometimes than an utter lack of imagination."

"Has Guy moved in yet?"

"Oh, yes. Yes he has."

"How is it, living with Guy?"

"Like a dream."

"You sound overwhelmed with joy."

"I never knew bliss could feel this way."

She has no sense of humor, but she laughs well. She is a grand audience, she is Ed McMahon if Ed McMahon wore a size four. I make wisecracks, and she pretends they are funnier than they really are, and I let her. We tell stories of our childhoods and treat them like revelations, when all they are are stories culled to hide the revelations. I tell her how my mother left when I was still in my boyhood, how she now lives with some alcoholic cowboy in Arizona. I tell her how my father still cuts lawns even with half a lung. She tells me of the tragic death of her father.

This is what I learn of her past, the bones of her life as she relates them to me. She was born in West Virginia, on the western edge of the Appalachian Mountains. Her daddy was a Cajun who came north looking for work in the lumber mills. They went to church every Sunday, had a house with a verandah on the high side of the river. She walked to school with her sister, came home to a plate of cookies and milk each afternoon, played in the park across from the courthouse. She was eight when a load of timber came loose during stacking and crushed her father to death.

There was no pension, no payout. He had been working all those years as an independent contractor. There was insurance, but barely enough for the burial. Her mother worked, but even so, things grew very hard very quickly and although she was still only a child at the time, in all her years after, she never forgot the bitter taste of financial desperation. In order to help out, her mother's brother moved in and joined his wages with his sister's. No family of his own, a drinker and gambler, her uncle settled down long enough to help raise the family. Eight years he lived with them, until the strain became too much and he disappeared, presumably to start again with the drinking and the gambling. But by then his job was complete, the girls were almost grown.

Hailey was popular, pretty, a prom queen who walked the high school halls arm in arm with the star halfback. Awarded a church scholarship, she left home to attend a small college in Maryland, and for the first time she concentrated more on her studies than on her social life. To her great surprise she discovered that she was good at academics. Dean's-list good. Good enough for the church scholarship to be extended to graduate school if she wanted to attend, and she did. She never forgot what had happened to her father and family, never forgot how an unfair contract and unsafe conditions had left her family on the brink. It was that experience, she told me, that had sent her into the law, and when she said it, there was none of the ironic tone that normally left you looking for the explanatory footnotes. A law school in New Jersey gave her enough aid so that with the scholarship and loans she could make a go of it. Three years later she landed an associate's position with a small but profitable plaintiff's firm in Philadelphia. Four years after that, when an affair with the managing partner created a scandal, she took a stack of files and went out on her own.

"It all sounds so damn inspiring," I say. "Rags to riches."

"Yes, I'm the American dream."

"How did you meet Guy?"

"At a seminar on proving and defending the medical malpractice case."

"I always knew CLE had to be good for something."

"That's what I get for trying to improve my mind."

"You think you deserve better?"

"I think I'm getting exactly what I deserve. Another martini, please."

"When do you have to get home?"

"After this drink."

"Then make it a double."

I SENSE in her the grand design of some awesome inevitability. I don't know from where it emanates, maybe it comes from having your father crushed beneath a load of pine, but its symptom is a weary resignation.

"Why don't you just end it?" I ask.

"But I like seeing you."

"I mean with Guy."

"Oh, I couldn't do that."

"Because you love him?"

"Why else?"

"I don't know."

"See. It's so simple, isn't it?"

She is committed to Guy, absolutely, she tells me so all the time, there is no other option. But still, when I call, she picks a place.

"I am so tired," she says. "Do you ever get so tired?"

"No," I say. "I'm too frightened all the time to be tired."

"Frightened of what?"

"Of learning that the best is behind me."

"Sometimes I have this urge to just start over," she says. "Be something new."

"Don't talk about it, do it. Guy has, apparently. You can, too."

"But I already have. This is it."

"You thought you'd change your life with Guy?"

"No, Guy was something else."

"And what am I?"

"You are an indulgence. Something not good for me, like a cigarette or a drink."

"Hazardous to your health."

"If only you knew."

WHAT SHE sees in me, I can only guess. What I see in her, besides the obvious beauty, is a sadness, palpable but elusive, a sadness that reaches into my heart like a claw.

I'm not struggling to understand why her sadness touches me as it does, why I feel about her what I feel; it doesn't take Jung to dredge up the suspects. My mother drinking gin late nights in the kitchen, drumming her fingers on the Formica, wondering how she ended up married to this man, living in this tattered house in this decaying suburb, shackled to this brat with his whine like a siren. Or my father, in his chair in front of the television with a can of Iron City in his hand, sitting in the chair in the dark after his wife left him alone with his son, on his face the dazed expression of a car-crash victim staggering out of his wrecked vehicle. Why is it that children of alcoholics find themselves mysteriously attracted to the alcoholic personality? Answer that and you might understand why I found myself, many years before, engaged to a sad, sweet girl named Janice, who fulfilled all my greatest fears by breaking the engagement and running off with a forty-seven-year-old urologist named Wren. Or why, a few years after that, I prostrated my heart and my career on the altar of Veronica Ashland, a sad drug-addled woman whose betrayal was as inevitable as the thunderstorm at the end of a brutally sweltering day. Or why I find myself obsessively attracted to the sadness in Hailey Prouix. Is it that I see in her sadness a chance to ease my soul, to do for her what I could never do for my parents as they tore their lives apart? Or is it just that she is with my dear friend Guy and so hot my blood is boiling at the wanting?

IT IS usually me who calls, who tells the receptionist it is Victor Carl to talk about the Sylvester matter. That is our code case, the

Sylvester matter, in honor of her silver-screen hero. It is usually me who calls, so I am surprised when I return from a court appearance to see a message in my box pertaining to the Sylvester matter. When I phone, she speaks to me in a whisper.

"Are you free for lunch?"

"Yes," I say. "Of course."

"When can you shake loose?"

"Now. Where do you want to meet? What are you hungry for?"

"Oh, pick a place, Victor. Any place, any place at all."

She is waiting for me at the sandwich joint. There are little tables crowded into a long, narrow room, and the tables are filled with men and women talking loudly and stuffing corned beef specials into their mouths, strands of coleslaw hanging from their teeth. She is leaning back in her chair, arms crossed.

"What looks good?" I say as I sit.

"Everything," she says.

"The corned beef seems to be it."

"Nothing for me, thank you."

"Are you okay? What happened?"

"The most wonderful thing," but her voice is anything but glad-dened. "What are we going to do, Victor, you and I?"

"Have lunch?"

"Is that all? Because lately that seems like all."

"I've been following your lead."

"Well, I'm a lousy dancer."

"Did something happen between you and Guy?"

"Yes. Something happened."

Just then the waitress comes to our table, her pad out. "Are you ready?"

"Victor, are you ready?" asks Hailey.

"I don't know."

"Can you give us a minute," says Hailey. The waitress rolls her eyes before rushing off to grab an order in the kitchen.

"I'm not hungry," she says. "Are you hungry?"

"Not anymore."

"Then let's go for a walk."

"Where to?"

"Anywhere you want."

Outside, it is damp and chill and the temperature brings a rouge to her cheeks. She wears a gray overcoat atop her lawyer's garb, her hands tucked into the pockets.

"Do you want a drink? You look like you could use a drink. I have some beers in my apartment."

"Yes," she says. "Let's do that."

"Is it about work?" I ask. "Is it about Guy?"

"Yes."

"Which?"

"Aren't you sick of talking? Aren't you sick to death of talking? The more I talk, the less I know. The words are so fuzzy they turn everything into a lie, and then the lie becomes the new truth and I don't know anything for certain anymore."

I begin to say something, some comforting inanity, but the hungry look of tragedy in her eyes stops me midword, and so we walk in quiet through the noontime crowds toward my apartment.

It is a mess, like it is always a mess. I leave her standing in the living room as I gather up the clothes on the coach, the towel on the door, gather them up and dump them all into the hamper in my bathroom. She stands motionless as I work, still in her coat, hands still in her pockets. When it is almost presentable, I stop and look at her standing still in her coat, and the sadness that is always there is pouring out of her. I can see it, a dark blue pouring out of her. She looks at me, and her eyes beneath her glasses are moist, and the blue is pouring out of her, and I am helpless to stop myself from going to her and wrapping my arms about her and squeezing, as if I could squeeze out the sadness.

She feels thin beneath my arms, bones and nothing more. She smells of jasmine and smoke. I tell her it will be all right, even though I don't know what is troubling her and I suspect it will turn out badly. I tell her it will be all right, and I touch my lips to the top of her head in a brotherly kiss.

"I'm so bad."

"No you're not."

A brotherly kiss to the soft of her temple.

"I am. You don't know."

"I know what I need to know."

A brotherly kiss to the soft ridge beneath her eye, and I taste the salt of a tear.

I pull away. She lifts her face to me. Her eyes are wet, her nose red, her mouth quivering. She is the picture of desolation, and I can't help myself. I don't want to help myself. Something has happened between her and Guy and that now is enough for me. I take her biceps in my hands and squeeze, even as I kiss her gently. Even as our lips barely touch. There is no mashing, no gnashing, just the gentlest touch. The gentlest touch. A saving touch, I think, I hope. Our mouths open slightly, the touch of our lips staying just as gentle, and nothing slips between them, no tongue, no moisture, nothing, but not nothing, because there is a commingling of spaces, a creation of something new, and in the enclosure formed between our gently touching mouths I feel an emptiness flowing and growing, hers, mine, ours.

I WANT it to be slow.

I had fantasized about the two of us together, often, incessantly, it had been my nighttime preoccupation since our first meeting, and it had always been hard, rough, full of laughter and grabbing, she seemed that kind of lover, but in the presence of her overwhelming sadness I want this now to be slow, as gentle as our first kiss.

I brush my lips again upon her temple, upon her cheek, take her lips gently in my teeth. We are naked now, kneeling on the bed, our hands gently brushing each other's arms, sides, backs, thighs.

She is thinner than ever I thought, so thin and fragile and, without her glasses, so seemingly vulnerable, so in need of protection. And that is what I want to do, to protect her.

The afternoon light slices in through the blinds, her smell of smoke and jasmine is charged by the sharp edge of musk.

I slide closer. I am pressed up against the flat of her belly.

I glide my hand around the contour of her breast. I lift its weight in my palm.

I kiss her shoulder, I kiss the line of jaw, her neck. A tremor rises from her throat and with it a sound soft as a spring drizzle. I kiss the bone of her clavicle, I kiss the hollow beneath the bone, the first swell of her chest, the soft skin, the excited pink areola. The sound rises, stretches, widens to fill every inch of space.

I want it to be slow, but suddenly there is a presence in the room other than the two of us. A hunger, a need. Something foreign and relentless, primordial, with a rhythm of its own, a breath hot and dank, a power, and I don't know from whence it came. Is it mine, hers, is it an entity of its own invading our lives? I don't recognize it, I don't understand it, I've never felt anything like it before, this hunger, this need. It is brutal and violent and immortal, and before I know what has happened, it has taken control.

I want it to be slow, but what I want no longer matters.

And when it is over, she lies on her side, covered in sweat and sheets and I lie behind her, in a shocked silence, sore and uncertain, my arms wrapping her like a stole.

"That was insane," I say.

"It always is." There is a twang in her voice, a slight shift west and south into the hillocks of her West Virginia home, as if whatever it was that roared through us took her back into her past.

"No, it was a like freight train was in the room with us."

"That's what I meant."

"So you felt it, too?"

"Shhhhhh."

"What was it?"

"A vestige."

My chest is pressed into her back, my hips are pressed into her thighs. She doesn't want to talk about it, and I don't understand what has happened. I hold her tight and feel the sadness and hold her tighter, but with the shift in her accent for a moment I am not certain anymore whom I am holding.

"What was the thing?" I say. "The thing you wanted to tell me about."

"Nothing important."

"Tell me."

"Nothing you should worry about. Nothing that affects you."

I don't say anything. I hold tight and wait. She wanted to tell me before, she wants to tell me now, so I wait.

"It was last night," she says. "Guy. We were together in the Jacuzzi. There were candles, rose petals."

"I don't want to hear the details."

"He thought it was romantic. The candles. Like a commercial or something."

"Really, I don't want to hear."

"Then he asked me to marry him as soon as the divorce goes through. To marry him."

She says nothing more, and I say nothing, and the silence swells and stretches until it is as taut as an overinflated balloon that I can't help but prick with my words:

"And what did you say?"

"What could I say? I said yes."

PART TWO

WITH PREJUDICE

1

I COULD barely look at Guy as he sat next to me at the defense table, still in the clothes of the night before, the clothes, like Guy, now rumpled and stinking. I could barely look at his puffy face, his red eyes, the way his hands trembled. I could barely look at the fear that overwhelmed him as he began to understand the abject consequences of his single moment of uncontrollable rage. Whenever I looked at him, I wanted to strangle him, so instead I looked around the courtroom, at the bailiff, the guards, at the bored reporters scattered in the otherwise empty seats, at the detectives sitting in the front row behind the prosecution table, Stone leaning back, arms stretched out, Breger hunched forward in weariness. It was still early, the judge was not scheduled to arrive for another quarter of an hour, but it pays to be prompt when they are arraigning your client for murder.

The Montgomery County Courthouse was an old Greek Revival building with porticoes and pediments and a great green dome, all set in the county seat of Norristown. They had put us in Courtroom A, the building's largest room, with its high ceilings and wood paneling and big leather chairs at the counsel tables that squeaked with righteousness. The courtrooms in Philadelphia are fresh and spanking new, modern and streamlined, with a sense of the assembly line about them, and so it felt good to be in a place with heavy wooden benches and red carpeting, a place that exuded harsh justice of the old sort. That's the kind of justice I was hoping to find.

I let my partner, Beth Derringer, coach Guy through the procedure so I could stew blissfully in my own emotions. "This is just a formality, Guy, you know all this," she said quietly. "We'll waive the reading of the indictment, plead you not guilty, and get started building your defense."

Beth was not just my partner, she was my best friend. Sharp, faithful, absolutely trustworthy. So of course I couldn't trust her with all that had happened between Hailey and me and what had been decided the night before.

And what exactly had been decided? Justice, vengeance, take your pick, they both felt the same to me.

It all would have been simpler had I been able to go it alone, but this would be a trying case, I would need assistance, and so I had asked Beth to assist. And having Beth on my side had another distinct advantage. She could be my canary in the mine shaft. If I could keep her in the dark about what had happened and what I had decided to do about it, I believed I could keep everyone else there, too.

"What about bail?" said Guy. "I've got to get out of here. Do you have any idea of what it's like in prison? Do you have any idea of the way those animals inside look at me?"

"No," said Beth. "I don't. We'll try to get you out, Guy, but it's a murder charge, and you were trying to run. The judge will grant either no bail or one absurdly high. But how much could you put up if bail is set?"

"I don't know. There's money in the account, there's Hailey's life insurance, there's the house. It's worth a mil or so."

"Whose house?" I said while still looking away.

"Mine. Leila's. Our house."

"That's not your house," I said.

As soon as I said it, Guy understood. We sat side by side in Property Law, I cribbed off of his notes for my outline. In Pennsylvania, when any real estate is owned by a married couple, neither spouse has any individual property interest, it is owned by the couple itself, and any disposition of the property must be agreed to by both spouses.

"Will Leila agree to put it up for bail?" asked Beth.

"Yes, of course. To get me out of jail, of course. Let me talk to her."

"Do you think she'd put up your children's house to give you a chance to run and leave them homeless?" I said without looking at him so he couldn't see the expression twisting my features. "Do you really think her father would let her?"

"Talk to her, Victor. You can get her to sign."

"I'm not that persuasive."

"Talk to her for me."

"All right."

"And tell her I want to see the kids. I need to see the kids."

Before I could respond, Beth continued. "You mentioned an account. What kind of account?"

"A brokerage account."

"In whose name?"

"In my name. And Hailey's."

I turned suddenly and stared at him, his pleading eyes, his mouth, jerked now and then by a twitch that had never marred his features before his arrest. Not so handsome anymore. "How much?"

"I don't know exactly," he said. "Depending on the markets, maybe half a million."

"Where the hell did you get half a million dollars?"

"Hailey had a big case before we got together. Medical malpractice. The settlement was huge."

"If it was Hailey's money, why was your name on the accounts?"

"Because we were in love. We were going to be married, so we put all our money together. I added some, too. Part of it was mine."

I stared at him, suddenly even angrier than before, and then turned away in disgust.

"Do you know where the account is?" said Beth.

"Schwab. Hailey did some trading online. I let her keep track of everything. I didn't even know the password."

"That's okay, Guy. We'll find out exactly what's in there." She reached into her file and pulled out a piece of paper. "We'd like you to sign this power of attorney. It will allow us to access information about your financial accounts. It doesn't provide us the power to withdraw funds, but it will let us learn what we need to make bail or to convince the judge to set something reasonable later on."

I watched out of the corner of my eye as Guy reviewed the document. He had said the fee would be no problem, I wanted to make sure. I watched until he signed and handed it back to Beth, and then my disgust forced me to turn away again.

"And you said there was insurance?" asked Beth.

"Life insurance. I already had a policy where I switched my secondary beneficiary to her. She took a policy on herself and named me the beneficiary."

"Where are the policies?"

"I don't know. Hailey had them, maybe in her office or something."

"Okay," said Beth. "We'll find them, too. After the arraignment they're going to take you back to the county lockup, so we won't be able to talk right away. We'll set something up as soon as possible. What we need to know right now is if you have any idea who might have done this, if you have any leads you think we ought to investigate?"

I swiveled my head slowly until I was staring straight at him once again. This time he looked at me as if he were pleading for some answers. I had none, at least none he would like.

"I don't know," he said. "Everyone loved her. She was great. No one wanted to hurt her."

"Had there been anything unusual? Did you notice anything out of the ordinary in the past few months?"

"No. Nothing. There were some calls at the house, you know, calls I answered and then the caller hung up. Stuff like that. They ended about a month ago, but maybe something was going on. Maybe there was someone else I didn't know about."

I stood and left the table so he wouldn't hear the snort of disbelief that came unbidden from my throat. It was all too much to take, Guy professing his innocence, casting about for suspects, especially the thing about the phone caller who kept hanging up when he answered, since the phone caller who kept hanging up when he answered was me.

In the peanut gallery behind the bar, a tall man with a suit and a briefcase was standing in the aisle, talking to Breger and Stone. I took him to be the prosecutor and I stepped over to make the introductions. We were going to be a good team, I was sure, he and I, working together as we were toward a common goal.

But as I got closer, I realized the prosecutor and two detectives weren't talking so much as arguing. Stone was keeping her voice low, but her disgust was evident. Breger looked away, his mouth set with a disappointment that seemed expected yet still painful, like a kid on Christmas morning who finds beneath the tree a puzzle and not a pony. When Stone saw me approach, she stopped talking and gestured to the prosecutor. The tall man with the suit and briefcase turned around.

"You're Victor Carl?"

"That's right," I said. He was a handsome man, lean and athletic, and I thought he looked familiar but I couldn't be sure.

"Yeah, I recognize you from the paper." He was talking about this morning's *Daily News*. Beneath the headline—SHOT THROUGH THE HEART—was my picture, hand out warding off the camera, looking as guilty as a politician in a strip club.

"They didn't get my good side," I said.

"Well, you were facing the camera," said Stone.

Breger, staring now down at the floor, bowed his head sadly at his partner's impudence even as his shoulders shook with stifled laughter.

"Now, is that nice?" I said. "Here I am, trying to be pleasant, trying to forge a working relationship with the officers of the law, and you return my overture with insults."

"That wasn't an insult," said Stone, showing off her healthy teeth. "If I was meaning to insult you, I would have started with your tie."

"What's wrong with my tie?"

"Please. It's like you and Breger frequent the same thrift shop."

"I was just about to compliment Detective Breger on his neckwear. It's rare to find a man brave enough to wear a plaid jacket and a plaid tie to go with it."

"If I may interrupt the soirée," said the handsome man in the aisle. "I'm Troy Jefferson, chief of the trial division in the DA's office here. I'll be prosecuting Mr. Forrest."

I looked up at him. "I saw you play," I said. "I saw you light us up for thirty-five when you could barely walk."

"You went to Abington?"

"I did."

"Did you play yourself?"

"No. I was barely coordinated enough the climb the bleachers."

"That's one game I'll never forget. I had an operation the next week and was never the same."

"You were a beautiful player."

"Thank you."

"Nice to meet you."

"Likewise."

I smiled at him. He smiled at me. I reached out my hand and he shook it. Troy Jefferson was the basketball star in our conference when I went to high school. He was fast, aggressive on the dribble, with a sweet jumper from the top of the key. He had led his team to a state championship as a junior, and before his knee collapsed on him had been talked about as the surest thing since Wilt. He played college ball, I remembered, but was never the same as before the injury and went undrafted. I had heard he played in Europe for a few years before going to law school and becoming a prosecutor. Word was he was waiting for the right moment to turn political and leap into some public office, maybe attorney general, maybe higher. He had been a high school superstar, I had been a high school nothing, and now here we were, face to face in a courtroom, each of us smiling. We were going to like one another, Troy and I, we were going to be best friends. Who would have thought it a decade and a half before?

"Have you already entered your notice of appearance?" he said.

"Yes."

"Good," said my new friend Troy. "Do you have a minute, Victor? I have something I want to talk to you about."

I glanced at Breger and Stone, who glared not at me but at Troy, and then followed him out of the courtroom. We found a private perch on the marble stairway in the courthouse atrium, beneath a green stained-glass ceiling.

"I just wanted you to know that we're going to oppose any bail in this case," said Troy Jefferson.

"I expected as much."

"That thing with the suitcase and the passport sealed it. And we're still debating whether to ask for this to be a capital case."

"That's your decision," I said, being as helpful as possible.

"The evidence against your client is overwhelming, and a lot of people, including the detectives in this case, think we should push for death. They don't like the fact that she was hit before she was shot. Neither do I. And in case you didn't know, the only fingerprints we could lift from the gun you handed over were your client's."

"He picked it up after the killing," I said perfunctorily, because, as a defense attorney, I was supposed to say things like that, but I must say I admired Troy's righteous indignation. Juries respond well to righteous indignation.

"Can we keep this conversation absolutely confidential?"

"Yes, of course," I said.

"Good." He looked up and down down the empty staircase. "Victor, we haven't finished our investigation by a long shot, and a lot of people want us to wait before we do anything. But this appears to me to be a crime of passion. Your client and Miss Prouix were fighting, there was a scuffle, your client couldn't control himself, and he shot his fiancée. It's a common enough story, and it's sad, truly, but it's not worth death. Right now, to me, it appears like nothing worse than man one. Something in the ten- to fifteen-year range. I've talked this over with the DA, and we'd be willing to accept a man one plea right now. Your client could be out, with good behavior, in eight to ten years."

"That's generous of you," I said. And it was, shockingly.

"But you should know, Victor, that as our investigation continues, there is no telling what we might find. Stone and Breger are not happy with the offer and they are going to scour the landscape looking for more of a motive. You don't want them to find it. If they dig up even the hint of a motive beyond the heat of the moment, I'm going to have no choice but to yank the offer and go for murder one with death as a possibility. I know it's a lot to think about, and you don't need to decide today, but you don't want to wait too long either."

"I understand."

"So talk it over with your client and let me know."

"I will," I said. "Thanks."

"It was nice meeting you, Victor. Breger said favorable things about you, which is rarer than you can imagine. Let's see if we can work something out." He smiled his charismatic Troy Jefferson smile, patted me on my shoulder, and headed back into court. I watched him go, trying to hide my shock.

What the hell was he doing? A woman was murdered in cold blood by a smarmy asshole and he offers up man one, ten to fifteen years, out in eight to ten? Where was the justice in that? I had half a mind to read Troy the riot act. I wouldn't, of course, it was not the place of a defense attorney to complain of an offer as being too lenient—but still. But still. I had no choice now but to present this abomination to Guy, with the chance that he might just accept. And any normal murderer would accept, would jump as if for a lifeline, which, in fact, this offer was. But this was not a normal murderer, this was the killer of Hailey Prouix. It was a good thing I was not a normal defense attorney either. I would present the offer, yes I would, but I would also use all my powers to present it in such a way that Guy would turn it down. It wouldn't be so hard, it was all in the presentation. They don't have the evidence, Guy, they're running scared, Guy, we can beat the charge, Guy, we can give you back your life, Guy. If I couldn't turn an offer of man one into a first-degree murder conviction, then I might as well hand in my ticket to practice law and become a dentist.

OUTSIDE THE courthouse, after I had done my bit for the television cameras, Beth and I climbed down the wide front steps. I couldn't help but notice that bulbs in the flower beds were blooming, birds were atwitter, buds were sprouting in the trees lining the street. It was as if the rain of the night before had washed away the remnants of winter and spring had suddenly swooped down with its special light to spread its finery. And yet it felt to me, for some reason, on those gray, sunlit steps, that I was still standing in the murky gloom, within a landscape of shadows and secrets. I wanted to get away just then, to find a place where the sun might burst through my own personal fog and warm my face, when Detectives Breger and Stone stepped in our way.

"Got a minute, Mr. Carl?" said Stone.

I gestured for Beth to wait and walked off with the two of them. Stone wasn't smiling now, a bad sign I figured, but Breger wasn't staring at me either, which seemed to be his way of showing respect. I suppose you spend enough years staring down suspects in the interrogation room, you end up staring away from those you consider respectful and law-abiding. A habit that must make for lovely family dinners.

"You mind if we look at your hands?" asked Breger.

"My hands?"

"If you don't mind."

I put down my briefcase and held out my hands. Breger took one each in his big mitts and carefully examined the knuckles before letting them drop.

"Thanks," he said as he turned his gaze to survey the street. "Troy Jefferson gave you a pretty generous offer."

"Yes he did. He also told me you said some nice things about me. Thank you."

"You should know we both opposed the offer. We think it is far too lenient, man one for a homicide like this. Is your client going to accept it?"

"He pled not guilty in court."

"I know, but is he going to accept the offer?"

"He says he didn't do it. I relayed the offer and he rejected it outright. Says he didn't do it."

"That means the investigation is still moving forward," said Breger, his eyebrows raised.

"I suppose so," I said.

"Then we have to ask you a question, Mr. Carl," said Stone, "about the night of the killing, because something confuses us."

"That must happen often, Detective."

"You said that Mr. Forrest called you at your home and then you came right over."

"That's correct."

"Except we got a look at the phone logs from Mr. Forrest's line just before court and we found something peculiar. Your call to 911 showed up, as expected, and there were other calls to you from earlier dates, as expected since you were a friend, but there was no call to you registered from the night of the killing."

"Is that a fact?"

"Any idea why that is?"

"Phone company made a mistake?"

"Is that what you think?" said Breger sharply, and as he said it he turned to stare at me. "The computers of the phone company made a mistake?" It was the first time he'd ever looked at me straight on, and I noticed now that one of his eyes wandered slightly. The effect was strangely disorienting and I didn't like it, the variance in his gazes seemed to suggest a variance between the truth and my words. His gaze itself acted as an accusation.

"Does your client have a cell phone?" he said.

"I don't know. I suppose if he does there are records."

"I suppose there are. You didn't happen to see his cell phone when you were up in that bedroom?"

"No, sir."

He looked at me for a moment longer and then turned again to survey the street. "You said you were watching a game when he called. What game was that?"

"The Phils were in Atlanta. I slept through most of it, but they were down when I left."

"They scored two in the bottom of the ninth to beat the bastards."

"Good," I said. "Is that all?"

"That's all. Thank you for the help, Mr. Carl."

"Call me Victor, Detective Breger."

"No, I don't think so."

"You know, Vic," said Stone, "when we asked you about Miss Prouix, you described her as sweet and nice. We've been running the usual inquiries and I have to tell you, we've been talking to a lot of people who knew Miss Prouix and they all seemed to have a lot to say, but not a one of them used the words 'sweet' or 'nice' when talking about her."

"Maybe I didn't know her all that well. What was the thing with the hands all about?"

"Last night one of our Forensic Unit technicians was heading into the house to redo a few tests," said Stone. "A man rushed out and ran her over, a man dressed in black with a watch cap pulled over his face. When she grabbed his leg, he turned and beat her in the face pretty badly."

"So you checked my hands?"

"Just routine, Vic."

"Call me Mr. Carl, Detective Stone."

"She is still in the hospital," said Breger.

"Good thing then that I didn't scrape my knuckles on a cement step this morning."

"Yes it is."

"Probably just a burglar who knew that the house was empty."

"Probably," he said. "Just like the phone company computer probably made a mistake."

"Bye-bye, Vic," said Stone with a little wave of her fingers. "We'll talk again."

As I walked away from them and down the steps, they huddled together, discussing something or other, apparently not pleased, apparently not pleased at all.

Beth slid over and walked down with me. "What was that all about?"

"Nothing," I said. "It was nothing. Detectives Stone and Breger were just asking about a phone."

8

IT WAS my phone the detectives were looking for, the same phone that I had picked off the crate beside the corpse of Hailey Prouix and placed in my pocket the night of her murder. My phone. That was why I had taken it that night, why I didn't want it found anywhere near that house. My phone. Sitting now in my kitchen drawer. Registered in my name, with the bills and records going to my apartment. But I wasn't willing to wait for the end of the month to see what calls had been made. As soon as we returned from the arraignment, I phoned my service provider and requested that it print up a record of calls for the past month and fax it to my office. The lady on the line was most agreeable and said she'd get right on it. I couldn't complain about the service, they'd do anything they could to help you out, so long as you let them slip a fifty from your wallet every month.

I told Ellie, my secretary, that I was waiting for a fax.

"I HAVE something for you," I say to Hailey. This is a month before her murder. I had tried to stay away when I learned about Guy's proposal and her acceptance, tried to forget the smell of her, the feel of her, the tang of her tongue on my own. I tried, really, but the

Sylvester matter kept showing up in my in-box and my dreams grew torrid and haunting. I had tried to stay away, but she pursued me like she needed me and I couldn't help believing that maybe she did. She understood intuitively my weakness, I am most easily seduced by need. I had tried to stay away, and I had failed and I was glad.

"I have something for you," I say to Hailey. We are in bed, after, the same huge presence having roared through us the way it always roared through us, leaving us exhausted and dazed.

"Diamonds?" she asks, that twang again in her voice.

"Better."

"What could be better than diamonds? So flashy, so bright, so readily turned into ready cash."

"What about me?"

"You?" She laughs as she lifts her legs and twists them locked behind my back, twists them tight so I can't move in or out, here or there, trapped. "But I already have you, Victor, and you won't look half so pretty hanging from my ears."

Hailey in her normal life is a hard piece of work, flinty, sardonic, infected with a nervous bundle of habits that act as sword and shield to protect her inner sadness. She is both desirable and detached, which of course only makes her more desirable. It is impossible to get a straight answer from Hailey Prouix. Ask her a question and she deftly directs the line to something less threatening or, instead, asks a question of her own that puts you smack on the defensive. She is, remember, a lawyer. But after sex, oh after sex, after the two of us are run over by that charging train of hunger and need with its own strange pulse and rhythms, a train that seems to come from neither her nor me but from elsewhere, after all that, it is as if her defenses fall like the walls of Jericho under Joshua's horn. The easy, drawly vowels replace the clipped, big-city cadence she has adopted in her adopted city and her flinty defensive manner turns richer, her emotions show through almost unguarded.

"I bought you a phone," I tell Hailey that afternoon.

"I have a phone. I have too many damn phones."

"But I've been having a hard time reaching you at night. How many times can I hang up when Guy answers?"

"So that was you."

"Who did you think it was?"

"I was hoping it was you."

"How come you don't answer your cell phone after hours?"

"Because my clients call. They call to complain about their pains. They call to say they can't sleep. They want to tell me they're taking their medicine, they want to tell me they're not taking their medicine. They call to have me verify their paranoia. They call because, like everyone else, they're lonely and scared and know I'm not charging by the hour. I leave my phone in the office with the rest of my workday because if I don't, my clients will drown me."

"But I'm not a client."

"So why do you need to reach me?"

"To say hello. To let you know I'm thinking about you. To ask what you are wearing."

"In other words, so you, too, can tell me you can't sleep."

"Exactly."

"I'd rather have diamonds."

"But it's really cute, and I got it in red to match your lipstick."

"Red?"

"Shocking red."

"And who else has the number?"

"Just me."

"So it's our own private hot line."

"That's right."

"I feel like the president."

"And best of all, my number is already number one in the speed dial."

"For now." She laughs, her hearty, throaty laugh, but I can tell she likes the gift even though she can't hang it from her ears, I can tell because after she laughs she starts devouring my mouth the way she does when it is time to end our talking, hungrily, meatily, in a way that still tingled even as I remembered two days after her death.

"THAT THING you were waiting for?" said my secretary, sticking her head in my office door. "Is it from the phone company?"

"Yes," I said, with more excitement than I meant to show. To cover myself I added, "Thanks, Ellie. Just put it on the chair and I'll get to it when I can."

She laid the paper on the seat, closed the door, and I leaped out from behind my desk to get my hands on the three stapled sheets.

I started at the last page, the last call. It was registered at 10:15 the night of Hailey's death, made to my number. It was Guy, telling me that something horrible had happened. Guy. Why had he used the cell phone to make the call?

I sat down hard on the chair and thought it through. It made no sense. No sense, and that might be the only explanation. So undone by his murderous act, he picked up the first thing he could grab, the bright red phone, left out on the end table by Hailey for some reason. Picked it over the regular phone for no special reason, picked it up and dialed my number and made the call. He didn't even remember that he had used the cell phone, hadn't mentioned it when he told me the story, would probably swear he had used the regular phone, but he was mistaken, and here was the proof. It was a simple enough explanation, and it would certainly calm Detective Breger's concerns, and so all I had to do was give him the fax.

Except I couldn't. Because then I'd have to explain why a phone registered in my name, with the bills going to my home, was in that house the night of the murder. And I'd have to explain all the calls made to my number, and all the calls registered going from my number to that phone, all also listed and on the record. And with that explanation I'd surely be off the case as an attorney. Off the case as an attorney, yes, but still on as a witness or, more precisely, as a suspect. Ah, there it was, the foul root of the problem. If Guy's unthinking, nonsensical act was discovered, I'd be a suspect. I'd be a suspect that could be used by any competent defense attorney to raise doubt, maybe even reasonable doubt. Wasn't it I who was having a deceitful relationship with the deceased? Wasn't it I who had possession of the gun until I dropped it in the laps of the police? Wasn't it I who had lied about everything so that I could stay on the case as defense attorney to lay blame at the feet of the innocent Guy Forrest? The closing as much as wrote itself. How ironic that I might, in the end, be Guy's route to freedom. What I held in my hand was reasonable doubt as to Guy's guilt, except I knew I didn't do it, and I knew Guy did, and so I had to be sure that no one, no one, would ever be able to see this record.

I'd have to burn it.

I opened my office window and took an old pack of matches out of my desk drawer. Just a little fire, nothing to set off the sprinklers, I hoped, just a little fire. I lit a match. A breath of wind came through the window and killed it. I lit another and placed the flame at the document's corner. Just as it was catching, just as the blue flame turned yellow and began to curl the three pieces of paper, I noticed something.

I tried to blow out the flame, but it grew and began to devour the pages. I dropped them to the floor and stamped, stamped, stamped out the fire. The office smelled like a cigar bar. I picked up the now blackened documents. Half of each sheet was gone, on the other halves the printing could barely be discerned. But barely was enough.

There were calls on the phone made to two strange numbers. Calls made every other afternoon or so. To a number in area code 304 and then to a number in area code 702. I grabbed my phone book. Area code 304 was West Virginia, Hailey's home state. That made sense, calls to family or an old friend. But what about the number in the other area code. 702. Nevada. Who was she calling in Nevada?

"Desert Winds, how can I direct your call?"

"Desert Winds?" I said into the phone. "What exactly is Desert Winds?"

"Desert Winds is a full-care retirement community in Henderson, Nevada, just minutes outside exciting Las Vegas. Are you interested in a brochure? I could direct your call to Sales."

"No, not quite yet. Do the residents have phones in their rooms?"

"Of course. Do you know the member's extension?"

"No, I'm sorry. I'm calling about a woman named Hailey Prouix. P-r-o-u-i-x."

"One moment while I check, please. No, I'm sorry, there is no member by that name."

"Member?"

"At Desert Winds we treat all our guests as if they are members of a very exclusive club."

"Are there any members named Prouix?"

"No, not currently."

"Okay, thank you."

"Are you sure I can't direct you to Sales?"

"Do you have shuffleboard?"

"Oh, yes, tournaments and everything."

"Well, in that case, maybe a brochure would be just the thing."

9

BERWYN IS the story of American sprawl writ across a rolling suburban landscape. At first it was farm county, supplying the big city
with its corn and tomatoes. But early in the nineteenth century a
few grand estates were carved out by the aristocratic wealthy as
necessary places of refuge from the hurly-burly hoi polloi of the
city. Of course the estates needed staff, staff that lived in the city, so
the railroad, coincidentally owned by those with just such estates,
built a train line to ferry the staff back and forth from their meager
urban dwellings. It was the railroad that serviced these estates that
became known as the Main Line, a name that soon came to desig-
nate the entire area. But the raw plow of progress always follows
transportation, and it wasn't long before developers began to sell
neat little houses not far from the stations, promising easy train
commutes to the city. As the years went on, the suburban outcrop-
pings grew, some would say metastasized, spreading outward, invading farmland like a heartless disease, until only the original
great estates were left intact. But who anymore could afford to
maintain an eighty-acre estate in the middle of the 'burbs? One by
one the estates were sold, subdivided, developed, and turned into
the very creatures they had spawned, but with a difference. No typical suburban split-levels were to be built upon these blue-blooded

grounds. It was as if their aristocratic origins infected the new developments, and what was created instead were strange imitations of the great manor houses, with falsely majestic fronts and grotesquely shaped wings all out of proportion to their three-quarter-acre lots.

Welcome to the Brontë Estates, luxury homes starting in the low $800,000s. McMansions for those whose aspirations had outlived their times. The American dream on steroids.

I remember when the Forrests first moved into their new house in the Brontë Estates, showing off the seven thousand square feet of luxurious, state-of-the-art suburban space. The ground was still packed hard from the heavy vehicles, the land barren of all but the youngest, barest twigs planted by the developers, most lots were still construction sites, but Leila and Guy were proud as new parents. They had chosen the Heathcliff model, with the extra bedroom, the cathedral ceilings, the oversize great room, the atmosphere of continual yearning. A house, they said, to grow into. Leila talked of all her decorating ideas, and Guy fiddled with the new lawn mower, though his sod lawn had yet to be laid. They had lived in an apartment in the city until Leila had become pregnant with their second child, so they exuded that special glow of freshly minted suburbanites ensconced in a McMansion of their very own. The grass would arrive on a truck, the skinny trees would grow, how could the future be anything but lush?

"Hello, Victor," said the former Leila Peale at her front door. "I was wondering when you'd arrive."

"Mind if I come in for a few moments?"

"Of course not. I always have time for an old friend."

I thought she was being facetious. When Guy had left his family for Hailey, the family friends were forced to make a choice, Leila or Guy. Leila, being the more sympathetic figure and having the older connection to their social set, seemed to end up with everyone but me. I had known Guy long before his marriage and, though I thought what he had done was despicable, I ended up, almost against my will, on his side of the aisle. That he had told me everything before he left his wife and I had said nothing to her only cemented my place outside her circle. I hadn't seen her, hadn't spoken to her, since the separation, so when Leila called me an old friend I thought she was making a joke. But she surprised me by ushering me not into the formal parlor with its stiff French furnishings reserved for painfully polite conversation but through the open kitchen area into the spacious, vaulted informal room used by family and friends.

So there we were, perched in the plush green furnishings, two iced teas on coasters atop the coffee table, chatting like, well, like old friends. I wanted to pat her on the knee and assure her that I was taking care of everything, that Guy would pay for all he had done, but it was better to maintain my secrets. When she looked at me, I supposed she saw the bastard lawyer defending her bastard husband. When I looked at her, I supposed I saw an ally.

"I saw you on TV, Victor, giving your little speech as you left the courthouse."

"It's part of the job."

"Well, it doesn't look as if you hate it."

"No, can't say I do."

"And they do seem to like putting you on."

"Such is the burden of startling good looks and a winning personality."

She laughed at that, a deep, good-natured laugh, and curled her legs beneath her on the couch. It reminded me of better times, when Leila and Guy were my mature married friends and I played the part of the unsettled single guy. Leila was a big-boned women with an inviting, if not beautiful, face. Friendly and warm with a lively sense of humor, she had made a nice contrast to the serious and humorless Guy.

Slowly her laughter subsided and her face darkened. "How is he?" she asked.

"Not so good."

"I didn't think so. Guy sometimes pretended to be a hard guy, as if the tattoo prepared him for anything, but he is not the prison type."

"Who is, really? How are the children handling it?" They had two: Laura, a lovely, quiet girl, aged six, and Elliott, a terror who never outgrew his terrible twos, aged four. "Do they know?"

"Not really. It's not as if he had been much of a presence in their lives after he left anyway. I told them their daddy is in trouble but that it's all a mistake and he'll be with them soon."

"He wants to see them."

"I don't think that's best. After the trial, if he's convicted, I expect we'll have to work something out about visitation, but until then I don't think it healthy for a six- and four-year-old to see their father in prison. I've talked it over with the pediatrician and she agrees."

"I'll tell him. He'll be disappointed, but I'm sure he'll understand."

"He should write letters. They'd love to hear from him and Laura, at least, can write back. Is there anything else I can do? Anything? I'll do what I can."

"That's sort of why I came, but I'm a little surprised at the offer. I thought a part of you would be glad it turned out like it did."

"He's still my husband, Victor, the father of my children. I don't want him in jail."

"And Hailey?"

She winced, as if she had just chewed a rotten morsel of beef. "I don't wish anyone dead, but I won't mourn Hailey Prouix. Somehow she turned Guy against himself, and that's a crime. You know, Victor, I was suing her."

"Suing her?"

"Alienation of affection I think is the legal term, but basically I was suing her for stealing my husband. There have been successful suits just like it all over the country. One woman I heard won a million dollars."

"Sounds like the lottery."

"I was suing that witch for every penny she had."

"What good would that have done, Leila?"

"Other than the money?" She laughed again. "Oh, I suppose in some bitter way it would have cheered me. I wanted to take something from her that she cared about, just like she took Guy from me."

"He had something to do with it, too."

"He was bewitched."

"Leila."

"Well, it wasn't love. What Guy and I had together was love, what he had with her was something else. I think love is more than just a one-way obsession, don't you, Victor? Doesn't it have to be based on some sort of understanding of the other? Doesn't it have to be reciprocated in some way to be real?"

"I don't know," I said, and in that moment I could have sworn I caught a whiff of jasmine, Hailey's scent, and I remembered, suddenly, an afternoon we spent together just a few weeks before her death. I blinked the memory away before it overwhelmed me. "Reciprocated or not," I said, "the emotion feels just the same either way."

"Yes, that's just it. It feels the same either way, but it isn't the same. One is real, genuine, an emotional coming-together that forms the basis for everything meaningful. The other is a solipsistic delusion, not so different from a teenager with a crush on a rock star or a stalker obsessed with his prey. Whatever those emotions are, no matter how strong, they are not love. Guy was obsessed with her, I know that, and I can understand it, but it wasn't love. Whatever trouble he's in, it arrived because in the midst of his obsession he thought she was feeling what he was feeling, when she was incapable of returning what he felt with anything but scorn."

"How do you know what she was capable of?"

"So defensive, Victor. It's charming, your trying to defend my husband's emotional life, but I know her. I know how she met my husband and why. And I had a run-in with her on my own. After the complaint was filed by some young attorney in my father's office, she called me. Out of the blue she called me, and what she said . . . Victor, I was third-team all-American as a swimmer in college and let me tell you, a swimmers' locker room can be pretty raucous—some of the girls could shame a sailor—but still, I have never heard language coming from a woman like I heard over the phone. When she hung up, I was too startled to be angry. What I was, actually, was sorry for Guy."

"What did she say?"

"I won't tell you word for word, I don't use that kind of language in my home, but it was something to the effect that if I wanted him back so badly, I was welcome to him. But then she warned me that with the taste of her still in his teeth there was no way in hell he was coming back to me. I'll give her this, at least she knew where her power lay."

"So you hated her."

"No, it wasn't so personal. I wanted it to be personal, me against her, then maybe the lawsuit would have given me true satisfaction, but it wasn't like that. She was more a force of nature, like a sudden raging storm or a tornado. You don't hate it, but you sure as hell feel sorry for anyone in its path."

I winced. I couldn't help it. It was easy enough to dismiss Leila's disparagements as the words of a woman scorned, because take away the informal setting and the apparent calm of her voice and that was what she was, a woman scorned, whose husband had left her for something sweeter. It was easy enough to dismiss all she said, except that Leila herself was a presence not easily dismissed.

"Leila," I said, wanting to change the topic, "Guy is pretty shaken. He says he needs to get out of jail until the trial, but it looks like he won't have enough assets to put up for bond if bail is set."

"I thought there was money?"

"There is some, yes. We're in the process of tracking it down, getting an exact figure, but, from what we can tell so far, there were apparently some bad investments and some unaccounted-for withdrawals."

"Bad investments and unaccounted-for withdrawals." She repeated my words, as if to imprint the new idea in her consciousness. "No money? There's no money?"

"We haven't tracked down the exact figure yet."

The exact figure apparently didn't matter. She started laughing, as if some great practical joke had been played for her benefit. "Well, you don't have to bother. I can guess all right. There's no money. So much for my lawsuit." Her laughter continued, ratcheted up in intensity. "So much for Juan Gonzalez."

"Who? The ballplayer?"

"Forget it. Nothing." She kept laughing until she noticed me sitting there glumly and regained her composure. "But, Victor, if there's no money, how are you getting paid?"

"I don't know."

"The loyalty of an old friend?"

"Something like that."

"I wonder if Guy knows how lucky he is to have you."

"The point is, Leila, that Guy wants to know if you'd put up the house for his bail. It might not be enough even if you could, but he wanted me to ask, and I said I would, even though I—"

"Yes."

"Excuse me?"

"Yes, I would put up the house to get him out of jail. Will it be enough?"

"I don't know."

"The mortgage is pretty high, and I don't know how much equity there is, but whatever I can do I will do. I also have some investments we could use."

"You know he was trying to run when they arrested him. He could try to run again."

"He won't. His life is here."

"And he might have actually killed her."

"If he did, he had good reason. Is there something I have to sign?"

"You might want to talk to a lawyer before you do anything. If he runs, you could lose the house. You might want to talk to your father."

"I know what my father would say and I don't care. You bring to me what you want me to sign and I will sign it. And you tell Guy I'm still waiting."

"Waiting?"

"He'll know."

"You're waiting? For him?" My eyes opened wide with my incredulity. "You're waiting for him to come back?"

"This is his home, too."

"You still love him, even after all he did?"

"It's not like a faucet, Victor. You don't just turn it off."

"You ever think he's not worthy of it?"

"Every day."

"And that if he does get out, he might not choose to live with you again?"

"Victor, everything you say makes a great deal of sense, and thank you for your sage advice, but I'm willing to take my chances. Sometimes in the middle of our lives we don't realize that our dreams have come true. It's only after it all disappears that we know. I want it back the way it was before ever we heard of Hailey Prouix. I want my husband back, my children's father back, my life back. I want everything the way it was."

"It can never be that way again, Leila. Whatever it is, it will be different."

"Maybc better, who can tell? She's dead, isn't she? You bring me the paper, I'll sign what I need to sign."

I hadn't thought of it before, it hadn't seemed a possibility before, but now how could I avoid it? Even knowing what I knew, even with all my certainties, how could I avoid it?

"On the night Hailey was killed," I said, "where were you around ten o'clock?"

"That's funny, Victor. The police asked me the very same question."

"They've been here?"

"Two detectives. An athletic woman, who might have been a swimmer herself. She did most of the talking. And another, an older black man, a Detective Breger, I think it was, who spent the whole time pacing the room, snooping into every corner. I'll give you the same thing I gave them." She stood, walked to the phone table, wrote down a number. "His name is Herb Stein, a very nice man. We had dinner in a Belgian place by the library that night. The mussel sauce splashed all over his tie. He wiped it spotless with a napkin."

"Don't be a snob, Leila, I wear polyester ties myself."

"Well, then, Victor, you can date him. Or Ted Jenrette, with his nose hairs, or Biff Callender and Chip Cannon. What is it, Victor, with men who keep their nicknames from summer camp? My friends are so eager for me to start a new life, when all I want is my old one back. Not very Buddhist of me I know, but, hell, I was raised Episcopalian."

"Did you ever think, Leila, that your current love for Guy, being completely unrequited, is as solipsistic a delusion as you said was his love for Hailey?"

"I have an appointment, Victor, that I just can't miss. May I show you out?"

"I know the way," I said. "I don't mean to keep you. Can I ask one more thing?"

She glanced at her watch and nodded.

"What made you think that Hailey had enough money to be worth suing?"

"I just supposed. I guess I supposed wrong. You'll bring those papers for me to sign."

"I'll bring the papers. But can I give you a word of advice, as a friend?"

"No."

"Be careful what you risk on him, Leila."

It was the best advice I could give, but she wasn't listening. She wasn't listening. All she wanted was for me to take my truths out of her life so she could pursue a past that had receded into fantasy.

Nostalgia is a fire fueled by failures of memory.

10

DRIVING HOME through the narrow suburban streets, I wasn't smelling the freshness of newly mown grass or marveling at the variety of roadside flora blooming with a fertile exuberance, azaleas and dogwoods, cherry blossoms, forsythia. Something blocked the sun of the afternoon from my sight, something turned the brightness into a gray murk that spread out from me in dusky waves. And in the midst of that gloom the memory that had invaded me at Leila's returned to work its black magic in my consciousness, and this time I didn't blink it away. This time, as I drove, I let it overwhelm me. I am smelling her perfume and tasting the salt of her shoulder, feeling the striae of rib beneath her breasts. She is in control, pressing her knees against my sides, licking my breast, her dark hair tickling my chest.

"Do you love him?" I ask.

She raises her head just quick enough to answer, "No."

"Then why are you with him?"

"Must we?"

"Yes."

"I needed him."

"And now you're going to marry him?"

"It's what he wants. Suck my thumb."

"No."

"Just do it."

"It's because you don't want to talk about him, isn't it?"

She places her thumb in my mouth, scratches my tongue with her nail, fish-jerks my head to the side and bites my neck.

"How can you marry him if you don't love him?" I ask later. She is facedown now on the bed, her knees beneath her. I am atop her, moving slowly, methodically, waiting for the train to come through and take control. It has become something akin to an addiction, that train, that strange locomotive of primordial emotion that roars through us and speeds us along on its frenzied uncontrollable ride.

"Last thing I ever want to be again is in love," she says. It is a shocking statement. It stops short my rhythm.

"You're lying. The whole world wants to be in love."

"The whole world is wrong."

"And you know better than the world?"

"Oh, yes. Oh, yes, I know."

"Were you ever?"

"Yes."

"And it ended badly?"

"Hiroshima."

"Who was it? The halfback? The philandering partner?"

"It was the wrong man."

"Maybe all you need is the right man."

"Shut up, Victor."

"Maybe all you need—"

"Shut up," she says as she rolls away with a loud, sucking thwap and I am left dangling stiffly. "I'm done."

"I'm not."

"Well, then," she says, her back now to me as she walks to the bathroom, "don't let me stop you."

Before she leaves the apartment, she stands over me as I lay still naked in my bed. She is fully dressed now, panty-hosed and pow-dered, buttoned up tight, tall in her heels, glasses on, her face hold-ing the stoic impassivity of a suffering soldier. And she tells me something I remembered with utter clarity as I drove away from Leila's house.

"I'm sleeping with one man," says Hailey Prouix, her voice an emotionless monotone, "engaged to another, emotionally entrapped with a third, mourning forever a fourth. I have no illusions about the tragic mess of my life. But I tell you, Victor, everything I have become has been forged by a love so fearsome it has seared my soul. Don't waste your time trying to understand it, because it is mine and it still baffles me, but don't for a minute think I want anything like that to happen to me again. Only the deranged want to be struck by lightning twice. In the end you're no different from Guy, you desperately want love while having no idea what it is. You say love and you think something else, you think of affection tinged with desire, you think of friendship, comfort, you think of someone to cuddle while you watch videos, to help you choose your linens, someone to make you the man you hope to be. That's all fine, nothing wrong with that, but don't pretend such watered milk to be love. We fuck and I like it, and maybe I like you better than Guy, and maybe if I were free to choose I'd choose you to watch videos with and help me pick out towels for the master bath, but don't delude yourself that it is love, Victor, because it is not, thank God. If you knew what love was, what it could do, if you really knew, you wouldn't want it either. In love there is no choice, no freedom, no dignity, no happiness, no joy, nothing but hunger and burn that eats away at the flesh. Who in their right mind would want that? I'd sooner die than go through it again. I'd sooner you shot me through the heart."

It was not the kind of declaration you forget, Hailey's confession of the fearsome love that had singed her soul, but it was not the kind of thing you let get in the way of a healthy sexual obsession either. I wanted Hailey and so I played deaf, assuming her hard stance was merely another attempt to deflect my attempts at intimacy. Who knew better than I all the tricks of the trade in keeping emotional distance? Who knew better than I what soft yearnings lay behind the pose of unconcern? But coming back from Leila's, after Guy's wife had spoken to me of the secrets she had learned about Hailey and Hailey's inability to return Guy's love, I began to wonder if maybe Hailey had been spilling more of the truth than I had realized. In her lawyer's garb, in her unimpassioned voice, without the least hint of her cynical smile, maybe she was opening up more than ever I had realized. What had happened in the past, I wondered as I drove through the suburbs and onto the expressway, to wound her so badly? And how did that past intersect with the moment when Guy had aimed his gun and shot her, just as she wished, right through the heart?

11

"**SO WHAT** do you think?" said Beth.

I was sitting in my office, remembering Hailey as compulsively as if I were worrying a loose tooth, when Beth strolled in and collapsed into the client chair opposite my desk. A document of some sort was clutched in her hand.

"Think about what?" I said.

"About whether Guy killed Hailey Prouix."

"It's not our job to figure that out."

"I know, I know, I know, but still." Her eyes widened. "What do you think?"

"I think he's presumptively innocent," I snapped, pretending to concentrate on something on my desk. "I think we should leave it at that and not act like amateurs."

"Don't get snippy about it, Victor. Are you okay? You look like hell. Maybe you need a break. Maybe you should make a date with that mysterious woman you've been seeing."

My head jerked up and I stared at her, bewildered. "Who?"

"I thought you were in the middle of a big romance, sneaking out of the office in the early afternoons, coming back all bleary-eyed and full of sated smiles. You didn't say anything, but I could tell."

My nerves contracted in on themselves as I tried to look calm. I had, of course, never told Beth about Hailey, I had never told anyone—there were reasons in the middle of our affair and there were stronger reasons now—but how could I not have figured that she had known I was at least seeing someone?

"It ended," I said. "Badly. She wants to be friends."

"Oooh, that's hard."

"And not even good friends, more like distant acquaintances who, if we happen to see each other in a theater, nod but make no effort to say hello."

"That's really hard."

"Just to be sure, she changed her number. I think she might have even changed her name. Last I heard she was on a tramp steamer to Marrakesh, which is pretty much a distance record to avoid seeing me again."

Beth laughed, which was what I wanted. Both of our love lives were in perpetual states of ruin and we liked to comfort one another by detailing our most recent disasters. "Didn't one of your old girlfriends join the Peace Corps?" she said.

"Yeah, but she was assigned to Guatemala, which is at least in this hemisphere."

"Maybe that's why you've been acting like you've been acting," she said.

"How have I been acting?"

"A little strange, a little mysterious. Doing things no one would expect from you, very un-Victor-like things."

"Like what?"

"Like taking this case without a retainer."

"He's a friend. He said money would be no problem."

"Is that what he said? And you believed him?"

"I've a trusting soul."

"Right. And Emily Dickinson was a party girl. And then you up and turned the murder weapon over to the detectives."

"I was obligated," I said. "I'm an officer of the court and I held material evidence."

She leaned forward, stared at me as if she had those X-ray spiral glasses they advertise in the back of Archie comics. "And far be it from you ever to mess with your obligations as an officer of the court."

"Far be it. What are you getting at?"

"I don't know, Victor. What should I be getting at?"

I shrugged, but my canary in the mine shaft was making like Pavarotti. If she suspected something, she who knew me best, someone else might, too. I had to get a grip, I had to start assuaging suspicions, I had to start now.

"I'm sorry if I was short," I said, as sweetly as I could. "I've been on edge about this case, but I shouldn't take it out on you. Maybe I think Guy's really in trouble. Maybe I'm feeling pressure because he's a friend. Maybe I'm not handling it as well as I should. You want to know whether I think Guy did it? Well, I think his story about the headphones and the Jacuzzi and hearing nothing is well neigh unbelievable."

"What about the gun? Maybe it was silenced, maybe he couldn't hear it."

"The gun was a revolver," I said. "You can't silence a revolver. And anyway, the biggest trouble is that nobody else seems to have a motive."

"What about his wife? Hailey stole her husband. Is there a better motive than that?"

"Well, she was angry, for sure. She was even suing the victim."

"Really?"

"Yes, but that works against her doing it, doesn't it? I don't think you just off the object of your lawsuit. You already have an outlet for your anger, and it makes it hard to collect damages. But there's more. I just got off the phone with a Herb Stein. He was with Leila on a date the night of the murder, at a place called Cuvée Notre Dame on Green Street."

"Good mussels."

"So he said. I don't think we can pin it on her and, frankly, I don't know who else, besides Guy, might have been involved enough to want her dead." I leaned back in my chair, stared at the ceiling. "Except, of course, Guy doesn't have much of a motive either. It's the weakest part of the government's case. The why. Why would he be so angry at her as to shoot her through the heart? As long as they don't have an answer, Guy has a chance." I took a quick glance at Beth. "That's why I advised him to reject the government's offer. There is means and opportunity, sure, but you also need motive."

"Interesting, because the coroner's report came in while you were out." She waved the document in her hand. "Bullet through the heart, like we knew, a bruising on her cheek, like we knew, tubes tied, like we could have expected."

"Really?"

"And there was one thing more, one quite interesting thing more."

I raised an eyebrow and waited.

"They found traces of semen inside her."

"No surprise. She was living with Guy."

"Yes, except that they did preliminary tests on the sample pending DNA typing. It turns out the semen came from a secretor, so they could do a quick determination of blood type. Type A."

"That's common enough. What is it, a third of the population?"

"Forty-two percent, according the report. But we don't care about the general population, we're not representing the general population, we're representing Guy. And that's where it all starts looking hinky. Guy is type B."

I bathed my face in false surprise.

"She was cheating on him, Victor. There was another man."

I stared at her, fighting to remain impassive. "Did he know it?"

"I don't know."

"I suppose we'll have to find out."

"I suppose we will. But, Victor, Hailey *was* cheating on him, that is a fact. He can deny knowing it all he wants, but no one has to believe him. Hailey was cheating on him and there, Victor, on a fine silver salver, is your motive."

I stared at her, stared at her as the case against my client strengthened immeasurably right before my very eyes, based ironically on my own blood antigens, stared at her as Guy Forrest took three giant steps toward a life sentence, and the whole time I was fighting the urge to smile.

12

"**WHO DO** you think killed her, Guy?" asked Beth.

"I don't know."

"You have to have some idea. Hailey's dead and you're on trial for her murder. You knew her life better than anyone. You have to have some theory."

We were in one of the lawyer-client rooms at the Montgomery County Correctional Facility, a squat, sprawling building of orange brick, with a green ribbed roof and shiny loops of barbed wire, set out more for their aesthetic appeal than for security, a prison built for five hundred inmates but holding more than twice that amount. The room itself was slate gray, with a metal table, walls of cinder block, a solid steel door, and it had that lovely prison smell of ammonia and sweat and fear, with the faintest undertone of urine, which may have come from the surrounding halls or may have come from Guy himself, who was certainly distraught enough. In the week or so since his arrest he had grown gaunt. His hands shook slightly even as he held them on the tabletop. His eyes were like a bleary red smear. There was a welt beneath his left eye, blue-black against his gray pallor, fitting, since Hailey's corpse held the same kind of welt, and the tic that jerked his upper lip to the right at arraignment was developing nicely.

I crossed my arms over my chest and leaned against a wall in the corner of the room and let Beth handle the questioning. This was all pro forma, something we had to do, keeping Guy fully apprised of what was happening to him as we asked him for as much information as possible. There were no surprises here. He continued to maintain his innocence as I leaned against the wall and watched the lies spill out.

"The only answer," said Guy, "is that someone came in while I was in the Jacuzzi. I didn't hear him because of the headphones. That had to be what happened."

"Who?"

"I don't know."

"Why?"

"I don't know. They were mad at me, not at her."

"Who was mad at you, Guy?"

"Leila was upset when I left, and so was her father."

"Jonah Peale?"

"Yes. Do you know him?"

"Only by reputation," said Beth.

"A hard son of a bitch. Scary. He told me to stay away from Leila and stay away from him or he'd shove a pitching wedge down my throat and take a swing at my spleen."

"Can you blame him?" I said.

Guy shot me a look of annoyance. "There was also an investigator who did some work for the firm, an ugly little lizard named Skink. Phil Skink. He had a rough reputation, and I never understood why the firm used him. There was a time, before I met Hailey, when he tried to buddy up with me for some reason. I blew him off. Frankly, he creeped me out. And then, after I left everything for Hailey, I started running into Skink in strange places."

"Where?"

"Outside my new office, in a bar. Once I was pissing at a urinal in a restaurant bathroom. The son of a bitch came out of nowhere, sidled up next to me, and gave me that gap-toothed smile of his."

"Phil Skink?"

"Yeah."

"Did he threaten you?"

"Not directly, he was too sly for that. But he did mention some files I had taken with me when I left Dawson, Cricket. I told him to stay the hell away from me, and he laughed. Once, when I was walking up to Hailey on the street, from afar I saw her talking to some man. As I got closer, I realized it was Skink. It sent a shiver through me. When he spotted me, he simply walked away. Hailey would never tell me what he said."

"You think he threatened her?"

"That's what I assumed. Maybe he was the one making the calls and then hanging up. Maybe he was the one who killed her."

"Phil Skink?" I said.

"Yeah, maybe it was him."

"Yeah," I said. "Maybe." Or maybe O.J. was in town, I thought.

"Did you lock the front door of the house before you went upstairs?" said Beth.

"I usually did, bolted the door and locked the windows. We're still pretty close to the city where we live. Lived."

"And that night?"

"I think so."

"The windows were locked when the police came, but the door was open. Did you unlock the door when you went outside?"

"I don't remember."

"Was it locked or was it open? After you climbed out of the Jacuzzi, you saw her on the mattress, you picked up the gun, you searched the house. Then you called Victor and went outside to wait for him. Is that all correct?"

"Yes. Yes."

"When you went outside, did you have to unlock the door?"

"I don't know."

"Think about it, Guy."

"I don't remember unlocking it. I just opened it. It must have been unlocked. It must have been unlocked." He opened his eyes wide, as if he had just discovered a wonderful, liberating secret. "The killer somehow unlocked it and left it unlocked. That's it. That's the proof."

I stared at him from my corner, Beth stared from across the table. We didn't say a word, didn't a move a muscle.

"Why don't you tell them? That's the answer. The door was un-locked. That proves everything I said is true."

"And the evidence for that is?" said Beth, softly.

His gaze shifted crazily around the room, and then, as if her question had been a pin inserted into his abdomen, his body deflated.

I pushed myself off the wall and walked to the desk until I stood over him, my arms still crossed. "Tell me again about your relationship with Hailey," I said.

He looked up at me. "We were in love."

"Still?"

"What do you mean, still? Yes, of course."

"Did you have sex the night she died?"

"No."

"The night before?"

"I don't know, I don't remember."

"The night before that?"

"I don't know specifically. We had an active sex life."

"Is that why the Viagra?"

"Yes." Pause. "But I didn't need it."

"Has any company ever made more money selling a drug that nobody claims to need?"

"Its just that . . . that . . . Hailey liked to keep going. The pill helped. She made me get it."

"She made you? When was the last time you used the Viagra?"

"I don't remember. Is it important? Why is this important?"

"Were you and Hailey fighting? Did you have any fights?"

"Some, sure. Everyone does. We did, too. About the usual things. She was fiery when we were fighting and then again when we made up."

"Did you ever hit her?"

"No."

"Did you hit her the night of her death?"

"No. Stop it. What are you saying?"

"There was a bruise on her cheek."

"Maybe the killer—"

"Did you fight the night of her death? Did you hit her the night of her death?"

"No. Hit her? No. Never. Why would I do something like that?"

"Out of raw anger."

"No."

"Because she was sleeping with someone else. Because she was fucking someone else, Guy, and she wasn't fucking you."

He stared up at me, horrified and pained. "You're wrong."

"Am I?" I said.

Beth's calm voice broke through the fierce flow of testosterone coursing through the room. "The coroner found semen traces in her vagina," she said. "Such traces don't last more than a day and half, two days maximum. The coroner swabbed out a sample and took a preliminary test. It doesn't match your blood type, Guy. They'll perform other tests, but that will only prove it more convincingly. Hailey Prouix was cheating on you."

Guy didn't say anything for a long time, nothing, and then he lied. "I didn't know," he said.

I stood over him for a moment longer before, ignoring Beth's questing gaze, I turned and strolled back to the corner.

Guy's head shook as if it were struggling to take in a new bolt of information. It was a treat, actually, to watch him work. He was dramatically sliding through the appropriate emotions like a ski racer sliding through the gates, first one, then the other. He was giving us an approximation of the emotional reaction of a man learning for the first time that his dead fiancée had been cheating on him, and a rather awkward one at that, except for the verisimilitude of the setting and situation. And then he glanced up at Beth, he glanced up as if to make sure that his emotional slalom run had been duly noted and admired, before saying:

"He did it."

"Who?" asked Beth.

"The bastard who was doing her. You asked me who did it. I'm telling you right now. It was him. I have no doubt about it. She was staying with me, and he didn't like it. He knew how to get in. Maybe she had even given him a key to the house. Maybe she had even shown him the gun. He did it. He did it, damn it. We have to find him. He's a murderer. He killed Hailey."

I stared at him with disgust, even as I thought the theory through.

It wasn't bad, it had promise. Guy had never been a legal scholar, but he was a trial lawyer himself and had always been a clever strategist. And now he had come up with a damn clever strategy. Just what I did not need.

"It's a theory," I said, "but there's no evidence to support it."

"*Find* the evidence. Find the bastard. He did it, I know it. Find him, and if you can't find him, that doesn't change a thing. He did it. That's what I want you to argue, Victor. That's what I want you to prove. That's our theory."

"Without proof it's a loser," I said.

"I don't know," said Beth. "It sounds pretty good to me."

"If you make the lover the issue," I said slowly, as if instructing a first-year Criminal Law class, "you just throw Guy's motive in the jury's face over and over and over. Every time you mention the lover, Guy's reason to kill her becomes more evident. And of course, if we make the lover the issue, then Jefferson will put every resource into finding him. And if he does find him, and there's an alibi, then you might as well check the guilty box on the verdict form yourself."

"Guy, have you thought any more about the deal?" asked Beth.

"Some. Maybe I've been thinking about it a lot."

"Don't lose your nerve here, Guy," I said.

"I can't spend my life in here. It's been only a week, and already I'm a wreck."

"Don't lose your nerve," I repeated, ignoring Beth's gaze.

"Okay."

"Everything still looks solid," I said.

"Okay, okay. I'm sticking with you, Victor. So when can I get out of here? When can I get a bail set?"

"That's also what we came to talk about," said Beth. "You remember, at arraignment, when the judge set no bail, she indicated that she might reconsider if we could come up with a complete financial profile so she could set a figure high enough to be sure to deter flight. To that end we began to examine your economic resources, using the authority you gave us when you signed those documents."

"Then let's get moving. If I have to spend another night in here, I don't know if . . ." He stopped speaking. He clasped his hands tighter to stop the shaking.

"We found your account at Schwab." Beth reached into her briefcase and took out a statement. "It was registered in your and Hailey's names, as joint tenants, as you told us, and we wanted you to have a look at it and maybe explain some things to us."

"Fine," he said, holding his hand out for the statement.

"Before you look," I said, "can we go over again why you and Hailey had a joint account?"

"We were committed to each other, Victor. That's the way you do it when you're going to spend the rest of your lives together. She had some money from a case, I had some money for me to live on after I left Leila, we put it together."

"What case did she get the payment from?"

"I don't know, some big medical malpractice case."

"When did it settle?"

"Last year or something."

"You don't know the name?"

"I don't remember."

"Who was the defense attorney? He'll know the name."

"I don't know who it was."

"Didn't you discuss it with her at all?"

"Sure. War stories, you know."

"And you don't know the name of the opposing counsel? Because when I tell my war stories to other lawyers, I always mention who was on the other side. It makes the tale of victory so much sweeter."

"I don't remember."

"How much was in the account?"

"Maybe half a million."

"Who had access to the money?"

"Hailey mainly. I let her deal with it. Didn't we already go over this? Can I see the statements?"

"You said you fought with Hailey now and then about the usual things," said Beth. "The most usual thing for couples to fight about is money. Did you ever fight with Hailey about the money in the account?"

"No. Maybe. I don't remember. Maybe."

There was a pause, which neither Beth nor I deigned to fill.

"Yes. Once. Or maybe more than once. There was some money missing. I called up the brokerage. I wanted to make a payment to Leila for the house without Hailey knowing. It was silly, but she had been complaining about having to sign checks for my wife, so I thought I'd wire some money right to the mortgage company to take care of a few months and everything would be fine. But I was surprised at the amount they said was available. It was less than I thought it should be, about half, actually. I asked Hailey about it. She told me it was none of my business, that she was taking care of it, that some of her investments hadn't worked out."

"Did anyone hear you fight?" asked Beth.

"No, I don't think so."

"Was it at home or in a public place?"

"Maybe a restaurant, I don't know. I decided after to take some cash out of the account, just to be safe."

"The cash you had in the suitcase?"

"That's right. Can I see the statement?"

"Do you know a man named Juan Gonzalez?" I asked.

He stopped, made a show of searching through his memory. "The ballplayer?"

"No. Not the ballplayer. Someone else."

"I don't think so."

"What about Hailey? Did she ever mention someone by that name?"

"No. Never heard of him. I would have remembered. The name rings no bell." Pause. "Where did you hear it?"

"From your wife. She's actually willing to put up the house for your bail. She still loves you."

Guy didn't respond, he merely shrugged, as if it were expected.

"She also said she had sued Hailey Prouix."

"Yes," said Guy. "Alienation of affection."

"She said she thought that Hailey had all this money that made her worth suing, and as she said it the name Juan Gonzalez slipped out."

"Well, as usual, when it comes to Leila, I have no idea what she's talking about. Don't take anything she says too seriously. Can I see my financial statement now?"

I stood there for a moment and then nodded. Beth handed it over. I watched carefully as he examined the document, watched him screw his face into puzzlement and scratch his head, watched his eyes shift from uncertainty to fear.

"What happened to the money? There's nothing here." His voice dropped from his normal swift confidence to something scared, to something desperate and caught, like a furry animal trapped in a corner discovering that its escape hole has been cemented shut. There was nothing of the deliberate sliding through the expected here, this was real and desolate and terrifying, and his whole body shook as his voice whined like a siren, "Where is my money? Where is it? Where?"

After the guard led him away, Beth and I sat quietly together in the conference room for a moment.

"Things grew a little heated there," said Beth.

"It's going to get more heated if he takes the stand. It was time for him to get a taste of what it will be like."

"I had a dog once," she said. "A bichon frisé, a pretty little white thing we called Pom Pom. I had begged so shamelessly for a dog for so long that my mother finally gave in. But she insisted Pom Pom stay in his little crate in the mud room whenever he wasn't being walked on his leash. Pom Pom hated his crate, cried incessantly, whined and yipped and snapped at all of us whenever he was let out for brief reprieves. You could hear his moans all through the house. He had an eye condition common to the breed, so his eyes were surrounded with a red crust that only made his whining all the more pitiable. Then one day after school my mother picked me up in the car and held me tight and told me Pom Pom had been killed by a car."

"Now, that's hard."

"No, it was a relief. I grew to hate that dog and his desperate whining. It made me feel guilty every time I looked at his red runny eyes behind the barred door of his crate."

"What suddenly brought to mind your old family dog?"

"He should take the plea."

"It's his choice."

"It's a good offer. He should take the plea. His lover theory isn't bad, but something's not right about the money."

"I know."

"He's not telling us something."

"I know."

"And when they find out about it, and they will find out about it, it's going jump up and bite him in the ass."

I didn't say anything, but I knew she was absolutely right. It was going to jump up and bite him in the ass, and all I had to do was figure out what it was. All I had to do was figure out what it was, and I knew where to start the figuring.

Juan Gonzalez.

"Funny thing about that dog," said Beth. "It wasn't until I was already in college that I began to wonder. If little Pom Pom was always locked in his crate, how did that car manage to drive into our mud room and squash him flat?"

13

JUAN GONZALEZ.

A name that meant nothing, except that Leila had mentioned it offhandedly and then Guy had made quite a show of knowing nothing about it. Too much of a show for me to leave it alone. A name that meant nothing except that it meant something, surely.

Juan Gonzalez.

Beth had said it for me: Something was not right about the money. Why had everyone thought there was once so much of it? Why had Hailey, who was startlingly unsentimental about love and romance, allowed it to be put into a joint account? To where had it disappeared? Something was not right about the money, something that would cause grievous harm to Guy's cause if discovered, and so my number-one priority was to discover it. I didn't know yet what it was, that secret, but I knew enough to lead me to its shelter. I knew its name.

Juan Gonzales.

First name Juan, John in Spanish. Family name Gonzalez, might as well be Smith. Juan Gonzalez. John Smith. How was it possible to find a connection between such a name and Hailey Prouix? Was it business or personal? Was he a lawyer or a client? Was he a friend or a relative. Was he a lover of Hailey's or Guy's or both? The possibilities were endless. All I knew for sure was that he wasn't the ballplayer, but whoever he was, he was important enough for Guy and Leila to want to hide the truth, and so he was important enough for me to find.

"Never heard of him," had said Guy. "I would have remembered. The name rings no bell." When he told us this he was lying. Guy thought he had a secret without realizing that there is no such thing. There is always a trail, always a betrayal of some sort of another. To say you have a secret is only to say that you know something no one cares enough yet to figure out, But I cared, I cared like hell.

"Leila," I said into the phone. "I have a question."

"How is Guy?"

"About as you would expect."

"Did you tell him what I agreed to do with the house? Did you tell him what I said?"

"Yes, I did. I have a question."

"What did he say when you told him?"

"He shrugged, Leila."

"He's distraught still. He needs time."

"Yes," I said. He needs about thirty to life, I thought without saying. "Juan Gonzalez. You mentioned that name."

"Did I?"

"Yes, you did. Who is he?"

"I don't know, Victor. You said he was a ballplayer."

"Not the ballplayer."

"Then I must have misspoken."

"You didn't misspeak. Who is he?"

"Do you have those papers for me to sign? Does it look like he'll be out of prison soon?"

"Leila, if I'm going to defend Guy, if I'm going to do right by Guy, I need to know everything. I need to know about Juan Gonzalez."

"No, Victor. No you don't. I heard the prosecutor made an offer."

"Yes."

"If he accepts the offer, when would he be out?"

"Somewhere between eight and ten years. Maybe less."

"I'd be forty-five or so."

"I need to know about Juan Gonzalez, Leila."

"Tell him I'd wait. Will you tell him that?"

"Why don't you tell him?"

"He's not taking my calls."

"Isn't that answer enough?"

"I have to go. I have to pick up Laura at school."

"Juan Gonzalez."

"Tell him what I said, Victor."

In the Philadelphia phone book there were three listings for a Juan Gonzalez, five more for J. Gonzalez. I would call each one and ask if he knew a Hailey Prouix or a Guy Forrest. If that didn't work, I'd expand my search to include the suburbs, then New Jersey, then Delaware, spreading out nationwide in a great arc of inquiry. There were also records to check, computer databases to consult, sources to pump. It would take days, weeks, it could tie up my office for months, but still I wouldn't stop until I had the answer. And I would find the answer, I had no doubts, because Guy thought his secret was safe without realizing that no secrets are safe. A secret has weight, it feasts and swells, it fills voids, it invades sleep, it withers joy, it darkens the landscape and presses down upon the soul and grows ever larger until it is too great to be contained. Then it crawls out into the world, hiding in dark places, waiting to be found.

I would check the files and peruse the records and follow the slime trail. One by one I would turn over the rocks, one by one, until underneath some seemingly irrelevant hunk of granite there it would lie, like a fat, wriggling worm. A worm with a name.

Juan Gonzalez.

14

I WASN'T sleeping. I couldn't figure what was the problem, but somehow my circadian rhythms had come undone, and I wasn't sleeping.

At night, in my bed, I would feel myself slipping, falling delightfully into sleep. And then something would happen, something hard would seize my fall. I couldn't figure what it was, but something would happen and I would end up staring at the ceiling, seeing the darkness separate into pinpricks of matter, each hurtling away from me with fierce velocity.

In desperation, to pass the night, I'd pick up the book on my bedstand. In college, how many how many times had I fallen asleep at my desk, my head resting on the pages of a book from my Nineteenth-Century Russian Literature class? Just a few philosophical diatribes from one Karamazov brother or another and I would be gone. But such was not the case with *Crime and Punishment*. I found all of it compelling, all of it enthralling, all of it somehow resonant. *Taking a breath and pressing his hand against his thumping heart, he immediately felt for the hatchet and once more put it straight. Then he began to mount the stairs very quietly and cautiously, stopping every moment to listen for any suspicious noise.* I thought it would put me to sleep, the old Russian master spinning out his words by the bushelful, but each night, after hours of the toss and turn, I lit the lamp and opened the book and dropped into old St. Petersburg. And what does it tell you about my state of mind that, even as I struggled to ensure Guy's conviction, I was rooting for Raskolnikov to get away with murder?

Then, in the mornings, more exhausted than I was the night before, I would wash the sleeplessness from my eyes and step out into the dreary morning and head to the diner. It was at the diner, in the netherworld between my sleepless nights and my surreptitious days, that I found some respite. I'd sit undisturbed at the counter, spread my paper across the countertop beside me, eat my eggs and home fries, coffee up, read the sports page and comics. The front page was too depressing, but the Phils were winning and though "Doonesbury" had grown tepid over the years and "Family Circle" was too cloying to bear, there was always "The Piranha Club," "For Better or for Worse," and that bastion of old values, "Rex Morgan, M.D." And then of course there was the Jumble.

So there I was at the diner, safe within my exhaustion, struggling to form a word from the letters TOZALE, when a man in a brown suit, with a face like a battered hardball, sat down smack beside me.

"What's good in this here joint?" he said. He spoke slowly, his voice soft and throaty, as if his larynx had been scarred by fire.

"About what you'd expect," I said as I eased away from him so our elbows wouldn't knock.

"What you got there, the eggs?"

I looked down at my plate, the yolks of my easy-overs broken, the yellow spread like thick paint over the home fries, and then looked past him at all the empty stools he had chosen to ignore when he set down next to me.

"Yes," I said, turning back to my paper. "The eggs."

Unless it is crowded at the counter of a diner, no one sits next to another patron. As the stools are left vacant and then occupied, the crucial spacing of two or three stools is maintained as if the rules were written on the blackboard above the swinging chrome door. People sit at the counter of a diner to stare into their plates, to read their papers undisturbed, to be left alone. I turned slightly, showing my back to the stranger, and leaned close to the paper.

"I used to love my eggs and bangers," said the stranger, ignoring my body language, "toast sopping with butter. Every morning. But then my cholesterol, it shot higher than Everest, it did. My dentist told me it was time for a change. You might ask why my dentist, but I don't gots no other doctor. The rest of me I let go to hell, but you gots to take care of the choppers."

He smiled at me, showing off his bright whites, with a large gap between his two front teeth, before slapping on the counter for Shelly. When I said he looked like a battered hardball, I didn't mean a sweet major league ball with one single smudge, I meant one of those ruined remainders we used to play with as kids, brown, mis-shapen, waterlogged balls we kept banging on even as the stitching came undone and the gray stuffing leaked from the seams. His face was flat and round, his ears stuck out like handles, his nose was the Blob, there was even heavy stitching on the line of his jaw. He was so ugly it was hard to look away from him. His face was like an accident on the side of the road.

"Hey, sweetheart," he called to Shelly at the other side of the counter, "a bowl of oatmeal here. That's right, with some skim milk and a joe. Thanks. Oatmeal, that's what I'm reduced to. It's a sorry sight when a man with teeth like mine is wasting bicuspids on oatmeal, innit? The dentist, she told me. It's the fiber what cleans out the arteries, she said. That and garlic. I was eating the garlic raw for a while, but for some reason people stopped talking to me, so nows I take the pills. They say garlic does wonders. At least that's what they say now. Next week they'll be telling us something different, like the best thing for your heart is smoking stogies and wanking off."

"Excuse me?"

"Smoking stogies and wanking off. Wouldn't it be something if for once they tell us that the things what are actually good for you are the things everyone does anyway?"

"Not everybody," I muttered, my face back in the paper.

"What, you don't fancy cigars? Let me guess, you're a lawyer, right?"

"That's right."

He slapped the counter. "I got you, didn't I? First time, too. I got a knack for these things. Used to sell cars. Buicks, Olds. I got so I could pick out who was what just by the way they sashayed into the showroom. Lawyers would come in like they was daring you to try to sell them. And you never saw a lawyer come in and say 'I'll take it.' The lawyer was always sniffing here, sniffing there, and then he'd check six other showrooms to see if he could save a nickel. If I spotted a lawyer walking through them doors, I'd say, 'Joey, why don't you take this one.' And then Joey would waste his afternoon with the lawyer in the three-piece while I would grab the guy with the grease beneath his fingernails who would buy that big red Buick on the spot. Zealot."

"What?"

"The word, in the Jumble you're stuck on. TOZALE is zealot."

"Do you mind?"

"Not at all. The next one, SORIAL, is sailor. I used to do them Jumbles every day. I was like the Michael Jordan of the Jumble. It's a talent I got for taking things that are all mixed up and putting it in an order that makes sense. That's how I got into my new line. But I still got friends in the car biz. Hey, you looking for a new car? I could set something up."

"All I want is to finish reading the paper in peace."

"Yeah, I notice a lot of guys come to places like this to be left alone, but I never understood that. I want to be alone, I'll eat my oatmeal standing by the sink in my skivvies. It's like in the car business. When I was working the shop, no one wanted to be jammed by a salesman right off. They wanted to be able to browse around la-di-da on theys own. But I figure, why come into a sales center if you don't want to be sold? You let the bastards browse around on theys own, next thing you know they'll be browsing their way over to the Toyota place across the street.

"Thanks, sweetheart, and more coffee when you can. Javalicious. Hey, could you pass the sugar? This one is all lumped up. Yeah.

"Funny thing about them lawyers in the salesroom, though. When it came down to negotiating a deal, they was like virgins in a sailors' bar. They would do theys research, sure. They'd come in loaded with papers, figuring they knew everything they needed to know, when really they knew nothing. Because what was important wasn't all the crap they brought in, it was how much the dealer was paying in the first place, how desperate was the cash-flow situation, what the boss's girlfriend was whining for that week, all stuff that ain't in *Consumer Reports*. Is the slurping bothering you? Good. The oatmeal is better with the milk, makes it like a soup. Anywise, the lawyers would bypass the salesman and sit down with the assistant manager, which is like bypassing the pilot fish to deal directly with the shark. Frigging lawyers. By the time they got finished with the assistant manager and with the F&I guys, they was getting it up the arse, down the throat and in both ears."

By now my face was out of the paper and I was staring at the man beside me. The hairs on the back of my neck prickled.

"You know what they should teach you first thing in law school?" he said. "They should teach you that maybe you don't know everything you think you know. They should teach you that if a deal for some reason seems too good to be true, then maybe you should jump off your arse and grab it afore it disappears. Maybe sometimes you should take the damn deal before something bad happens, before something awful happens that will absolutely ruin your day. What the hell do you think of that?"

"What line did you say you were in now?" I asked.

"Nowadays I solve bigger puzzles than the Jumble. Things what don't add up, I find the sense of the things and make them add up in a way that everybody wins. Even me. Especially me." He reached into his jacket pocket for a wallet, took out a five, and slapped it on the counter. Calling to Shelly, he said, "Here you go, sweetie. You keep what's left."

"You got a card?" I asked.

"Nah, those what need me know where to find me."

"Can I ask you a favor?"

"Shoot," he said.

"Next time you want to send me a message, do it by fax."

He stared at me for a long moment, the geniality leaking out of his face. "Don't get too smart on me, I'm liable to change my whole opinion of the profession." Then he let out a belch that shook the plates on the counter before us. "There's the problem with the oatmeal, right there."

"What do you want, Skink?"

"A bowl of oatmeal. A cup of joe. A chance to pass a few friendly words. I'm doing you a favor here by giving you an honest piece of advice. Forget your snooping around about this Juan Gonzalez. He ain't important. What's important is that you do the right thing. Take the deal. It's a good deal. It ends everything and keeps everybody happy."

"Who sent you?"

"See, here's the thing, Vic. You think you knew her, but you didn't know the first thing about her. You think you understood her, but you understood nothing. She was like a fancy gold watch, she was, simple and slim on the outside, but inside was wheels within wheels within wheels. And you never had the frigginest."

"And you did?"

"Me and her, we understood each other. Me and her, we got along like long-lost pals. We had things in common. She talked to me."

"About what?"

"You know. About her affairs and such."

I didn't say anything, I just stared. He smiled and leaned so close I was glad he had stopped eating his garlic raw, leaned so close his whisper was like a roar.

"I know," he said.

"Know what?"

"You know."

"No, I don't know."

"Your little no-no."

"My no-no?"

"Oh, I know," he said. "Yes I does. I know."

I stood abruptly, as if the secret itself propelled me off my stool. I stood, but I didn't say anything and I didn't leave. I stood and listened.

"She told me so herself," said Skink. "I assure you, Vic, I'm not here to hurt you, I'm here to help. It's safe with me, your little secret. I got no wish to spread it around like butter on a stack of flapjacks. But don't be like those lawyers in the showroom with their lawyerish ways. Take the deal. It wasn't no picnic getting Jefferson to go for the plea. Don't think we can keep it on the table forever.

Forget about Juan Gonzalez. Take the deal, put everything right, so no one ends up knowing nothing and we all go home happy."

He nodded at me, pushed himself off his stool, and headed for the door. He had a strange, waddling walk, like he'd just jumped off his horse after riding for a fortnight. Then he stopped, turned, and waddled back.

"You was in the house alone after she was doffed, wasn't you?"

I said nothing.

"An item is missing, a small item. No bigger than a key, if you catch the drift. It wasn't logged in by the police detectives, and it seems no longer to be in the house."

"How would you know?" I blurted out, my gaze dropping down from his eyes to his hands, which were now hidden in his pockets.

He ignored my question. "You didn't happen to pilfer the item whilst inside the house, did you? You didn't happen to palm it for your own invidious purposes?"

I couldn't answer, too frightened and stunned to even try to deny it. I stood there shaking, mute, my eyes watering involuntarily as they hadn't done in years. I couldn't answer, but it wasn't the type of question that demanded an answer. I got the sense that Phil Skink didn't need many answers from anyone, especially from me.

"G'day, Vic," he said with a click and a wink.

I watched him push open the door, head out to the street, and then I wheeled around in terror.

15

HE KNEW. That bastard, Skink, he knew. I could have brazened it out with denial after denial, but that wouldn't have altered a thing. The truth was in his ugly puss. He knew. How was it possible? How? Why? Because Hailey . . . because Hailey had told him, so he said. They had had an understanding, so he said. They had things in common. Hailey Prouix and Phil Skink. What the hell could they have had in common? But Skink knew, no doubt about it, and there was no telling the kind of hurt he could put on me with what he knew.

I stared into my plate, filthy now with the yellow of smeared yolk and the paprika of the potatoes. The greasy slop in my stomach turned and I gagged with a sudden nausea. There is always a faint tinge of nausea after a heavy diner meal, as if the high heat of the griddle renders cheap grease into a mild emetic, but this was something different, something far richer and justly deserved.

What the hell was I doing? I had slept with my friend's fiancée, I had taken evidence from the scene of her murder, and now I was defending her killer to the worst of my abilities. In the heat of everything, when it played out only in my consciousness, it had all seemed so logical, even so inevitable. But now, when my perfidy played out also in the consciousness of the world's sleaziest private eye, the end result was humiliation. How had I looked to him? I could see it in his eyes. I had put myself into a position to be ethically condescended to by the likes of Phil Frigging Skink. I was a fool, I was in far over my head, I was making mistake after mistake.

I closed my eyes and let the nausea slide through me and waited for it to fade. But it didn't fade. It grew and twisted inside my stomach, reached out its arms and stretched. Unsteadily, I made my way past the empty stools and into the lavatory, turned on the light, locked the door behind me. It was filthy and small, the floor was wet, the trash bin jammed with paper towels even this early in the morning, and it smelled like, well, like a toilet. I leaned on the sink, looked in the mirror at my face, oily and green. I was getting sicker by the second. My breaths were coming now in panicky gulps. I had to figure out what to do. I had to figure out my options. Had to. Had to. Now.

Give it up, let my plan of vengeance fade, back away from the trial and disclose the affair and hope it all turned out right? Yes, yes, I could do that, yes. Except that it wouldn't go away and nothing would turn out right. Skink might disappear, true, but Guy's new defense attorney would blame me for the murder, Guy would strut out of jail, and I, stripped of my membership in the bar and humiliated in the press, would be the new chief suspect of Detectives Stone and Breger.

Ignore the bastard and continue on as I was continuing on? Yes, yes. Maybe that was it, maybe I should just brazen it through. I bent over the sink, splashed water on my overheated face, felt the hard living thing in my stomach bubble and belch, rise into my chest and then fall again. Skink had said the secret was safe with him, that he only wanted to help. But he wanted something from me, and he was not the kind to give up on what he wanted. There would be more visits, more threats. It would never end, never, end, until the bastard broke me in two.

"Oh, God," I said as I banged on the wall.

Of course, of course, there was another route. Give him what he wanted, take the plea. Skink wanted it, Beth wanted it, even Guy was inclined. That was it, the easiest way out and the most obvious. Good, yes, but . . . A plea would hardly avenge Hailey, and even with a plea, Phil Frigging Skink would still hold his sword of knowledge over my head. How much would I have to pay him in the future to keep his mouth shut? What would it be like to have another partner?

Derringer, Carl and Skink.

What kind of name was Skink anyway?

No, it was all bad, there were no options. I was lost, I was sunk, there was no solution to that bastard Skink, nothing to be done except throw up. I lurched over to the scummy little toilet and in one quick spasm gave up my morning's feed.

I stared at my red-rimmed orbs in the mirror. My face looked like a tawdry country music song. I dampened a paper towel and wiped my face and then pressed it onto my overheated forehead and let the cool seep through my skin. I rinsed out my mouth, one spit, two, wiped my teeth roughly with the paper towel. I felt better, yes, I felt much better, and my emotions settled. Slowly I began to calm, and as I did, I sifted through the detritus of my panic, searching for one thing, anything, on which to grab hold. And what I came up with had the face of a battered hardball.

Skink.

What was his game? I knew enough about guys like Skink to know the Jumblemeister wasn't after honor or love or sense of self in a world beset with meaninglessness—he was thinking of one thing only: money. And he seemed to have a route to it all his own. Wasn't it funny that in a case I had thought turned only on passion and rage there seemed to be an underlying theme of money? The cash in the envelope. The cash in Guy's suitcase. The funds mysteriously absent from the brokerage account about which Guy and Hailey had fought. The strange untapped relationship between Leila's vindictive grab for Hailey's money and the name Juan Gonzalez. I had still no doubt as to who had pulled the trigger, but Guy's motivation might not be as simple as I had imagined. Maybe my personal involvement had twisted my thinking on the why, maybe it wasn't that he loved her too much, maybe it was that something he loved too much was missing. I remembered the look on his face when he learned that the brokerage account was empty. Money money money. How could ever I be surprised to learn that money ran through a story of murder like the sewers run through Paris?

Skink.

What was his relationship to Juan Gonzalez? Why did he want Guy to plead? And how did a piece of slime like Phil Frigging Skink get the estimable Troy Jefferson, with his overt political ambitions, to offer a lowball plea in the first place? The answer was, he didn't. The answer was, someone else did. He had used the first-person plural, and my guess is that Phil Frigging Skink was not the type to routinely use the royal "we."

Guy said Skink had worked for Jonah Peale, Guy's father-in-law. Odds on, that's who he still was working for. Maybe Jonah Peale was the other part of the "we." Maybe I should go right at him, barge in, make all sorts of threats, see what I shook up. Except I knew Jonah Peale, had met him at Guy's wedding to Leila and had spotted him since around town. He was a short, bellicose man who nodded at me brusquely as he passed me in the street, not quite sure, I could tell, who I was or how he had met me, but quite sure he didn't care. Whatever he was, he wouldn't shake easily. I didn't know enough yet to go after him. Something was eluding me, something basic that explained much.

I took a deep breath and then another, let the oxygen flow rich through my veins. Good, see, panic was useless. With my breakfast down the toilet, I could think things through calmly and coolly.

Skink.

Juan Gonzalez.

Jonah Peale.

Skink.

Juan Gonzalez.

Jonah Peale.

Three names. Three. Somehow they were connected. How? Why? Three names. Or was it more than three names? Wasn't it also Guy Forrest? Wasn't it also Leila Forrest, née Peale? Wasn't it also Hailey Prouix? What was it that could link them all together?

It came to me in a flash of empathic insight. It came to me because I was standing in a stinking shithole, having just thrown up in disgust at myself, and understood how low it was possible to fall. It came to me because I was treading the same path for Hailey that had already been trodden before me, for Hailey, and so I could see the footsteps of the prior traveler as clearly now as I could see my own. It came to me, and when it came to me, it seemed so obvious that I could barely believe I hadn't seen it with utter clarity before.

It would be nothing to confirm, and I would confirm it, but I would do more. For not only did I suddenly understand exactly who was Juan Gonzalez, but also exactly what he could do for me. He was probably dead, or as good as dead, but that was no matter. Juan Gonzalez would single-handedly get Skink off my back and bring Jonah Peale in line. Juan Gonzalez would be my enforcer. But there was more.

If it was played just right, Juan Gonzalez would also convict Guy of first-degree murder as if he himself were the decisive witness, as if he himself had seen Guy fire that shot into Hailey Prouix's heart. All I needed was to bring his name, and his story, to the proper authorities so that the insulting plea offer would be withdrawn forthwith. All I needed was a way to introduce Juan Gonzalez to Troy Jefferson without it seeming as if I were the matchmaker. All I needed was a sly plan, too clever by half, that would do by proxy what I couldn't do in person. The plan would have to be dirty, base, vile. The plan would have to exhibit a complete lack of moral fiber in the soul of the deranged maniac who dreamed it up.

I was just the man for the job.

STANDING AT the reception desk on the ground floor of the Dawson, Cricket and Peale building, I could feel them working above me, the swarm, buzzing and fussing, drafting and faxing, answering phones, answering complaints, answering insults with insults, investigating, inventing, tendering offers and refusing offers, wheeling, dealing, hustling, bustling, holding firm, holding firmer, shopping for experts, shopping for forums, shopping online, filing interrogatories, answering interrogatories, deposing, defending, coaching witnesses, browbeating witnesses, browbeating secretaries, snapping pencils, complaining with righteous indignation, responding with moral sincerity, filing motions to dismiss, filing motions for summary judgment, filing motions for sanctions, responding to motions for sanctions, exploding with anger in calculated bursts, filing trial memos, filing witness lists, hiring jury consultants, conducting mock trials before focus groups, meeting, discussing, shuddering with fear, settling, settling, always settling, quickly, before the next complaint arrived. Standing at the reception desk on the ground floor of the Dawson, Cricket and Peale building was like standing beneath a hive of drones and feeling the vibrations of a hundred thousand wings beating in crazy disorder toward the common goal of honey, honey, and more honey.

"Jonah Peale," I said to the receptionist. She presided over a desk beside the elevator, an armed guard behind her, and behind him the firm's name spelled out in steel. Between the elevator and the front door sat a large marble fountain, a huge copper fish leaping out of the water with a foul spray erupting from its mouth. The spitting of the fish was almost loud enough to drown out my words.

"Is he expecting you?"

"No."

"Then I'm sorry, but Mr. Peale has a very busy—"

"Get him on the phone. He'll see me," I said. "Tell him it's Victor Carl. Tell him I'm here to talk about his beloved son-in-law."

Peale grabbed my arm as I came out of the elevator on the sixth and top floor. He was ten inches shorter than me, but his grip was iron and so was his voice. "I'm meeting with clients in my office," he said as he pulled me into the conference room. "We'll talk in here."

The room was large, long, with a huge wooden table and a wall of windows. Peale was wearing a black pin-striped suit with a bright red tie bursting with flowers. He sat me down and then walked around the table until he stood directly across from me, his arms straight, his fists resting on the tabletop as he leaned forward. With the light streaming in from behind him, he seemed taller, the red tie glowed with power. I felt like a trash hauler negotiating a union contract with the chairman of the board.

"We've met before," he said.

"At Leila and Guy's wedding."

"Feh." Disgust twisted his hard features as if a piece of gristle were stuck in his teeth.

"Maybe you should be more careful in vetting your recruits."

His eyes flashed anger. He had a way of speaking as if every declarative statement were a barroom challenge. "I wasn't recruiting for Leila. What you want in a litigator is very different from what you want in a son-in-law. But I was wrong about him as a lawyer, too. What the hell kind of man gets a tattoo like that on his chest?"

"The kind that good daughters inevitably fall for."

"To their regret. Your friend betrayed my daughter, he betrayed my grandchildren, he betrayed his vows. That he finally betrayed his lover by murdering her is no great surprise. I hope you received your fee in advance, or he'll betray you, too."

"How can you be so certain?"

"It's his nature to cheat."

"I'm not talking about my fee, I'm talking about the murder."

"How do I know? Because he's family." His tongue moved angrily within his cheek, still searching for the gristle.

"If you're that certain, Mr. Peale, then why are you so anxious for him to plead to a lesser charge?"

"Am I?"

"Yesterday morning a man named Phil Skink" —I left out the adjective that had become for me like a middle name—"invaded my breakfast at a neighborhood diner."

"Skink? Phil Skink? Don't know him."

"Really, now. In our conversation this Skink wanted me to plead your son-in-law out to manslaughter. In fact, he wanted it so badly he bound the request in a threat. I assumed he was speaking for you, since Guy had told me Skink did some work for your firm. If he wasn't speaking for you, then the detectives investigating Hailey Prouix's murder would surely want to speak to him about his peculiar interest in the case. I thought I'd check with you before I gave the information to the police."

I stared calmly at him and he stared fiercely back. He was a little man with a little mustache, but his eyes beneath his wire-frame glasses burned with intensity as bright as his tie. I remembered then that his wife was exceptionally large and the two of them made a comically proportioned couple, but no one ever dared laugh. I remembered then that he had been caught in some scandal involving a congressman and his aide a few years back and that the congressman's aide was a tall, full-size blonde named Agatha.

"Mr. Skink," he said finally, "is occasionally contracted by this firm to provide investigative services. He may have taken it upon himself to voice my concerns about the effects of a lengthy murder trial on my family."

"He threatened me."

"That's unfortunate."

"I don't like to be threatened."

"Things happen to all of us that we don't like. I'll be blunt. I don't want that bastard's picture in the papers staring at me for the next six months. I don't want the articles talking about my daughter. I don't want her forced to testify. I don't want my grandchildren used as pawns. I don't want the tragedies of my family played out in the tabloids. I want it to be over. Is that clear enough for you?"

"Your familial concern is touching."

"So you're touched. Is that all? Because I have a client in my office."

"Give him the newspaper. Tell him to do the Jumble while he waits. I have more questions."

"I have no more answers. You can send any request for further information to my lawyer. Good day, Mr. Carl. We are through." He started the long walk around the table.

"Do you want a subpoena, Mr. Peale? Because I have one in my briefcase with your name on it."

"I'll quash it."

"I'll quash back. I was a Division Two quash champion in college. And then, when you're under oath, maybe I'll start asking about the promises you made to support Troy Jefferson's future political aspirations in exchange for a quick plea."

He stopped. "There were no promises."

"Call them what you will. The only way a political opportunist like Jefferson backs away from a high-profile murder trial is if the political payoff is higher than all those appearances on the six o'clock news. What does he want to be, DA? Attorney general? Lieutenant governor? What does he want to be, the big man himself?"

"Troy Jefferson is a young man with sterling qualities who would be an asset to the commonwealth in any public role."

"Yes, and he had a nice jump shot, too, but that's not what's going on, is it? Why are you trying to end this case before it starts?"

"I told you. My family—"

"No. Try again."

"My daughter—"

"Sorry, wrong answer."

"My grandchildren—"

"I don't think so. Not unless you have a grandchild named Juan Gonzalez."

Peale pressed his thin lips together, his head jerked within his starched collar. He took hold of the closest seat and sat down. His voice, when it came, had lost its iron edge. "I don't know what you're talking about."

"I understand why you wanted it kept secret. Red Book Insurance is your largest and oldest client. It bought this building for you, paneled your offices. It keeps you in feed, and not chicken feed at that. If you had told them what happened right at the start, you could have weathered it, maybe, but you kept it from them, kept it your little secret. For them to find out now would destroy the relationship irrevocably. They'd leave, for sure, and the scandal would convince others to leave, too. Who could ever trust your firm after this? It would be over for Dawson, Cricket and Peale, except at the unemployment line."

"You're barking off half-cocked."

"I can tell I'm right, you're mixing metaphors. What I don't understand is how you expected it to stay a secret. It wasn't hidden, really. All it took was a visit to the clerk's office, a review of the case files, the discovery of a medical malpractice action entitled *Juan Gonzalez* v. *Dr. Irwin Glass et al.* The whole story is there right on the docket sheet. I found it all yesterday, after my little breakfast meeting with Skink. Representing the plaintiff: Hailey Prouix, Esquire. Representing the defendant doctor and insurance company: Guy Forrest, Esquire. Oh, not only Guy, your name was at the top of the list of lawyers, you were the billing partner, I suppose, but Guy did the work. It was on that case that he met Hailey, wasn't it? It was during the length of the litigation that he dined her, romanced her, seduced her. And after the settlement, after the three million dollars were handed from the insurance company to the plaintiff, about the going rate for a man entering the hospital for routine prostate surgery and leaving in a coma, Guy ditched his wife, his children, your firm, to move in with Hailey. Living on her share of the award, her one-third, a cool mil."

"It was a solid case," said Peale. "The settlement was a fair one. I oversaw it all. For the three million dollars Red Book escaped ex-

posure to a much larger amount, an amount that could have crip-
pled its operations."

"Maybe, but I think not. I think there was something there that
would have won the case for Red Book, some hard piece of evidence that Guy hid until after the settlement was signed and the
money paid and Guy and Hailey had a million dollars to start their
lives together. Otherwise he would have dropped off the case once
the relationship started. Otherwise Hailey Prouix would have insisted on it. Why allow even the tinge of impropriety to hazard the
settlement somewhere down the line? Why put a million dollars at
risk? Unless it was the only way to get the million dollars in the
first place. I had wondered why Hailey's big fee was placed in a
joint account, and now I know, because they both earned it. And
you knew, didn't you? You knew and tried to keep it quiet. That's
why you wanted the plea accepted. That's why you sent Skink to
threaten me."

I was guessing, this last part about the hidden evidence, but it
was a guess that made sense, and Jonah Peale's reaction, a sort of
head swivel of frustration, told me that my guess was spot on.

"You have no proof," he said.

"I don't need proof right now, all I need is to know I'm right. It
won't be too hard to find what it was Guy hid, now that we know
what to look for. And wouldn't Red Book be interested as hell in
seeing it for themselves?"

Jonah Peale's face turned pale and then paler still. He lost so
much color I thought he would collapse, right there before me, collapse and fall off that chair. Then, suddenly, he composed himself,
as if a knob had been turned. He took off his spectacles, cleaned the
lenses with the tip of his bright red tie. "It would destroy this firm's
reputation," he said calmly, "destroy the firm I've put my life into.
I can't allow that to happen."

"So it's not the family you're concerned about, is it?"

"We all have our priorities. Why are you here?"

And there it was, the negotiation had begun. It was a pretty im-
pressive performance by Peale, he had taken the shot, recovered,
and now was ready to take control of the situation. Good for him,
good for me.

"We both have an interest in keeping this information quiet," I said. "If it becomes public, it could be damaging to my client's case. As long as I control the disclosure, and the spin, I think I could manage it. I could even turn it to Guy's advantage, paint Hailey as a schemer out for the money, reduce the natural sympathy for the victim. But still, it complicates things as far as motive. And, of course, to you it would be devastating. So I believe it is in our interests to work together to keep it quiet."

"Agreed. What do you want?"

"I want Skink off my back."

"I'll tell him."

"I don't want to see him again. I don't want him talking to anyone about this case in any way, shape, or form. It would be best if he took a vacation until this whole thing is cleared up."

"He will be so instructed."

"I see him, I hear word one from him or about him, then I'll let out the information my way, and Red Book will know not only what Guy did but that you were hiding it from them."

"You've made yourself clear."

"I also assume there are documents showing what Guy discovered and hid. I assume there is a file."

"Maybe there is."

"If we agree to keep it quiet, I can't afford to have it slip out when I least expect it. I don't want anyone to control that information but me. I want the file. I want all copies of it."

"That may prove difficult."

"I don't want to hear excuses."

"It may prove difficult," said Jonah Peale, "because if there is a file, I don't have it."

"Where is it?"

"I don't know."

"You're kidding me."

"I'm not the type, Mr. Carl."

"It must keep you up at night."

"Yes, well, with the way my wife snores, I don't get much sleep anyway."

"Any ideas what happened to it?"

"Ask your client. Anything else?"

I sat for a moment, tapped my chin. "One more thing, I suppose. I like your tie."

"Thank you."

"I want it."

He stared at me, hard. I was going way overboard, but there was a purpose to it. His face reddened with anger and then the color subsided. "I'll messenger it over tomorrow."

"Actually I was going out tonight, and it would go marvelously with my blue suit."

He stared at me a moment longer, bloody daggers in his eyes, and then he reached a finger into the knot. As he worked the tie loose, his thin lips spread in an approximation of a smile. "You know, Victor, may I call you Victor? I suspect, Victor, that in the end we'll work well together. I'll make sure Mr. Skink is cooperative, as we discussed, but you might want to rethink Troy Jefferson's offer. Hell, it really is the best that asshole could ever hope for. It would be to everyone's benefit for this to go away. And as for your fee, which your expression told me had not been paid for in advance, if he takes the deal, I'll make sure your fee is paid in full. Whatever the invoice says, no questions asked. He is family, after all, at least until the inevitable divorce."

I slapped my thighs and stood. "Talk to Skink."

He held out the tie. I stepped forward to take it. "Done," he said.

"Good." I turned to face the door and then stopped, turned around again. This was the moment, the crucial moment. It had to seem incidental, offhand. "By the way, you mentioned the inevitable divorce. Don't be so sure about that."

"What are you talking about?"

"Your daughter wants him back."

"Of course she doesn't."

"I visited her just last week. She wants everything returned to the way it was before. Her husband back in her happy home, sharing her bed, raising their children."

"She . . ." His voice softened. "She can't be serious."

"Oh, she is. Quite. She has even agreed to put up the house for his bail."

He didn't react like I expected. Instead of exploding in anger, he looked away from me, toward the windows, and creased his forehead in thought. "She can't," he said matter-of-factly. "It's not hers to put up."

"I don't understand."

"I cosigned the mortgage. She can't do a thing without my agreement, and I won't put up a penny to get that bastard out of jail. Not a penny." He turned quickly to stare at me. "You wouldn't insist that I do that, too, would you? You wouldn't do that."

The pleading in his voice was almost pathetic. I made a gesture of thinking on it for a moment before smiling to myself. "No. Better not to tip our hand. If you agreed to bail him out, it would look suspicious."

"She really wants him back?"

"As soon as I acquit him."

"How could she be such a fool?" he said, his voice now almost wistful, his gaze back to the window.

I said something or other by way of ending the meeting, but he didn't respond, just kept on staring, and so I left without another word, though on the way out I have to admit I skipped a step or two. Call me Satchmo, seeing as I had just played Jonah Peale like a cornet.

In the lobby I stopped in front of the fish leaping out from the marble fountain. The fish's fish lips were puckered and spitting out the nasty little stream. Someone, somewhere, thought the effect was pleasing, but who? How? Maybe that was the biggest mystery of all. I wrapped Jonah Peale's red power tie tight around that ugly fish's neck and stepped into the street.

17

"**YOU KNOW** if this leaks," said Beth after I had told her of my discovery about Juan Gonzalez and my meeting with Peale, minus the bit about Skink, "it would devastate Guy's defense. He wants us to pursue the lover as the killer. Fine. In a lover's triangle it's easy enough to point the finger at the missing member."

"Speaking metonymically, of course."

"But money trumps love. If the prosecution can show a monetary motive for Guy's anger, like being cheated out of the money they had stolen together, they'll have a much easier go."

"I know," I said.

"And if Troy Jefferson finds out what you found out, he'll withdraw the plea offer in a second."

"I know that, too."

"Then maybe we should accept it before it disappears."

"Maybe, but we need to talk to Guy first. We need to give Guy a chance to tell us his side of the story."

"Guy stole the money, didn't he?"

"Yes."

"And Hailey transferred it out of their joint account, didn't she?"

"Yes."

"Then what is there that he could tell us to alter those fundamental facts? His explanation won't change the government's ability to turn that into motive. You add this to his fingerprints on the gun, the improbability of his story, the evidence of another lover, the lack of evidence of a break-in, you add it all up and the sum is a guilty."

I avoided her gaze and shrugged. "Convictions happen."

She stared at me. I refused to stare back.

"You look terrible."

"Thank you," I said. "That's so sweet."

"You have bags under your eyes the airlines would make you gate-check."

"I've been staying up late reading."

"Must be something good."

"A classic."

"I've been wondering why you haven't pushed Guy to accept the plea. At first I thought maybe it was because you like appearing on the evening news and it had been a while since you had a case that put you there. Then I thought you just wanted to keep the case alive so you could bury yourself in work and forget your failed romance. But I never thought it was because you believed Guy is innocent. Do you, Victor?"

"What?"

"Believe he's innocent?"

I turned my head to look at her straight on. "It shouldn't matter."

"But it does, doesn't it? I can feel it in you."

"Let me turn it around. How would you feel if you learned that Guy was absolutely guilty? How would you feel then about defending him? How would you feel then about getting for him a sweetheart deal?"

"I'd feel lousy about it."

"But you'd still defend him to the best of your abilities?"

"Yes. I would. That's the job."

"I know the job. I'm not talking about the job. I'm talking about what you *think* of the job."

"Sometimes I think it's rotten."

"There you go."

"So you do believe he did it."

"I'm saying it shouldn't matter, but sometimes it does. I'm saying that I'm in a tough situation, but I'm doing the best I can. I'm saying that all I need from you is a little faith that I'll do the right thing."

"You usually do."

"Thank you."

"But sometimes," she said, "you do it for all the wrong reasons."

I didn't want to ask her what she meant by that, so I ignored the comment. She scratched her neck and tilted her head as if she were trying to work it out, trying to find the missing piece that would explain everything. But she didn't have it, I knew, and she wouldn't get it if I had anything to say about the matter. What had been between Hailey and me was a secret, and even if Skink knew, that was where it would end. I had seen to that.

But I could still sense her unease. It was time to bring her tacitly on my side, time for her to see the absolute truth. It was time, finally, for Guy to confess, if only to his lawyers. Nothing admissible in a court of law, of course, but enough to get Beth working with and not against me. Time for Guy to tell the whole truth, and I knew just how to squeeze it out of him.

Juan Gonzalez.

IT WAS like cracking a walnut.

Guy again denied knowing anything about Juan Gonzalez. Guy again denied knowing the specifics of the case in which Hailey had won her big contingency fee. Guy again explained that the only reason Hailey's money was in a joint account was that they were in love and that's how lovers treat money. Guy again said he wasn't really upset that some money from the account had been missing because most of it was Hailey's money to begin with. Guy again claimed that he didn't kill her, that he loved her and couldn't have hurt her.

Beth and I listened to it all with straight faces, and then, slowly, I brought out the lever.

We placed the docket sheet for the Juan Gonzalez case on the table in front of him. He looked down at the paper, up at us, back down at the paper. His gray face turned grayer, the twitch in his lip became grotesque.

"Who knows about this?" he said in soft voice.

"Just us," I said. "And of course your father-in-law."

"Oh, God," he said.

"Leave Him out of it."

"I didn't kill her," he said.

"You can't tell us that and then lie about the rest," I said. "We don't have time to play around anymore. We have to know everything. From the beginning. We have to know everything about you and Hailey."

He stared down at the docket sheet and closed his eyes. Beth and I waited in silence. He kept his eyes closed for a long time, and when they finally opened, he said, "I made a decision. It turned rotten."

I nodded. "Leaving Leila and your family for another woman."

"No," said Guy. "Before Hailey. The decision at the heart of it all, to become a lawyer."

18

GUY FORREST

THERE IS a story I don't want to get into, a story about a motorcycle, a guy named Pepito, who weighed, it must have been three hundred pounds, and a stripper from Nogales named CiCi. It's a bad story and it makes no sense, just like the way I was living made no sense.

After college I lost seven years trying hard not to be ordinary, chasing something, I never knew what, falling into a squalor I can't anymore imagine. I grew sick of the carelessness, the drugs, the greasy food, the bad grammar. There had to be a better way. Had to be. I was living then on the outskirts of a college town, and some kids we were dealing to were talking about the LSATs, and I figured I was smarter than they were, so I signed up, too. It was a lark, but it wasn't a lark, because underneath I knew what it was pointing to. And I did all right, better than the college kids. So when Pepito walked through my door, just walked right through it, wood crashing down around him, waving a sawed-off shotgun in the air, misusing adjectives as adverbs, I knew it was time to change everything.

Law school was hard. I didn't take to it like you did, Victor, too many rules based on imprecise language, too many leaps of twisted logic, but that's not what made it so hard. It was hard because it wasn't just a few years of professional training for me. I was re-inventing myself. I knew what I would be falling back into if I didn't make it. I worked harder than I ever thought possible, kept my nose clean, changed my whole way of living. I saw some of our classmates right out of college hanging in the bars, trying to act cool, and I just shook my head. I knew cool, I nearly froze to death in the desert from cool. That's why I liked you. Beside the fact you could explain things to me, you weren't trying to be something other than you were, you weren't cool. See, every day I was pretending to be something less than I was. I kept everything buttoned, everything tight and grim. I was going the other route one hundred percent. I was keeping my head low, because any day Pepito could burst again through my door.

I was tempted to go in with you after law school, Victor, it would have been fun, but the law for me was not about fun. It was about security, about money, about gaining some status starting from nothing. It was about leading a different life. At Dawson, Cricket and Peale, straight was the only way to play it. I put my head down and sucked up the hours, the workload, the bland social obligations. When the thing with Leila came along, I figured it had happened, the change, that I was someone shiny and new. And in no time there we were with the big house, the country club, the kids, the life. The goddamn life. I'm not claiming to be a victim here, none of this was done to me, the whole thing was my choosing, but even so, something was wrong. The clue was, I suppose, that after eight years I still wasn't comfortable in a suit and tie. I hated my job, hated the work, hated the firm, yet my grandest ambition was to become partner. The schizophrenia of it was tearing me apart. Do you know the word "anhedonia?" I suffered it, I was plagued by it. After eight years I looked up and realized I was living in black and white.

It was in a hospital room. There had been a bad result to a simple surgery. The doctor had notified the insurance company, Red Book, and they had notified us. In my briefcase was a contract that I was to have the wife sign, a contract that would guarantee the patient's medical care in exchange for an agreement to arbitrate any dispute over his prior care and a waiver of any claims for pain and suffering. Hey, bad things happen, and some bad things that happen are nobody's fault. That was our motto there at Dawson, Cricket and Peale. For a while I sat alone in the darkened room with the patient. He had intravenous lines leading into his arms, he had a catheter leading from his prick, he had a respirator tube snaking down his throat. The bellows of the respirator rose and fell, over and over, like a torture machine. Allow me to introduce you to Juan Gonzalez.

Once he had been a handsome man, he had played minor league baseball, he had raised a family by the strength of his hands. Now I looked at him lying near lifeless in the bed, and in a way I envied him. For him, at least, it was over, the maneuvering, the arguing, the rushing here and there for results that meant nothing. That was how far I had fallen—I envied the man in the coma—when Mrs. Gonzalez walked into the room.

She was a nice lady, sweet and terrified, devoted to her husband, worried about his future, her ability to continue his care. Her insurance had a limit, it would run out, it would run out, and then what would she do? I commiserated. In my job I had become excellent at commiseration. I was wearing a dark suit, an overcoat, polished black shoes. I must have seemed the bearer of very bad tidings, but I was there to help, I told her. In any way I could.

There was an order to things. You couldn't just presume, you couldn't just go in waving dollar bills. You needed to follow the order of things. If you showed any eagerness, they would want a lawyer of their own, and once they found a lawyer of their own, it became a whole different game. I learned that from my clever father-in-law, Jonah Peale himself. So I moved in slowly.

"Are you happy with the room?" I asked. "Are you happy with the care, the nursing? Anything we can do to help in this most difficult time, we will do. Just ask. Please. Anything. You shouldn't worry about the limit on your medical insurance, Mrs. Gonzalez. I will personally make sure that no transfer takes place until you are satisfied that his care in the new facility will be as good as the care here. We want to take care of you. How are things at home without Mr. Gonzalez's salary? Are you managing? If you need anything, I want you to call me. There are people who can help. I'm on your side. Tell me what I can do to help. Anything. Anything."

It was going well, so well that I opened the briefcase and took out the long piece of paper. It was always the crucial moment, the opening of the briefcase. You didn't open the briefcase unless you felt the deal, and once it was open you didn't leave the room until the deal was closed. The briefcase was open, the papers were out, Mrs. Gonzalez was on the verge of signing. Pushing her would have been as easy as pushing aside a curtain, I could feel it, but I didn't push. That was not the way it was done. It had to be her choice, and she was choosing to sign. The pen was in her hand, and she was choosing to sign.

When a voice from outside the room said, "Stop."

I turned to see a pair of bright crimson lips set upon a pale face, a flash of color so vivid it cut like a Technicolor knife through the gray scale of my world. They were smirking at me, those bright red lips, and yet I couldn't look away, I couldn't help myself from staring, soaking in the color. There was the body, too, of course, small, frail, even in the black suit, even with the briefcase and in the heels, but it was the crimson of the lips that caught me off guard, a flash of color so vivid it startled me.

"This is a private room," I stammered, "and this is a private meeting."

"Not anymore," said the woman.

The lips widened, showing now teeth, white and even, and between the bright teeth the pink tip of her tongue. She was sticking her tongue out at me.

"Your daughter asked me to come, Mrs. Gonzalez," she said. "I'm a lawyer." When she said that she adjusted her serious, dark-framed glasses as if to emphasize the point. "Your daughter asked me to speak to you before you signed anything." She looked at me. "It appears I've come just in time."

I tried to get rid of her, get the meeting back on track, but in that flash of a moment it was over. The woman explained to Mrs. Gonzalez the consequences of the contract, and it was over. I put the paper back in the briefcase, snapped it shut. The closing of the briefcase. I stared impassively for a moment at the lawyer's bright red lips as they unsuccessfully fought a smile, and then I turned to Mrs. Gonzalez.

"I hope everything turns out well for you and your family," I said, and then I started out of the room.

"I'll be in touch," said the woman lawyer to my back.

I hesitated for a moment, fought the urge to turn around, and then I continued out the door, and what I was seeing as I walked down the hall was not the failure of my meeting but shades of red, the crimson of her lips, the pink of her tongue. She had said she'd be in touch, and I was hoping then that she would keep to her word.

She did.

Hailey Prouix.

IT WAS Hailey who placed the calls, at least at the start. She asked questions about the case. She made demands for settlement even before she filed, ridiculous demands. And then there were other calls, not strictly necessary for the business at hand. And all the conversations ended on a note light and flirty.

I began thinking of her in odd moments, those lips, those cheekbones, the intonations of her soft laughter over the phone. In the grays that had become my life, she was a splash of color. Her calls became the highlight of my day. It was inevitable that we would meet for lunch. Inevitable that after a few lunches we would meet for drinks after work. It happened slowly. It wasn't something I didn't want, but it wasn't anything I pursued either. I knew the costs, I knew the dangers, and still it happened.

She filed her lawsuit on behalf of Juan Gonzalez and his family. I responded. In our offices the litigation moved apace, but in addition to the business calls we left each other more personal messages about the Willis case, named for her favorite movie star at the time. After work almost every other day we met somewhere and sopped up martinis and avoided talking about what both of us were thinking. We sat close while we drank, we shared cigarettes, our knees bumped. We never talked about anything too personal, but we talked. Every day I found her more lovely, every day I found the sadness that enveloped her like an exotic perfume more intoxicating. I stared at the red of her lips, the blue of her eyes. Starved as I was for color, I couldn't help myself from gorging. I came home later each evening, my family life dimmed. But in the middle of the night, for the first time since I'd entered the law, I began to dream again in more than black and white.

It was after work one evening, at the bar of the Brasserie Perrier, when, in the middle of a conversation about something meaningless, like the weather or the Supreme Court, she said simply, "What are we going to do?"

I knew what she meant, but I didn't want to answer, so I said, "Have another drink."

"I don't want another drink."

"What do you want?" I asked.

"I want to not want anything. I want to pretend we are simply two lawyers on opposite sides of a case."

"That's all we are," I said.

"I'm glad. It makes everything easier." She picked up her purse, gathered up her things. "It's time we both go home."

"I don't want to go home," I said, and I didn't. I didn't.

"Go home to your children."

"They're already in bed."

"Kiss them gently while they sleep," she said. "Go home to your wife, on whom, as you've told me over and over, you've never cheated."

"She's waiting up for me," I said. "She always does."

"Then make love to her."

"When I do, I think of you."

"How satisfying for me." She downed the last of her drink, stood from her stool.

"I kiss her breast," I said without looking at her, "and I think of the swelling flesh beneath your blouse. I kiss her thigh and I think of the softness beneath your skirt. I kiss her neck and smell the jasmine of your skin and my heart leaps."

"Then hurry home."

I grabbed her wrist. "I want you so badly my kidneys ache."

She shook her arm free.

"Go home, Guy," she said. "Go home to your family and your life. Just go home."

When she left the bar, I had the urge to chase her, but I didn't. I let her leave, I let her leave, and instead I caught the train, dark and dreary, to the station, to my car, to my house. The children were asleep. I kissed them each, gently. Leila was reading in bed. I slipped beneath the covers. She closed her book. I responded to her questions. She reached a hand to me, and I felt a chill. It was like the hand of death. It touched me and I felt all the color in my body bleed out through the touch. I had the urge to jump out of bed, to run from the house, but I didn't. I stayed in the bed, frozen from the touch. I stayed with my wife for that night and the next and the next. I stayed with my wife and let her hold me as she slept, let her nuzzle my neck with her cold chin, let her reach beneath my tee shirt with her cold hands. Those nights I dreamed again in black and white.

A few days later, after being able to hold off no longer, I left Hailey a message about the Willis matter. When I met her that afternoon for lunch, there was no lunch.

IT WAS Paris after the liberation.

It was champagne and abandon, laughter, twisting tongues, drunken revelry, teeth-clattering sex. Oh, don't make a face, Victor, don't be such a prude. It was amazing, amazing, like some strange brute force was running through as we pounded away. And it was like she didn't merely want it, she needed it, more and more of it. Thus the Viagra. But it was more than just great sex. She freed a part of me that had been imprisoned for ten years, the part that Pepito had sent fleeing off to law school.

I tend to rocket too far in any direction I head off in, that was what happened after college and again when I went on to law school, and this was no different. I wanted, that first afternoon, to give over everything to my lover, to end it with Leila, to flee parenthood, to quit the firm and the law, to move in and start it all again with Hailey. I wanted the new sense of freedom to be instantaneous and irrevocable, right then and there, but she wouldn't have it. Not until some things were settled, not until the Gonzalez case was over, not until my family situation had sorted itself out and we had some money to make a go of it. And I understood. I would lose my job for sure, as soon as it all became public, I couldn't wait to lose my job, but then what would happen to us? What would happen to my family, my children whom I would still need to support? She was the one who brought me back to my responsibilities. We had to move slowly, she said, surely, and I loved her all the more for her sensible sensibility in the midst of our hard passion.

So instead of embracing an earth-shifting freedom, I fell into the patterns of simple adultery. I left my messages about the Willis case, I snuck out for long lunches, I led a double life. It was so much easier this way that I didn't fight it, no need to tell Leila, confront my children, no need to deal with my father-in-law. My unthinking love for Hailey was just as strong, maybe even stronger, for all the wanting, but it hadn't transformed my life as I believed it would, it had only complicated it.

Still, there was the future. It would happen in the future, she assured me. As soon as we had some money, as soon as the Gonzalez case was over. She joked that we would live off her share of the Gonzalez settlement, and I laughed. But it was a big case with a high potential value for the plaintiffs; I had been involved in cases just like it that had settled for millions and saw no reason why this one would not. So the next time she made the joke, I didn't laugh. We stared at each other, and without the passing of a word it became understood that once the Gonzalez case was settled we would make the move, take the fee, go off together somewhere and start over. "Costa Rica," she said one late afternoon as she lay in my arms. "I've been thinking about Costa Rica." I knew what she meant, the two of us living the expatriate life in Costa Rica, sun, sand, excursions deep into the verdant forest, or, hand in hand, scuba diving beneath the perfect turquoise surface of the sea. I couldn't think of anything sweeter. Juan Gonzalez would be our ticket out.

It was shortly thereafter that the file came.

AT THE start of the Gonzalez case I had made all the routine inquiries and received the routine answers. Gonzalez had lived for a time in

Denver, so I contacted his old employer for his insurance records and used those to track down possible hospitals where he might have been treated. From those hospitals I requested any medical records they might have had on the man. I had sent out my requests, backed by threat of subpoena, before the thing with Hailey turned into what it became. And then, after everything had changed, out of the blue a package came from Denver. I closed the door and, with shaking hands, I opened it. It was Juan Gonzalez's medical file with a copy of my request inside. He'd had pains in his head, there was a scan taken, they had found an aneurysm, ready to burst at any moment. There was nothing to be done, no operation that was not too risky. The advice was to leave it alone and pray, and that is what he had done.

Juan Gonzalez had a preexisting medical condition that he had not disclosed to his doctor and that had caused his grievous injury. Bad things happen, and some bad things that happen are nobody's fault, and this time I could prove it.

Before I showed the file to anyone else, I took it to Hailey. She didn't seem terribly surprised. She took off her glasses, read it through, shrugged her shoulders, smiled sadly. "I suppose Costa Rica will have to wait," she said.

To her credit, she didn't push. She didn't even so much as suggest. She could have, and I would have gone along. Pushing me would have been as easy as pushing aside a curtain, I could feel the weakness in myself, but she didn't push. That would have changed everything, and she knew enough not to change anything. So it was my idea to tell no one, to bury the file, to continue moving the case toward settlement. My idea, my choice. And it wasn't even that hard a choice.

In my mind I was already free of my family, my career. I had broken every rule for the love I felt for Hailey, why should one more transgression make any difference? Leaving my wife, my children, that would be hard. But in my mind I had already fled my career, ditched the law, to which I discovered I was constitutionally ill suited. To ditch my fiduciary responsibilities and work it so that Red Book Insurance compensated the Gonzaleses for the bad result visited upon their patriarch, and to finance my freedom in the

process, seemed nothing in comparison to what I had already decided to abandon.

I handed her the file.

She said she would destroy it, and then she kissed me, she kissed
me, and whatever feeling of dread I felt washed out of me with that
kiss, along with something else.

What would I call it? Innocence? No, not innocence, something
else. Hope maybe. I had held the hope, foolish certainly, but still the
hope that everything would work out perfectly, that my wife would
serenely accept my defection and move on with her life, my children would adjust without any damage, that Hailey and I would
sail off into the pure waters of unadulterated happiness. Can there
be unadulterated happiness in adultery? Yes, there can. I felt it in
those moments when, naked, we pressed against each other, when
I hugged her so tight it hurt, because I wanted us to be as close as
two could possibly be. I felt it then, and I held true every hour to the
fantasy that such would comprise our future. I suppose my final
hope had been that Hailey would tell me to not to hide the file, to
give it to the insurance company, to start our lives clean. Maybe that
was the most foolish hope of all.

When she said not a word as I handed it to her and then gave me
her kiss, the hope bled out of me, all my hope, and I saw with utter
clarity what lay ahead: disillusion, bitterness, separation, devasta-
tion. I saw it so clearly, and yet there was nothing I could do to stop
it. Because I loved her, Victor, and I had no option but her. I was
ready to lose everything for a hope I now knew was false. I now
knew it was false, impossible, ruined already by my own hand, and
still I had no choice.

What does a degenerate gambler do when the luck dies and he
loses everything, when he knows the tide has turned and he has no
chance at all? He doubles the wager and bets his life.

IT WAS never the same after that. Never.

I convinced Red Book to settle, and once the papers were signed
and the check cleared, I went about the grim task of extricating myself from my grim legal life. Leila took it badly, melodramatically,

played it out in a series of ugly scenes; the children took it better than I expected, which was somehow even worse. My father-in-law went stone cold with rage. He knew enough to suspect something about the Gonzalez case but did nothing, except send Skink after me looking for any files I might still have. The one he wanted, though, I had already given to Hailey. To Hailey. And I decided, as a cover for the money we had stolen, to stay in the law, at least for a time. I started my own practice, forged anew my old chains. I figured I would find my great transformation not in a new profession but solely in Hailey.

But even before I moved in, she had changed, grown mysterious. I still loved her so much it ached, but she had changed. I tried to step out a bit, start a new life with her. I introduced her to you even before the move and to some other of my former friends after, but something was wrong. We stopped making love, she came up with excuses every night. She would take pills to go to sleep and drift off into something closer to a coma than a doze. It drove me crazy, her denying me and slipping away from me like that, and strangely it made me want her even more. As she lay drugged beside me, I fantasized about her and grew painfully overheated. I forced her once, and she was too drowsy to stop me, telling me in that drugged girlish voice to be quiet, be quiet, they might hear. I hated myself after that and didn't again, ever, but that didn't stop the wanting.

She started coming home late, coming home half drunk, as I had come home half drunk when I started seeing her. I sensed she was becoming involved with someone else. Feeling desperate, I acted desperately. It had always been my plan to wed after the divorce, and so I set the scene with a hundred candles surrounding the tub. I filled the Jacuzzi and tossed rose petals onto the surface of the water and I waited. She looked at the scene strangely when she came home, as if disgusted at the overt romantic display. I told her milady's bath was waiting. She sneered at the corniness of the line and then undressed as if facing an execution. She immersed herself so deeply I was afraid she would drown. When she came up for air, I fell to my knee and asked, and she said yes, a sad, stone-faced yes.

But nothing changed. We still made no love, she still took her pills to get to sleep, I still lay beside her, my mind a riot. She was distant, distracted. There would be days when she disappeared entirely without explanation. I grew certain that she was seeing someone else. I snooped through her drawers, her effects, I found baggage receipts for the airport in Vegas. I imagined she had gone there with her new lover and it drove me crazy. Our relationship had turned into a nightmare even before I discovered that most of the money was gone.

I won't go blow-by-blow with you, how I found out, how I confronted her, how she reacted, and how I reacted back. There were arguments, bitter fights, threats, tears, more fighting. It wasn't the money I was upset about, it was her. I was losing her. We fought about the money because it was easier than fighting about what was really happening. If I confronted her about her lover or Vegas, I feared it would be over, I feared she would throw me out, and so I kept it to the money only. But she never told me what she had done with it, what she had spent it on, and my shouts only strengthened her resolve to stay silent.

I threatened to call the police about the theft. In response she threatened to turn over to them the Gonzalez medical file. "You destroyed it," I said. "Did I?" she said. Her eyes narrowed when she said it and she grew cold, cold as ice, frighteningly cold. It was like she was another person entirely, somebody hard and damaged and capable of horrible things, and still, Victor, I was desperate not to lose her.

I think by then it was not her I was afraid of losing but the vision of myself that she had liberated, the vision of a man wild, daring, brave enough to live his own life, a man eternally free. I couldn't give her up because that meant giving up on that part of myself.

TWO WEEKS before she was murdered, she disappeared, another of her jaunts with her lover, I supposed, but when she came back, things had changed. She was suddenly loving again. We had sex again, and it was as amazing as before, even if tinged with a strange sadness. She spoke of our future, our married life together. She asked when the divorce would be finalized. She even mentioned again Costa Rica. Have you ever been to Costa Rica, Victor? I hear it's magical. She asked me to buy tickets to take us there for a vacation, and I did. I figured that she had been dumped by her lover, and I was thrilled. There's the sign of how gone I was. I had projected so much onto her, had sacrificed so much, made so many choices based on our future together that I couldn't imagine going on without her. It would mean facing what I had done to my family, my life, the false fantasies that had led me once again astray. Anything that kept me from facing my failures was reason for celebration.

Then one night she came home late, very late, and acted strangely when she saw me, as if she didn't know who I was or what I was doing there. She even gasped when she saw me waiting for her. It was peculiar, and a fear gripped me like a fist around my throat. I figured she was out drinking again, back with that other man again, or maybe someone new. That night she went back to her pills, even pricking the capsules to make them work more quickly. And the next night, when I came home, she was waiting for me.

"There is no kind way to say this," she said, "so I won't try to make it kind. It's over."

She was lying on the mattress, smoking, glasses on, staring at me as if I were a thief. I'd like to say I took it with a profound stoicism, but that would be a lie. I begged, I cried, I threatened to kill her, I threatened to kill myself, I broke down, I refused to let it be over.

"Oh, it is," she said. "Believe it. You need to make arrangements to move out as soon as you can."

No, I told her. I wouldn't. I couldn't. What about our future? What about Costa Rica? What about the money? The money, damn it. I shouted, I pleaded, I lost control. "There's someone else, isn't there?" I said.

"Yes," she said.

"Tell me who?" I said.

"Someone who fucks like a railroad engineer," she said, smiling coldly. "It's all aboard and then on to Abilene."

That's when I hit her. I leaned over and smacked her face with the back of my hand, and when I did, something snapped inside me. She just lay there and took it and curled her lips into that hard smile, but something had snapped inside me. I think maybe in that instant when my flesh smashed against hers, I saw, as if from a distance, the whole thing, the scene, the relationship, my folly, saw it all at a distance as if it were someone else hitting her, someone else who loved her, someone else who had given up the world for her.

I stood back in horror at what I had done.

With that smile still in place she rolled away from me and said simply, "Put out the light."

So I did, without saying another word. I turned out the light and went into the bathroom and filled the tub with scalding water, as if I needed to be cleansed. I put Louis Armstrong into the Walkman and rolled myself a joint. I stripped and lit up and put on the headphones and slipped into the tub, turned on the water jets and thought about what I had seen from the distance as I hit her. I had seen a fool, desperate and lost. I had seen a runner who had run from everything and was still running. I sat in the tub and closed my eyes and thought my way through into a future without Hailey, without my family, without my career, without my money. In front of me was a door I couldn't open and behind which was a life I couldn't fathom. I felt a dark desperation overwhelm me, and I thought of dying, the freedom, the peace of death. But there was something about the music, something about the jazz, the brassy trumpet, the joyous spirit marching through hard times. I sat in the tub and smoked the dope and listened to Louis Armstrong, and I thought my way through the blackness, through the blackness, toward the door I couldn't open. And I imagined myself putting my shoulder to it, pressing against it, breaking through it, crashing through the door like Pepito himself into something approaching equilibrium, and I felt strangely peaceful. And tired. Maybe it was the reefer, maybe it was that I hadn't slept the night before, maybe it was the release of all those tightly clenched expectations, but I felt strangely peaceful and tired, and with the headphones on and the heat of the water soothing my bones, I fell asleep.

When I awoke, it was into a nightmare of blood.

I LISTENED to his story with horror, and when he stopped speaking I shook my head as if shaking myself back into the world. The room was the same as before, still gray, still lit by the fluorescent lights humming in the ceiling. The barred window still looked out upon another block wall. The room was the same, but the universe had shifted.

If life is lived in that normally narrow and disappointing region between expectation and actuality, then those moments that most change our lives play out in the great gaps where expectation and reality veer wildly apart. Listening to Guy Forrest tell his story was for me like falling headfirst into one of those gaps. I had expected the story to be self-serving, and it was that, though not to the degree I had thought, but I had also expected it to be a tale of Guy's depredations, of Guy's machinations, of one arrogant step after another that led, inexorably, to Guy's moral disintegration and his explosion into murder. What I saw instead were the depredations and machinations of another.

It was the bumping of the knees that did it. The innocuous detail that sounded like a siren for me. They are at a bar, he is not sure what they are doing, not sure what he wants or why he is there. Betrayal is the unspoken message that swirls about them like the smoke from her cigarette. Their conversations approach and then veer away from the topic at hand, but as they drink and talk their knees touch, in a gesture both awkward and intimate, their knees touch, and the spark sends a complex wave of emotion through Guy. It is contact charged with meaning and yet maybe no meaning at all. It promises so much and yet it embarrasses him all the same. It is intimate, but is it, really? Or is it instead an accident? The uncertainty raises the level of everything it conveys, lust, confusion, desire, fear, all of it. I know, because the same accidental touching of the knees sent the same wave of emotion through me. The accidental touching that was not so accidental.

She had known about Juan Gonzalez's prior medical condition from the first. "Don't mention it," she must have told the family. "I'll take care of it," and she did. The slow seduction, the promises of a future, the whispers of Costa Rica, all of it was the buildup toward the crucial moment when Guy discovered the fatal flaw in her case. It can take years, decades waiting for a case so rich to walk into your office. Negligence without massive damages is penny common and worth about as much. Cases with massive damages and clear negligence usually go to the big names with the big reputations. How does a young solo practitioner get her hands on a case like that? Luck. And if luck is not with you? Then make your own luck. Take a case with a fatal flaw and find a way to make the flaw disappear.

Hailey Prouix.

But what had she wanted from me? She had laid on me the same slow seduction, the same banging of the knees that made it seem it was I doing the seducing. But it wasn't my doing, was it? She followed the script, for some unknown reason of her own devising. What was it that I could have offered her? Why was I worth using?

The questions came crashing down upon me, along with the realization.

"You didn't kill her," I said to Guy, as a statement not as a question, though he took it as the latter.

"No, I told you, no. I didn't. No."

I glanced at Beth with a nervous hesitation. I wanted to see if belief was on her face, too, and I wanted to see something else. Had she figured it out, the madness behind my method? Had she matched his chronology about Hailey's secret lover with the bare bones she knew of my failed relationship? Had she matched the dates when both started and both flamed out, filled in the gaps and taken a guess at my motives? She was staring now at Guy and I could read nothing in her expression.

"Why not?" she asked Guy. "She had stolen your money, taken another lover, left you without your family, your career, without a cent or a future. She had used you like a rented mule. Why *didn't* you kill her?"

He looked at her strangely, as if it were a question he never considered before. "Because I loved her?"

"Please," I said loudly, in a voice overflowing with exasperation. "Who loved better than Othello? In the history of the world love has caused more murder than ever it stopped."

"What stopped you?" said Beth softly.

He didn't answer right off. He stared off to the side, his face twisted in puzzlement. I expected him to come up with something soulful and religious, something all surface, like the answer of a beauty pageant contestant. *I didn't kill her because I believe that love can make the world a better place and we should shower our fellow humans with affection, not violence.* But that's not what he said, what he said instead was:

"Because it never occurred to me."

It never occurred to him? It never occurred to him? How could it not have occurred to him in this post-Holocaust, post-9/11 violence-saturated, blood-soaked-blockbuster age of ours? It never occurred to him? He had come up with the perfect answer, because it rang so true. It never occurred to him. Isn't that what keeps us on the razor's edge of the straight and narrow more often than not, that falling off never occurs to us? With that answer the vestiges of my doubts were routed. I now believed him. I now believed his entire story.

I had been wrong, wrong from the start, dead wrong.

I had been wrong enough to leap at a false assumption, wrong enough to chase a man through the wet streets of the city, wrong enough to seek to consign a friend to a life in jail or, worse, an execution. I had violated every precept of my lawyer's oath, had tried to railroad a guilty man, to elevate justice over form, to sacrifice means to an end, and all along I had been flat-out wrong.

There's the rub with taking the law into your own hands. There may be things upon which to stake your life, at least you should hope so, but upon what can you hold absolute enough to stake the life of another?

It is not enough to suspect, to surmise, to sort of kind of believe. It is not enough. Maybe that's what due process is, a method, devised over millennia, to allow us to treat our guesses as certainties. We can put you in jail without absolute certainty after we've jumped through all the hoops and played the game as fairly as we know how. Due process is not a way toward certainty but a way to handle uncertainty, and when you forget that, you begin to forget that uncertainty is all we ever have.

To the question of how you can represent a man you are certain is guilty, I give this answer: Who the hell can be certain of anything in this world?

So here I was in a universe different than that into which I awoke, representing a man who I now believed was innocent and whose defense I had relentlessly sabotaged from almost the very moment of the crime. Now what was I to do, now how was I to save him, to save myself? Whatever it was, I had to do it quickly, before the wheels I had set into motion fell like a hatchet, smack on Guy Forrest's head.

"I have to tell you this, Guy," I said, trying to hide the desperation in my voice. "The evidence against you is overwhelming. Your gun, your fingerprints, the bruise, which you'll have to admit to if you testify, your attempted flight. They don't know yet about the money, but if they do, it becomes even worse. I don't believe you did it, and I'm willing to defend you to the best of my ability, no holds barred, but it might be time to seriously consider their offer."

"You said we should fight it."

"Yes, but that was before I learned about Gonzalez. You might win the murder case, but you'd still be up on fraud on the Gonzalez case. You'd still end up in jail. Look. Troy Jefferson offered up man one. You'd serve eight to ten years. I might be able to shave some months off. And I'll make sure it covers what you did in the Gonzalez case, too. It's not great, but you'll be out before you're fifty, with nothing hanging over your head and a chance to start over."

"I didn't do it."

"I know that, Guy. I believe that. But you did cheat the insurance company. And if you go to trial and lose, which with the Juan Gonzalez stuff is more likely than ever, they could keep you in jail for the rest of your life, or even kill you."

"What about the other man?"

"We can argue he did it," I said, "and we will. But it cuts both ways. It could also be a reason for you to kill her, jealousy, anger. It's a dangerous game you want to play. Eight years is hard, but it's not the end of your life."

He turned to Beth. "What do you think?"

"I think it's a generous offer," said Beth. "From what I understand, your father-in-law set it up to avoid a trial and the bad publicity. And to avoid any mention of Juan Gonzalez. I think it makes sense to pursue it."

"Can I think about it?" said Guy.

"No," I said. "There isn't time. If Jefferson gets word of the Gonzalez mess, the deal will disappear. We have to decide now, this instant. Every second is dangerous. Give me authority to make a deal."

"I don't know."

"You don't have the luxury not to know. You have to decide, now. I strongly suggest you make the deal. Beth strongly suggests you make the deal. It is your decision, but if you don't decide now, it won't be there later, and that could be the end."

"I don't know. I don't know."

"I need an answer now, Guy. Now. Yes or no. What do you say? Yes or no."

THE RECEPTIONIST behind the glass window made us wait in the waiting area.

Mr. Jefferson, the receptionist said, was still in his meeting.

I had called right from the prison and had been told by that self-same lady that Mr. Jefferson was tied up. I told her it was important, I told her it was urgent, I told her it was about the Guy Forrest murder case and that Troy Jefferson would very much want to speak to me right away.

She repeated her demurrer: "Mr. Jefferson is unavailable at the present instant."

"I'll be right over," I said. "Don't let him leave before I get there."

And now here I was.

The receptionist smiled from behind the glass like a civil servant at the end of a long day and told us to please sit and wait. So we sat and we waited.

The waiting area for the DA's office was in the elevator lobby of the fourth floor of the courthouse. It was a stark and uncomfortable space. It appeared they had bought the furniture secondhand from the office of a failed dentist. You could almost hear the echoes of the screams. A single door with frosted glass, its lock controlled by the receptionist, led to the offices. I tapped my watch, tapped my foot.

A heavy woman walked out of the elevator and was immediately buzzed through by the receptionist. I worked on the Jumble in the newspaper left out on the table along with a *Newsweek* months old. CEZAR was craze. THICY was itchy. But DUGAY, DUGAY. I was stumped on DUGAY. Where was Skink when you needed him?

"Gaudy," said Beth, looking over my shoulder.

"Enough about my damn ties," I said even as I filled in the blocks.

The door opened, a man in a suit with a briefcase the size of a filing cabinet stepped through.

"Could you tell Mr. Jefferson again that we are here?" I asked the receptionist.

"I've told his secretary," she said.

"Could you remind her?"

She smiled at me. "She knows. She asked that I have you wait."

I picked up the *Newsweek.* I read the review of a movie already out of the theaters. I read of a rising star already fallen. I read of a disaster in China already replaced in our finite capacities for horror by a disaster in Cental America.

The door opened, a small man in a suit stepped through, and I jerked to standing even as my heart sank sickeningly, like the NASDAQ on earnings fears.

"Peale," I said.

Jonah Peale wore a pained expression like a mask. Behind him, holding the door, stood a smiling Troy Jefferson.

"I'm surprised to see you here, Mr. Peale," I said.

"Priorities," said Jonah Peale, nodding brusquely as he brushed by. I was too stunned to say anything, just watched him go.

"Are you ready for me, Victor?" said Troy Jefferson.

"Yes," I said, though I suspected I was too late, too, too late.

Beth and I followed the prosecutor through the door, down a narrow hall, into his small office. He walked with a slight limp, still. In his office, exhibits and files were piled on the floor, maps were taped to the walls. Among the clutter were two flags, standing next to each another, the flag of the United States of America and the flag of the Commonwealth of Pennsylvania. All the documents on the desk were facedown. Leaning against a file cabinet were our detective friends, Breger and Stone.

This was not good, I knew. This was not good at all.

"How's it going there, Victor?" said Troy Jefferson after we all had situated ourselves in the proper seats. "You getting ready to rumble?"

"That's what I came here to talk to you about."

"Of course we'll cooperate to the full extent required by law, give you everything you're entitled to. But I must say, this case suddenly has my competitive juices flowing. I get the same sense of nervous anticipation before every trial as I had when I played ball. I still play, I suppose. I just play in a different court now. With justice as my goal."

"We're not reporters," said Beth. "Save the patter for the press."

He grinned and shrugged as if he were already in the statehouse.

"We met today with our client," I said. "We discussed everything once again. He continues to profess his innocence, but, in light of the overwhelming evidence facing him, he asked I explore further the plea offer you made at the arraignment."

"Yes, well, I am sorry about that," said Troy Jefferson.

"Sorry?"

"When I made the offer, it was contingent on our finding no information that would indicate a motive other than the heat of passion."

"That's right," I said. "But we've received no notice that you have discovered such information."

"I faxed notice to your office twenty minutes ago."

"Twenty minutes ago? We were in your waiting room twenty minutes ago."

"Were you? We didn't know." He reached for one of the overturned papers on his desk, checked it, offered it to me. "Here it is."

Without looking at it, I said, "We are accepting the offer."

"I'm sorry, Victor, but it has been withdrawn."

"You can't."

"We have."

"Offer and acceptance. We have a contract."

"I don't think so. All material terms were never spelled out in full, the offer was at all times contingent, the contingency failed, and the offer was withdrawn well before you accepted. Pleas are not governed by the laws of contract but even if they were, your claim would fall."

"We'll see what the judge has to say about it."

"I suppose we will."

I stared at him. He grinned at me.

"What did you find?" asked Beth.

He leaned back in his chair, webbed his hands and placed them behind his head. "Juan Gonzalez."

"The ballplayer?" I said, a false confusion in my voice.

"No, not the ballplayer," said Jefferson.

By the file cabinet Stone laughed lightly. Breger, gazing up at the ceiling, kept his broad face free of expression.

Beth's features betrayed her shock. I tried to replicate the expression, though it was hard. It was hard. The moment I saw Jonah Peale come out that frosted-glass door, I knew. Of course I knew. I had set the whole thing up.

"Mr. Peale will be added to our witness list," said Troy Jefferson. "He's an interesting man, Jonah Peale, with an interesting story to tell."

"He'll ruin his practice," I said.

"Yes, I expect his testimony might do serious damage to his law firm, but still, he feels compelled to tell the truth, the whole truth, and nothing but the truth. At one point he wanted to avoid publicity but now he is interested only in seeing that Mr. Forrest suffer the full force of justice."

"I don't understand," said Beth.

"It seems, somehow, that Mr. Peale learned his daughter wants her husband back. Imagine that. Mr. Peale would prefer to lose his business than to allow a murderer to move back in with his daughter and grandchildren."

I closed my eyes, fought back the nausea. This was all my doing, I had just destroyed my client's chance to live at least part of his life out of jail. "He didn't do it," I said.

"And you'll have every chance to prove it, Victor. But what we really have now is a simple case of fraud where the co-conspirators fell out over money. Stone here has checked out the finances."

"Were you aware of the withdrawals by Miss Prouix?" she said.

"Yes," I said.

"Do you know where the money went?"

"Attorney-client privilege forbids me from saying anything. But I can say that my client was aware that money had been withdrawn and he had no problem with it."

Breger snorted.

"Sure," said Stone. "What's a million bucks among friends?"

"We believe," said Troy Jefferson, "that we finally understand what happened. They stole the money together, she transferred it out of the joint account for her own purposes without telling him. In a rage over the stolen money, and her dalliance with another, shown by the DNA, he killed her. It happens all too frequently, a sad tale often told. And we'll tell it well."

"It's not the truth," I said.

"It's as close as we need to get. I hope your preparation is moving apace, Victor, because the stakes have been raised. Man one is off the table. Tomorrow we're filing the Commonwealth's Notice of Intent to Seek the Death Penalty. The game is on, my friend. Oh, yes, the game is on."

AFTER THE meeting I stepped out onto the courthouse steps, blinking at the bright sun shining through the perfect blue sky. The air was fresh, spring was strutting its stuff, and for the first time in a long time I noticed it. I noticed it all.

"What are we going to do?" said Beth.

"I don't know what we're going to do." I took a deep breath, let the oxygen soak into my lungs like an elixir, and then loosed a great yawn. "But I think what I'm going to do is go home and take a nap."

"Victor? Are you all right?"

"I'm just a little tired. Just a little. I haven't been sleeping. I'll drop you at the office first and then I'm going home. Could you tell Guy the bad news?"

"Victor?"

"I would do it myself, except I need to close my eyes. Just for a few minutes."

It was still afternoon when I got home, stripped off my suit, slipped between the covers. It was still bright outside, sunlight was leaking through the gaps betwcen my window and my shade. I stared at the ceiling for a moment. It didn't break apart, it was inert, safe. I closed my eyes and slept like a dead goat.

When I awoke, it was dark and silent and I knew exactly what I needed to do. I might not have known what the hell I was doing before, I had never before contemplated doing what I had contemplated doing to Guy, but now I was on more comfortable ground. A girl was dead, my lover was dead, and she left me now a mystery to solve, a simple mystery. Who the hell had killed her? To save Guy and enact my vengeance both I needed only to unlock the mystery, ferret out the motive, and find the murderer. And I believed just then I already had the key.

I was wrong, of course. There was nothing simple about the mystery of Hailey Prouix's death, just as there was nothing simple about Hailey Prouix herself.

But damn if I wasn't right about the key.

FIRST PHILADELPHIA, Market Street Branch, Allison Robards speaking."

"Hi, Allison. Tommy, Tommy Baker, over at First Philadelphia, Old City. How you doing today?"

"Fine. Tommy, is it?"

"That's right. Tommy, Tommy Baker."

"Tommy Baker, that name is familiar. Did I meet you at the Christmas party?"

"Remember the fellow in the checked jacket dancing that dance?"

"The bald one?"

"I'm not bald, I'm follicularly challenged."

"I thought the name was familiar. Tommy. Tommy Baker. How are you, Tommy?"

"Great. Doing great, except for our computers. Are you guys up, or is the whole system down?"

"No, we're up. What do you need?"

"I got a police detective in here asking about one of our accounts. The name is Hailey Prouix."

"Hailey Prouix? Isn't she . . . ?"

"Exactly. But with my computer down, and it's been happening a lot. Someone is screwing up. Who's the vendor, you know?"

"Not my department."

"They said her office was near your branch, so I thought you might be able to help."

"Okay, sure, Tommy. What was the name again?"

"P-r-o-u-i-x. Hailey. With a suburban address."

"Here it is. Account number 598872. We are the home branch. She opened the account here two years ago."

"All right, great. What's the balance?"

"One-oh-three-four-two and fifty-six."

"Any recent activity?"

"Checks, nothing strange. Except . . ."

"Go ahead."

"A wire transfer about two months ago, February eighteenth. Big amount. Whoa. Four hundred thousand."

"You don't say. Where to?"

"Don't know, location isn't listed here. It's number WT876032Q. You'd have to check Wire Transfers for specifics."

"Okay, that's great, thanks. And as the home branch, you guys have her safe-deposit box, too?"

"Let me look. Hold on a sec, I'll have to check the cards."

Long pause.

"No, no, we don't have a safe-deposit box registered in her name."

"All right, thanks a load."

"No problem."

"And, Allison. Have a nice day."

THE KEY.

It sat on my desk, the little chunk of metal, one end rounded like a clover, the other jagged like the teeth of one of the winos on North Broad Street. And stamped into its head the words DIEBOLD INC./CANTON OHIO. Canton, Ohio, the birthplace of football and home to the pro football hall of fame. Also the home of Diebold, Incorporated. From the moment I first laid eyes on it in Hailey Prouix's desk drawer, I knew what it was. Diebold didn't make just any old lock and key. Diebold didn't make filing cabinets or desks or padlocks or cars. Diebold made vaults, bank vaults. This was the key to Hailey Prouix's safe-deposit box, the hiding place for her secrets, both personal and financial. A man in black had searched the house after the murder, apparently looking for this very chunk of metal. And in my vomitous encounter with Skink, he had told me that he knew I had it and that he wanted it, wanted it badly enough to let me know he wanted it. I had taken it on a whim but suddenly, in my desire to save Guy's life, I had a great need to know what was inside its box.

I used the phone I had given to Hailey, to keep the records off my office line, and geared myself up for the role, shaking my neck, jiggling my arms, breathing like a prizefighter about to enter the ring. What I needed was the right voice. A job like this depended on voice. With the right voice you could work wonders. Tommy, Tommy Baker. With my rumpled suits, my spreading rear, my comb-over. I had risen fast at the start, but then my career had stalled, along with my life. My wife had gained thirty pounds, my daughter had pierced her tongue, my car smelled like a cat, and I was trying to make that new teller but she didn't seem interested. My weight was high, my blood pressure higher, I drank too much because by my age my father was dead. What I needed was a tone of overt jocularity covering a vast sea of despair. The jocularity I could fake, the despair I didn't need to.

"FIRST PHILADELPHIA, Ardmore Branch."

"Hi, this is Market Street. Who am I speaking to?"

"Latitia Clogg."

"Hi, Latitia. This is Tommy, Tommy Baker. Allison Robards over here suggested I give you a call."

"Allison?"

"She said she had some questions for you before and that you were a great help."

"Allison? Oh, yeah, Allison. Pretty little blond girl."

"That's the one. Look, I have something you might be able to answer. I have been getting some information requests from Legal about account number 598872, which was opened by a Hailey Prouix in this branch about two years ago."

"Isn't she . . . ?"

"That's right. What was the *Daily News* headline: SHOT THROUGH THE HEART? What do you think of that, huh? Makes you wonder, doesn't it?"

"Wonder about what?"

"Fate. Life. The price of bananas. Who knows? But Legal, man. You should see the mess of forms they want us to fill out. It's going to take a week."

"I bet. First thing let's kill all the lawyers, right?"

"Who said that?"

"Wasn't it like Nixon or somebody?"

"Probably. Look, Latitia, they've been asking us, in addition to the account information, whether there was a safe-deposit box in her name. We've got nothing here on that, but I understand she was living not too far from your branch, so I was wondering if you could check whether she had a box there or not."

"Of course, Tommy. Just wait a minute, I'll check the cards."

Long pause.

"Nope, nothing. Sorry."

"No, that's good, that's easier. Thanks, Latitia. By the way, I have to check out some other things, too. You know anyone in Wire Transfers I could get to help me out?"

"Kelly Morgan."

"She knows her stuff?"

"Oh, yes. Tell her Latitia sent you."

"Thank you, you've been great. Did I meet you at the Christmas party?"

"I was there with my husband."

"Why is it, Latitia, that all the good ones are already taken?"

ALONG WITH the key, I had taken Hailey Prouix's expired driver's license from the desk in the room of her murder. It was the only picture I had of her: guilt-ridden lovers don't take snapshots. In my office, the door closed and locked, I looked hard at the tiny photograph on the card, but it was like looking at a stranger. There had been a wonderful plasticity to her face, her mouth always teetering on the edge of a smile or a frown, her eyes widening or contracting, her face alive with the currents of emotion flowing beneath the surface, but all that aliveness was missing on the photograph. She looked plain, even mousy on the license, her hair pulled back, her glasses hiding the sharp ridges of her face instead of accentuating them. She looked like no one I had ever known. The raw statistics were there, birth date, sex, her height was listed as five-two, her eyes blue, but she was missing.

I closed my eyes and tried to conjure her. I had been haunted by the specter of Hailey Prouix from the moment I discovered her corpse—it had driven me first to exact a punishment from Guy and now, having discovered his innocence, to search for the real killer— but just then, sitting at my desk between calls, I couldn't see it. The image was blurry. I thought I knew her, we were intimate in more than one way, I thought I knew her, better than her fiancé, I was sure, but now her image was blurry. What was causing the distortion?

Every damn thing. From the moment of her death I had been learning more and more about her. Detective Stone had said that of all those who knew her, the words "nice" and "sweet" had never been mentioned. Leila had told of her spitting out the most vile slurs. I always thought she was hard, but that hard? And then a slime like Skink thought he knew her better than I did, and I suspected he was right. Wheels within wheels within wheels. The final twist was Guy's own story, which showed how she had used Guy for her own corrupt purpose and then, for some other purpose, used me. It was as if whatever I thought I knew about her was shattered by the revelations of a darkness deep within her character that I had never before glimpsed. I closed my eyes and tried to conjure her and failed. Who was Hailey Prouix?

I suspected that behind that answer crouched a murderer.

"WIRE TRANSFERS."

"Hi, I'm looking for Kelly Morgan."

"One moment, please."

Soothing music.

"Kelly Morgan."

"Kelly. Hi. Tommy, Tommy Baker, from the Ardmore branch here. Latitia Clogg said if I had some questions I should get hold of you. Said you were the only one up there who knew what the hell was going on."

"She's right about that. How are you doing?"

"Good, better than good. I got—let me see—five hours left and then I'm out of here for a week's vacation. And let me tell you, Kelly, I could use it."

"Couldn't we all, Tommy, couldn't we all."

"Here's my problem. Before I get out of here, I have to finish up a ream of paperwork sent to me by Legal. You ever get mixed up with that crew?"

"I try not to."

"I hear you, Kelly. Well, there's this account they've got questions about. It's that Hailey Prouix, you hear about her?"

"Not that I know of."

"Girl shot in the heart out here in Ardmore?"

"Oh, yeah, the boyfriend did it, didn't he? What was he, married to someone else and he shacks up with her and then kills her?"

"That's what they say."

"Nice guy. Sounds like the ones I end up with."

"Not you, Kelly."

"You don't want to know, trust me. What do you need?"

"Apparently she wire-transferred some funds out of her account on February eighteenth of this year. Account number 598872, wire transfer number WT876032Q. Legal wants to know where they went."

"Hold on a second, let me see here. Account number . . . ?"

"598872."

"Yeah, I see it. Went to a bank in Las Vegas, something called Nevada One. Into account number 67ST98016. The branch address is Paradise Road in Las Vegas, 89109."

"That is so great, Kelly, thanks."

"Anything else?"

"No, this is enough to get Legal off my back."

"Enjoy your vacation, Tommy."

"Believe you me I will."

OUR LIFE stories are always lies. How could we be the heroes of our lives if all we told was the truth? We shade an incident here, invent a rationale there, leave out the telling detail that changes everything. Is there anything less reliable than the memoir? Eichmann was following orders. Clinton did nothing wrong. Our life stories are our great fictions, and so I knew to take, even as I was hearing it, Hailey's life story with a bucket of salt. Oh, I could fill in some of the gaps. Her high school years were probably not so idyllic— are anyone's? College was not the grind she claimed—college girls who look like Hailey don't live hermits' lives. And I could imagine that the affair with the partner at her first law firm was more torrid, more painful, and ended with more difficulty than she let on. Oh, I had no trouble believing that her life story was more fiction than truth, considering she herself told me not to trust anything she said.

"Why do you care?" she asks me as we lie side by side in the bed where we pass our stories like kisses atop the pillow, the shades pulled to keep out the afternoon light, her scent swirling about me like a drug.

"I want to know you," I say.

"No you don't."

"I don't?"

"All you want is to confirm what you already believe. Last thing you want are any surprises."

"Are there any?"

"Do you want them?"

I think on that for a moment. Do I want the surprises? Do I want to peer at the sad, unvarnished hollows in her heart? It all comes down to what are we doing in that bed? Are we playing out a fantasy in our otherwise reality-drenched days, or are we looking for a piece of the real in a life of artifice?

"I don't know," I say.

"Then there aren't any."

And she laughs, as if my indecision justifies everything.

But now she was dead, and the mystery of her death had become my new reality, and I very much needed to learn every secret, every truth, everything she had never wanted me to know. It was time to go behind the lies.

"NEVADA ONE, Paradise Road Branch. How may I direct your call?"

"Customer Service."

"One moment, please."

"Gerald Hopkins here."

"Hi, Gerald, this is Tommy Baker at First Philadelphia Bank and Trust. I wonder if you could help me. I have a client sitting right here at my desk who also has an account at your bank. She had us wire in some funds on—what was it?—oh, yes, February eighteenth of this year, and she wants to be sure everything worked out. Could you check that for us? Her name is Hailey Prouix and her account number with your bank is 67ST98016."

"What was the date of that transfer?"

"February eighteenth."

"All right. Let me check that out for you."

"What's the weather like out there?"

"Hot. Spring here lasts about a week. Okay, yeah, here it is. We got the transfer on February eighteenth. Money went in that day, went out a few days later. Everything looks fine."

"You have a balance on that account, Gerald?"

"Yeah sure. Twenty-seven thousand, six hundred and sixty seven."

"Good, that matches what she expected. One last thing, she wants to know if the fee on her safe-deposit box is overdue? She doesn't want to miss a payment."

"Let me see. No, it's fine. The fee was paid last month out of the account."

"Perfect. Thanks, Gerald."

"Oh, and Tommy. Give Ms. Prouix my regards. I remember her well, I personally opened her account for her. How is she doing?"

"Fine, great. I mean, I can't say anything about her personal life, but she looks like a million bucks."

"That she does."

"I'll send along your regards, Gerald. Thanks."

I STARED for another long moment at the picture of the stranger on the driver's license. It didn't look like Hailey, but it looked like someone. I didn't know who, but it surely looked like someone. I told Ellie I'd be right back and I stepped out of my building and into the bookstore right next door. From the rack of reading glasses I searched among the pairs until I found one that matched, somewhat, the glasses in the photograph. Then I went back up to my floor and entered Beth's office.

"Do me a favor," I said. "Pull your hair back and bind it with a rubber band."

"Why?"

"Just do it."

She looked at me like I'd gone over the edge and then went into her drawer and took out a rubber band. Beth's hair was black and shiny and fell down about to her shoulders, so she was able to make a short ponytail of it.

"All right," I said, "now put these on."

She took the glasses and peered at them for a long moment. "What's this all about?"

"Humor me," I said.

When the glasses were on, I compared what I saw with the picture. It wasn't a perfect match by any means. Beth's eyes were green, not blue, and she was slightly taller. But there was a resemblance, an undeniable resemblance.

"How are you feeling, Beth? You a little tired?"

"No."

"Worn down by your frantic pace? At the end of your rope?"

"No."

"Are you feeling overwhelmed by life?"

"Not at all."

"Funny, I am, too. You know what we should do? We should

chuck it all for a bit and get out of here. Not just the office but the city, the state. Aren't you sick of the East Coast?"

"Victor, what are you talking about? We have a trial to prepare for. Did someone spike your morning coffee? Are you sane?"

"Actually no, but that's not what's going on. Clear the weekend, partner, because you and I, we're taking a road trip."

PART THREE

DESERT

WINDS

AH, LAS VEGAS. Neon, flash, the crush of crowds opening for long-legged women in boots and short skirts. Artificial light, artificial air, proud entrances, meek exits, announcements, lines, doors hissing open and shut, chrome, chrome. The bells and whistles of the slot machines, the silver clatter of coins, the snarl of old ladies with cigarettes dangling feeding in quarter after quarter. Giant video screens advertising the latest shows, the fattest buffets, the newest hotels. Wheels spinning, luggage flying, money passing in every handshake, limos lined up like black lemmings at the doors. The infinite sense of promise in those arriving, the weary defeat in those departing. Signs, shops, restaurants, uniforms, joyous laughter cackling over the grand cacophony as a jackpot hits and the lights start flashing. Ah, Las Vegas.

And that was only the airport.

"Could you wait here a minute?" said Beth after we had departed our plane and were headed to the tramway into the main terminal. "I could use a pit stop."

I stood in the gray concourse and looked around. The usual mall-like stores and fast-food joints intermixed with slot machines. Nothing of too much interest, until something in the window of a kiosk with a great neon Mardi Gras head on top captured my attention and knocked it cold. While Beth was taking care of business, I went to check it out.

It was a sports jacket, hanging on a rack just beside the snow globes with the Vegas skyline doused in glitter. I found one in my size and felt its material, the lapels a satiny black, the body a rough and sparkly gold lamé. Gold lamé, how apropos. It wasn't well made—it had no lining, threads were fraying already from the shoulder seams—but it had pockets big enough to hold five jack-pots and it glistened so brightly it should have had a switch. I slipped it on and did a spin in front of the narrow mirror and had to shield my eyes. It was money, baby.

"You sell many of these?" I asked the cute salesgirl with the green hair and the ring though her eyebrow.

She curled her lip. "Hardly."

"It's a little bright, hey?"

"A-yaah."

"Could you think of anything tackier?"

"Not really."

"Perfect. I'll take it."

Seventy-eight bucks, and worth every dime.

"By the way," I said to the salesgirl as I left the store, the jacket packed safely away in my briefcase, "I like your hair," and I meant it, and she blushed, which was like hitting three sevens on the slots.

While Beth waited for our luggage, I took the shuttle bus to pick up our rental car. A convertible, red, as cheaply made as the jacket, but still topless and red. Before I drove it back to the airport, I dropped the roof. I shucked on my new jacket despite the oppres-sive heat. I slipped on my sunglasses despite the fact that it was long past dark.

When I pulled in front of Beth at the loading curb, I was smiling like an idiot.

"Welcome to Vegas," I said.

"You look like you're about to do a very bad version of 'Feel-ings.' "

"This city brings out the best in me."

"I'd hate to be with you in any city that brings out your worst."

"Boca Raton, where I break out my Sansabelt slacks and white shoes?"

"Victor, Sansabelt slacks and white shoes would be six steps up from that jacket."

"Hop in, sweetheart, the night is young and my stake is burning a hole in my pocket."

She dropped our bags into the back seat and opened the door. "I didn't know a buck sixty-four could get so hot?"

"Let's go shoot craps."

"Do you know how to shoot craps?"

"No," I said, "but I understand they teach you how to play right on the television in your room. How nice is that?"

"It's going to be an expensive night, isn't it?"

I squealed my tires on the blacktop and tore out of the airport, into the desert night.

Vegas was not in my normal route between the office, the diner, and my apartment, but I had been there before. After college, on the obligatory cross-country road trip, I had stopped in Vegas on the way to L.A. and stayed longer than I ever expected. I remembered the $1.99 breakfast buffet at Circus Circus, great troughs of eggs, mountains of bacon. I remembered the shabby old pool at the Dunes where I could sneak in without anyone caring enough to do a thing about it. I saw Wayne Newton at the Hilton, I saw an Elvis impersonator sing "Viva Las Vegas" at the Imperial Inn. I lost thirty bucks on a queen-high straight playing poker at Binion's. I spent a Sunday afternoon in the Caesar's sports book, sitting in a helmet, watching nine NFL games at once. I bought the little yellow card that detailed perfect blackjack strategy and still lost more than I could afford and then won half of it back on a royal straight flush at a video poker machine. It was a great tacky carnival and I loved it, and that was why I was in high spirits despite the grim nature of our errand.

Yes, we might be there to break open the safe-deposit box of my murdered lover, but, hell, I was going to have myself a time. It was, after all, still Vegas.

Or was it?

It had changed. It was no longer dominated by the hopelessly tacky, now it was all flash and pomposity. The Dunes had disappeared, spectacularly razed to make way for the Bellagio, with its great sign in front advertising the Picassos and Manets held in the hotel's private museum. Just on the other side of Caesar's was the Mirage, with its high-toned lobby and volcano out front. We could have stayed at Paris with its Eiffel Tower, at the Venetian with its Grand Canal, at the Monte Carlo or Mandalay Bay or the Rio or New York, New York. There was the MGM Grand, there was the sinister Pyramid of Luxor with its message beam of pyramid power soaring out to the heavens, there was the Excaliber. As we drove down the glory of the Strip, the city was different from how I remembered it to be, a place that now aspired to be something grander than the tacky heart of the American wasteland. It didn't look like it was succeeding, but even the attempt was disappointing. My God, I wondered if it still had whores.

"This is amazing," said Beth as I drove her down the Strip. She had never before been to Vegas and her head wagged as we passed all the shiny new hotels.

"I don't understand," I said. "Why do they have to ruin everything?"

"I've never seen so many lights in my life. It's like the whole city is a parade. What is that?"

"The Pyramid of Luxor," I said. "But they have a better one in Egypt."

"And look, look, the Statue of Liberty."

"The one in New York Harbor is cooler."

"And what's that? Oh, my God, the Eiffel Tower."

"Yeah, but the one in France is bigger."

"Look at the sign. 'Now appearing, Picasso'?"

"That's where the Dunes was. Now, that was a Vegas hotel. You want to talk seedy, that was seedy. There were rats nibbling the food trays left outside the rooms at night, and they had this thing shaped like a spaceship with rows and rows of nickel slots. That was my Vegas."

"But look how bright it is."

"It used to be brighter."

"Why do I suddenly have the urge, Victor, to rub lemons on my breasts?"

I had booked us rooms at the Flamingo, which was decidedly old school, the first casino ever built on the Strip. But it had one of the biggest neon displays, which I liked, and it was also three hundred and fifty dollars a night cheaper than the Bellagio, which I liked a lot. The hotel was very Miami Beach, old-time Miami Beach, crowded with an aged clientele drawn to the same bargains as was I. We ate dinner in their restaurant, the Flamingo Room, since Beth refused to wait in a long line for a buffet, and took a stroll down the Strip to the Venetian, where we saw the gondoliers, and then it was time. I went back up to my room, put on my new lucky jacket, checked my wallet, cracked my knuckles, picked up Beth at her room, and together we took the elevator down to the casino. It was nine-thirty in the evening, Las Vegas time, and I was ready to play.

By ten-fifteen I had busted through my bankroll and was mournfully hanging, like a disconsolate teenager, around the nickel slots.

The only thing more pitiful than stories of great gambling winnings are stories of great gambling losses, so I'll spare you the details of the debacle, but let me just ask one question: Why is it that whenever you jump-raise your blackjack bet to a level higher than you should, you end up with a pair begging to be split, and then, after you've doubled the already stupidly high bet, why does the dealer always seem to pull that six she needs to turn a dead fifteen into a killer twenty-one? Why is that? Why? Answer me that. Does that seem fair to you? Or does it seem fair that Beth, who as far as I knew had never played before, who was merely following the rules of the little yellow strategy card instead of well-honed instinct, was doing spectacularly well, her stack of chips rising and turning colors while mine dwindled and disappeared? It was almost enough to make me lose faith in my lucky jacket. Almost.

So I was mournfully hanging around the nickel slots, feeling like I was living dangerously if I punched the "bet max" button and put a quarter on the line, when I saw it.

A flash of sparkly color. Gold lamé. My jacket.

Just the sight of it on someone else cheered me. It was like finding a grade school soul mate in the glittery wasteland of the new Vegas. Only someone who appreciated the Vegas I had first known could appreciate that kind of jacket. I wondered if my friend was having any better luck with his jacket than I was with mine. Maybe I had taken the wrong jacket off the rack, maybe the lucky one was the one he took. Good for him. Maybe I should pat him on the back, just for laughs. Without anything much else to do, I followed the flash of gold through the pink sheen of the Flamingo's casino. I glimpsed it snaking in and out among the craps tables, and I kept after it. I could only catch sight of it here or there, losing it among the crowds or in the aisles. Who was he? I wondered. A hard-core gambler or a tourist like me? His hair was black, I could tell, there was a cigar, but I never got a clear glimpse of him. And strangely, as I hurried to catch up, the jacket seemed to hurry away from me.

I sped up my pace. Past the craps tables, the blackjack, the Let-It-Ride, the big wheel. I could only now catch glimpses of the jacket rushing out of this crowd, around this row of tables, catch a glance of its reflection in the shiny side of a slot machine.

Who was in the jacket? Did he know me? Who did I know whose taste was as tacky as mine, and why was he avoiding me?

I had a final glimpse of gold slinking out the corner doors to the Strip, but when I stepped out into the thick night air with its crazed electricity, he was gone.

"IS THAT him?" asked Beth.

"No, I told you, he was a smarmy-looking man."

"He looks smarmy."

"That's not smarmy, that's just old."

"He has a mustache."

"So did Stalin," I said. "But he wasn't smarmy."

"Maybe we have a different definition of the word."

"But only one of us is right," I said, "and that guy is not smarmy. He looks like Art Carney."

"I always thought Art Carney looked a little smarmy. When was Hopkins leaving for lunch?"

"They said he leaves about twelve-thirty. We have time yet."

"Is that him?"

"What are you, kidding?"

"Maybe you're right. It's hard to be smarmy shaped like a fire-plug."

"So how much did you win?"

"A few hundred, nothing much. Maybe ten."

"A thousand? You won a thousand? And you've really never played before?"

"Well, maybe a little in Atlantic City."

"Ah, so now we get the truth."

"A few jaunts now and then with an old boyfriend."

"Which one?"

"Dieter."

"Dieter, the German computer scientist. Dieter was smarmy."

"So that's what you mean."

"I didn't know Dieter liked the cards."

"He played slots. I suppose your jacket wasn't lucky after all."

"Oh, no, the jacket was lucky, but I wasn't. It did okay for you while you were sitting next to it."

"Yes, it did."

"And I won a pot on the nickel slots."

"They make you sign a W-2 on that one?"

"Wait a second."

"Is that him?"

"Wait a second."

"Now, he's smarmy."

"There we go. Yes, that's our boy."

We were in a strip-mall parking lot off Paradise Road, just west of the Flamingo, watching from the convertible, with its top up, as Gerald Hopkins left the bank. I had stopped at the bank earlier in the morning to scope out what he looked like. Then I made a call from Hailey's cell phone to say I'd like to meet with Mr. Hopkins after lunch and to ask about his normal lunch hours. The bank people were ever so helpful. Everything was done to ensure that when we walked in with Hailey Prouix's identification card and safe-deposit key, Gerald Hopkins, who asked me to give his regards to Hailey, would not be in the bank. I was hoping that when he left for lunch he wouldn't be walking to the Indian restaurant a few doors down for the $5.95 buffet and a quick return. I almost willed him into the parking lot and, thankfully, he obliged. There was a white Cadillac a few rows down and he opened it with his key and ducked inside. A few seconds later he passed right by us on his way out of the lot and onto Paradise Road.

"How do I look?" said Beth, with her hair now back and the glasses on.

"You look great," I said, "just great. Now let's hope that no one's reported yet to her Vegas bank that Hailey Prouix is dead."

WE SAT at a desk and waited as the service specialist went off to get the card for the safe-deposit box. Beth fingered the key, trying to hide her nervousness. The woman, a Mrs. Selegard, heavy and smiling, talking all the while to her friend at the other desk, hadn't blinked when Beth gave Hailey's name and the box number stamped on the key.

"Here it is, Miss Prouix," said Mrs. Selegard as she came back with the card. "I'll need to see your identification and then have you sign."

Beth reached into her bag, pulled out a wallet, unfolded flap after flap as if searching for something long hidden away. I thought she was laying it on a bit thick, but finally she pulled out the driver's license and Mrs. Selegard started taking down the information.

"Do you have a home here, Miss Prouix?" asked Mrs. Selegard offhandedly.

"No, I live in Philadelphia. But my parents live here and I keep some things for them."

"I hope they're in good health."

"Still," said Beth, rapping on the wooden desk.

"We have experts in estate planning if they're looking for someone to talk to."

"Thank you, but I think they have a lawyer here working on it."

"Good, that's smart. No reason for Uncle Sam to get more than he must. I see, Miss Prouix, that your license has expired."

"Has it?"

"Yes." Mrs. Selegard looked up at Beth. "A year and a half ago."

"I gave up my car when I moved to Philadelphia, so I suppose I hadn't noticed."

"You should take care of that." Pause. "It says here your eyes are blue." She looked at Beth for a moment. "They don't look blue."

"In some lights they're bluish," said Beth.

Mrs. Selegard examined the ID again and then Beth's face. "Well, in some lights," she said, "I'm a size six."

The ladies laughed at that, sharing a little piece of vanity among themselves. I could tell that Beth wasn't a natural at playacting. She was giving too much information, seemed to have an answer to everything when answers weren't required. If it were me with the fake ID, I wouldn't have been chatty with the account-executive lady, I'd have acted as if none of it was any of her damn business. But I had to admit, the "In some lights they're bluish," line was genius.

"If you'll just sign here, Miss Prouix," said Mrs. Selegard, handing her the card. There were a series of lines on the card, with some signatures by Hailey, all duly dated. Without hesitation, Beth signed. She had been practicing all morning in the hotel room, writing out the name based on the signature on the license: Hailey Prouix, Hailey Prouix, Hailey Prouix. It wasn't a perfect match, but the flourishes were the same, and it was close enough, and after their little laugh together Mrs. Selegard barely glanced at the card before standing from her desk.

"Is your friend coming, too?" asked Mrs. Selegard, gesturing in my direction.

"You mean Raoul?" said Beth. "Sure, why not?"

I tossed Beth a "what the hell are you doing?" expression as we followed Mrs. Selegard to the vault, but Beth, feeling good after having passed her test, only smiled.

The door was a foot thick, the vault itself a closet-size opening walled on either side with the fronts of boxes, two locks on each. Mrs. Selegard placed a key in one of the locks of Box 124, and Beth placed her key in the other, and they both turned at the same time. The metal box slid out of its opening. Mrs. Selegard handed the long, narrow box to Beth and led us to a small room beside the vault with two chairs and a narrow shelf. When the door closed behind us, Beth placed the box on the shelf and we both sat in front of it and stared.

"That went well," said Beth.

"Raoul?"

"It just came to me."

"I don't look like a Raoul. I always thought when I turned gigolo my name would be something more like Giorgio."

"I wasn't thinking gigolo, I was thinking cabana boy. Aren't you going to open it?"

"Sure. Soon. But suddenly it feels weird, doesn't it, looking into a dead woman's safe-deposit box?"

"You couldn't have thought of that in Philadelphia?"

"But now we're in Las Vegas, land of morality."

"And all of it cheap. But I think maybe we should check it out before the smarmy Gerald Hopkins comes back from lunch."

She was right, of course, and I stood again, but before I opened the box's lid, I hesitated. It wasn't that I thought I was violating Hailey Prouix's last hiding place. Someone would eventually open this box, some investigator would eventually cotton to the knowledge that it existed and get some court order and scour it for clues, and so I rationalized that the initial scourer might as well be me. Who, after all, was working more in her interests than myself, sworn as I was to see her killer punished? But still I hesitated, and why was not a mystery to me even then, in the middle of the hesitating, when things suddenly seemed so confusing. "Last thing you want," she had said, "are any surprises." I used to think I knew what I needed to know about Hailey Prouix, I used to think I knew the basics, that maybe I knew her heart. But I didn't think that anymore, and that's what forced my hesitation. Because as that box with its secrets lay before me, I was deathly afraid of what it was I might learn.

"Go ahead, Victor."

And go ahead I did. I slipped on a pair of rubber gloves. I took hold of the box. Slowly the top slid off, and there it was, Hailey Prouix's safe deposits. What lay inside were clues to a whole brutal world I would just as soon had stayed closed to me forever, a world that told me more than I ever wanted to know about a woman named Hailey Prouix and the strange murderous past where were born both her sadness and her death.

23

HENDERSON, NEVADA, used to be a little desert town between Las Vegas and the Hoover Dam. I say "used to be" because now it's a boomtown, in the truest sense of the word, its growth fueled not by a discovered silver mine or a new technological industry but because the Boomer generation is looking for someplace to retire, and tens of thousands have decided that Henderson is it. It's got sun, it's got Lake Mead, it's got the Las Vegas Strip not six miles away. Henderson is now growing so fast they can't print maps speedily enough to keep up with the newest walled developments. It is growing so fast it is now the second-largest city in Nevada, leaving Reno in the dust. They've trucked in palm trees by the thousands to line the boulevards, housing prices are rising like helium, people are moving there at the rate of twelve hundred a month. And it's not as if the city has discouraged the grand influx. Seattle's motto might just as well be "Stay the hell in California because we don't want you here." Henderson's motto is "A place to call home."

I suppose that was the idea behind Desert Winds, a huge, first-class assisted-living facility built on the edge of the vast desert that leads to Lake Mead. Located on a flat spread of desert rubble with wide pathways and small patches of green grass, more intimations of lawn than lawns themselves, Desert Winds consisted of a series of large buildings in the ubiquitous Spanish Colonial style, with red asphalt roofing and barred windows. The campus was Disney-fascist, a relentlessly upbeat place to wither and die. Despite the evident number of rooms, the landscape was deserted. Maybe it was the heat, or maybe the intended clientele hadn't yet ripened. The Boomers moving to Henderson weren't ready yet for a nursing home. They wanted developments like Sun City, where the houses were built side by side and the residents could drive their personal golf carts to the clubhouse and the card games and the golf course and the pool. They had come for the active lifestyle promised in the brochure. The Boomers moving to Henderson weren't ready yet for a nursing home. Not yet. But it was only a matter of time. In that great Nevada tradition, the owners of Desert Winds were betting on the come.

The office was in a separate building in the center of the campus.

"Are you here for a tour?" chirped the cheery receptionist as I signed in.

"No," I said. "We came to visit one of your residents."

"How wonderful. Our members so love to have visitors. Are you expected?"

"No, not exactly."

"If you tell me the name of the member, I'll see if a visit can be arranged."

"Lawrence Cutlip."

"Oh, my, isn't Mr. Cutlip having a busy day. Sit down, Mr." — she turned the book around to check my name—"Mr. Carl, and I'll see what we can arrange."

"Should we go to his room?"

"That won't be necessary. Many of our members have private aides to help them during their event-filled days here at Desert Winds. Mr. Cutlip is one of the lucky ones."

Lawrence Cutlip. It was a name in a file I had taken from Hailey's safe-deposit box and put into my briefcase. I had taken a lot of things from that box. I had taken old photographs; I had taken letters, love letters not addressed to me; I had taken a maroon folder with the medical file of Juan Gonzalez, surprise, surprise; I had taken cash—not all the cash, and there was quite a bit there, over eighty thousand, but enough to provide a retainer for my defense of Guy. Taking the cash was only fair, I figured, since the money was undoubtedly part of the funds transferred out of Guy and Hailey's joint account by Hailey's unilateral act, but I left even more cash than I took to allay suspicion. When the detectives eventually searched the box, they'd have to assume nothing was taken. I mean, what kind of jerk would empty a safe-deposit box and accidentally leave fifty thousand dollars?

The file in which I had found Lawrence Cutlip's name contained two life insurance policies, the very policies Guy had been searching for. One was made out in the name of Guy Forrest, with Leila Forrest as the main beneficiary. Accompanying that policy was a copy of a change-in-beneficiary notice that made Hailey Prouix the new beneficiary to the extent the law allowed, since some funds would still, by law, go to Leila, the wife. The other was a policy made out in the name of Hailey Prouix, with the sole beneficiary being not Guy Forrest, as Guy had expected, but one Lawrence Cutlip. Who was this Lawrence Cutlip, important enough to Hailey Prouix to be the sole beneficiary on her life insurance at the expense of her fiancé? Lawrence Cutlip. I had never heard the name before but I had a guess who he was. And I also had a guess as to exactly where I'd find him, a guess confirmed with a quick phone call. Which was why Beth and I had taken the convertible east on Interstate 215 to Henderson and the Desert Winds retirement home.

We were directed to one of the large buildings off to the side and then led through a hallway with a thick blue rug and no smell of piss or green beans. That was how you could tell for sure it was an upscale old-age joint. It smelled instead like a summer meadow, it smelled of daisies, it smelled like a preview of coming attractions.

"What exactly are we doing here?" asked Beth as we followed our guide.

"Hailey Prouix transferred the money missing from her and Guy's account to the bank we visited this morning. In addition, she made a number of calls to right here, undoubtedly to this Lawrence Cutlip."

"How do you know that?"

"I have my sources," I said. "They're very flexible as to payments here at Desert Winds. You can either pay your exorbitant monthly bill in advance, or pay an even more exorbitant lump sum up front, which works like an annuity. My guess is that the Gonzalez money went into a lump-sum purchase of Cutlip's spot at this lovely facility. And he's the main beneficiary on her life insurance instead of Guy. I want to know why."

"To what end?"

"To save Guy, we need to find a killer. To do that, we need to learn what we can about the victim, to see if there was something in her life that caused her death."

"Blame the victim."

"Or find someone else to blame, anyone but Guy."

"We already have the mystery man she was sleeping with."

"When it comes to suspects, it's like the invitation list to a college keg party: the more the merrier."

We were led outside the building to a little walled courtyard with a flooring of red brick. It was a sunny day, as relentlessly sunny as the staff was relentlessly cheerful, and Beth had put on her sunglasses, but with a few well-tended trees and bright umbrellas, much of the courtyard was in shade. We sat at a small table beneath the ethereal leaf network of a twisting mesquite tree and waited. It was quiet, remarkably so. No wind in the flora, no calls or hoots from the fauna. All of Henderson was quiet, I had noticed, as if exuberance had been outlawed by the city fathers as nonconducive to further growth. We sat at the table and waited until a swinging door swung open and a tall, snaggletoothed man with long blond hair and bad skin wheeled what was left of Lawrence Cutlip into the courtyard.

You could tell that at one point in his life Lawrence Cutlip had been an imposing man, tall of limb, broad of shoulder, with a heavy jaw and stern dark eyes, but he wasn't imposing anymore. He slumped in his wheelchair like a sack of bones, his stockinged feet resting on the risers like lumps of clay. A thin plastic line lay just beneath his nose, feeding oxygen into his nostrils from a tank attached to the rear of his chair, and his mouth was perpetually open, as if the effort to close it was too much now to bear. In the ugly open maw could be seen irregular clumps of yellowed teeth. But despite his evident decay, his eyes were still stern and dark and very much alert. Hailey's uncle, I assumed.

"Leave it here, Bobo," said Cutlip in a gruff country voice, wheezing all the while, as the attendant placed his chair facing us.

Bobo, remaining behind the chair, began scratching at one of his wrists. Both of Bobo's arms were covered with scabs from his fingertips to the short sleeves of his white shirt, as if he had a colony of chiggers breeding like crazy beneath his skin.

"You here to see me?" said Cutlip.

"Yes, sir," I said.

"What can I do you for?"

"We came to talk to you about your niece."

"Which one?"

"Hailey."

"Yeah, well, she's dead, ain't she?" Cutlip fought to catch his breath even as he spoke, and his wheeze grew louder. "What else is there to know?"

"I wondered if you were aware, Mr. Cutlip, that you were named beneficiary on her life insurance policy."

His eyes widened for a instant and then he smiled. "Course I knowed. I was wondering when one of you clucks from the insurance company was going to show 'round here with the check. Hand it on over."

"I don't have your check."

"What the hell's keeping it, then? I been waiting days and days."

"I suppose nothing's going to happen with the check until they figure out exactly who killed her."

"They arrested that bastard boyfriend of hers, didn't they? I told her he was no good, I told her she was making a mistake." He coughed and fought for a breath and his coughing calmed. "She wasn't the marrying kind, Hailey. I don't know what the hell she was thinking. Then again, I never did know with her. But I ain't surprised that he kilt her. She could drive men crazy, Hailey could, drive 'em straight out of they right minds. I almost feel sorry for what he walked into. Almost. And now I hear he got himself some smart Jew lawyer that's aiming to give him a walk."

"That would be me," I said.

"Son of a bitch."

"My name's Victor Carl, and yes I am."

His face grew red and he struggled for air. "Let's get out of here, Bobo."

"I think you'll want to talk to us, Mr. Cutlip."

Bobo started to pull back the chair, but Cutlip raised his hand. "Why the hell is that?"

"With me is my partner Beth Derringer. We represent Guy Forrest, and we have some questions."

"What makes you think I got any answers I'd be willing to share with a peckerhead like you?"

"Because I figure we're both after the same thing, trying to find out who it was who really killed your niece and make sure he's punished."

"They done found him already."

"No, they didn't. They're wrong."

"And I'm supposed to believe you, a lawyer?"

"A Jew lawyer to be precise, and yes."

"How the hell?"

"Because I knew her, Mr. Cutlip. I knew her before she was murdered. What happened to her was wrong and needs to be punished."

I saw something just then, something in those stern, dark eyes, just a flutter come in an out, like a snake's tongue slashing in the air. I stared at him, and he stared at me, and the thing in those eyes got brighter and glowed until he turned away from me and looked at Beth.

"I thought this was all up and finished already," he wheezed out. "I thought you was going to take the plea and put the son of a bitch in jail so we can all rest easy?"

"You knew about the offer?" said Beth.

"Of course I knowed about the offer. I ain't blind out here in the desert. It's damn generous, that offer, too damn generous. I thought it was a done deal." So he, too, had been anxious for me to accept Troy Jefferson's offer. That was more than passing strange. Didn't it make sense for Hailey's uncle to want the greatest measure of justice for the murderer of his niece? You would think. And wouldn't a trial with a punishment of death waiting at the end be more to his liking? You would think. But that's not how he was acting. Instead he said, "I don't know why the hell you folks ain't snapping at it."

"Because it's been pulled," I said.

"Is that a fact?" he said, a smile growing. "I guess now they're going to go through with a trial and kill that sumbitch."

"Our client says he didn't do it," said Beth.

"I can't do nothing about the lies he tells you."

"The story I heard was that you were a gambler, Mr. Cutlip," I said.

"Is that the story?"

I looked around at the lovely courtyard. "You must have read the odds pretty damn well to be able to afford this place."

"Oh, I could, yes I could, when I wasn't drinking, though that wasn't much time total, was it, Bobo?"

The attendant smiled and nodded stupidly.

"But that's not how I can afford this. Hailey paid for it. And she paid for Bobo, too. What with her being a lawyer, it wasn't too much a strain."

I looked around again at the high-toned surroundings. "I'd expect it would be a strain for anyone. And she called you frequently?"

"Sure she did. We was close, we had a bond. Hailey and me, we had history. It warn't no picnic raising her and her sister after the father died. Warn't no picnic at all. We had us some tough times, some times we both of us would rather forget. But we can't, can we? I mean, the past it just jumps out and bites you in the ass whenever it gets itself real good and hungry, don't it?"

"What kind of past, Mr. Cutlip?"

"I don't know, the past. The past. Maybe it's best it's just forgot. What about my check, my insurance check? When's that coming?"

"You'll have to ask the insurance company, Mr. Cutlip. But I'm glad to see you're not so overwhelmed with grief that you can't keep your mind focused on the more important matters, like your check."

He stared at me. His lips quivered. "Why you son of a . . ." came out of his throat until it was choked back by an acute breathlessness and a rising flood of anger that filled those dark eyes until they swelled with something else, something else, and then I could see that the something else they swelled with was tears. Whatever salty anger he had been aiming at me disappeared as if dissolved by the tears, and he came apart in front of us, his once huge body shaking with sobs, gasping for breath, the back of his still-large hands trying to wipe his cheeks dry and failing. And out of his trembling lips came one sentence, over and over again.

"My Hailey. My Hailey. My Hailey."

Bobo leaned over the wheelchair and whispered in Cutlip's ear and Cutlip nodded before tossing Bobo a withering glance. Bobo jerked back and stood straight. Beth and I glanced at each other and rose from our chairs, about to leave Cutlip with his grief, when he raised a hand in the middle of his sobs to stop us from leaving. Slowly the jag subsided, the tears abated, his breaths slowed and then deepened, the loose flesh of his palms pulled away whatever wetness still lay on his face. He coughed loudly as he slowly gained control.

"I'm sorry," he said, waving one of those big hands as if to cover his face. "It happens sometimes when I think, when I remember. I'm sorry. Sit down. It's just it's . . . it's . . ." It appeared as if he were about to start again.

It seemed genuine, his grief, it seemed deep and painful and more than I ever would have expected, and it caught me off guard. I turned and frowned at Beth as we both sat again. She had taken off her sunglasses and was staring at Uncle Larry with deep interest.

"How were you and Hailey related, Mr. Cutlip?" she asked.

"She was my sister's daughter," he said as he wiped again at his eyes. "But I didn't have nothing much to do with her until her daddy died in the accident."

"When was that?" asked Beth.

"They was eight, the girls, when it happened. After that, I could see they was having troubles. After that, I could see they was near to starving. Little eight-year-old girls with no one much taking care of them, raggedy dresses falling off their bones."

"What about the mother?"

"My sister Debra was a sweet, pretty thing, but she didn't have what it took to do it all by herself, and when her husband died, she sort of broke apart. They needed somebody with them. So I moved myself in. Never had a steady job before, never needed one or wanted one, could always cadge a drink or find a game with a couple of fish that would keep me going for a spell. But I moved myself in with Debra and the girls and found a job and for eight years I didn't miss so much as a day at the plant carving carcasses, grinding meat, stuffing casings. Stood ankle deep in blood just so I could help those girls be raised."

I saw the image just then, Lawrence Cutlip as a younger man, tall, dark, broad, hip boots on, wading through a wilderness of blood as he hacked away at the carcasses passing by him on a conveyer belt of hooks, a wild man who had tamed himself so that two little girls who weren't his own could have a decent start. The man wading through the blood, I knew, was the uncle that Hailey had told me about, the uncle who was the hero of her life and whom she had put up in this luxury nursing home as a way of offering thanks. My opinion of him shifted as fast as the image came and I felt a sudden swell of affection for the old coot. His grief had been real, his sacrifice true, his gruff, hard exterior a way to hide the caramel inside.

"That must have been hard, doing all that for them," I said.

"It was, sure, but I ain't never regretted it. It was the rightest thing I ever done in my life."

"And looking around at this place, Hailey seemed to appreciate it."

"Them girls, they needed a firm hand in that house. Now, Roylynn, she was a good girl, a little on the quiet side with all her big ideas, but Hailey, she was trouble, more than her mother could ever hope to handle. There was something about her that was catnip. No man could resist her. Those boys couldn't walk close as five feet without losing control of they bowels and shittin' themselves. They swarmed around her, like she was some kind of queen bee, and she let 'em. She let 'em. I tried to swat 'em away, but it wasn't they fault, it was just the way she was."

"Did she have boyfriends?"

"Course she did. She didn't tell me things like that, personal things, she wasn't one to kiss and tell, but sure she did, though they never lasted too damn long. There was Grady Pritchett, who was older and I didn't like him hanging around the way he was. And there was that Jesse boy, but he was kilt out near the quarry when she was fifteen. She and Jesse knew each other since grade school, and they was more like friends, not boyfriend girlfriend, but still, that was hard on her. After that there was that Bronson boy, the football player, but it was a halfhearted thing at best. Turned out he was more interested in standing over his center than being with Hailey, if you know what I'm saying. And he wasn't even the quarterback. If you know what I'm saying."

Old Bobo, standing still behind Cutlip, snickered, his twisted teeth catching bits of yellow light.

"But I can't rightly say too much about that one. When the girls they was fifteen or so, I figured I was done, that they could make it on they own. Had some opportunity out here and I took it. I had a lot of drinking to catch up on and I did. Didn't I, Bobo?"

Bobo nodded. "Oh, yeah," he said. "It was party time."

"Bobo was just a kid when I first met him, a runaway, come to sin city to make good. I showed him around, helped him out. Now I got him this job."

"Mr. Cutlip's been good to me."

"That's my Bobo. He's from out your way, some beach town in Delaware, ain't that right, Bobo?"

Bobo smiled and nodded. "Dewey Beach."

"Sure," I said.

"Inland from there."

"But he ran into trouble and came out here and I sort of adopted him. I take care of him like I took care of them girls."

"You kept in touch with Hailey, Mr. Cutlip?" I asked.

"I did, yeah. For a while, right after I left, I lost touch, but then she came out and found me. After that, we kept in touch. We was closer than the normal uncle and niece, you know, me and Hailey."

"You ever visit her in Philadelphia?"

"Nah. I don't travel much no more. I like it right here in the desert. Nice and hot, nice and dry."

"Did she tell you about Guy Forrest?"

"Just that she had decided to marry. I told her it was a mistake.

The Hailey I knew wasn't the marrying type. And when she told me they was fighting over the money she spent to put me in this place, I knew it would all go to hell. But Hailey, you could never tell her nothing. I would have told her to stop the fighting, to forget about the money, but I needed someplace. You ever hear of beriberi? It tears you apart from the inside, paralyzes you piece by piece as you swell to twice your size."

"Beriberi?" said Beth. "Like sailors used to get?"

"That's it. Strange to catch it in the desert, ain't it? Nothing I could do, it came and ran through me and destroyed half my insides. I needed this place."

"There are plenty of places," said Beth.

"Yeah, I knowed. I was happy just out in that motel I was living at, but she said I deserved a place like this. Couldn't talk her out of it. She said I deserved it, and said she knew how to get it for me. And she said I deserved having Bobo to push me around, and that I figured was all right, since I had pushed him around long enough."

"Did she tell you about anyone she was seeing besides Guy?" I asked.

"There was someone else, she said. But she never told me who. Was it you, you Hebrew son of a bitch?"

"No," I said, stunned and trying not to show it.

"You sure?" The old man stared at me for a moment, and I thought again I saw that snakelike flutter.

"I'm sure."

"Good." He smiled and then he turned to Beth. "It could have been him. It could have been anyone. To know Hailey was to want her, and even when she was with someone, they was always someone else. But she didn't tell me things like that. Never did. From the time she was fifteen or something, she just closed right up and told me nothing."

"Did she ever mention anyone named Juan Gonzalez?" said Beth.

"Is that the other fella she was sleeping with? Is that the fella, some Mexican? Had she fallen that low?"

"I don't think that was the other man," I said, relieved that his suspicions were so wild as to alight on any name tossed out.

"I wouldn't put it past her," he said, staring at me again. "Never had no idea what kind of scum riffraff she'd end up with."

"In your conversations before her death," said Beth, "did she mention to you that she was scared of anyone?"

"No, Hailey wasn't scared of no one."

"Do you have any idea who might have wanted to do her any harm?"

"Nope, none, except she was aiming to marry one man and sleeping with another and that's a dangerous proposition in our part of country."

"In our part of the country, too," I said. I looked at Beth. She put her sunglasses back on. I slapped my thighs and stood. "I think that's everything. Thank you for your help, Mr. Cutlip."

He lifted one of those big hands and pointed at me. "You said you was going make the man who did that to my Hailey pay."

"Yes I did."

"Don't be acting like a lawyer. You be true to your word there, boy."

"Count on it, Mr. Cutlip."

"I aim to."

I nodded at Bobo, standing behind the man with a smile fixed dully on his face, and started heading for the door when Beth asked a final question.

"That boy, Hailey's friend. You said he died out near some quarry?"

"Jesse was his name. Jesse Sterrett. That's right."

"How did it happen?"

"It's a mystery, ain't it? Don't nobody knowed what he was doing there. All they knowed is that somehow he cracked his head and fell into the water sittin' there at the bottom."

"They ever find out who killed him?"

"Coroner ruled it an accident."

"But no one believed that, did they?" said Beth.

"Don't know what no one believed. Coroner said he slipped and cracked his head before he fell off the ledge they all used to hang out on. That's what the coroner said, and how the hell you all the way over here fifteen years later can think something different is a goddamn mystery to me."

"Just like that," she said. "Fell off a ledge just like that."

"That's what he said, good old Doc Robinson. Best-loved man in the county. Good doctor, bad cardplayer. Ruled it an accident."

"What did Hailey think happened?"

"She didn't much say," said Cutlip. "We done never talked about it. She wasn't much interested in legal stuff then."

"Only after. Thank you, Mr. Cutlip," said Beth. "You've been a big help."

24

OUR PLANE didn't leave McCarran International until late that evening, we were red-eyeing our way back to Philly, so I took the scenic route west toward Lake Mead. The narrow two-lane road, with shoulders soft and gravelly, twisted through hills and canyons. The desert here rose on either side in great piles of singed rock. There was a sign, LAST STOP BASS 'N' GAS, there was a sign warning of the danger in an abandoned mine, and then just the road. In the desert, with the top of our convertible down and the wind rushing over our heads, the world seemed still raw and the Strip far, far away, even though at night its gaudy lights would fill the sky like a hundred thousand beacons.

Beth hadn't said much during the drive, and that had been fine by me. There was much I had to think about, the young Hailey with tattered dresses hanging from her bones, the uncle exiling himself to the slaughterhouse to keep his nieces and sister fed, the boyfriend dead in the quarry, Hailey's subsequent tepid relationship with the football player who preferred showering with his teammates to pitching woo with his girl, the long, improbable haul through college and law school, only to end at the wrong end of a gun. It all seemed to amplify the tragedy of Hailey's story, turning the bare bones of what she had told me into some sad Gothic opera.

Beside me Beth shuddered, as if she were thinking through the same things, and then she chuckled.

"So you're the mystery man who was sleeping with Hailey Prouix," she said.

I played it nonchalant. "Except when she was out on the town with Juan Gonzalez."

"He looked at that moment when he made his wild accusation as if he wanted to strike you dead."

"Like a protective papa bear."

Beth didn't reply.

We were driving slowly on the road, enjoying the scenery. A big black Lincoln, with its windows up and air conditioner undoubtedly blasting, blew by.

"I had this image when he was talking," I said, "of him in the slaughterhouse, surrounded by carcasses, ankle deep in blood. It was something, what he did, sacrificing almost a decade of his life so his sister and his nieces could live decently. However he wasted his life before or after, and it seems he wasted it badly, at least he did that one noble thing."

"Was it noble?"

"You don't think so?"

"I don't think," said Beth, "I've ever met a more vile man."

I was stunned by what she said. He seemed ornery, sure, small-minded and bigoted, with a foul word for everyone, but nothing worse than expected from a decrepit old goat. "You're not serious."

"Something about him, Victor, creeped me to the bone. His fake tears when you pressed him about being more concerned about the check than the death of his niece."

"I thought they were genuine."

"Please. And his little protestations of sacrifice, of how hard it was to take care of that family, of how much his firmness was needed."

"You don't think it was a sacrifice?"

"Do you remember in *David Copperfield* when David's sweet mother marries Murdstone, and Murdstone comes in with his sister and takes over the house, bending everyone to his will until he destroys his new wife and forces David out?"

"Murdstone with the big black sideburns?"

"Yes. What did Uncle Larry say, the girls needed a firm hand in that house? I shivered when I heard that."

"Your imagination is running amok. This explains her travel to Vegas. She didn't go with a lover, she went to visit her uncle. And I was curious why Hailey transferred the bulk of her Gonzalez fee, after taxes, to Las Vegas, and now I know. To pay for the uncle's nursing home."

"But why?"

"Loyalty."

"Maybe," said Beth. "But if you ask me, there's something else going on. Something that ruined him, too. Do you know what beriberi is?"

"Some exotic South Seas disease, it sounds like. How do you think he caught it in the desert?"

"Beriberi is not a virus. It's a vitamin deficiency that sailors used to get because of unbalanced diets. You can also get it from drinking, but not just a little light tippling. They see it in drunks who drink so much that nothing matters but the drinking and the forgetting, who drink so much they forget to eat."

A flight of warplanes flew low overhead, banking to the left, blowing away the soft rush of the wind with the roar of their engines, leaving thin trails through the pale blue as if the fabric of the sky itself had been ripped.

"Remember when I kept asking about the death of that boy?" she said. "What was his name?"

"Jesse Sterrett."

"That's right. You know what we should do? We should go back to Hailey's old hometown and find out what really happened to him."

"He said it was ruled an accident."

"Maybe it was, if you can trust old Doc Robinson to know the difference between an accident and a murder."

Behind us a white muscle car, its windows darkened, came up on us at a high rate of speed and shifted into the passing lane.

"If you ask me," said Beth, "I'd guess there was a link between Hailey Prouix's murder and the death of that boy. If you ask me, there's something malignant that was alive back then that still exists, just as strong, today."

"You're creeping me out, Beth."

"He creeped me out, Victor."

"I don't understand why."

"Neither do I. But you know what? It gets me to wondering. It gets me to wondering if maybe we don't have it all wrong. It gets me to wondering if maybe—"

Just then the white muscle car roared alongside us. It was a Camaro, the noise of its engine exploding without the restraint of a muffler. I expected it to zoom on past, but it didn't, it stayed even with us, like a shadow.

I pulled my foot off the accelerator and slowed down to let it go on by, and it slowed down with me.

I sped up, and it kept pace.

I tried to peer inside but the windows were tinted so dark it was impossible to see who was driving.

I glanced at the road in front and saw a huge red pickup truck, hauling a motorboat, coming our way in the muscle car's lane.

The truck blared its horn.

I sped up.

The muscle car veered away to the left and then, as if it were a yo-yo on a string, came back and slammed us hard in the side.

The crash of metal, the crack of glass, the horn of the red pickup, and then a strange sound like the flap of a huge wing, followed by silence.

The straight road twisted sharply to the left, the soft shoulder tossed us, the great singed desert opened its arms to us, and, like children of the earth, we fell into them, spinning into the arms of the earth as the pale blue of the sky and the rocky surface of the desert revolved one around the other and became for us as one.

MY FIRST words when I came to were for Beth. I called her name, I called her name and heard nothing. The sun was brutal in my eyes, three dark things circling about it in the sky. My back ached so badly I thought it was broken, but I realized that as long as it hurt like hell it was still together, still together, and I called out for Beth.

From behind I heard voices. I twisted my head and saw the car, our car, the convertible, on its side, twisted grotesquely, the windshield shattered, fingers of flame lapping out the side of the hood. The red pickup truck was parked off a ways in the distance, the huge boat still hitched behind it. A man in jeans and a tee shirt stood in front of it, talking into a cellular phone.

"Beth," I called out as loud as I could. "Where's Beth?"

And then a face appeared over me, blurry and in shadow against the harsh sun. A man's face, round, with its ears sticking out.

"She's all right," came a soft, scarred voice, strangely familiar, though badly out of place. "I think something in her arm, it snapped, but other than that she's doing fine. You, too, mate. You was both wearing seat belts, good thing, or you'd be vulture bait."

"The car . . ."

"I hope you took out insurance on your rental, is all I can say."

"Beth's all right?"

"Yeah, Vic, she's fine. Just fine. I took her out of the car first, you second. Didn't want to move you but I had to with the engine burning like it was. What's that?" he called out to the man on the phone.

He turned to hear what the truck driver had to say and the sun lit up his face and I recognized him, I recognized him. That bastard.

"The ambulance will be along any minute. Don't worry, Vic. Don't you worry. I'm here to help. I'll take care of everything."

And he would, I was sure. I recognized him all right, no doubt about it, and I knew he would take care of everything, that bastard, just like he promised.

Phil Frigging Skink.

26

IN A curtained alcove of the emergency room of the St. Rose Dominican Hospital in Henderson, Nevada, a uniformed police officer took my statement as I waited for the results of the X-rays. They had strapped me to the stretcher in the ambulance to ensure I wouldn't further injure my back, and the doctor had urged me to lie still on the table until he could review the film.

"Any sudden movement could cause irreparable injury," he had said.

So I was lying as motionless as I could manage while the cop asked her questions. She was slight and cute, and I would have flirted her up in any other circumstance, but just then she was not at all what I wanted to see in the way of law enforcement. Just then what I wanted to see in the way of law enforcement was a burly bruiser who would take Skink by the scruff of his neck and toss him straight into the slammola. I told the cute police officer what happened with the white Camaro, about the way it smashed me in the side and sent me spinning off the road and how I was ready to sign a complaint for attempted murder as soon as she had it prepared.

"The truck driver said you did a full turn in the air before hitting the ground and spinning onto your side," she said.

"Degree of difficulty six-point-nine." Well, maybe I couldn't help doing a little flirting, and she did have a pretty smile, and I always admired a woman in a uniform with a gun strapped to her hip.

"You were damn lucky, Mr. Carl. If you had dropped upside down, you likely both would have been crushed."

"That's just how I feel, lucky lucky lucky. It's because my lucky jacket was in the trunk."

"Is it bright?"

"Blinding," I said.

"Lovely. Did you happen to see the license-plate number of the Camaro?"

"No, I'm sorry, I was busily spinning in the air as it drove away."

"Did you see the driver?"

"I couldn't see inside," I said. "The windows were a dark blue, but it was Skink driving."

She flipped through her notepad. "You mean the Mr. Skink who gave the statement?"

"That's right, Phil Frigging Skink."

"Calm yourself down, sir."

"Sorry. But it had to be him. He obviously followed me here to Vegas. There's something he's desperate to hide, desperate enough for him to try to kill me. My guess is he was in on a murder that happened in Philadelphia and he knows I'm hot on his trail."

"A murder?"

"That's right."

"In Philadelphia."

"Yes."

"You're talking about the Mr. Skink who ignored the smoke pouring from the front of your hood and dragged you and Miss Derringer out of the vehicle and maybe saved your lives?"

"Exactly."

"And you think he's a murderer?"

"Doesn't what he did prove it?"

"Why would he try to kill you, Mr. Carl, and then save your lives?"

"I don't know. Ask him."

"I will. But I have to tell you, the truck driver who saw the whole thing said Mr. Skink drove up in a blue Taurus about three minutes after it happened, moving in the same direction as the Camaro, so he couldn't have been involved in the accident."

"Accident? It was no accident. The damn Camaro slammed into me."

"The truck driver said the Camaro was trying to pass and it looked like you sped up and blocked it in."

"I was speeding up to get away from him."

"And the truck driver said the Camaro tried to get out of the truck's lane but you stayed in its path and that's why it tapped you."

"It wasn't a tap."

"No, sir, going as fast as you were, it must not have seemed like a tap at all. Do you know how fast you were going?"

"No. I don't."

"The speed limit on that road is fifty-five."

"Is that so?"

"The truck driver said you were flying."

"I was trying to get away."

"From whom, Mr. Carl?"

"From the Camaro."

"I see. We are of course looking for the Camaro, leaving the scene of an accident is a very serious charge, but often we find in these types of incidents that both parties are somewhat at fault."

"I didn't do anything wrong."

"Maybe not, sir, but I'm going to have to ticket you for speeding nonetheless."

I bolted up off of the examination table and ignored the scream of pain in my back. "You're going to ticket me?"

"Yes, sir."

"*I* get run off the road and you ticket *me*?"

Just then the doctor came back into the room. When he entered and saw me sitting straight up, he stopped short and gave me a stare. "Good to see you up and about, Mr. Carl."

My head grew suddenly woozy and I lay back down on the table. "I don't feel so well," I said.

"Is that so?" The doctor gave the officer a knowing look, and I thought, Hey, no flirting with my cop. "Everything looks fine," said the doctor. "Nothing broken, just bruising. I see no reason to keep you in the hospital, so we're releasing you."

I struggled slowly to sit up again. "What about my friend?"

"We're going to keep Miss Derringer overnight for observation. In addition to her broken wrist she's having headaches and might have a concussion. We'd like to be sure of her situation before we let her go."

"We took your luggage from the car, Mr. Carl," said the cop.

"And my briefcase?"

"Yes, that, too. You can pick it up as soon as you sign all the paperwork here. Is there anyone in Philadelphia you want me to call in reference to this murder you were talking about?"

She had a benign expression on her face, as if I were a lunatic she was trying to mollify. I thought of the discussion she would have with Stone and Breger, the three of them laughing together at my expense, and I involuntarily winced.

"No. No one."

"Good," she said. "I always strive to be thorough. This is for you."

She handed me a slip of paper and I knew without looking what it was.

"What happens if I just rip up the ticket and refuse to pay?" I said.

She gave a smile, a charming, heart-stopping smile, aimed at the doctor. "Then we hunt you down and kill you."

BETH HAD already been admitted as a patient. I took an elevator to the third floor and limped down the hallway to pay her a visit. It wasn't a big hospital, a white circular building on the eastern edge of Henderson, and it wasn't at all crowded. Beth's eyes were closed when I entered the room, her left arm with its shiny white cast rising and falling atop her stomach. I didn't want to wake her, so instead I stepped over and brushed away a lock of hair from her forehead. I don't know why I did that, it never does any good, the lock always falls back, but I did it, and it made me feel better, and maybe that's the reason right there. Whatever the cause of what happened, whether a simple accident or a brutal attempt on our lives, I still had been driving. She had been my charge, and I had failed her.

I sat down beside her and waited. After a while I took out Hailey's phone and made some calls, pushing to the next afternoon our flight back to Philadelphia, reserving another night at the Flamingo, informing the rental-car agency of the little mishap and the total destruction of their automobile. When my calls were over, I sat and waited by Beth's bedside.

My family had disintegrated like an atom split, my old high school and college chums had drifted like driftwood, my law school classmates had gone on to promising careers and gladly left me behind, all but Guy, and we know how well that had turned out. I didn't have many people in this world with whom I had a mutual caring relationship. My father, maybe, though you could never tell by the tense words we passed back and forth. My sometime private investigator Morris Kapustin, whom I was keeping far away from this case because he knew me too well and could see right through me, when right now I didn't want anyone seeing right through me. And there was Beth. Beth, my partner and best friend, the woman who shared my adventures, both financial and legal. There had been a time when we had contemplated something romantic happening between us, but it wasn't there, at least for me, the primal spark, and so we never tried it, and I am so glad. I am the Wile E. Coyote of romance, I keep chasing, keep chasing, only to end up, always, standing still in midair, the edge of the cliff behind me, the bomb in my hand, fuse burning low. But whatever tragedy befalls me, there has always been Beth to crack a joke and rub my neck and keep me from plunging into total despair. What would I do without her? The mere contemplation left me fighting tears.

"Hey, cowboy," she said. "Why so sad?"

Her eyes were open and she was smiling.

"I was imagining the worst and trying to calculate the price of new letterhead. How's the wrist?"

"I can't feel a thing with all the Novocain they pumped into it."

"How about your head?"

"It hurts so much I can't tell. Too bad they can't inject Novocain into the brain."

"You want the nurse?"

"Nah, not yet. They'll only give me more drugs, and you know how I am about drugs."

"Yes, I know. I'll go get her."

The nurse came in and checked the chart, took Beth's temp, and told her it wasn't time yet for her medication. Beth flirted, the nurse shook his head, Beth pouted, the nurse remained resolute, Beth pled, shedding all dignity, and finally the nurse said he'd ask the doctor. When the nurse came back with the little paper cup of pills, Beth gave me a triumphant smile.

"I should be ashamed of myself," she said. "When am I supposed to get out of here?"

"Tomorrow, if everything goes right. I changed our flight."

"I wonder if my head will explode at high altitude."

"Just in case, I booked a seat ten rows behind yours. That way I can see it happen without it ruining my jacket."

"Your lucky jacket. Is that why we survived?"

"Absolutely. Did you see what happened?"

"I suppose I did, but I don't remember." She closed her eyes and slowly opened them again. "I don't remember anything. Last thing I recall, we were driving into Henderson to talk to the name on the insurance document. And next thing, I was looking up at some really ugly man who was being very sweet and my arm really, really hurt."

"I think someone tried to kill us."

"Really? Who?"

"I don't know. Some guy in a white Camaro slammed me off the road. The cops think I was speeding and it was simply an accident."

"Were you?"

"Only after I spotted the Camaro coming after me."

"Do you think you only imagined it?"

"Maybe, but imagined or not, I'm through driving in this town, I'll tell you that. Last I saw, the car was slowly burning."

"I hope we still have the briefcase. I'd hate to have wasted the trip."

"The cop said the briefcase and the luggage are waiting for me in the hospital office."

"Did we meet the guy in Henderson?"

"Yes."

"Interesting?"

"Not really. Hailey's uncle. Do you need anything?"

"A toothbrush would be nice," she said. "I'd like to brush my teeth before I fall asleep again."

"Consider it done."

I stood, leaned over to kiss her on the forehead, and went off to find our luggage.

It was stacked behind the desk of an admittance clerk in one of the small cubicles they had off the lobby. An older woman smiled at me when I demanded my luggage and sweetly asked for my identification and insurance information. Very clever. They were holding our luggage hostage to our Blue Cross number. I thought of complaining, just for the sport of it, but the old lady with the sweet smile had the eyes of an IRS agent, and so, meekly, I took out my insurance card.

Ransom paid, I lugged our two suitcases and my briefcase into the lobby. I looked around furtively and then checked the briefcase to make sure everything was there. At first glance it all appeared to be in order. The photographs, the letters, the insurance file, the maroon medical file, the envelope in which I had stashed the cash, all there, all seemingly undisturbed. I let out a sigh of relief as I checked the details, one by one, the insurance file first. Guy's policy was still there, but . . . but Hailey's now was missing. Damn it. Damn damn it. Quickly I pulled out the maroon folder. Where there should have been a medical file detailing the treatment of Juan Gonzalez, there was nothing, nothing. And then I noticed that the money envelope was sickeningly thin. Thirty thousand dollars, where was my damn thirty thousand dollars? I ripped open the envelope and found not the sweet hundred-dollar bills but instead a single scrap of paper with a note scrawled in a rough, barely legible hand.

> Feeling like a little lamb?
> They braise a nice shank at the Bellagio.
> Nine o'clock reservation in your name.
> Jacket required. Bring your wallet.

It wasn't signed, but it didn't need to be. I knew who had written it, the same man who'd set up the accident, I now was certain, the same man who had in all likelihood killed Hailey Prouix.

Phil Frigging Skink.

27

"**WHERE THE** fuck is my money, you scabrous piece of shit?"

Skink was already sitting at a table, beside a thick gray curtain, beneath a painting of a naked woman with her hand demurely covering her crotch. The joint was papered with maroon velvet, the corners were graced with great metal urns filled with ivy and denuded branches in arresting arrays. The chairs, upholstered also in velvet, had large brass rings hanging from their backs. It felt, the Prime Steakhouse on the lower level of the Bellagio, Roman and gangsterish at the same time, a place where Tiberius Caesar and Sam Giancana could dine together on great chunks of charred oxen and laugh about conquered provinces and rigged elections. A place where grasping lieutenants who had skimmed the empire's profits could be taken care of with a single blow from a pepper mill the size of a baseball bat.

Sitting before Skink on the peach-colored tablecloth was a huge crystal shell filled with ice, covered with an array of plump fresh oysters. Skink eyed me calmly as he sucked out the insides of a nacreous shell. The maître d' had brought me through the fabulously decadent dining room to the table and was standing aside as I ignored the proffered seat and confronted the slurping Skink to no great effect. It was disconcerting that Skink seemed to be enjoying himself immensely despite my rage. It was doubly disconcerting that he was wearing the same gold lamé lucky jacket as I was.

"You're a bit late, Vic, so I hope you don't mind I started without you."

"I want my money and my documents, and I want them now."

"We look like a backup singing group here, don't we, Vic? You and I in the same jacket, like a couple of Pips. Or maybe like two homosexual types with the same taste in clothes. I wonder if everyone here thinks we're a couple of poofs having ourselves a lover's spat."

"Hand it over."

"Calm down," he said. "Sit. Eat first, talk later. That's a plan, innit? Let's keep things all clean and private."

He glanced to the side and I did, too, glanced at the maître d', still holding my chair. I felt a stern French disapproval of my table manners, which was interesting, because the maître d' was neither stern nor French. She instead was a lovely American with long, straight hair who calmly waited for my diatribe to conclude. There was no shock in her face—her restaurant served meat in the bowels of a casino, there wasn't much I expect she hadn't seen—still, her presence there settled me enough that I finally dropped down into the chair and accepted the great burgundy menu.

"You like shrimp, Vic?" asked Skink. "Who don't, right? Bring him an order of the grilled prawns to start with while he reads the bill of fare, will you, sweetheart?"

The maître d' smiled, nodded, swayed away.

"Lovely girl, that. Wouldn't mind ordering her right off the menu."

"There's enough to buy in this town, if that's what you need to do."

"I don't need to do a thing," he said. "Just like I don't need to pick up my skim milk in the 7-Eleven. It's the convenience, is all."

"I want my money and I want my documents."

He picked up another oyster and slurped. "There's the root of the problem, innit? None of thems is yours. You pocketed it all from a dead girl's bank deposit box, didn't you?"

"Jonah Peale promised you'd leave me alone?"

"He told me to go on vacation, and here I am. But even so, I'm nobody's boy. I'm what they call an independent contractor. Key word being 'independent.' I do whatever I want, work for whoever I damn please."

"For whom exactly do you work? Lawrence Cutlip? Is that why you took the insurance policy? The receptionist at Desert Winds said Cutlip was having a busy day. I'd bet you were the other visitor. I'd bet you showed up there before I did. I'd bet you were squatting there behind the mesquite tree, eavesdropping on our meeting."

Skink smiled as he sucked down another oyster.

"And Guy's father-in-law, Jonah Peale? That's who you took the Juan Gonzalez file for, isn't it?"

"It would be a violation of my ethical duties to be disclosing the names of my clients."

"It's so nice to see you concerned about your ethical duties."

"At least one of us is." He peered at me over the great crystal shell.

"What about the money? Who was that for?"

"A man's got to eat, don't he? You want an oyster? I could order more."

I shook my head no. He lifted one of the shells, elbow pointing high, and slurped. He chewed and swallowed and let out a soft sigh.

"There's nature's goodness, right there," he said. "It's like taking in a swallow of the sea."

"You almost killed me. You almost killed Beth, which is even worse."

"Is that where all this hostility comes from? You think it was me what ran you off the highway?" He seemed surprised, even hurt. "I had nothing to do with it. I was as shocked as anyone to see the carcass of your car tilting there on the side of the road. In fact, I was thinking it was I who saved your life. And what thanks does I get? Nothing but this diatribe of accusation."

"If it wasn't you who tried to kill me, who was it?"

"That's a question, innit? Though that cute little copper thought it was just an accident. Said you was speeding, driving reckless."

"But neither of us believes that, do we? You threatened me if I didn't take the plea, said something awful would happen."

"Come now, Vic, that's right there in the private detection hand-book, technique number nineteen: the idle threat. It gets the juices flowing, gets the pot stirred. Make the threat, stir the pot, follow the mark until he leads you to something worth your while."

"And that's why you're in Vegas, following me."

"I even gave you a hint of what I wanted you to look for."

"The key."

"I knew it was missing, and I suspected where it might be. By the way, you done terrific work in finding the box. My compliments. But all the time, the threat was idle. It's one thing to put a scare in a person, quite another to actually back it up with murder."

"And you're not capable of that?"

I stared at his eyes, beady, ugly things, stared at his eyes to see whether there might be murder there. He stared back for a moment as if he understood where lay my deepest suspicions and then shrugged.

"Didn't say that, only said it was quite a thing. You should gan-der the menu, Vic. They've got nine different types of potato. Un-fortunately, with my cholesterol problem, I can't order a one of them. Nothing for me but the oysters and a single filet mignon, well done. A lean cut of beef that is, and after they burn it, not a scrap of fat left. But you, you should help yourself there, since it's you who's treating."

"Why me? You have the money."

"True, true, but it's mostly earmarked already, expenses and such. How about some creamed spinach, Vic, some rack of lamb? A bargain, too, the whole thing costing less than a proper craps spread at a ten-dollar table. You play craps?"

"No."

"Well, then, maybe you should learn. I gots myself a system."

"You've got a system?"

"Oh, yes. Yes I do. Yes, yes. With a few quick lessons maybe you could earn it all back and more. You know what the good book says: Give a man thirty thou, he's rich for a day, but teach a man to play craps, well, then, he's got something for the rest of his life, don't he?"

Just then a waiter laid a plate in front of me. It held four large crustaceans, split and grilled, a wild assortment of antennae and legs sticking helter-skelter from the shells, the whole thing looking like some bizarre Klingon meal served to interstellar diplomats on the USS *Enterprise.*

"How do I eat this?" I said.

"With the saffron mayonnaise, I would suppose," said Skink.

I reached my fork into one of the shells, pulled out the meat, dipped it into the yellow sauce.

"Oh, my."

"I hear they're quiet good," said Skink. "Although on my diet, I'm afraid . . ."

I didn't wait to hear what he had to say, and I didn't offer him one either. I pulled out another, dipped it in the sauce, snapped it clean between my teeth—marvelous. All day I'd been running around like a crazy man, stealing into a safe-deposit box, interrogating Cutlip, getting sideswiped in the desert, being examined at the hospital, sitting by Beth's bedside, taking a cab back to the hotel, checking back in, performing a quick run-through of what had been left me in the briefcase. With all that running, I hadn't eaten since the morning and wasn't aware how hungry I was until I bit into that first prawn. Then the second, then the third. I was ravenous, starved. I stopped only long enough to scan the menu and choose what else I wanted to stuff inside my gullet. Skink was wrong about the potatoes, there weren't nine choices, there were ten: shoestring and gaufrettes, ginger sweet and mashed, roasted fingerlings, french fries, truffle mashed, grati dauphinion, St. Florentine, and the simple, classic baked. With the waiter hovering, I ordered the lamb, the spinach, both the shoestrings and the ginger sweets. Then I attacked the final prawn.

"You want mint jelly with that lamb, Vic? My mamma, she always served mint jelly with her lamb."

I nodded.

"And how about some wine? Something red, good for the heart. A little merlot? How does that sound? This is a business meeting, it's all tax deductible. Let's have some wine."

I nodded again. Skink ordered. The waiter took away the menu and bowed.

"You surprise me, Vic. I had taken you for the tightest of arses, but you're more fun than I expected. I'm beginning to see what it was she saw."

I had come into the restaurant homicidally angry at Phil Frigging Skink, angry at him for trying to kill us, angry at him for stealing my files, strongly suspecting that he had been the one to shoot Hailey Prouix. Hatred is a soft word for what I felt toward him, but while I was sitting at that table, eating prawns and then lamb, the spinach and potatoes, drinking the Merlot, which was excellent by the way, smooth and dark, while I was sitting at that table, my emotions softened. He was a creep, clearly, but a pleasant little creep, pleasanter still as we started into the second bottle of wine. And I had to admit, I admired his taste in jackets. It would be a shame if I were right about him.

"Tell me something, Phil." He was no longer Phil Frigging Skink, he now was just Phil. "Did you ever in your life sell cars for a living?"

"Never." He laughed, and I laughed with him. "That would be a honest day's work."

"And who the hell needs that?"

"There you go."

"Well, you'd be good at it nonetheless. Most of sales is bullshit and you're a master. But something confuses me. How many people are you representing, and how do you stop from getting all their differing agendas confused?"

He paused, took a sip of Merlot. "It's all a matter of lines and angles, of anticipation."

"Like billiards."

"Now you're getting it, yes you are. You like stories?"

"Who doesn't?"

"Well, fill your glass, Vic, sit back, and listen up. I got me a story you might want to hear. Yes, you might at that."

28

"**A MAN** sets up a meeting, wants me to spy on his wife. Oldest story in the world, but with a twist. He's a fancy-dressing man, you know what I mean, handkerchief sticking out his suit jacket, his finger-nails manicured and glossy. I hate him at sight. And here's the thing, not a whit of nervousness or upset about him. Generally a Joe thinks some other Joe is doing his wife, he's all flippy, but this Joe he's an absolute cuke, an arrogant cuke, if you catch my drift. It doesn't feel right. But like Sam says, never believe the client, believe the money. So's I take the retainer, write the information in my lit-tle book, and sets about tailing the wife.

"She was once a pretty thing, I can tell, but she'd gotten no younger over the years and the things what happen to women as they get older, the thickening thing, happened to her just as you would expect. But, see, with her I can tell she knows it, with her you can see the vulnerability. She shops, plays tennis, lunches at the club with the other ladies, la-di-da. Don't know why that's the life all the birds want, it'd be enough to bore my pants right off, I was them, and I figure maybe that's the trouble. So Thursday is lawn day, the boys in their cutoffs, whipping the mowers over the client's three football fields, and there's one boy wearing no shirt, who I tell you is frigging gorgeous. Dark complexion, thick curled lips, straight

narrow nose, a perfect nose, with a ballplayer's arse and a swimmer's body, thin but with muscles chiseled and abs, oh, my, the abs.

"Now, I ain't that way, I want you to know, don't be getting no
ideas, me in this jacket and all, but I can still appreciate the male figure and I can tell you he's a frigging rock star. And next thing you
know, he's talking to the missus. She brings him a lemonade.
Sweat's dripping from his tits as he takes the glass. He lifts his chin
to drain the drink, his Adam's apple bobs, one of his pecs twitches.
She reaches out and almost touches his shoulder but pulls back. Obvious, innit? The attraction between 'em is so thick you could lubri-
cate your dick with it. So they all leave, all the lawn boys, but at
three he comes back in a ratty old car and starts searching around
like he lost something. She comes out to help him, they search
around together, side by side. And when he happens to find it, the
shirt he planted there that morning, he doesn't put it on as you
would expect, but tosses it over his shoulder and waits there, like
waiting for an invitation in, and she gives it, how could she not?
Next thing you know I got myself a roll of film, job done, fee
earned.

"But something's not right, and I don't like it. So I gives off following the lady and start to following the lawn boy. I meet up with
him in a bar on Twelfth Street, a funny bar, you know, where we
with our jackets would fit right in. I buy him a beer, buy him another, he thinks I'm an old poof interested in that swimmer's bod,
and I can tell that he's willing to be interested, too, as long as I'm
paying. So I go out back with him, into the alley behind the bar. It's
dark, damp, rubber johnnies littering the asphalt, a place where if it
could talk, you'd cover your ears and run out screaming. Lawn boy
puts his hand on my hip and smiles his charming smile. I lift my
elbow and break his nose. Sounded like someone snacking on a
taco. So much for perfect. Now he's on the ground, hands covering
his face, blood leaking through his fingers. I leans down and I tell
him what I want to know, and he spills. Everything. It was the husband what put him up to it, the husband what paid off this trick to
do his wife while I was there whole time with my camera.

"I figure the bastard, he wants a divorce on his terms, wants the
pictures either as bargaining leverage, hoping to unsettle her so

she'll agree to poverty, or to show the judge in a custody fight when he grabs for the kids. Either way a nasty piece of business. So of course I goes back to the missus and shows her the pictures, and she breaks down, begging me not to give them to her husband. I tell her how I got no choice, I was paid for them in advance, I got my ethics to consider, but then I tell her about lawn boy and about how her husband paid him off and how she ought to get herself checked, because there's no telling what kind of vile organisms lawn boy passed on to her. She's collapsed into a heap, sniveling, crying, moaning out, 'What am I going to do? What am I going to do?' Beautiful, right? So's I go and tell her what it is she is going to do, and she spots me another retainer.

"I'm back on the road, following husband this time. Is this a great job or what? It turns out husband, he's a lawyer, surprise, surprise, driving a Jaguar, lunching at the Palm with political heavies, and spending stray afternoons in the Bellevue with some little chippy from his law firm. It's harder getting pictures from a hotel like that as compared to a private home, but with the right equipment, including a pinch of cash for the staff, you can get yourself anything, and it ain't long before I can a roll of that son of a bitch with his arse hanging out and his socks on giving that chippy his prima facie best.

"Now the two parties, husband and wife, they're back on level turf, and I'm feeling pretty good about things, but why stop there, why stop with two? It's a triangle, innit? So I decide on following the bird from the husband's law firm, a good-looking thing, I must say. I was just curious, mind you, not knowing what I'd find, but just trying to figure out what pitch to make and where to make it. I read her as a typical spoiled brat, never wanting for nothing, fancy college, ambition driving her into the law, setting up her yuppie lifestyle, not minding grabbing another woman's husband if it helps her climb a peg or two. A little pressure and she'd be willing to pay anything to make it go away. It all seems so obvious, except this girl, she ain't obvious.

"One night I follow her to a dive of a bar in South Philly, where she meets up with some shady sailor type. Next night I follow her into some church, where she stays an hour before rushing off to meet the husband. Night after she has dinner in some ragged seafood joint alongside some scumbucket from Kensington with but three teeth to his name, and after that she ends up again in the church. I go in behind her this time. She slips a buck or two into the box, buys herself a candle, then it's off to a pew by herself. She doesn't hit her knees, she's no papist, I can tell, but I look around, seeing who she's meeting, and there's no one. Might as well have been praying, for all I know. And then I trail her until she disappears into some lesbo bar in Old City. That's a switch, huh? But I can't go in there without getting marked, so I wait outside in my car. An hour later she's on the street with some bull dyke in a black leather vest, and while they're clinching and kissing, and not like cousins neither, while they're chewing each other's tongues, she opens her eyes and gives me the stare from across the street. Then she's off, alone, heading away from me. I gets out of my car and follow.

"It's an old section of the town, narrow streets, lots of turns and twists. It's raining lightly, there's a mist, I see her go down one alleyway, I catch a glimpse of her turning down another. I have no idea where she's going, but I'm curious, right? Who the hell is she, right? This ain't no yuppie like I ever saw before. Another turn, across a bigger street and into another alley. All the time I'm seeing just bits of her, never the full thing. I catch just the flash of her heel as she turns down a narrow cobbled street. I make the turn, and next thing I know I'm on the ground, a knee in my crotch, a knife at my throat, and the bull dyke staring down at me with a look that lets me know she'd do it, she'd do it, and damn if slicing my throat wouldn't be the most fun she could ever have with a man. And behind her, calmly leaning against a wall, smoking, stands the girl.

" 'What do you want?' she says.

" 'A word, is all,' I says.

" 'Go ahead,' she says.

" 'Let me up first,' I says.

" 'No,' she says, and the dyke presses the knife a little harder at my throat.

" 'Fine,' I says. 'At my age I can use a little time off my feets.'

"And then I tell her, I tell her about the husband coming into my office, about the missus and the lawn boy, about the pictures of the two of them in the Bellevue. When you're in a situation like that, it don't pay to hold nothing back. You give it all, the whole of it, and hope they get so lost in the details they don't know what to do. But this bird, she knows what to do. She starts to laughing.

" 'Is that all?' she says. 'I hope you caught my good side.'

" 'From what I could tell,' I says, 'that's all you got.'

"And the bull dyke, she stares down at me and says, 'Don't make me puke.'

" 'All right, Tiffany,' says the girl. 'Let him up.'

"The bull dyke lets me up. I look at her in her leather vest, shoulders bulging, Doc Martens, and all I can say is, 'Tiffany? You gots to be kidding.'

"The dyke snarls, the girl laughs, and the next thing I know the girl and I, we're in that lesbo bar, downing vodka martinis, trading cigs, laughing like we was the oldest of old pals. I ask her if she wants to get married to the lawyer. All she says is 'Please.' I ask her why and she shows me her pinkie. Then she turns her face away and says in the saddest voice I ever heard, 'Besides, it would end up bloody.' I asks her to explain. She shakes her head. Then she writes a name on a napkin and tells me before I meet with either husband or wife I oughts to find out what I can about it. For her. The only requirement is that no one knows it was she what set me on the name. And right there she writes me a check for my retainer. My third retainer.

"You would think it would be a trick with just a name to go on, figuring what there was to learn. You'd think. But I look up the name and then knocks on a door and some old lady, she just invites me in, pours me a cup of herbal, puts out a plate of biscuits, and starts chatting off my ear. Nice old lady she was, old for sure, what with her skin like tissue paper and me being able to see the blue veins pulsing in her neck. Never had no children, she tells me, but she was married for forty years to Morty. I hear a lot about Morty. He fought in the war, occupied Japan, through no fault of his own came down with some tropical disease transmitted by the mosquito that left him sterile. A senseless tragedy, she says, though I'm thinking that if Morty can convince her that the clap is transmitted by the mosquito, then what couldn't she be convinced of? So I asks about her estate and she tells me it's all taken care of, handled by a very sweet young man who calls her every day. She's going to give it all to the nunnery, that's what she plans, and every day the sweet young lawyer calls and tells her how the market moved that day. It's going to be a tidy sum, yes, it's going to raise some eyebrows, oh, yes. There'll be a building at the nunnery named after Morty, oh, yes, oh, yes. Won't that be something?

"No, it won't. Because there's nothing left in the trust account, is there? Nothing left, the sweet young lawyer has taken it all. Except he's not so sweet, not so young. All he is is a frigging lawyer. And, of course, he's the husband.

"So's I go back to the chippy, though by now I know she's no chippy, and tell her what I found, and she's not the least bit shocked. And here's the tripper, she tells me to give it to the wife, the name and the story, to let the wife do with it whatever she wants. I toss her a look like she's crazy, like she can do a lot better for herself with the information, but she just tells me to shut up and do what I'm told. Well, that's what she's paying me for, and so that's what I do. I give the pictures of the wife and the lawn boy to the husband. I give the pictures of the husband and the chippy to the wife. And with those pictures I give the name, address, and story of the old lady.

"Now, I can't say for sure what happened in the meeting with the lawyers once the husband told the missus he wanted the divorce. I wish I was there, it must have been something. But in the end the husband and wife, they stayed married after all. In fact, they went on a European holiday for three months after. The north of Italy, the South of France. They would have gone to the coast of Luxembourg, excepting Luxembourg's got no coast. It must have been lovely, and it was quite the shopping spree if my sources were right. And funny thing, I ran into the missus a little while after she got back, and she was happy as an oyster, had even lost some pounds and was looking rather svelte. Rather svelte. I'd of done her myself, I would, but now she was happily married.

"And the chippy that wasn't no chippy? Listen to this. The wife, she insists, insists that the chippy leave the husband's firm. And the chippy, she balks. No way in hell she's leaving without a little something to remember him by. The husband, now desperate to keep the wife happy, gives the chippy a slew of cases, some profitable ones, too, I might add, and some money if she'd just leave. And so she does. Starts her own place, turns those cases into cash, begins to make a name for herself. She did quite well, didn't she? Lost a arsehole and gained a practice all in one swell foop.

"It was my kind of case, it was. Three clients, three retainers, and the outcome, in a rough sense, was just. But the best thing was meeting the chippy. We became partners of a sort. I did her investigations, working on the sly mostly, helped those fees of hers roll in. And she, she was something, she was, special, and far too smart for the likes of me. Wheels within wheels within wheels."

"Hailey," I said.

"She was a hell of a girl, and I miss her."

"So do I."

"I believe you do."

"I thought you might have killed her," I said.

"I knows you did. I could see it in them peepers of yours. And me, I was wondering what kind of man represents the killer of the girl what he's doing the old Friar Tuck to every chance he gets? I thought you was going to use some insider knowledge to get him off the hook and get your face all over the papers. I didn't like that idea, wasn't so happy with that. I figured I owed the girl enough to not let that happen. That's why I came on so hard over my oatmeal. But after watching you for the last couple days, I gots a different idea."

"Go ahead."

"This is what I thinks." He leaned forward, lowered his voice. "I thinks at first you weren't taking the deal because you thought it too sweet. You thought the bastard did it, and you was standing by your Guy just to be sure he paid the ultimate price. That was what your meeting with Peale was all about, wasn't it? Setting him up to tell the coppers all about our Mr. Gonzalez. You're taking our little murder all personal like, playing at being being the Lone Ranger."

"And you're not?"

I stared at him, he stared back.

"You're a piece of work, ain't you, Vic?" he said. "But you don't think he did it no more, do you?"

"Nope."

"Something switched in your head."

"Like a light turning on."

"What changed your mind?"

I picked up my wine, stared into the deep crimson before taking a drink. "Hailey changed my mind. I finally learned the whole sad story of her and Guy. She was in control. From the very first, when she met him in that hospital room, to the very last, on the night of her death, when she told him it was over, she was in control. Total control. Guy never had a chance."

"Not much a one, no."

"And you helped set him up, didn't you? Hailey needed to know all about the man defending the Gonzalez case to lay her trap, and you gave her what she needed. And when Guy thought you were threatening her, you were really just giving her little tidbits to help her scheme."

Skink didn't answer.

"Well, if she was so much in control, how could she have ever let it happen? How could she have miscalculated so? Unless she didn't and he didn't. Tell you what I think, I think he was in thrall to her to the very end. I think he was too whipped to kill her."

"Or maybe he fooled her like he fooled you. He's a harder piece of work than he lets on. You should a seen how viciously he cut down the claims of the poor injured wretches what fell in his path. Not an ounce of mercy. He left his wife and kids at the drop of a skirt and stole a million in the process. That bastard is capable of anything. You was right from the first. It was Guy what done it."

"Nope, it was someone else. And I have a pretty good idea where I need to go to find who."

"Where's that?"

"You much interested in history?"

"Julius Caesar?" said Skink. "The bloody fall of the bloody Roman Empire?"

"No, the recent past. Hailey Prouix's past. I'm taking a trip, and that's where I'm headed." I stared at his ugly mug for a moment, thought of his story and the tenderness behind it, and then said softly, "You coming?"

Skink tilted his head.

"I was looking through what you left me in the briefcase," I said. "Keepsakes from her past. I have some questions."

"What kind of questions?"

"The usual. An idyllic childhood that might not have been so idyllic. An accidental death that might not have been an accident."

"And you think all that has something to do with what happened to Hailey?"

"Now that you're no longer a suspect, maybe I do. That's what I'm taking the trip to find out. You coming?"

"Where to?"

"Pierce, West Virginia."

"Her girlhood home."

"You coming?"

"You won't find nothing."

"Sure I won't."

"It's been too long."

"Far too long."

"Nobody no more knows nothing."

"You coming?"

Skink sucked his teeth for a moment. "I charge two-fifty a day."

"A hundred."

"Two hundred."

"One-fifty. Plus expenses."

"I'll need a retainer."

"You got thirty thousand already."

"Did I?"

"I need to settle a few things first. Take care of Beth, do some trial prep. But then it's West Virginia ho. You coming?"

He paused a moment, reading my face as if reading the newspaper, and then he broke into a gap-toothed smile as wide as the Mississippi and reached out his hand.

I took it and shook it, but before I let go, I turned it over and checked the knuckles. Rough and hairy, each as ugly as a slag heap, but no scrapes, no bruises. Still holding on, I said, "How'd you know the safe-deposit key was missing from her house?"

"Private sources."

"You weren't the lug in black who beat the hell out of that police technician?"

"Me? Nah, I'm a lover, not a fighter."

"You understand if you work for me, your mouth stays shut. Our little secret remains our little secret."

"Vic, sweetie, if we're going to be partners, we need to trust each other."

"I already have a partner," I said as I finally let go. "And the idea of trusting you is enough to get my stomach roiling."

"I seem to have that effect on you, don't I?" said Phil Skink with a laugh. "Don't worry, Vic, I'll play it your way, all buttoned up, while you convince yourself that your friend really done it and deserves whatever he gets. Now, take care of the check and we'll go on up and have ourselves a time. What say I teach you how to play craps?"

"I don't think so."

"Not to worry, Vic. We're sporting our lucky jackets. How can we lose? And better than that, I gots myself a system."

PART FOUR

BLACK
HOLES

29

I HAD never imagined, before driving into it, how amazingly beautiful was West Virginia. The steep mountain faces, the slender valleys carved by winding rivers, the roads twisting like snakes, the lovely white churches sitting beyond every bend. When Skink and I dropped south out of the long left arm of Maryland into West Virginia, it was like dropping into the landscape of a purer age. Even the sound track was purer—all we could get on the car radio was gospel stations. There were houses all along the route, some fine, some trailers beautifully maintained, some out-and-out hovels, but all seemed to flow naturally from the contours of the landscape. We followed the main road as it crossed a green metal bridge and twisted low through a fertile valley dotted with livestock and then turned off onto a smaller route that started a slow, inexorable climb into the mountains.

The car struggled until it reached the top of Point Mountain, with its inevitable white church just off the peak, and then fell as the road switched back and forth down, down. After a few minutes, to our left, we could catch glimpses through the leaves of something green and narrow and far beneath us, something that seemed, from that distance, more legendary than real. A valley, busy with farms and houses and lumber mills, isolated and lovely in its crevice in the western reaches of the Appalachians. We shared the road with pick-ups and beat old logging trucks as we continued down into the heart of that valley. Here and there, where the map showed a town, were mere scatterings of houses, a church, a lumber mill, clouds of sheep, another lumber mill, a collection of commercial buildings, a food mart, a Laundromat, a Chrysler-Dodge dealership. This was not a wealthy county, and there was the occasional shack, the rusted-out frame of a swing set, the boarded-up store, but still it was undeniably beautiful.

And then the valley widened and the road rose from the tumbling river and we saw a wooden frame, studded with the signs of the Lions Club, of the Kiwanis Club, of the Chamber of Commerce and the VFW and the various and sundry churches. On the frame, beneath the signs, the following words were affixed:

WELCOME TO PIERCE, POPULATION 649.

H.

I don't want you to be thinking to all the crap that Tina she spits out. She's just that way, always stirring up the pot once it stops a boiling. I like you, sure, like I like a lot of others, but I don't think you're like special or nothing, not like she says. Everyone knows that you're with Grady and he's with you and I don't want you thinking nothing like what Tina says. I like hanging out with you, is all. It's bad enough with Grady always on my ass. I don't be needing you to get all weirded out too or anything. You looked at me yesterday like I was some alien from Mars or something and that's why I'm writing this.

I maybe have a hard time talking about things. I find it easier sometimes to say what I feel when I'm alone with my mom's old L. C. Smith. Face to face it's harder, it's like my tongue twists in on itself and I get all stupid. I'm not the sharpest spade, I know, as Mr. Perrine makes sure to tell me in front of everyone, but I'm not as dumb as I sound when I talk which is why I'm writing this instead of talking to you at school or on the phone or something.

That time in the quarry I wasn't leaving cause I was sad or anything. I was just tired, I don't know. And I feel weird when everyone starts lighting up. I know you say it's cool that I don't and no one says they mind but I feel weird. It's like suddenly everyone's at a party that I'm not invited to. And when everyone starts to laughing I don't like that I don't see nothing funny. I feel less alone sometimes when I'm alone, if you know what I mean. That's why I up and left. And Grady saying all them things and making jokes about my leaving, that's all right. I know Grady, he's just like that, but I only wanted to be alone. Which is why when I first saw that you were following me maybe I wasn't so nice and all. But I was glad finally that you did.

I didn't know someone else felt as different and out of place as I do, though I have a hard time thinking you really do. I mean you're so pretty and you're with Grady and it's like you fit in more than anyone. But I guess that goes to show. Some people think because I play ball I'm all this way or that way but I'm not any way like that, I'm my own way, which is, I guess, the problem.

Anyway, thanks for walking and for asking about Leon. I didn't say much, I guess there's not much to say, but it still was nice. It's like now that he's dead and with what happened and all it seems now no one wants to talk nothing about him. Maybe they're trying to make it easier on me, I don't know, but in a way it just makes it worse. Like he's some huge secret when all he was was a kid. I miss him every day, but if I mention him now my dad just yells at me to put it behind me and move on. Move on to where, I want to ask. Where the hell am I going? He was my best friend, more I guess, and I feel real lost still without him even though it's been already two years.

So that's all I wanted to say. I don't want you acting all weird around me. I'm hoping we can just be friends and hang out a little and maybe you'll watch me play. That would be something nice.

J.

From the moment of Hailey's murder I had assumed that Guy, somehow, was at the heart of the story leading to her death. He was my contact in, my secret rival, the third point of our triangle of betrayal, and so I couldn't conceive of his somehow not being to blame for her murder. But after hearing Guy's story I suddenly had a different sense of it all. Guy was a pawn, so was I, and the master strategist was Hailey herself.

So my focus now was where it should have been from the start, on Hailey. The answer to her death lay somewhere in her life, and she had given me a map to its most significant moments. In her safe-deposit box she herself had chosen what I would see. The photographs and documents that she had left for me would be my lever to pry open her past. And included among them were the letters, mash notes typed or scribbled by a boy long dead, words that bristled still with raw emotion.

H.

I know you're mad at me and you got good reason and so I got nothing to say but I'm sorry. I'm sorry for everything. I don't know what got into me. It was for a time like the only place I felt free was with you or on the ball field and now, after the fight and the suspension, there ain't no place left. My dad he blames you for everything and tells me I'm not to see you no more and I tell him to go to hell and that also is on the razor's edge of blows. So it all keeps getting worse and worse and I don't know why. We're just friends, just friends, why can't everyone see that? What's going on between you and Grady got nothing to do with me and what happened between Grady and me got nothing to do with you neither. We've been cruising toward this for years, Grady and me, only so many times you can hear yourself being called mountain trash without doing something about it. This has been coming since our boyhoods, you was just his excuse.

But I'm not here writing to apologize about Grady. It's the other thing, the thing that got you pissed at me in the first place. I can't be like you want me to be, I can't be all chatty and confessional, it's not in me. I know plenty of folk who go around telling their life's story to anyone who happens by but I've got no urge to puke my guts out on anybody's front porch.

We all got a secret. I know you got yours, I can feel it, large and dark, but I got mine too. When I think about what I keep hidden it's so large it dwarfs me. Whatever you see on the outside is just some sort of a lie, it's the insides that matter and that's got to stay inside. Sometimes the secret is so heavy I feel about to be crushed, but it's never hard keeping it. I might as easily just rip out my insides and let you take a look as to start blatting about like a sheep. It's me, it's what I am, I wouldn't want to survive without it but like a kidney it ain't nothing I want to be showing around neither. I don't want you getting pissed at me but it won't do me no good talking about it, that won't change a thing. It's there and I live with it every day, and there's nothing to be done. So when you say I'm not communicating well there it is. I ain't. And if that's gonna keep you mad at me, so be it.

I don't know when I'll be back in school. Coach wants me back out there soon as he can the way Delmore's been booting the ball around short but it's not up to him. Grady's due out of the hospital in a few days and Chief Edmonds says I have to wait until he's out to see if they are pressing charges. They won't let me back in school until then so if I'm gonna see you before I'm going to have to sneak out but I'm willing if you are.

Just take a little pity on me and don't ask too many questions cause right now things are such a mess I don't know what I'm going to do and I don't know how I'm going to do what I need to do if you stay mad at me.

J.

Along with the letters in the box were the photographs, heartrending because I knew how it all turned out, how but not why. There was a picture of two girls, young girls, just kids, arm in arm, blond in their shifts, frowning both. I could see her face in the picture, Hailey's face, the cheekbones not yet pronounced, the eyebrows not yet arched, the lips not the full buds they would become, but there it was, her sad face—twice. I knew she had a sister, I never knew she had a twin. Roylynn and Hailey.

I didn't glimpse the pictures once and quickly, like moving through a friend's photo album. Instead I thumbed through them often, obsessively, time and time again. It was a strange sensation, this examining of the photographs, unseemly in a way, like pawing through the dresser drawers of some other family's memories. But they were a part of my route into her past. Roylynn had stayed in

West Virgina and Hailey had left, Roylynn was still alive and Hailey was dead. How had that happened? They had shared each other's features, but what else, what history? I wondered if the pictures would provide a clue. I stacked them and restacked them, I shuffled them randomly and went through them again, trying to find, in the differing orders, a sense behind them, trying to divine the story.

Here was one, the nuclear family, twin girls, still just babies with their mother and their father, their poor doomed father, short, swarthy, his forearms thick and meaty. What little girl wouldn't feel safe in those forearms? They were smiling, the parents, in that picture, and the babies had that satisfied contempt on their shapeless faces that marked them as happy. This was the "before" picture. Another, burned into my memory, Hailey dead and bloody on the mattress thirty years later, was the "after."

A photograph of the father, alone now, in a uniform of some sort with a peaked cap, his truck driver's uniform. Smiling, cocky, gladiator of the road, master of his destiny, hero of country-and-western song, off to haul his cargo of lumber until a load shifted and a brace failed to hold and he was gone.

Where was the sense in the order?

I shifted them around, and now the father was replaced by another. It was a picture of one of the girls holding the hand of a man, not the father, a tall, rawboned man with a grizzled beard. Oh, I recognized him, yes I did. Lawrence Cutlip, younger and harder, not a man to be messed with for certain, but there, holding on to that girl when she needed him most. Who was the girl, Roylynn or Hailey? I couldn't tell, but there she stood, the girl in the picture, her father gone, squeezing, as if for dear life, the hand of the man who now was her sole protection against an oblivious world.

H.

I am flying, I am floating through the air and I don't never want to come down. Never. I always thought when it came it would be heavy, leaden, that it would clutch me at the throat like it did before, but this is like drinking freedom pure. I am soaring, held high by something so magical it has no name. The moment we left apart I ran home, to my room, to my desk, so I could write all the things I found it impossible to say in the moment.

I know I'm still in a world of trouble but that don't have grip on me no more. When you hit a ball solid on the meat of the bat there is an instant when the whole force flows though you like an easy wave. It's why I love the game so, the feel of that easy wave that flows through you for the instant it takes to finish the swing and send the ball a flying. But now I feel like I am riding that wave, surfing it like a Beach Boy's song all sweet and sure. All I can think about is you, your smile, your soft hands, the red of your lips, the silver tang of electricity I tasted in your mouth. How did this happen, I keep asking myself, how? One moment we're in the quarry, talking about something that happened in the past, huddling on the rock, talking as friends, leaning close, our knees butting up one against the other like friends, talking in near whispers, and the next moment I am overcome with something so powerful that it starts me to shaking and has me shaking still. There was a switch and I don't know how it turned or why but suddenly everything changed and the world was lit with a light I didn't know existed and I am flying. I don't know how it happened, I only know I have never been happy before, never, not like this, no, never.

I was wrong when I said there was no use talking. I can't find the words to say what it felt like to finally trust someone enough to tell it all to, to tell it all and to see a reaction so different than ever I expected. There was no disgust or hate or even pity, you was just listening and nodding like, yeah, okay, and then what. You weren't sitting there like a judge, you were there like a friend and that meant so much even before the wave hit. And I was wrong when I said I was nothing but the secret because this is so strong, what I'm feeling now, and so outside what I had ever felt before that it makes me doubt whether it was so dark a secret in the first place. Maybe it was like you said, maybe we was young and feeling things we didn't understand and ended up doing things that meant nothing except that we loved each other in the best way. Maybe like you said it's common, it happens, and then you move on. And maybe we would have if Leon hadn't gotten so scared like he did and then played that game with the train that he knew he'd lose. Or maybe it wasn't just the talking that cured me, maybe you chased it out too, chased it with your kiss, like an angel chasing out something evil in my soul.

Whatever it is I am ready to face what comes next. I know Grady's been talking about me, talking out of that wired jaw, and so he'll try something. I know that I even so much as cough in class I'll be out on my ear. I know that the only reason I'm back on the team is because I was hitting .467 and that if my average drops or I start fumbling at short coach will bench my ass and smile when he does it. I know all that, but I'm not afraid, I'm excited. I can't wait. I can't wait to go to sleep tonight so I can wake up to-morrow and see your face and then after school and after practice run to the quarry so I can cover you in kisses till it's dark and we have to go home and then do it all again the day after and then again and then again.

J.

Another photograph. The two girls again, older now, young, good-looking girls, high school girls.

Is there is something primordial in the attraction of high school girls for the male of the species? When we are younger, say, in jun-ior high, they are the unavailable avatars of desire. What would Juliet have been in the Verona High School, a sophomore? We can barely wait to grow older, to gain confidence, to take our turn with them. But when we ourselves are in high school, most of us find, to our shock, that the years did not bring the confidence or skills we expected to have come as our due. They are there, waiting for us, the high school girls, and yet we fumble our way into disaster after disaster and leave them unsatisfied and confused and looking for college boys. And then later, when we are old enough so that our skills and confidence have caught up with our desires, the high school girls are once again unavailable. We give them their own slang, jailbait, and prudently cross them off the list of possibilities. But does the desire ever die? Do we ever see a pretty high school girl walk by with her pleated skirt and young high breasts and not sigh in disappointment?

And now here, in the photograph, we have the orgasmic fantasy of every red-blooded heterosexual male on the planet earth: two great-looking high school girls who happen to be twins. But instead of desire, this picture provoked curiosity in me. One was dressed prim and proper, books held in front of her body like a shield, smiling shyly. The other stared straight at the camera, arms on hips, hip cocked, leaning slightly forward, defiantly, but without a smile. It was a sad defiance. Look at what I am, it said, look at what I have become. Oh, yes, two girls, twins, but now I could tell them apart. I knew nothing about Roylynn, but this girl, this girl staring with sad defiance at the camera, this girl was my Hailey. And so the question: Why the difference? What had come into their lives and pressed them in so very different ways?

One other picture grips at me. A boy in a uniform, a baseball uniform. He's on one knee, arms leaning on his bat, posing like a major leaguer. Solid, handsome, either serious or sad, it's hard to tell in the old black-and-white. Jesse Sterrett, I presume.

In the letters it was clear what had developed between Jesse Sterrett and Hailey Prouix, something strong and indelible, passionate enough to have its great joys and great troubles. On a fragment of paper, a ripped portion of envelope, written in a hand overcome with some long-vanished remorse, he pleaded with her from the bottom of his soul.

It's killing me ever day, ever damn day that we're not together. My heart weeps in the wanting. I'm less than a man without you, a carcass already near dead, dying of lost love. You done this to me, you stole my world like a thief. Don't listen to what they are saying, it's nothing but lies, lies and damn lies. I'm sorry for what I done but I never had no choice, I only done what I had to. Never a love been so fierce or fearsome, never has it cost so high or been worth the entire world. It'll kill me, it will, and damn soon. I'm dying for damn sure without you. Yes, I surely am.

The love was fierce and fearsome, seemingly worth every sacrifice, and I hoped so, because I knew how it ended, knew where Jesse Sterrett breathed his last breath and where he died. But why?

What secrets had torn them apart? Jesse had a secret, something between him and Leon, his friend, something that dragged at Jesse's
soul and drove Leon possibly to his death. It wasn't too hard to figure it out, two boys, two best friends, down by the tracks, the
changes happening to their bodies, to their thoughts, waking up
with strange sensations, two boys experimenting. Oh, it wasn't too
hard to figure it out, Jesse's dark secret that wasn't so dark, his
strange encounter that was less strange than he could ever have
imagined. But Jesse also mentioned Hailey's own secret, large and
dark. What was that, and how did that turn her in the direction of
her life? Were the two deaths two decades apart linked in any way?
Could learning the truths behind that death shed any light upon
Hailey's? And why had Hailey, with a ragged line of pencil, slashed
a brutal zig-zag-zig through the last of of Jesse Sterrett's letters, as
if she were a deranged Zorro trying to deface the words?

H.

I am so angry I could strangle a porcupine, and scared too, so
scared, impossibly scared. I love you so much, want you so much,
but now I have learned that secret you've been hiding, my anger
burns least as bright as the love.

I don't know what to do, but I got to do something and there is
only two answers that I can see. One is to stay and fight. Take my
word on this, if I do stay there is no way it won't turn to blood. My
rage is so murderous now I couldn't stop with one blow here or
there. Remember how I was with Grady on the ground that time,
how I couldn't stop myself from slamming his grinning face, how
the only reason I didn't kill his ass was that you stopped me? The
way I feel now is ten times worse, twenty times, a hundred, and
nothing, no power, not even what I feel for you will stop me. I'll
kill him, I will, and they'll lock up my ass even though the bastard
had it coming, and that would be fine by me because I would have
done right by you which is all I care about.

But there is another answer, to run, to leave, to up and get the
hell out of this town, this state. I know we got nothing, you and
me, nothing but the burden of our pasts, but we can make a go of
it. What we feel one for the other will get us through. The scouts

have been sniffing. I'll be up in the next draft and till then I can play semipro somewhere or in some unaffiliated pro league where they'll sign anyone, no questions asked. I'll talk my way into a try-out and smack the apple all over the yard and they'll sign me, I know they'll sign me. And if they find us and come after us we'll go down to Mexico and change our names and I'll play down there. They got leagues down there that play all year. And when I'm seasoned enough I'll make the bigs, I know it, and we'll be so rich we'll have a swimming pool the size of this entire county.

All I'm asking is that you trust me. All I'm asking is that you put your faith in my feelings for you. I got a truck from my cousin Ned, a beat-up old thing but it runs, and I've packed what I need and I'm ready to go. But I ain't going without you.

I'll be at the quarry tonight, I'll be waiting for you. If you trust me enough to come I'll dedicate my every waking hour of the rest of my life to making you happy, I will. I swear. But if you don't come, if you won't run away with me, then I'll do it the other way. I'll do what I need to do to protect you and whatever conse-quences that come my way I'll bear gladly because I'll be bearing them for you. Tonight, I'll be waiting. Tonight.

J.

PIERCE, WEST VIRGINIA, was a county seat, and to prove it, on a hill smack in the center, they had set the county courthouse, a blocky brown building with a single turret, built of sandstone quarried out of a ledge of rock at the far end of the town. To one side of the courthouse the city climbed the slope of the mountain, to the other it fell gently toward the river and then reached across to the far bank, where scattered houses sat in the shadow of another steep rise. The main street, imaginatively named Main Street, jogged around the courthouse. It was built up with brick buildings, squat and aged black, all pressed together along the narrow street as if real estate had once been a prized commodity in the county. The buildings had signs from the middle of the last century, stylized neon banners advertising gifts and flowers and the Courthouse Hotel, signs that hearkened back to a prosperous past. But Pierce didn't look prosperous now. It looked as if nothing had been built in fifty years, except for the modern and unpleasant Rite Aid that sat just before the turnoff. Something had slipped away from Pierce, some vitality. In its buildings and slumped posture you could sense the vaguely disturbing notion that Pierce was at the heart of an American dream that had suddenly shifted.

We drove around a bit to get our bearings and then took the Hailey Prouix tour of the city. Our first stop was the high school, stretching out on the banks of the river, home of the Fighting Wild-cats. It was big for the town, too big, and the buses in the lot told us that children from all over the valley attended. This was where the likes of Hailey Prouix could mix with the wealthy Grady Pritchett as well as mountain trash like Jesse Sterrett.

Our second stop was up the hill from Main Street, a lovely little house painted white with a porch that wrapped around the front like a generous ribbon. The lawn was neatly trimmed, the flowers in the beds were blooming brightly, a swing set could be seen in the side yard. It was the all-American home, it even had a picket fence. The sign said THE LIPTONS, and it seemed as if the Liptons had lived there for generations, but that was an illusion. This was Hailey Prouix's girlhood home. I wondered how it smelled when she was young, whether the paint then was peeling, the lawn untrimmed, the beds brown and weed-ridden. I wondered what I could have seen through those windows had I been here twenty years before. But time had bleached that house clean of whatever then went on inside. Nothing to be learned here.

And, finally, nothing to be learned either at the quarry on the far edge of the town. I was directed to it by a kid at the Sunoco who eyed me suspiciously when I asked, as if it were a sacred place that I was intending to desecrate. I took a road that twisted up into the moun-tain and stopped at a turnoff the boy had described. There was a fence, and there were signs warning of dangers and signs prohibiting trespassing, and there was a gate wrapped with chains and fastened by a lock. But the lock was rusted, the signs defaced, the fence torn apart at certain edges. It didn't take a thing to slip through.

It was getting dark now, but we could see the contours of what had been left after the stone had been ripped from the earth. The walls formed a shoehorn-shaped canyon browned by age, with bushes and scrub trees growing in the cracks, weakening the stone as the plants fought for purchase. There was a wide ledge below us and a path that seemed to travel down to the ledge, a path that re-quired grabbing hold of certain bushes and the roots of certain trees as you made your way down. The ledge was uneven, rough, and lit-tered with beer cans and cigarette packs and graffiti. JK & FS. CATS

RULE. JOHN G. LOVES TINA R. I wondered if there was a GRADY LOVES HAILEY or maybe a HP & JS, but I couldn't spot such from where we stood. And then, beneath the ledge, at the bottom part of the quarry, was a road that rolled out to the river, to take the mined stone to the trains. Between the great stone walls and the road was a reservoir of sorts that seemed to be filled deep with water. I could imagine it all, hanging on the ledge and swimming in the reservoir, a few beers, a little laughter, high dives and skinny-dipping, shrieks of abandon, a little tonguing under the cover of the night, or maybe something a little more than a little tonguing. It was almost enough to make me wish I were seventeen again. Almost. This was the lake, I supposed, that drew the local kids on hot summer nights. And this was the lake from where they dragged the body of Jesse Sterrett.

"So what's the agenda, mate?" said Skink as we stood over the edge and looked into the dark water.

"Go in town, ask some questions, find the truth about that boy's death."

"Sounds simple, it does. So simple, you'd have thought someone would have done it by now."

"You'd have thought."

"We just stop anyone on the street, or do you have a plan?"

"I have a plan."

"That's encouraging."

Pause.

"Don't you want to know what it is?" I asked.

"Not particularly."

"Not even curious."

"Only thing I'm curious about is why you brought me along."

"A lawyer always brings an investigator when he questions witnesses."

"That he does. But my guess, Vic, is you don't want me nowhere near that courtroom."

He was right, I didn't. As far as I knew, only Skink could connect me to Hailey Prouix, and that I couldn't allow. "Maybe not. Maybe I just like your company."

"I am charming, I am. But if I was a hundred and fifty dollars a day charming, I'd be in another line of work. You don't know what the hell you're getting into, do you?"

"Nope."

"And you wanted to bring some muscle."

"Something like that."

"All right, then."

"Don't you want to know my plan?"

"Nah," he said, turning from the edge and heading back for the path up the hill. "Far as I'm concerned, you're chasing here after your own tail. I don't need no plan. I'll just sit back and watch the show."

31

"**COURSE I** remember," said Chief Edmonds as he wrapped his meaty hands around a coffee cup. "How could I forget? A sight like that's not something slips away so easy. When they pulled him out of the water, he was bloated and white like a German Wasserwurst and the back of his head was cracked open like a walnut."

I tried to ignore the unpleasant food imagery as I finished my breakfast.

We were in Kim's Luncheonette on Main Street, a large, barren café that, with its high ceiling and uncomfortable spaciousness, seemed to have taken over for a failed hardware store in one of the city's squat brick buildings. The plain Formica tables were sparsely filled with grizzled patrons, who slumped over their meals and drank their coffees in silence.

"How was everything, Harvey?" said the woman behind the counter when a man stepped over to pay for his eggs.

"Just fine."

"That'll be a dollar eighty-six."

"Uh-oh, I ain't got it."

"Then it will be four-fifty."

They both shared a laugh as he handed over his money. Behind the counter at Kim's was a large stainless steel milk refrigerator with one serving spigot, the red sign above the spigot holding a single word: WHOLE.

Edmonds and I finished up our breakfasts: eggs, ham, grits, and biscuits with white milk gravy. Skink pawed with his spoon at his milkless oatmeal. The dress code required blue jeans and baseball caps advertising various farm implements, and so Skink and I stood out more than a bit, Skink in his brown suit, me in my shirtsleeves. The chief sat stolidly in his flannel shirt and green John Deere baseball cap. Edmonds's name had been in Jesse's letters to Hailey. It hadn't taken much to look him up in the Pierce telephone directory, and it hadn't taken much more to get him out to Kim's. Edmonds, now retired, seemed to welcome the company and was willing enough to talk about Hailey. Trying to get people to speak to me was pretty much the extent of the wondrous plan I had wrought: I would take my cue from the letters, talk to the principals involved, try to shake something loose.

I said I had a plan; I didn't say it was brilliant.

In the middle of breakfast I had dropped the picture of the boy in his baseball uniform onto the center of our table. I figured that might start things shaking, and maybe it did. When Edmonds saw it, he closed his eyes for a moment and exhaled the name. "Jesse Sterrett."

"What happened?" I asked after he had described the corpse.

"Who the hell knows?" said Edmonds. "That damn quarry. In Jesse's time they necked and did their drugs there. In my time we necked and drank our beer there. Now they neck and do who knows what there. We've got a fence all around and signs warning everyone to stay away, warning that the rock faces have grown unsteady over time, but I suppose there never was a danger sign that teenagers didn't ignore. We were forever patrolling, shining in our spotlights, but it didn't do any good. It was only a matter of time before something happened. Best as we could tell, he fell down, cracked his head, and then tumbled into the water."

"An accident?" said Skink.

"Yep."

"Everyone thought so?" I pressed.

"All that mattered, me and the coroner."

"Doc Robinson."

"That's right."

"How about the boy's father?"

"You know parents. If a kid crashes the car, it must be a dangerous turn that should have been fixed years ago. If the kid busts a
knee in football, it's the coach's fault. Always looking for someone
to blame. How else could you lawyers stay in business? Jesse's dad
didn't want to believe that his son was out at the quarry smoking
that marihuana and just got careless."

"Jesse Sterrett didn't smoke marihuana," I said.

Edmonds was taken up short. "How do you know that?"

"And didn't you find it peculiar that a week after Jesse is in a brutal fight that puts a boy in the hospital, he's found dead?"

Chief Edmonds squinted his hard blue eyes at me. "Come again
with what you're doing here?"

"We're just trying to understand what happened to Hailey. We
have the idea . . ." I glanced at Skink. "I have the idea that there
might be some connection between what happened to Hailey and
what happened to Jesse Sterrett."

"I'm sorry as hell about Hailey. I knew her father, played cards
with her uncle, and what's happened with her sister is just plain
sad. I'm sorry as hell, but I'm not surprised. She had a wild streak
no one could tame."

"What is it that happened with her sister?"

Edmonds looked at me and pursed his lips. "I'm willing to tell
you what I know about Hailey, but that's as far as I go. Though I'll
tell you this for free: There's nothing between what happened to her
and what happened to that boy."

"Weren't Hailey and Jesse going together when he died?"

"Not as I recall. I seem to recall that Jesse had other interests."

"Like baseball."

"Just other interests. And as I remember it, Hailey was seeing
someone else at the time. That fight, it was just something between
two boys. It's not unusual 'round here. This one just got a little out
of hand. From what I learned, they had been at each other's throats
for years."

"Jesse and Grady," I said.

"That's right. Grady Pritchett. He was like a spur in Jesse's side, never gave it a moment's rest. Two guys hate each other like that, you don't need a reason to fight. From what I could tell, the fight was Grady's doing. That's why we let Jesse go back to school and play ball after just a few days."

"And you never thought there might be a link between the fight and the death?"

"Like I said, it looked like an accident to us. But we did our jobs. Police work's the same out here as anywhere else. We brought in Grady for questioning. Said he knew nothing about it, said it convincingly, too. He'd been in trouble before, and he had lied to us before, and this time looked to me he wasn't lying. But still we checked him out. Oh, we did ourselves a full investigation. Doc Robinson insisted, and I wouldn't have it any other way. On the night of the accident Grady said he was with someone at the time. We went out and proved up his alibi. Witness we talked to was as definite as could be. So that was that."

I leaned forward. "Who was the witness?"

Edmonds took a sip of his coffee. "Hailey," he said. "And she didn't have no doubt about it."

32

"**SO EXPLAIN** this to me," I said to Skink as we drove out of Pierce, following the path of the river. "Jesse is crazy in love with Hailey, he promises to protect Hailey from Grady Pritchett."

"This all from the letters?"

"From what I could tell; Jesse wasn't exactly a Hemingway when it came to clarity. So he puts Grady in the hospital, and it sounds like the next thing he's going to do is put Grady in the morgue. And then, boom, Jesse is found dead and Grady's alibi is Hailey."

"Dames," said Skink.

"Dames? Dames? Who uses the word 'dames' anymore?"

"I do."

"What were you, a sailor?"

"My daddy was. Anyways, you never can tell with a dame. First they blow hot, then they blow cold. It's all the same to me, just so long as they're blowing."

"Your level of enlightenment is dazzling."

"Thank you."

We took a right at the Foodmart and drove over a one-lane bridge, as per our instructions. There were three roads leading off to the right, we took the one with the steepest climb up a ravine jutting into the side of the mountain. The road switchbacked once and then again as it climbed the ravine. With a sudden jolt the asphalt gave out, and we were riding now on dirt, soaked with grease and hardened with pebbles. I checked the directions once again as the car shimmied and shook in its climb.

"It should be just up ahead," I said, and then there it was, a ragged metal mailbox with the the address on the side, two ruts shooting off sharply to the right creating their own switchback as they rose deeper into the yaw of the ravine. A sign was posted on a tree by the drive, the words painted roughly in red:

NO TURNAROUND

I checked the address and then looked over to Skink. "Guess it's all right to go in, since we have no intention of turning around."

I steered the car into the drive and slowly rumbled up the pitted ruts. At a sharp turn in the climb there was another sign, this one nailed onto a post:

NO SALESMEN

"You selling anything?" I asked Skink.

"Not me, mate."

"Me neither."

I continued up, moving now out of the ravine toward the river, only much higher. The road was getting steeper, my ears popped, and I didn't like that there was no barrier on the far edge of the drive, that one bad bounce could send us tumbling. On the hill above us I spied a rusted old truck, wheels missing, suspended in a mad pursuit down the side of the mountain. God knows what was stopping it from skidding off the hill and crushing us. In its windshield was another sign, this one, too, painted in red, a blood red I now noticed:

NO HUNTING

"It's a good thing we left the shotguns and coon dogs at home," I said.

Farther up the road there was a scraggly grove of weed trees with a sign nailed onto a thin trunk:

NO TRESPASSING

"We don't seem to be welcome," said Skink. "What again is the purpose of our visit?"

"To trespass."

"I feel so much better now. Look up there."

Another sign:

GO THE HELL AWAY

"That's to the point, at least," I said. "Can't say he's not being clear."

I slowed down now, made two final turns up the slope, the car dipping into the ruts, its undercarriage savaged by thick weeds and loose rock. The drive rose through the trees until it ended at a turnaround. An old brown truck was parked there, facing us. Ragged wooden stairs led up to the left, and at the front of the path was one final sign:

BEWARE OF DOGS

I didn't have time to come up with another weak witticism before something hard slammed into my side of the car and suddenly, at my window, a giant snarling face was baring its teeth and yelping like a maniac.

I turned to look at Skink. His head was thrown back, his mouth a rictus of fear. On the other side of his window a savage face grimaced, saliva falling in streams from yellow teeth.

"Let's get out of here," he said.

"You don't like dogs?"

"Not ones that are trying to bite my noggin off."

"Oh, these little pooches don't mean any harm," I said as the black dog on my side continued its yelping and the brown dog on Skink's side snarled and snapped in frustration at the glass between his teeth and Skink's neck. "They just want us to rub them on their bellies."

"Turn around, mate, and get us out of here," said Skink, a real panic in his voice.

"Not yet." I banged the horn and waited. The black dog danced at the side of the car and kept up its yelping. The brown dog smashed its muzzle against the glass and snapped its jaws. The car rocked.

"Please, please," said Skink. "Turn around."

"What is it with you and dogs?" I said.

"Let's just say I had an unpleasant encounter with a bulldog in my youth."

"I hear once they chomp their teeth around something, you have to kill them to get them off."

"Get us the hell out of here."

Just then a shot rang out.

Skink and I ducked down and stayed down.

"Maybe you should pull out your gun to be safe," I said.

"I didn't bring no gun."

"I thought you were bringing a gun."

"Across state lines on a fool's errand? I don't think so, mate."

"What good are you without a gun?"

"Plenty damn good. I've got fists of iron and nerves of steel."

"Except when it comes to dogs."

I cautiously raised my head and peeked out my window. On the staircase leading up the hill a man now stood, cradling a shotgun, the dogs sitting calmly on the step beneath him. He was an old man, thick and unshaved, sparse clumps of hair standing out from his huge head. I sat up slowly, my hands raised to show I held nothing in them. I whispered for Skink to do the same.

I leaned over to open the window. The gun jerked in the man's arms. I sat up straight again, gesturing my intentions. The gun settled, and the man nodded.

"Are you Mr. Sterrett?" I said, sticking my head carefully out the now open window, my hands still in sight.

"Who's looking for him?" said the man.

"My name is Victor Carl. I'm a lawyer from Philadlephia, and I haven't come to help him or to sue him. I simply have some questions."

"Didn't you see them signs?"

"Yes I did, I surely did. But I'm not a salesman or a hunter. I didn't see a sign saying no lawyers."

"Guess I'll be putting one up tomorrow."

"But until then I'd like to ask Mr. Sterrett some questions about his son."

"Which one?"

"How many does he have?"

"Five boys, three girls."

I whistled. "And Mrs. Sterrett?"

"Gone now going on five years."

"I guess the eight kids wore her out."

"Not the ones still around, they didn't. It was worrying about the ones that warn't."

"I've come to talk about Jesse."

"He's one of the ones that warn't."

"I know he is, Mr. Sterrett. I'm trying to find out why."

"Hell, I can tell you why."

"I was hoping you could."

"You a connoisseur of fine wine, boy?"

"Not really," I said.

"That's handy, 'cause I ain't got none. But I got some corn liquor that I save for special occasions and, you being a lawyer and my dogs being hungry, I'm guessing this qualifies."

"Is it any good?"

"Course it ain't no good, but it works."

"It will pin our ears back, is that it?"

"Like six-inch nails."

"That would be just wonderful. Especially for my friend here," I gestured at Skink, "who could use a little cosmetic surgery. But I was wondering if you might help him out a bit. My friend is afraid of dogs."

"Afraid of these old hounds? Tell your friend Fire and Brimstone here wouldn't hurt a soul. All you need do is rub they bellies and they'll be your slaves for life."

THE HOUSE was just a ways up the path, perched on the hill as if it was getting ready to jump off and fly. Or maybe jump off and not fly. Its walls listed, its paint peeled, its porch sagged low in the middle. Weeds sprouted tall around it, and to the side sat a pile of old metal, twisted fencing, rusted buckets, a refrigerator with its door still dangerously on. We sat out on the wreck of a porch, avoiding the patches where the wood had collapsed through. We each held a glass jar of the corn liquor, a clear, toxic brew that burned all the way down the throat and then set fire to the stomach. I liked it, actually, and was afraid of it all at the same time. Sterrett sat on a big old setting chair, the jug resting by his side, I sat on a crate, Skink sat stiffly on a rocking chair, the dogs curled at his feet, as if Skink's discomfort was for them like an old familiar blanket. And the view from the porch, well, the view from the porch was astounding.

It flew down into the valley, capturing a swath of green pasture and the tiny sway of cattle before it picked up the flow of the river, with its white froth pouring around jutting rocks. A hawk soared beneath us on patrol, gliding between the sheer cliff faces of the mountains rising on either side. We sat and sipped and listened to the silence, which wasn't actually a silence at all but a riot of insectile rattles and bird twitters, the scurrying footfalls of rodents, the strange, forbidding rustle of the undergrowth.

"You could sell this view," I said.

"Yep," said Mr. Sterrett, "but why would I?"

"The dogs seem to like you, Phil," I said.

"My luck," he said.

"What was it that bulldog did to you anyway?" I said.

He scowled and didn't answer.

Sterrett said, "I heard tell once they get a bite on you—"

"I hear that one more time," interrupted Skink, "I'm going to burst a vessel."

"Skink apparently had himself some sort of childhood calamity," I said.

Sterrett looked at me, then at Skink, then back at me. "I know some about them childhood calamities." He raised his jar slightly. "You want more?"

I took a sip from my jar, felt the liquor roil down my throat and ignite the eggs and grits and grease of my breakfast, and shook my head no. Skink glanced at the dogs, drained his jar, and held it out for more. Sterrett hoisted the jug and poured.

"I understand that Jesse was a ballplayer," I said.

"Yep."

"Any good?"

"Damn good."

"Did you ever play?"

"Some, but not as good as him."

"It must have been hard, when he died."

"He didn't die."

I glanced at Skink. "No?"

"He was kilt. Simple as that."

"The police chief and the coroner ruled it an accident."

"Yes they did."

"But you don't believe them."

"No I don't."

"Why's that, Mr. Sterrett? What makes you think they were mistaken?"

"Warn't no mistake."

Sterrett took a sip from his jar and then rose without speaking and walked slowly off the porch and to the rear of the shack. I stood to follow, but one of the dogs, Fire or Brimstone, I didn't know which was which, raised his neck and growled, and I sat right down again. We waited a few moments and a few moments more. Skink looked down at the dogs and reached a hand slowly to touch the fur on the black dog's back. The dog picked up his head, Skink jerked his hand away. Sterrett came back around the side of the house, made his slow way up the steps and into his chair.

"So you think it was a conspiracy, is that it?" I said, starting right again where we had left off.

"Let's just say they was all in the game."

"I don't understand."

"The card game. High-stakes poker, every other Thursday at the Chevy dealership. Chief Edmonds, Doc Robinson, Gus Pritchett, Larry Cutlip, and whatever other fool they could get to join 'em. Word was sometimes even Reverend Henson sat in, throwing away his paycheck."

"Pritchett?"

"That's right. He owned the dealership, the five and dime, the Quick Mart, and most of the rest of the county, not excluding the judge."

"Let me guess. He's Grady Pritchett's father."

"Was. Dead now."

"So was he a winner or a loser in the game?"

"He was rich enough it didn't much matter. What mattered was that Doc Robinson was a drunk and Edmonds never saw a straight he wouldn't draw inside to, and the two of them was in so damn deep they couldn't see the stars 'cause they pants was pulled too high."

"They owed money to Cutlip, the gambler?"

"That's right. And the thing about old Larry was, he was a hard man."

"A man you didn't want to stiff."

Sterrett shook his head. "And right after my boy's death, Cutlip falls into money and busts out to them bright lights in Vegas, and them boys, they rule it all an accident."

Skink's hand was now halted in the air just above the black dog's back. He took another sip and then reached down, tentatively scratching the fur. "Who were they protecting?" he asked.

"That's the question, isn't it?"

"You said you knew who killed your son," I said.

"Never said such a thing. Don't know for sure."

"But you have suspicions."

"I might, yes."

"You think it was Grady Pritchett?"

"Ain't right to start spouting off without knowing for sure."

"But you think it was Grady and that his father bought off the chief and the coroner by paying their debts to Cutlip."

"Never said such a thing. Don't know nothing for sure. This man you're representing, did he really kill Hailey?"

"No," I said. "I don't think so."

"What do you think about it?" said Sterrett, talking now to Skink.

"Oh, I think he did it, all right," said Skink, bending over to scratch the underside of the black dog's neck. "I think he killed her dead, and now his lawyer is trying to wiggle his arse free."

I stared hard for a moment at Skink, hurt, as if betrayed.

"Well, he asked," said Skink.

"See there," said Sterrett, turning back to me. "A man never does know for sure. If I knew for sure, I'd a done something about it by now. But I can tell you this, it warn't no accident."

I didn't say anything, hoping he would interject himself into the uncomfortable silence, but he didn't. He stayed quiet, as if the silence wasn't uncomfortable to him, and we listened to nature settle into the afternoon as the corn liquor settled into our blood. We sat there for a long time in the quiet. The brown dog scooted around Skink's legs and whined quietly until Skink scratched his neck, too.

"You know where Grady Pritchett is now?" I asked finally.

"He owns a car lot out in Lewis County. Left to him by his daddy in the will."

"How's it doing?"

"Not so good, I hear," he said with a slight smile.

"You know what kind of car he drives?"

"Black Chevy pickup, front right wheel well all beat to hell."

"I bet, Mr. Sterrett, you know the license plate, too?"

"I won't deny it. No telling what things you might learn through the years that turn doubts into certainties."

"You know, maybe I'm crazed, but I could have sworn you told me you knew who did it?"

"No, I did not," he said, sitting back.

The black dog raised his head, let out a contented moan, and turned over to let Skink scratch his belly. The brown dog followed suit and Skink subdued them both with soft rubs. "He didn't say he knew *who* killed his son," said Skink. "He said he knew *why*."

I turned from Skink's seduction of the dogs to look back at the old man. "That's right, isn't it?"

Sterrett rubbed his thumb along the edge of the jar.

"So tell me, Mr. Sterrett, why did your son die?"

He waited a moment, took a drink, let the alcohol settle. Maybe he had taken too much of the liquor, because as he sat there and thought, his jaw began to quiver.

"I loved my boy," he said. "But it's not always an easy thing to show. And when you're working too damn hard and fighting to feed and clothe a family, sometimes you figure the showing can wait. When he was young, Jesse had a friend he could go to, but then they got confused about things and the friend died, and Jesse, I think Jesse was never the same. I tried, I did. But I knew things then maybe I shouldn't have known and wasn't under as much control as I might have been. How do you show a boy that you love him still when every look out of his eyes is full of sorrow and every word out of your mouth comes out in anger? I didn't know the answer, and I live with it every day of my life. It weighs me down like it weighed down my Sarah until she just let go. I thought I was showing what I felt by arguing with him. I thought he could tell from the volume how much I cared. But volume ain't enough. Listening maybe might have been better. That's why he died. 'Cause I didn't know how to show him that I loved him."

"You blame yourself," I said.

"What you don't find at home, you look elsewhere for. And generally you find it in the worst places possible. And that's what he done. He found hisself a girl that had nothing in her but pain and hurt and the seeds of destruction. You could almost tell it just by looking at her, that might have been the attraction, for all I know. But that's where he went looking for what he wasn't finding at home."

"You're talking about Hailey Prouix," I said. "You think she killed him?"

"Don't know who it was, I told you. But I know she was at the heart of what happened to him, know it in my bones. I won't say I'm not sorry she's dead, but I know where she's going. And I'll tell you this: Even the devil he best stay clear of her. Yes, sir. Even the devil."

I DROVE unsteadily down the rutted drive that fell from the Sterrett house, weaving more than I meant to and skirting the sheer edge of the ravine as we bounced around the ruts. The two dogs kept us company, running alongside, yelping their good-byes to Skink.

"You made yourself a couple of friends," I said.

"Steeling my nerves to cozy up to a pair of bloodthirsty hounds, I was. Best advice I ever got from my daddy: Muster your courage and face your fears."

"Looked to me what you were mustering was that corn liquor?"

"Nah, I was just being polite. But truth to tell, I could use myself a nap right about now."

"We've got someone else to see. You know, I can't get that image out of my mind, Lucifer sliding respectfully out of the way as Hailey exits the elevator at the bottom floor."

"That was the liquor talking."

"I don't think so. He truly thinks she was evil."

"He's entitled."

"What do you think?"

"Girl I knew," said Skink, "was hard as dog's teeth and twice as sharp, but she wasn't evil. There was a softness in the middle, is all.

There was too much need to her. When something's soft and needy like that, it ain't much of a trick to twist it around."

"You think she was manipulated?"

"Don't know."

"By Grady Pritchett and his rich father?"

"Money has a way, don't it?"

"So what do you think of our little murder case now?"

"You mean the boy in the quarry? The cop says it was an accident. The father says it was murder. Hard to tell, though what you told me of them letters makes it seem the father might be more on the right. Still, I don't see what this one has to do with the other."

"Neither do I. That's why I think it's time to go to church."

"You reduced to looking for a sign from the Almighty Himself?"

"Pretty much," I said.

THE BUILDING was solid and white with narrow arched windows and a steeple high enough for you to know it was a church but not so high as to look unduly prideful. Beside the door was the symbol of a cross with a red sail attached. PIERCE UNITED METHODIST CHURCH, read the sign out front. REV. THEODORE H. HENSON. SUNDAY SCHOOL 10:00 A.M. WORSHIP SERVICES 11:00 A.M. 1 AND 3 SUNDAY. WE BLESS HIS NAME, HALLELUJAH.

The Reverend Henson, as one would expect, was on his knees, but not in supplication. We found him outside in the rear of the church, tending to the flowers in the beds alongside the path that led from the church to its well-shaded cemetery farther up the hill. His hands were moving like creatures in the loam, weeding, smoothing, pulling out withered stalks to make room for those still thriving.

When he heard us coming, he looked up and his face registered dismay for just a moment, as if the harbingers of a doom he had long been expecting had just arrived, before his features lit up in an inviting smile. He was a short, thin man, with nervous hands and pointy features that had aged sourly. He stood up when he heard his name, brushed the dirt from his palms, reached out to shake.

"You'd be the gentlemen from Philadelphia," he said in a sharp, high voice.

"Yes, we are," I said.

"Good. I've been expecting you. Why don't you wait inside the church, give me a chance to clean myself a bit before we talk."

"Don't be changing for our benefit, Padre," said Skink.

"I was pretty much done here, but if you'd like instead, we could take a walk."

"That would be perfect," I said. We followed him through the path defined by the beds he had just been working in, and I made the introductions.

"I hope you don't mind if we take our walk here," he said as he led us into the quiet of the church's graveyard.

The headstones were a mixture of weathered limestone markers, narrow and thin, and newer, thicker memorials, the smoothed granite still shiny. The grass was long and uneven, oaks were scattered among the plots like sentinels standing ramrod straight.

"When I first joined this congregation a few decades ago, I was intimidated by this place. It wasn't the fact of death that it so starkly represented as much as the history. I didn't know these people, didn't know these families. My parishioners came to me as blank slates that left me feeling inadequate to their needs, and I felt that sense of inadequacy most strongly here, in this place, where the pasts of which I knew nothing were represented by these stones."

As he walked, he gestured to the stones and the names upon them: Carpenter, Bright, Skidmore, McKinnon, Perrine. The older had the dates of birth and death carved on them, though the printing on some was so weathered as to be unreadable. ROY CUDDY, said one I could just make out. BORN JULY 1907, DIED MARCH 1908. It was impossible not to feel the same history the reverend talked about as we walked alongside him.

"But now that I have a surer sense of the past, now that I recognize the names and the people buried beneath the earth, I find this to be a place of great comfort. As many as I've buried in this dirt, I've baptized more, boys and girls with the same surnames as on these stones. You want to learn of the circle of life, Mr. Carl, you don't need see a Disney movie. Just come and take a walk within any church graveyard in any small town."

It was a nice little talk from Reverend Henson, touching and real, but it was clear he had choreographed it for our benefit. Having learned from his poker buddy, Chief Edmonds, that we were in town, he decided to spend the day gardening so that we would find him out back and we could take this very walk and hear this very speech. Because the subtext of what he was saying was as clear as his words themselves. There is history in this town, Mr. Carl, centuries of history that you neither know nor could possibly understand. Be careful what you conclude, be careful how you judge, for in the scheme of all things you know nothing.

"I was so very sorry to hear about Hailey," said Reverend Henson. "She had such promise and had overcome so much."

"Overcome what?" I asked.

"The death of her father. He's buried over there, along with his wife." He pointed to a headstone in the corner of the yard. "The death of Hailey's friend Jesse, which I understand you've been asking questions about. That's his stone over there. He's buried next to his mother, brother, and sister Amy, who was born with serious problems and didn't make it past the third week, bless her tiny soul. Jesse's death had a profound effect on Hailey, I can attest, and sent her into a spiritual crisis I'm not sure she ever came out of. And then of course there was the general level of the poverty into which she fell after her father died, which drags down so many of our best and brightest."

"Were you close to Hailey?"

"I don't think anyone was ever truly close to Hailey. She was very tight within herself, but we talked on occasion, and I tried to help her as much as I could."

"Getting through his death."

"And other things, yes."

"I heard she won a church scholarship for her education."

"That's right," said Henson, beaming. "She was a very smart girl, and I was glad to get it for her. She deserved it."

"You mentioned a spiritual crisis."

"I did, didn't I, but I can't really talk about it now, can I? That was between Hailey and her God."

"You know I've been asking not only about Hailey but about the death of Jesse Sterrett."

"You believe there may be some connection?"

"I think there must be, yes. What do you think happened to Jesse in that quarry, Reverend?"

"I don't know, Mr. Carl. The police said it was an accident. Jesse's father has other ideas. All I know is that it was a terrible tragedy. I don't think it's my place to go around assigning blame."

"Do you think Grady Pritchett was involved?"

"No," he said quickly, with a sureness I hadn't expected. "No, he was not involved. And if there is anything you bring back from our conversation, I want you to know that."

"How are you so sure?"

There was a pause while Reverend Henson reached down and pulled out a weed that was sprouting next to one of the headstones. "He had an alibi."

"Hailey was his alibi."

"That's right," said the reverend. "And she wouldn't have lied to protect Grady if he had been involved."

"No, maybe not. I've been looking for Hailey's sister, what was her name?"

"Is. Roylynn. A very sweet girl, smart as a whip, smarter than anyone, maybe even than Hailey, but she was never as strong as her sister. I've tried to help her, too, but her problems proved to be beyond my talents."

"Do you know where I could find her?"

"Yes, I do."

"Do you mind telling us?"

"Yes, I do."

"Why is that?"

"Because, Mr. Carl, you are bringing trouble that she doesn't need. We're a strong town, we handled the deaths and we can handle your questions, but Roylynn has always been a fragile girl. We watch out for our own, even the weakest, and we tried to take care of her as best we could, but she was always very tender, too tender. She had pretty much slipped out of the world anyway when word came about Hailey. I fear its effect upon her."

"You don't know? You haven't spoken with her?"

"I have, yes, but the answers are not always clear. She is being well taken care of, that I know. She is in a place that's more home to her than here."

"Where?"

"Mr. Carl, I know you have your job to do, and I respect that. I have no opinion about who did what up there in Philadelphia, whether the man you represent really killed Hailey. I have faith in the workings of our legal system, and I'll leave it to that. And I don't mind you coming here and stirring pots, acting all self-righteous as if you're the only one interested in pursuing justice in a case fifteen years old, chasing after ghosts. We all do what we need to do. But I'm not going to send you on to that poor girl. I'm not. You'll break her in two without even knowing what you're doing, and then you'll leave and go back to Philadelphia, and who would be left to pick up the pieces? Leave her alone and let her heal."

I was about to tell Reverend Henson that I understood his concern, I was about to apologize for our intrusion and rudeness. He was right, I had been going on my little hunt without concern for whom it might have affected. And the news about Hailey's sister had thrown me. Why hadn't I been concerned for her? Why hadn't it ever crossed my mind how hard it must have been for a twin to lose her sister? He had succinctly put me in my place, shamed me, actually, and I was about to slink away like the worm under the rock I felt myself just then to be when Skink spoke up.

"You play cards, Padre?" asked Skink from the center of the graveyard. He had wandered away during my questioning, sauntered from grave to grave as if totally uninterested in what I was doing, but now here came his question, so simple and yet so sharply pointed: Do you play cards?

"I know how."

"I'm not talking crazy eights here," said Skink. "I'm talking poker. Seven stud, Texas hold 'em, Maltese cross. You ever play poker for money?"

"Not anymore."

"But you used to, didn't you, Padre? You played in that game, didn't you, with that fellow Edmonds, and old Doc Robinson, and

Larry Cutlip, and this Pritchett, the rich one we been hearing so much about?"

"I sat in once or twice, yes."

"How'd you do?"

Henson laughed. "Not so well, I'm afraid."

"How about the others?"

"Gus Pritchett knew how to handle himself, and Larry, well, he took it seriously."

"It sounds like a tough game, it does. Sounds like one I'm glad I missed. But here's the thing, Padre, did all you chums, you poker buddies, ever get together over a nice friendly hand of five-card draw, jacks to open, trips to win, ever get together and talk about Jesse Sterrett being murdered and Grady Pritchett being a murderer and what you all was going to do about it?"

"No, of course not. I told you that Grady did nothing."

"You sure? Because something here, it seems funny to me. You got Edmonds and Robinson deep in poker debt to Cutlip, a man who likes to get paid. And then this Jesse Sterrett gets his head smashed and he falls into the lake at the quarry. Edmonds said he looked like some pale German banger when they pulled him out. And it's after they pull him out that all the strange happenings, they happen. Like first Cutlip falls into money and leaves. And Edmonds and Robinson, their foul-tempered creditor suddenly gone from town, call the whole thing an accident. And then you tell us you know it's not Grady, like you know it for sure, and I begin to wonder *how* you could know it for sure, and then I begin to wonder how high was your gambling debts from that friendly little game. And to get me even more curious, I learn that Hailey stands up and alibis this Grady Pritchett. Grady Pritchett, who had just been put into the hospital by our friend Jesse, probably because of Hailey in the first place. See, I knew her, too, and she had that effect on men. Grady Pritchett, whose dad is the richest man in town. Grady Pritchett. Now, why would Hailey make up an alibi for Grady Pritchett if he killed her friend Jesse? She wouldn't, would she? Of course not, except after she alibis Grady, she ends up winning a church scholarship. How does that happen? How does a bare-arsed small-town congregation like this one happen to get its hands on enough money to give a girl like Hailey a scholarship? You don't even gots enough money to mow the lawn of your damn grave-yard, and yet there you are stuffing enough cash in her pockets to put her through college and law school. How does that happen, Padre? Tell us that."

Henson stared at him for a long time. "You've gotten it wrong."

"Maybe," said Skink, smiling broadly with his pearly teeth, a look of triumph on his scarred face. "But not all wrong, did I?"

Reverend Henson stood there for a moment more, rubbing his hands, and then said, "Well, now. This was a fine little chat, but I must be off. Pressing obligations. 'Twas nice to have met you both. Come again." And then, before we could respond, he turned and hurried out of the graveyard.

I walked over to Skink and looked down at the gravestone. In big letters carved into the marble was the name Sterrett.

"Quite a performance," I said.

"It's not the lying that gets to me—lying I can take, who lies bet-ter than myself? But I hate to be played for the fool."

"So what do you think?"

"I don't know. Who the hell knows? But I'd sure as hell like to learn who the padre is ringing up on the parish phone right about now."

34

THE LOG Cabin was a rough-looking roadhouse on the way to Clarksburg, just a gray shack off the side of an empty two-lane highway. The windows were dark, so you couldn't see whether or not there was anyone inside, but the sign advertising LEGAL BEVERAGES was lit, as was the neon MAC'S LIGHT sign. A few scattered vehicles were parked willy-nilly on the gravel parking lot that spilled out to the side of the building. I walked from my car, across the gravel, and patted the dented front wheel well of a black Chevy pickup. Then I loosened my tie, rubbed my eyes, mussed my hair, and headed inside.

The place smelled of sawdust and old smoke, of spilt beer and too many long nights that should have ended early. When I entered into the smoky red darkness, heads swiveled to get a look and then swiveled away with a distinct lack of interest. There was a couple drinking quietly in the corner, there was an old man at the bar hunched over an empty shot glass, there were two kids in a booth in the back, baseball caps drawn low, long legs stretched out arrogantly on the wooden seats. And then there was the man I had come looking for, sitting in the middle of the bar, sinking softly into middle age, a cloud of despair about his head. I had dismissed him as a possibility the first time I glanced his way, thought maybe my man was one of the kids in the corner, but then I realized those kids were not long out of high school. In my mind that's what Grady Pritchett still looked like, young and arrogant in jeans and baseball cap, full of piss and vinegar, even if with his family's money the vinegar was balsamic, but time works its black magic on us all. I eliminated one by one the other possibilities and was left with my man at the bar. I hitched up my pants and sauntered over to a stool one away from him.

"What'll it be?" said the bartender, a stocky gray man with a dented nose, who looked like he had seen trouble in his life and pounded it into submission.

"A draft," I said, pulling out a twenty from my wallet, "and keep 'em coming."

The barkeep nodded, and a moment later a coaster was spun in front of me, a full glass set atop the coaster, and the twenty changed into a pile of lesser bills and coins.

"Tough day?" said the bartender.

"They're all tough." I took a long draught and kept draining until the glass was emptied. I dropped it down upon the coaster. It wasn't a moment before the glass was filled again.

The bartender drifted to the end of the bar with the television turned to some lurid local news. The kids in the booth laughed out loud. I turned to the man next to me and said, "You know any good places to eat around here?"

"Where you headed?" said Grady Pritchett.

"Clarksburg."

"The Rib-Eye up the road a ways. They make a steak almost worth eating."

"Thanks," I said and took a long drink of my beer.

When the bartender came over to refill the beer, I gestured him to give the man next to me whatever he was drinking.

Grady Pritchett had a paunch and his hair was going. You could see he had once maybe been good-looking, but his face was now all bloated and shiny. He wore gray dress pants and a short-sleeved shirt with a tie, and there was a ring on his finger, but he was in no hurry to get home to the wifey-poo. Life had happened to Grady Pritchett in the worst way.

"Thanks, man," he said to me when a fresh Scotch and soda was placed before him. "Where you from?"

"Chicago."

"You come down this ways much?"

"First time."

Grady Pritchett raised his glass. "Welcome to paradise."

I was an investigator, working for a Chicago law firm that specialized in trusts and estates, seeking out missing heirs. That was the story. Generally we could do what we needed over the phone or on the Internet, but sometimes you just had get out there yourself and check the records that needed to be checked or, more important, meet up with the heirs and review with them their options. I dreaded these trips, the long roads and cheap hotels, the dust in the old county record rooms, the local lawyers who started sticking their noses in something that was none of their business. I didn't tell him all this in one swoop of words, that's not the way it's done. But it was there, the whole story, there in the sighs, the silences, the weary slump of my back. In Charleston I found the death certificate I was looking for. In a few small towns along the way I had talked to some people who needed talking to. In Clarksburg there was a lady who refused to tell me over the phone the whereabouts of another lady who was up for a pretty nifty sum. In Gettysburg I needed to check on a old man who'd disappeared from his nursing home six months ago. And then in Philadelphia I had the lovely task of trying to sift through three generations of Olaffsons to find the one that really mattered. I had been putting it off, this trip, letting the work pile up until I could put it off no longer. There were deadlines looming and commissions due, if certain parties that I found signed certain documents. So here I was on Route 19, making my way from Charleston to Clarksburg and thinking for the thousandth time I should find myself a more congenial line of work, like slaughtering pigs.

"You know any places to eat in Clarksburg?" I asked.

"The Holiday Inn ain't all bad."

"How about Gettysburg."

"Never been. They got that Civil War battlefield there."

"Yes they do. I'll be taking pictures for the kiddies. What about Philadelphia, you ever been in Philadelphia?"

"Sure. Lots of times."

"Business?"

"Sort of."

"That's the best kind, isn't it? I used to have a girl from Philadelphia with a mouth like wet velvet. I never been there, but it got so every time I heard the name Philadelphia I popped a woody."

"What happened to her?"

"Who, the girl from Philadelphia?"

"Yeah."

"Dead."

Grady Pritchett's face paled for an instant, and his mouth quivered.

"Cancer," I said. "It just ate through her insides like it had teeth, but she was married to someone else, so I was glad to let him hold her hand through it to the end. Still, when I hear Philadephia . . ."

There was a long silence, where Grady and I just sat and drank. Maybe he was thinking about an old girlfriend in Philly who now was dead. Maybe he was thinking about how it was that he had caused it. See, I had come up with a theory about Grady Pritchett. What if Hailey Prouix, in her youth, had concocted an alibi for Grady Pritchett in exchange for a college and graduate school education from his wealthy father? And what if, later, when pressed by Guy Forrest for some missing cash, Hailey Prouix had gone back to the source that had worked so well before, the Pritchetts, to fill her empty accounts? And what if Hailey Prouix had told Grady she needed the money and would recant the alibi if he refused, and what if Grady had decided that enough was enough, and what if he had gone to Philadelphia himself to finish the job? They say after the first killing it gets easier, and it seemed to me that maybe Jesse Sterrett was the first for Grady Pritchett, and so killing Hailey Prouix might not have been so hard after that. It was just a theory, sure, but I had to contain my anger as I sat beside the man who might have murdered Hailey Prouix.

"You from around here?" I said.

"You won't find too many tourists in this place. I live in Weston."

"Born there?"

"No."

"Where?"

"Pierce."

"Pierce? Pierce, West Viriginia? Now, how did I hear about Pierce?"

"You didn't."

"No, I did, I did."

"No one ever has."

"Let me see. Pierce. I think I heard about some family there up for a small inheritance. Is that possible? Nothing much, but it turned out one of the kids I was looking for died in a quarry."

Grady didn't say anything, he just stared straight ahead.

"He got his head smashed in and fell into the water there. You ever hear anything like that?"

"I think you're asking too many questions."

"Just trying to be friendly," I said, showing him my palms. "No need to come at me like a block of stone."

Grady gripped his drink and narrowed his eyes.

"I suppose that was an unfortunate term to use," I said, "considering the circumstances."

"I had heard there were two of you asking questions."

"Yeah, well, tonight I'm solo. So tell me something, Grady, which of your pals was worried enough to give you the warning?"

"Leave me the hell alone, okay? That's all I'm asking."

Just then the bartender leaned in between us, staring at me with his gray eyes even as he spoke to Grady. "Is there a problem here, Mr. Pritchett?"

"No, Jimmy, I was just leaving, thanks," said Grady, sliding off his stool and dumping some cash on the bar before turning to me. "This is what I'll tell you, same thing I told them fifteen years ago. I had nothing to do with what happened to Jesse Sterrett. Not a thing. There was bad blood, yeah, but still, I didn't have nothing to do with what happened. What happened to him destroyed me as bad as it did him, worse, because I had to keep living with all the doubts, but I had nothing to do with it. Believe me or not, I don't give a damn, but leave me the hell alone."

He wasn't halfway to the door before I jumped off my stool and started after him. He glanced back, saw me coming after him, spun around and punched me in the face.

The blow sent me reeling to the floor. The pain exploded from a dot beneath my eye to cover the whole of my face. I turned over onto my back, sprawled backward, and watched as the door slammed shut.

"Damn it," I said out loud. As fast as I could scramble to my feet, I followed him out the door. It had grown dark while I was inside, and the artificial light in the lot was feeble, but I could still see the front door slamming on the black pickup truck and Grady Pritchett's silhouette in the front seat.

I ran straight at it.

Grady was leaning forward, fighting to jab his key into the slot beneath the steering wheel.

I dashed at the truck, grabbed the handle, pulled. The door flew open and threw me off balance.

The engine turned over and shook to life.

I lunged at the open door, grabbed Grady Pritchett's collar, pulled him right out of the front seat until his face slammed into the gravel.

"That'll teach you to use your damn seat belt, you bastard," I yelled as I stood over him like Ali over Liston.

He rolled over slowly and looked up at me, fear smeared across his soft features like a stain, arms raised in defense. "Don't," he said softly. "Don't."

Don't what? What was I going to do to him? Hit him, kick him, beat him bloody until he confessed? What the hell had I just done, rushing out at him like that? I'd been pushing him inside the roadhouse, hoping for something to come loose, and instead he had acted perfectly reasonably. But still I had chased after him like a deranged avenger. What had come over me? I had lost my head, absolutely, and not for the first time since I found Hailey Prouix dead. Who was I so damn angry at? Him, for what he might have done to Hailey, or Hailey herself, for dragging me into this whole rotten story? I had lost myself in the anger of the moment and had no idea of what was supposed to come next.

I stepped back.

"I'm sorry," I said. "I didn't mean . . . I didn't . . . All I wanted was to ask some questions."

He looked so helpless, so pathetic, his arms raised defensively like a battered child's, that I backed off some more. But this time I backed into a wall where there shouldn't have been a wall. I twisted my head around to see what I had backed into. It wasn't a wall, it was Jimmy, the bartender with the boxer's nose.

He grabbed my arms and pulled them back so that he could hold them both with one of his thick arms, jerking my shoulders until they screamed with pain. The other arm he now wrapped around my neck and squeezed, only lightly, I could tell, but I grew suddenly woozy.

Grady Pritchett was still on the ground, but sitting now, hand to his forehead, legs outstretched like a young boy in a sandbox.

"I didn't mean to—" was all I could get out in a raspy gasp before Jimmy choked me into silence.

Grady pushed himself to standing and staggered at me, slowly, as if drunk, but he wasn't drunk, and maybe his stagger was an attempt at a swagger, because the next thing he did was rear back and slam his fist into my stomach.

The air flew out of my lungs so fast I could hear the whoosh. My body tried to bend over from the blow, but the granite grip of the bartender kept me standing straight even as my knees buckled from the shot of pain. Nausea flooded through me as Grady Pritchett gripped my hair with his left hand and cocked his right hand to finish the job he had started on my face.

I closed my eyes and heard the smack of something hard against something not so hard and felt my arms wrench and my body hurtle to the ground. I must have been unconscious already, I figured, because I couldn't feel the pain I knew had to be writhing through my face, the pain of ripping flesh and tearing muscle and collapsing bone. I thought I was unconscious until I opened my eyes and saw Grady Pritchett flying backward toward his black pickup truck as if propelled by some strange magnetic force.

Seeing him fly like that was right out of a comic book. I looked around dazedly for my comic-book hero. And there he was, brown jacket still buttoned, brown fedora still in place, white teeth glowing in the dim parking lot as if lit by black light, standing insouciantly with a large wooden oar in his hands.

Skink.

"How you doing there, mate?" he said, looking down at me.

I spun my head around to take in the scene. Grady was sitting on the ground, dazed. Jimmy the bartender was out cold on the ground, his arms still loose around me.

I squirmed from his grip and to my feet. "Am I bleeding? Did he hit me?"

"Nah, I nailed the bastard holding you afore our friend Pritchett had himself a chance to improve your face."

"You took your time."

"Well, I didn't know I'd be dealing with two, did I? I needed to find something to even up them odds." As he spoke, he tossed the oar onto the gravel. "But maybe we ought to make our getaway afore someone else charges out of that front door. Can you drive?"

I pressed my stomach, felt my ribs, my face. My eye was swelling from the first blow, my ribs were tender, my stomach was filled with an unpleasant cocktail of pain and nausea, but I could drive.

"I'll take Pritchett in his truck," said Skink. "You follow me."

"What are we doing?"

Skink walked to Grady Pritchett, on the ground by the black truck with its engine still running, and lifted Grady gently by the arm. Grady gave no fight. Skink helped him onto the bench seat of the truck and scooted him over so that Skink himself could get into the driver's seat. He leaned over solicitously and hitched up Grady's seat belt before quietly closing the truck's door.

"This is kidnapping," I said.

"Nah, that would be a federal crime," said Skink through the open window of the truck's front door. "Do we look like the type to commit a federal crime?"

I scanned his gangster outfit and battered features.

"We're just taking a ride through the countryside," he said. "We're going to find someplace nice and private where you and me and our good friend Grady Pritchett can have ourselves a friendly little talk."

"**YOU KNOW** that guy at every high school," said Grady Pritchett, "the guy with the rich father and fast car and best-looking girlfriend, the guy with the pack of followers that hang on his every last word and laugh at his every last joke? The guy that seems to have the whole school beat to hell?" Pritchett took a pull from his can of Coors. "That was me. Leastways, that was me before I got all messed up with Hailey Prouix."

We were surrounded by trees, not far from a stream whose gurgling we could just hear above the cacophonous calls of the insects all around us searching for love. Skink had stopped at a bar farther down the road and gestured me in to buy a couple six-packs, and now we were in the flatbed of Grady's truck, drinking. Grady had pulled a small electric lantern from the toolbox and we set that down between us like a campfire. We sprawled around its ghostly light and we talked. Or I should say it was Grady who talked. And the funny thing was, it didn't take much yanking to get the story out. Any hard feelings about the fight at the Log Cabin took wing as he started talking. It was as if the story had been festering inside him for all those long years, like the rotting core of a rotten tooth, and he was glad now, finally, to let it tumble out.

"I knew her and her sister before anything happened between

us," he said. "Pierce ain't no New York City—everyone in Pierce knows everybody's damn business—and everyone knew them Prouix sisters. Their father died when they was just girls and the uncle moved in to take care of them all. It was a touching story, and we all were a little sorry for them. But as they got older, they got cuter, and the sorry turned to something else, if you know what I mean. Now, Roylynn, she wasn't much interesting, she was like this porcelain thing you were so afraid was gonna break if you as much as breathed on it, but Hailey, well, Hailey grew up nice, with a flash of fire in her eyes. She was a couple years younger than us, but she had something, oh, yes. And when this girl Cheryl I was having some fun with decided she wanted to get all serious, talking about getting married and having kids, well, that was the end of Cheryl. So I was looking around for someone new, because when you're that guy at the high school you need to always have someone, and something about Hailey lit my fancy."

"She had that fire," I said, and the ghostly lit face of Skink stared hard at me as I said it.

"And remember now, she was only fifteen. But still. And so I asked her out, because when you're that guy, it ain't no big thing to ask some sophomore out, and damn if she didn't say no. Surprised the hell out of me, and it wasn't like a shy no, it was like a get-lost-you-asshole no. The guys, they got a laugh out of that one, but I wasn't laughing. You know how sometimes you see a girl every day of your life and it's just like nothing and then, when you decide you might like her, well, then every time you see her after that your heart just goes a little crazy? That's the way it was with Hailey when she said no to me. And after that, all I wanted in this world was her."

"She was playing you," said Skink.

"Maybe, but, you know, it was more like she really just wasn't interested, like there was nothing I could give her that she had any use for. So then I did like the full-court press, you know, being extra nice and getting her invited to all the parties and looking out for her all the time, like in the cafeteria and such. But none of it seemed to work. Until the reefer. I never expected her for that. Me, I started early, smoking with my mom."

"Your mum?" said Skink.

"My stepmom. My real mother, she left when I was young and took a chunk of my daddy's money, and then he got married again to someone not much older than me. And she was the one turned me on when I was just fourteen. My dad was out on business, and she came in wearing one a her outfits, which was not much at all, and looking damn good, and she up and asked me if I wanted to try something. Sure, I said. So we lit up in the backyard just like that, lying side by side in the chaises next to the pool, blowing smoke into the air, and ever since, that was how I had my fun outside of school, blowing reefer. It was why I eventually quit the ball team and started cutting school, because it was all getting in the way of my drugs. I mean, my future was set, I was going to work in my daddy's car lots and become as rich as him and spend my nights banging models and smoking the best weed money could buy. My future was laid out smooth as ice, and I was all for it. Well, asking Hailey out to the movies or some dance wasn't working, so one day, out of desperation, I sidled up to her in school and asked if she wanted to blow some dope down at the quarry, and what she did surprised the hell out of me. She looked up, smiled that wicked smile of hers, and said, 'Now you're talking.'

"So that's how we started together, hanging at the quarry with the rest, smoking dope. She pulled it in with this intensity I always remembered. The rest of us was just having some fun, but for her it was serious stuff, like the joint, it was a lifeline she was sucking at, like there was something dark she was trying to forget. I figured it was her father's death that was bumming her and I brought it up once and she told me to shut up in front of everyone, and that was the last time I did that.

"Now, it was clear that she was my girl, and at the quarry, with the others, she was all full of affection. I'd sit there with my arm around her and we'd act like a couple, and sometimes she would exhale the smoke right into my mouth and that got me harder than anything. But, you know, it never moved beyond that. When we were alone, she was cold, man. I'd sit there and try to kiss her and she wouldn't kiss back, her lips were like smooth slivers of marble. She'd let me grope her breasts, which was pretty nice, but when I tried to reach lower, she'd slap my hand away. I tried to force it once, and she kicked me so hard in the nuts I couldn't stand up for a week, and that was the last time I tried that, too.

"But I didn't sense like she wasn't that kind of girl. It was more she wasn't gonna be that kind of girl with me. Now, I'd been going all the way since I was fifteen, and Cheryl like couldn't get enough of it, but Hailey wouldn't give me a thing. Just to keep me happy she would jerk me off now and then, but she'd do it only 'cause I was begging and it wasn't so much better than me doing it myself, worse actually, because she was always acting like she was in a hurry for me to finish, which kind of ruined it. Anyone else, I'd a sent her packing, but her refusals just drove me more crazy. I even once said we could get married, and all she did was laugh at me like I was some zero asshole. It was humiliating enough to be a turn-on. So that's the way it was when Jesse Sterrett all of a sudden started hanging out at the quarry.

"Jesse and I used to be best friends. We played ball together all the time, basketball, baseball, everything. He was quiet and I wasn't, he was poor and I wasn't, he was humble and I wasn't. We was a perfect pair. But he turned against me when he started hanging with that Leon Dibble. I never liked that kid, thought he was strange in the brain and told Jesse so, and it was like Jesse near took my head off. Next thing you know Jesse's always off with his new best friend and I'm like nothing to him. It wasn't no surprise to anyone that Leon was as queer as a three-legged goat, and I figured that made Jesse the same. And he proved it to us all when Leon, he killed himself, it was like Jesse went into mourning. It was no use trying to talk to him after that, he wouldn't talk back. Got so the only way I could get a reaction from him was to needle, needle, and so I did, and he just took it and glowered, and at least that was something. But then he started hanging out at the quarry.

"I thought maybe it was me he was interested in, like as a friend, like he wanted us to be pals again. He wasn't there to toke, 'cause he didn't toke, and he wasn't there to joke around, because he didn't joke either. He was just there. And then I got an inkling he wasn't there for me, he was there for Hailey.

"Why is it that everything we most dread in this life we end up forcing on ourselves? I started making fun of him, needling him like I did, laughing at him for not reefing up with us, for being so quiet, for not liking no girls. Laughing at his back when he stormed off. And then one night, when he stormed off, Hailey, she gave me a look that froze my heart before she went off after him.

"It wasn't long before I realized something was going on, and it drove me insane. The thought of her doing all the things with him that she wouldn't do with me. I couldn't sleep. I started hanging outside her house at night, waiting to catch her with him. I never did but that meant nothing. Sometimes, in desperation, I called out her name and that uncle of hers, a brutal piece of man if ever there was one, would rush outside with his shotgun and tell me to get the hell away or he'd spatter me sure all over the county. I knew he would, too, it was in him, but it didn't mean a thing to me. I was insane. And then one day I just went after Jesse.

"I always was taller than him, stronger than him, and when as boys we wrestled, I always ended up on top forcing him to yell uncle. But he had kept playing ball and working out and the only thing I was exercising was my lungs, and this time it wasn't even close to a fair fight. I started it, he finished it, and I ended up in the hospital.

"My cheek was shattered, my jaw broken, my knee was busted up, I had bruises up and down my side. When I came in, the doctors said I looked like I'd been hit by a truck, but that wasn't the worst. Everyone knew what had happened, I had lost my girl to some closet queer, I went after him and he put me in the hospital. You know how in every high school there's that guy? Well, I wasn't him anymore.

"No one came visiting, not even my daddy, who was ashamed both that I had fought and that I had lost. Only my stepmom would keep me some company, staying by my side, wiping my brow when I hurt too much to move. And when I got out, it was like I had turned into something else, some ungainly cripple creature no one wanted to have a thing to do with. You can guess how I felt, like everyone had turned on me, and they had. And then there was my former girl and former best friend off together in their little blissful world, leaving me hobbling in the gutter. I wanted to kill them, I did. I wanted to kill them both, and I said so to anyone who would listen."

"And so when you knew he was planning to meet Hailey at the quarry," I said, "you were there waiting for him."

"No, I wasn't. I wasn't, that was it, what no one would believe. I wasn't there. I swear."

"Then where were you?"

"Someplace else."

"Where? With Hailey?"

He stopped talking, just shut down like a radio turned off for a long moment. He stopped talking and sat, and you could see the muscles in his face flinch as he considered which of his answers to tell.

"Yes," he said finally.

"Hell you was," said Skink. "Makes no sense that you would be, what with all the stuff happening between you and Jesse and her. You're just saying it because you think that's the surest way to keep your arse out of trouble. You're still worried about it, aren't you, mate? Even though it happened fifteen years ago and Hailey is dead, you're still worried they're going to think you done it."

"Yes," he said.

"But you didn't, did you?"

"No."

"And I believes you," said Skink.

He looked up at Skink with a strange hope in his face. "Do you?"

"Yes I do," said Skink, "but no one else did, did they?"

Grady shook his head.

"Your daddykins wouldn't believe a word from your face. He was sure you done it, wasn't he? He thought he had no choice but to bail out your arse. So he paid off his pals, the priest, the police chief, and the doctor, and worked a deal with Hailey. He worked a deal wheres he would pay for her college, pay for her to get the hell out of Pierce, so long as she made sure his boy didn't rot in jail for the rest of his life."

Grady Pritchett's eyes widened. "How do you know?"

"Because you're still in love with her, mate," said Skink.

"No I'm not."

"Don't even try. I can recognize the signs." Skink glanced at me. "It's a frigging epidemic, being still in love with Hailey Prouix. But you wouldn't still love her if she got you off for something you really done. That's not the way it works. If she had done that, well, you'd be blaming her now for every wrong thing in your life."

"She's the only one I can't blame."

"There you go."

"It was her idea," said Grady. "She came to me while I was still in jail for questioning. She came to me, and when I told her I didn't do it, like I told everyone I didn't do it, she was the sole one who believed me. It was she who came up with the idea of her being my alibi. She said she would work it out, so long as I agreed to parrot her story. And I did. Because I swear to God I thought they were going to fry my ass. I didn't know yet my dad had the fix in. Both for the charges, and for my life."

"What do you mean?" I said.

"It was never the warmest between us. And when I stopped playing ball, which was so important to him, it turned hard. But after this, after him thinking I had killed Jesse, where the hell could it go after that?" He stopped for a moment and wiped at his eyes, and his cheeks glistened in the pale light of the lantern. "He made me stay until the coroner ruled it an accident and the investigation was closed, made me stay in the house without a word passing between us. Then late one night he came into my room, just the shadow of him with the light coming in from behind. He was holding a drink, I remember, the ice clinked against the glass. And he told me to go the next day, to just up and go and to never come back. And so I did, the very next day." He wiped at his eyes once more. "I never did see him again."

He lifted his beer and drained it. Skink rescued another from the death ring of plastic and tossed it to him. Grady popped it right open and swallowed all the foam that spurted out and then drank half of that one, too.

"After he died, well, he left most everything to my stepmom, who went down to live in Florida with some guy named Lenny, and he left me nothing except for one stinking used-car lot here in Weston. I thought it was him giving me another chance, thought I could turn it into something like he would have wanted me to, maybe a whole chain of dealerships like he had built. But inventory sucked, and sales, they've never been what they should have been, and with the kids vacuuming up the money there's nothing left for expanding, and every day I go into that place it squeezes more life right out of me. I thought he was giving me a final chance, and now I know it was his final punishment for doing what I never did do.

"But I didn't begrudge Hailey what she got out of it, and I still don't. It wasn't her fault the way she was, and she never fooled me about nothing. In fact, in the whole mess, what she did for me in the jail was the one decent thing anyone did for me. In fact, we was still friends, even after she moved east. I sometimes would drive up to see her in Philadelphia. So maybe you're right, maybe I still had a crush. Hell, more than maybe. But she never encouraged it or let me do nothing about it. She was just always kind to me, and seeing her even for a little sometimes made me feel the way I felt before, when we was at the quarry at the start and I was still that guy and she was my girl and everything coming was going to be just so smooth."

WE SAT in that truck most of the night, finishing the beers. Just like it was Grady who did most of the talking, it was Grady who did most of the drinking, and I figured he had cause. I asked him if he knew who it was who really killed Jesse Sterrett, and he said he always assumed it was an accident after all. I asked him about Hailey's sister, Roylynn, and he told me he had heard she was in a place just south of Wheeling. And after I asked him that, we sat in that flatbed and drank up the beer and didn't say much of anything, listening instead to the rustle of the night. We stayed quiet and listened until the electric lantern dimmed and died and the stars overhead turned bright and cold and hard.

I drove him home. He wasn't in any condition to drive and I was, so Skink followed as I drove the black truck into the little town of Weston, to an old Victorian house that was nicely painted and well kept, hedges trimmed flat. When we pulled into the drive, a light went on in the upstairs window.

"Nice house," I said as I shut off the engine and handed him the keys.

"My wife takes good care of it."

"It doesn't look like it turned out all bad."

"She is sweeter than I deserve. And my kids, well, you know, they're my kids."

"Then why spend your nights at a dive like the Log Cabin?"

"All this ain't what I had in mind."

"Maybe it's time to grow up, Grady."

"Funny, that's what Hailey used to tell me, too."

"Where were you the night Jesse Sterrett died?"

"Nowheres."

"There's no such place."

"Sure there is. You just haven't spent enough time in West Virginia."

"Where were you?"

Pause. "You don't believe it wasn't me."

"I feel more comfortable with all the details nailed down."

He took a deep breath. The lights in one of the downstairs rooms turned on.

"She'd wanted it from the start," said Grady Pritchett, "I knew that, but I'd been good. Despite the temptations, I'd been a good boy. He was my daddy. But when things turned bad, she was the only one who came. And I grew so angry, so damn angry, that I couldn't even think no more except about hurting someone, especially him, so I stopped being good. She left word she was meeting friends at the club, but that's not where she was. She was with me, in a motel in a town down the highway, smoking reefer, getting down and nasty. I was still so banged up, it hurt so much, and that was the best damn thing about it."

I took that in. "You preferred your father to think you were a murderer than to know you were screwing his wife?"

"Wouldn't you?"

I didn't have an answer.

The front door of his house opened, and a slim figure clutching closed her robe stood leaning in the doorway.

"Anything else?" he said.

"That about does it. If I need you to testify . . ."

"Forget it."

"All right," I said. "I'll forget it."

He turned to me and smiled weakly and then opened the door and hopped out of the truck. He walked slowly down the driveway to the house, stopped to kiss the figure, and, without looking back, shut the door behind them.

36

THERE WAS one last place to visit in West Virginia.

The man in white led me through a well-lit hallway. He had broad shoulders, and his head was shaved, and his name was Titus. Titus didn't check behind him that I was following, but then he didn't need to. I was spooked, yes I was. It was not my normal venue, behind the walls of an asylum.

It hadn't taken much to find the place. I had simply called the West Virginia number on the singed records from my cellular phone and they had kindly given me directions. It certainly didn't look like what I had pictured a mental hospital to look like. From the outside, in fact, in its attitude at least, it suspiciously resembled the Desert Winds retirement home where we had met with Lawrence Cutlip in Henderson, Nevada. It was neat, well trimmed, seemingly deserted. A new, gabled structure with vinyl siding in a pleasing pastel, its grass freshly mowed, its bushes pruned into cute round balls. It appeared to be as much a spa as anything else, a place to restore the frazzled nerves of society wives. I could imagine that Hailey Prouix chose it personally, just as she personally chose Desert Winds for her uncle. She seemed have a thing for tidy places in which to store her various relatives.

The patients I passed as I followed Titus through the hallway were dressed in normal clothes, and they seemed pleasant enough, but I could tell they were patients. Some were impossibly thin and their jaws jutted with a strange prominence, still others wore long sleeves even in the uncomfortable warmth of the building, still others moved with an unnatural sluggishness. I tried to guess what they each were in for, anorexia, self-mutilation, schizophrenia. Look there, that older woman in the corner of that room, she was staring into the sky as if hearing the voice of God. Or was there maybe a television bolted into the upper corner of the room? And that woman there, wearing the long-sleeved blouse, look at her hands marked with cigarette burns. Or were they just birthmarks? And that woman sitting quietly in another corner, staring at her lap, was she a paranoiac ax murderess drugged into a stupor? Or was that a paperback book hidden in her lap?

Well, anyway, I could tell they were patients, absolutely I could. There was just something about them. And the something about them, I realized, was that they were here. But, of course, so was I.

Titus led me into a large common room and stopped at the entrance, waiting for me to step up beside him. "You can't take her from this room without prior approval," he said, his voice deep and commanding. "You can't give her anything without prior approval. You can't take anything from her without prior approval. There is to be no physical contact without prior approval. Do you have any prior approvals?"

"No, sir," I said.

"That settles that, doesn't it?"

"Yes, sir."

"What happened to your eye?"

"An accident."

"It accidentally got in the way of someone's fist?"

"Something like that."

"It doesn't make me happy, you coming in with an eye like that. Miss Prouix is a favorite of mine. Whenever I see her, it brightens my day. We all need a little bit of sunshine. I'd hate for anything to disturb her equilibrium."

"That's not what I'm here for."

"That doesn't mean it won't happen, does it? The supervisor said you had some questions for her."

"That's right."

"And I'm sure you'll be careful in digging for your answers."

"Yes, I will."

"Does she know you?"

"No. But I knew her sister."

"Well, then, go on and introduce yourself, Mr. Carl. She's over there, by the far wall."

A bright golden beam fell through the window, illuminating the slim woman on the coach in a halo of sunshine. She was leaning toward the glass, one leg curled under the other, one arm resting on the sofa's back. She was holding a book, thin and black, but the book was closed, and her face pointed toward the light. I remember quite clearly the bright golden light, but I'm wondering whether the magical beam exists now in my recollection much more vividly than it did that day. Maybe it was overcast, I seem to remember that it was. Maybe the light is an inventive trick of my memory, but I am not inventing that the woman on the couch was the very image of Hailey Prouix. And I am not inventing the emotion that clutched at my chest when I saw her there, across the room, gazing out the window, bathed as she was in gold.

What is love? It is a question that runs like a silver thread through this whole sorry tale, an elemental question that at each point seems to provide a very different answer. But if you had asked just then, as I stood beside Titus and saw Roylynn Prouix within that golden glow, I would have told you that love is a Pavlovian response to certain very specific stimuli. Because if I was feeling something for Hailey Prouix's sister, and I was, and I believe that what I was feeling was a shimmer of love, then it was based nothing on her, because I had never met her, and it was not a communal emotion flowing back and forth between us, because as of yet she didn't even know of my existence. It was instead an unavoidable remembrance of how I had felt before when I had seen that same face.

I glanced nervously at Titus, who smiled reassuringly and urged me on. Slowly, I made my way across the room to Roylynn Prouix.

She turned her face to me and smiled as I approached. It was a lovely smile, but different from her sister's. Where Hailey's had always been filled with a sad, calculating irony, this smile was guileless and genuine. I had adored Hailey's calculating smile, which evidenced so many strange depths, but after the multitude of ways I had been twisted and turned since first I saw it, I found Roylynn's all the more radiant.

"Miss Prouix?" I said.

She continued to smile without saying anything, and I began to worry.

"My name is Victor Carl."

No response, just that smile. Was there anything behind it? Was the guilelessness I had so admired just an instant before nothing but a lobotomized emptiness? I stared for a moment, overcome with a brief horror at what I imagined might be lacking in the woman before me.

"You, I suppose, are the visitor I've been told to expect," she said finally, in a voice curved by the same accent as affected Hailey's voice in her unguarded moments.

I breathed a great sigh of relief that someone was at home in the mansion. "Yes, that's right. I am so sorry about what happened to your sister."

The smile faded, she looked away to stare again out the window. "Thank you," she said quietly.

"I knew her in Philadelphia."

She turned quickly to peer at me. "Really. Tell me, was she happy in Philadelphia?"

It was a setup for a joke, but I resisted. "It's hard to say, she was a complicated woman, but I think there were moments of happiness."

She smiled again. "Well, I'm glad to hear that at least."

"Did she keep in touch with you?"

"Oh, yes. We talked frequently. She often called to see how I was doing, to ask about my day. She was always a very concerned sister."

"So you knew about Guy Forrest."

"Pardon?"

"Guy Forrest. Guy and your sister were living together. They were engaged to be married."

"No, she never mentioned him. I'm sure she would have, if she was really planning to marry him. But generally when we talked, she was more interested in how I was doing."

"Mr. Forrest was indeed engaged to your sister. There was a proposal, an acceptance, a ring. But now the state has accused him of killing her."

"Really? I hadn't heard. That is truly shocking. But I'm sure this Mr. Forrest did no such thing. Men didn't kill Hailey, they killed *for* Hailey."

I was taken aback by that comment, and the cheeriness with which it was dispensed.

"Sit down, Mr. Carl," she said, gesturing me to a spot at the other end of the couch. "No need to stand over me like that."

"You should know, Miss Prouix, I'm a lawyer representing Guy Forrest in the murder case. I've come to ask you some questions."

"It's not contagious, is it, being a lawyer?"

"Excuse me?"

"I won't start babbling in Latin or start charging for phone calls if you get too close, will I?"

"I can't guarantee it, but no, I don't think so."

"Well, then, I think maybe we can risk it." She gestured again to the other end of the couch, and I sat.

She shifted to face me, still holding her thin black book, dog-eared and dirty, still smiling, kindly now, with a deep assurance, and I thought suddenly that her being here had to be a mistake. Had to be. She was smart and charming and funny and full of kindness. It was quite a shift from my thinking her lobotomized only a few moment ago, but my whole experience in that place had proved disorienting, and the emotions I was feeling, the Pavlovian love that still clutched at me, made me certain. I didn't want at that moment to talk about Hailey or Guy or even poor dead Jesse Sterrett. My basest instincts kicked in and I wanted to talk about her. I wanted to chat her up like I would chat up a cutie in a bar.

"What's that you're reading?" I asked.

She took tighter hold of the black volume in her lap. "It's my favorite book. I read it over and over."

"It must be something fun," I said, twisting my head to read the battered spine. "Well, maybe not. *A Brief History of Time* by Stephen Hawking."

"Do you know of him?"

"Hawking. Isn't he that guy in the wheelchair?"

"Yes. He's marvelous. I think I'm a little bit in love with him, though I hear he's terrible to his wives. He has Lou Gehrig's disease, and he was supposed to have been dead years ago, but instead he sits in that chair and lets his mind wander out to the far edges of the universe. And the strange thing is that in writing about what he sees there, it is as if he is writing the story of my life."

"Your life?"

"Do you care much for physics, Mr. Carl?"

"E equals MC squared and all that?"

"Yes, and all that."

"No, I don't, actually. I don't understand it. But how is that the story of your life?"

"You know that the universe is expanding at tremendous speed. Of course you do. Can't you feel it? I can, every moment of every day I feel everything rushing away from me."

I thought suddenly of the way the points of darkness had rushed away from me during my sleepless nights and the terror that engendered. What must it be like to feel that every moment of every day?

"All this . . . disintegration," she said, "is an aftereffect of the big bang."

"The big bang?"

She leaned forward now, as if she had something urgent to relate to me, as if she were proselytizing about some great new religion that would save my soul. "The big bang. The very beginning of time, when the universe was formed out of a single great explosion. Before that, nothing happened that mattered, because it had no effect on what happened after. And after, nothing was ever the same again, because the explosion just kept hurtling everything far, far away."

"And that happened to you?"

"Yes. Of course. I thought you said you knew my sister. It happened to her, too. But at some point all this hurtling away is going to stop. It's slowing down already and the force of gravity is at work every moment and someday, someday soon, the universe is going to stop expanding and slowly, slowly begin to contract. And then the contraction will speed up, speed up, speed up, until boom." She smashed her palms together. "The big crunch."

"The big crunch?"

"Yes. And that will be the end of everything. The end of all time, because nothing that happens afterward will be affected by anything that happened before."

"And that's coming soon?"

"We can only hope," she said with a bright smile and a twinkle in her eye.

I wondered just then if she was putting me on. She must have been, and I smiled back at her even as I was feeling a confusing sadness.

"Is that what happened to Jesse Sterrett?" I said. "The big crunch?"

She seemed taken aback at the name. She turned her head and stared for a moment out the window.

"Is he in your book, too?" I said.

Without looking at me, she nodded and then looked down, opening the battered book in her lap. The pages were badly smudged, as if each had been fingered hundreds of times. She paged through the volume, stopping now and then, her attention caught by certain passages, in the way that some page through the Bible. She stopped finally and lifted the book to show it to me.

Chapter 6: "Black Holes."

"I think maybe," I said, slowly, as if to a child, "we should put away the book and just talk."

"Do you know what a black hole is? It is something so massive, something with a gravity so dense, that nothing can escape it, not even light. That's why they say it is black. Generally it is a star that collapses in on itself. It has to be just the right size, and then, when it is done burning, it just contracts into the tiniest ball of matter.

Anything that comes too close falls in and gets ripped apart before disappearing forever."

"And you say that's what happened to Jesse Sterrett?"

"Yes, of course. He fell into a black hole."

"Jesse Sterrett died in the quarry in Pierce. You think there was a collapsed star in that quarry?"

"No, of course not. Just because I'm in here doesn't make me crazy. But a black hole doesn't have to be formed only by a star. Anything with sufficient density can be a black hole. There are things called primordial black holes, formed in the very first moments after the big bang, formed of the very first pieces of the universe. It's right here in the book. Little bits of matter that have compressed into the tiniest shapes and float around the universe wreaking havoc. Think of something the mass of a mountain compressed into something no wider or longer than a million millionth of an inch. Think of that. A dark force from the very dawning of our universe. And they could be anywhere, anywhere, deep in outer space or just behind the moon or around the next bend in the road. They could be anywhere, floating here, floating there, leaving nothing but destruction. Anything that comes too close falls in and gets ripped apart before disappearing forever. The mass of a mountain in a million millionth of an inch."

I stared at her pretty face as she spoke, I gaped sad and incredulous, but at the same time, for some reason, I remembered the strange force that roared through Hailey and me in the middle of sex. It had seemed then, that force, something powerful, insatiable, devastating, ancient.

"And that's what killed Jesse Sterrett," I said, "a primordial black hole?"

"Yes. And Hailey, too."

"What are you talking about?"

"It's in the book."

"It doesn't make any sense."

"Of course it doesn't. Not yet, at least. No one's been smart enough to come up with a unified theory that explains everything. It is what Einstein spent his life searching for. It is what Stephen Hawking is traveling to the edges of the universe to figure out. One elegant equation that answers all the questions. Stephen Hawking is so close to figuring it out, they are all so close. And I am close, too. I know it. Each day I read over what he says here in this book and I feel myself growing closer and closer to an answer, closer and closer to figuring it out. And when I do, everything will become clear. Everything. Do you want to help me? Won't you help me?"

"I don't know anything about physics."

She reached out and grabbed at my shirt. "You said you knew her. You said you knew Hailey."

"Yes, I did."

"And you were asking questions about Jesse Sterrett. So you know more than you think you know. You are closer than you ever imagined. Will you work with me? Will you help me?"

She was shaking the fistful of cloth still in her grip. I took hold of her wrist and gently pulled her hand off of me. "That's what I'm trying to do. If you could only answer some questions . . ."

"All your answers are here." She waved the book with her other hand. "Whatever it is you want to know."

Just then a shadow appeared to my right. "Is everything all right?" said Titus, his deep voice filled with a solicitous concern.

I noticed then that I was still gripping Roylynn's wrist. I let go. She turned and smiled at Titus with the same bright smile she had given me only moments ago.

"Mr. Carl is going to work with us to find the unified theory," she said.

"That's good," said Titus. "That's very good."

"Titus has helped me so much already," she said. "We're getting so close, aren't we?"

"Yes, we are, we surely are."

"The world will be stunned when we figure it out."

"Yes, it will," said Titus. "You'll be getting yourself a Nobel Prize."

"We," said Roylynn. "You and everyone else who helped."

"Thank you, Ms. Prouix. That is so kind."

"All right, Mr. Carl?" she said. "Are you ready?"

"Do you miss her?" I said. "Do you miss your sister?"

There was a pause, where she seemed to carefully, willfully, compose her face into a smile. "How could I?" she said finally. "I never had the chance. She's in me, she always has been. She makes me strong. I've never been lonely a day in my life, because she is in me. I can feel her breath in my breath, her touch in my touch. When I look into a mirror, I see two faces. When I speak, I hear two voices. If it is all right, Mr. Carl, I like to start at the introduction. There are many clues there, I think." She opened the book. "Here we are. Are you ready?"

I glanced at Titus and then nodded into her kind, smiling face.

She began to read.

I nodded again and kept nodding as she read on and on.

There is something about a Southern accent that sends a comforting signal of assurance. The certainty in Roylynn Prouix's voice itself told me how important this all was to her, how surely she held to the belief that the answers to everything that had plagued her soul, and her sister's, were somewhere contained in that battered black book. So I nodded and stopped fighting it and let the syrup of her voice slip over me. I followed her through the words and the pages, I followed her through the simple equations and complex concepts, I followed her until we both were released from the bindings of gravity and flew free from this earth, this solar system, flew side by side past planets spinning and stars forming and stars collapsing and galaxies spiraling around great massive centers, past black holes glowing white-hot against all expectation, past all the strange, gorgeous phenomena, of which man can only as yet dream, toward the far far edges of the universe.

"ANYTHING?" SAID Skink when I met him in the lobby after Titus had come to take Roylynn away.

"No."

"What was she, Looney Tunes?"

"You could say that."

"What the hell you think you was going to get in a place like this?"

"I don't know. Something else. It's time to go home."

"Giving up, are we?"

"I've got a trial to prepare for."

"You still going to defend him after finding nothing?"

"Yes. He didn't do it, I'm sure of it now."

"You ain't convinced me yet."

"I don't have to convince you. There are only twelve that I care about."

"You're disappointing me, Vic. I thought if we found nothing, you'd go back to your original plan."

"It was a bad plan, flawed from the start. There's only one way to handle something like this. Straight up to the end. That's how I mean to play it."

"I didn't think you'd find a frigging thing down here, but I'll admit I'm a little disappointed it turns out I was right. It would have been nice to see things tidied all neat and clean, would have been nice to dig into the past to find our villain. But that ain't the way of it, is it, Vic? Things never do tidy up all neat and clean."

"I suppose not," I said. But even as I was saying it, I didn't believe it to be the truth. Even as I was saying it, I was remembering the strange interstellar journey I had just taken with Roylynn Prouix only a few moments before. And I couldn't help thinking that somewhere, out there, in the far reaches of the universe, somewhere in the great black space that I had traversed with Roylynn, somewhere lay the unified theory I was looking for, the theory that tied two victims, two murders, two mysteries together into one brutal solution.

PART FIVE

THE QUARRY

37

"IT WAS a quiet, rain-swept night on Raven Hill Road," said prosecutor Troy Jefferson in his smooth prosecutor's voice. "The kids were asleep, the cars were parked in the driveways and by the curb, the houses were dark. Everything was locked up tight, safe and sound. An unlikely night for—"

"Objection, Your Honor."

I was standing at the defense table, Guy Forrest sitting to my left and Beth, with a white plaster cast on her wrist, sitting to his. Judge Tifaro peered over her half glasses at me. The eyeglass chains hanging from her temples gave her pique a schoolmarmish edge. "We're only on the fourth sentence of Mr. Jefferson's opening, Counselor. Don't you think your objection is a bit premature?"

"Mr. Jefferson is implying that all the houses were locked up tight on Raven Hill Road the night of the murder, when he knows full well that there is no evidence that Miss Prouix's house was locked at all. When he knows full well there is no evidence to disprove the possibility that anyone could have strolled inside that house at any time for any purpose, whether—"

"Mr. Carl, that's enough. You'll have your turn to discuss any failures of proof in your closing. Objection overruled."

"Thank you, Your Honor," I said as I sat back down in my seat.

"Let me start again," said Jefferson, smirking at me before turning back to the jury. "It was a quiet, rain-swept night on Raven Hill
Road. The kids were asleep, the cars were parked in the driveways
and by the curb, the houses were dark. Everything was locked up
tight, safe and sound. An unlikely night—"

"Objection, Your Honor. He did it again."

"Mr. Carl, I overruled the objection. Mr. Jefferson can say what he
pleases. Sit down."

"Thank you, Your Honor." I sat.

"An unlikely night," said Jefferson hurriedly, "for murder."

"Objection, Your Honor."

"Oh, please," moaned Troy Jefferson, spinning around to give me
the eye.

"Mr. Carl?" said the judge, unable to conceal her exasperation.

"Whether or not there was a murder is a legal conclusion for the
jury to decide after receiving your instructions. Mr. Jefferson can
argue facts here, but an opening is not the time to throw all kinds of
technical legal terms at the jury in the hopes of pushing them at this
early stage to some legal conclusion that might not be warranted
by—"

"Overruled," said the judge. "Murder is the charge, and so he can
use the word. Sit down, Mr. Carl. I've had enough out of you already and we're only" —she glanced at her watch—"three minutes
into the proceeding. I fear this is going to one be of those trials, so
let make myself clear, Mr. Carl. I don't want you interrupting Mr.
Jefferson's opening again. I don't want to hear your voice even if
the building is on fire and you are the first to see the flames. Do you
understand?"

"Yes, Your Honor. Thank you, Your Honor."

"Don't thank me when I slap you down, Mr. Carl. It puts me in a
foul mood. And, Mr. Jefferson, when Mr. Carl is giving his opening,
I certainly hope you show him more respect than he has shown to
you."

"I certainly hope so, too, Your Honor," I said.

The jury laughed at that one, which I appreciated. I smiled as I
nodded their way. Some smiled back.

"Thank you, Your Honor," I said, to a few more chuckles.

Troy Jefferson glared at me before turning around and beginning again, but with his back now slightly hunched, as if anticipating the next interruption, and without the same lovely assurance in his voice.

God, I loved the courtroom.

I was in a strange, unsettled place just then, confused as to what had really happened or why to Hailey Prouix, confused by what I had learned in West Virginia, uncertain about who had done what to whom, certain only that the man I was defending was in a harder place than he should have been because I had screwed up in every which way. I was holding tight to a series of secrets that could destroy me and my client. I was keeping facts from Beth, my partner and best friend. I was playing a dangerous game. And yet, with all that, I still felt comfortable in that court of law, and the reason wasn't too hard to fathom.

My life to that point had been pretty much an unmitigated failure. I had little money, less love, a few good friends that I could count on, but only a few, and a career that, despite its evident lack of financial rewards, had somehow veered out of my control. My last romantic relationship fitted the pattern of all those that preceded it, a twisted affair that ended badly, although this ending seemed to rise to a new and unprecedented level, seeing how it ended in death. No, the whole my-life situation was pretty dim. Somehow, after all this time, I still had not figured out the rules. Where was the rule book? I needed a rule book. I thought that graduating from college would do it, turn my life into something lovely and joyful and successful, but, no, it did not. Then I thought that getting into law school would do it, and then I thought that passing the bar would do it, and then I thought that surviving in my own practice for more than five years would do it. Wrong, wrong, and wrong again. I didn't have the least notion of what was really going on. Others knew, others with fancy cars and big houses and lovely spouses and bushels of children, they knew how to play the game and come out winners. How did they get hold of the rule book while my hands still were empty?

But in court there was no such problem. Here there actually was a rule book, the Pennsylvania Code, and it contained between the many covers of its many volumes the rules of evidence and the rules of trial practice and the rules of criminal procedure and that great guidebook of human behavior, the penal code. In the course of my career I had spent enough time elbow deep in the law to learn these rules cold. And the other rules, too, the rules of dealing with your adversary, relating to the jury, bolstering your witnesses during direct examination, destroying their witnesses on cross. Outside the courtroom I was lost, inside I was slick. I'm not bragging, there were thousands just like me, it seemed to be an epidemic, lawyers helpless outside the courtroom while eagles within, and I don't claim to have been the best, or even close. Sometimes I would see a master go through the paces and grow sick with jealousy. So, no, I was not the best, but what I did best I did in the courtroom. It was the only place where I understood the rules.

So, in order to keep within the new rules laid out by Judge Tifaro, I spent the rest of Jefferson's opening restraining myself from objecting at every other word. It was seemingly a difficult task, I was halfway to standing many times until I openly noticed the judge's displeasure and meekly returned to my seat. I must have been a sight, squirming in the chair as I restrained myself, I must have been something to behold, and I know this because of the expressions on the faces of the jury members as they were beholding me, even as Troy Jefferson tried to continue.

It was a good opening, I must admit, laying out the facts that he would prove against Guy Forrest with a devastating simplicity. Motive. Guy and the victim had been involved with a fraud in the Juan Gonzalez case. Hailey had turned on him by stealing most of the money from their joint account and then sleeping with another man. Guy had every reason to be furious at her, murderously angry. And it showed. The night of her death Hailey Prouix had been hit in the eye before being shot to death. Opportunity. Guy was the only one we knew to have been in the house with the victim on the night of the murder. Means. Guy's fingerprints were on his gun, his gun, which the forensic evidence would prove had fired the bullet into Hailey Prouix's heart. And then there were those little factual touches that, like accent pillows on a couch, add so much. Instead of calling 911 for an ambulance after the shooting,

Guy had called his lawyer. And after the cops came, Guy tried to run away with a boatload of cash and a bottle of Viagra in his suitcase. Oh, the facts were clearly on Jefferson's side, and his opening would have been strong enough to clasp the iron shackles upon Guy Forrest's legs on its own if the jury hadn't been concentrating so much on my valiant efforts to restrain myself. In fact, it got to the point where I didn't even have to squirm like a snake to get their attention. Jefferson would make a point, the jury would glance my way, I would raise an eyebrow, and they would understand to take what had just been said with a jaundiced eye.

"MR. CARL," said Judge Tifaro, gesturing me to a space in front of the jury after Troy Jefferson had retaken his seat. "Don't make us wait."

Still in my chair behind the defense table, I patted Guy on the shoulder of his gray suit and then squeezed his arm in solidarity. "My name is Victor Carl," I said. "This is my client, Guy Forrest. Mr. Jefferson over there is trying to kill him, which is a serious thing. What, then, is Guy's serious crime? Mr. Jefferson says it is murder, but he is wrong. Guy didn't kill Hailey Prouix. Someone else did. Someone came into the house and walked up the stairs and shot Hailey Prouix dead while Guy was in the Jacuzzi with its whirlpools noisily whirling, wearing a set of headphones, listening to Louis Armstrong blow his cornet. That is what happened, no matter how strange it might sound. The police when they came found the Jacuzzi full, the Walkman by the side of the tub, the CD loaded and primed with Satchmo's lovely horn. When they checked Guy's hands the night of the murder, there was no evidence that he had fired a gun, because he hadn't. He was listening to Louis Armstrong, and when he came out of the bath, he found Hailey Prouix dead. He didn't do it. So why is Guy on trial? What is his crime, really?" I stood, stepped behind Guy, put a hand on each shoulder. "His crime here, the serious transgression for which they are putting him on trial for his life, is that he fell in love."

I walked slowly now as I spoke, moved toward the jury until I was standing right beside their box, close enough so I could reach out and anoint the foreheads of each of those in the front row.

"Guy had a life we all could wish for. A lovely wife, two children, a house, a big house, a job with a law firm that paid well and would pay far better when he made partner, which was a lock, believe me. It was a lock because the person making the partnership decision was his father-in-law, Jonah Peale, as you will learn when Mr. Peale testifies in this courtroom for the prosecution. Guy had a life we all could wish for, but he gave it up. Why? Mr. Jefferson will claim he gave it up for money, but don't you believe it. Prosecutors are paid less than they are worth and so they always think that money is at the root of everything, but not in this case, ladies and gentlemen. Whatever Guy Forrest did or didn't do, it had nothing to do with money. The evidence will show that Guy was in line to make millions and he gave it up, and when you see that, you will know better than to think it was money that motivated him. Instead he sacrificed his wonderful life, tossed aside everything he had, for love.

"Hailey Prouix was beautiful, smart, sad, alluring. Hailey Prouix was a siren calling Guy away from his comfortable life into the unpredictable waters of love, and he couldn't help himself. He abandoned his wife, his children, his job, his future, his very integrity—abandoned it all for her. Abandoned it all for love. I'm not saying he was right to desert his family and sully his profession—you have every right to condemn what he did, and he'll have to suffer the consequences for the rest of his life—but he did it for love, and love, at least in this state, is not a hanging offense.

"Now, you've already heard tell of the Juan Gonzalez case, as if that will prove that Guy killed Hailey Prouix. Let me tell you now that it will prove nothing. Juan Gonzalez, a poor man with a family to support, had entered the hospital for a simple operation and ended up in an irreversible coma. Hailey Prouix represented the Gonzalez family, seeking compensation. Guy Forrest represented the doctor and the insurance company, seeking to avoid paying the family for the disastrous result. There was a file that showed that Mr. Gonzalez had a preexisting condition and which might have won the case for Guy's clients, but Guy buried the file so that the family of Juan Gonzalez could get some money and so that Hailey Prouix, his love, could get some money, too.

"It was wrong what he did, I'm not defending it, but don't think he did it for the money. If he was thinking only of the money, he would have stayed married to Jonah Peale's daughter and become a partner in Jonah Peale's firm and stood in line to inherit Jonah Peale's fortune and ended up with more money than he could ever have spent. No, we can only imagine why Hailey Prouix got involved with Guy Forrest, we can only imagine as to her motivations, but when you hear the evidence, you will have no doubt as to what motivated Guy Forrest. He buried that file, failed his responsibilities to his clients and the law, stepped over the line for love. What he did was wrong, and maybe it was a crime, a crime for love, and maybe for that he should be tried. But he didn't bury that file for the money, and when Mr. Jefferson says he later killed his love for that same money, you will know he is wrong.

"And you heard Mr. Jefferson tell you that Hailey Prouix had another lover and that might be why Guy killed her. You would think Mr. Jefferson could figure out whether it was the one or the other, but that is what he has come up with. And the evidence will show how Mr. Jefferson discovered that fact of Hailey Prouix's lover, by reaching deep within Hailey Prouix's body and pulling out evidence, by testing that evidence with the most advanced scientific techniques, by comparing that DNA with Guy's own and showing that the complex DNA strands do not match. We will have no dispute with the accuracy of that test, but only with the idea that Guy Forrest could have conducted the same intricate scientific tests to learn that truth. It seems ridiculous, doesn't it? But Mr. Jefferson will rely on such an idea to show motive when there will be not a shred of evidence that Guy knew of this other lover.

"Mr. Jefferson assumes that Hailey was leaving Guy for this other man and that was why he hit her first and then killed her. But all we know for sure is that Guy and Hailey were living together, were engaged to be married, were planning for a future as man and wife. They were going to Costa Rica for a lovers' vacation. You will see the plane tickets in their names. Tell me, ladies and gentlemen, who was Hailey Prouix leaving for whom? You could equally assume the opposite of what Mr. Jefferson claims, that she was leaving this other lover for Guy and that was why the other man hit her when she told him it was over and then later killed her. The coroner will not be able to place exactly the time of the blow that caused the bruise. It happened before the killing, but we don't know for sure how far before, we don't know if it happened, maybe, at the time of the tryst with her lover earlier in the day when, maybe, she said good-bye and he lost control. And when you see Guy's name on the ticket to Costa Rica, maybe you will consider this possibility more likely.

"So maybe, possibly, probably it was this other lover that killed her. Now, ladies and gentlemen, you should be asking yourselves, what will you learn during the trial about this other lover other than his existence, which is beyond dispute? Will you learn who he was? No. Will you learn whether or not Hailey had given him the key to her house? No. Whether or not Hailey had shown him the location of the gun during one of their trysts? No. Whether or not he was murderously angry at Hailey Prouix for leaving him? No. Whether he has an alibi for the night of the killing? No. Whether he was, instead, lurking alone outside the house, waiting until his anger forced him through the door to the hidden location of the gun and then up the stairs, into that bedroom where he shot the woman he loved with a dangerous obsession, the woman who was abandoning him to his cold, cruel loneliness, shot her through the heart? Watch as this trial unfolds, and see if any of those answers are provided, and wonder why not.

"And ask yourselves about the mysterious patch of wet carpet found by the police beside the front door, and wonder who it was that came from outside and left something there, an umbrella, his boots, something, when we know for sure it wouldn't have been Guy. And ask yourselves about the strange man in black rushing out of Hailey Prouix's house the night after the murder, when Guy Forrest was already in police custody.

"This is what I believe the evidence will show. The evidence will show that Guy had no motive, but that another might have. The evidence will show the possibility that another had opportunity and access to the means to commit this crime. The evidence will show that the prosecution brought this case before they found the evidence needed to answer the crucial questions I have just raised, because they thought they had discovered the ultimate answer. They have accused Guy Forrest of killing Hailey Prouix because his is the only name they could come up with and the link between Guy and Hailey was powerful and undeniable. Love. He loved her. He had given up everything for her. That is why he is on trial today, because of that love.

"And so this is, finally, what I want you to ask yourselves, ladies and gentlemen: Whenever did love become a crime?"

WE STOOD as the jury was let out for the day, remained standing as Judge Tifaro followed. I put my arm around Guy's back, squeezed his shoulder, said a few encouraging words before the bailiff led him away for transport back to the county jail. So it was just Beth and me at the defense table as I packed up my notebooks, my folders, my omnipresent yellow pads, when something banged hard onto the wooden tabletop beside me.

Startled, I turned to find a large brown briefcase and holding on to it a grinning Troy Jefferson.

"That was pretty good," he said, "that song and dance of yours."

"Thank you."

"You should have lowered your voice and done a Barry White. I can hear him singing it: 'Whenever did love become a crime?' But it's not going to fly. Doesn't matter where you try to point the finger, the fingerprints on the gun are Guy's."

"We'll get to that in the course of the trial."

"I had thought blaming the lover might be your strategy, as good as any, but I didn't think you'd be so foolish as to spout it in the opening when any day, any minute he could walk right into the courtroom."

"Well, there you go, that's what we are, Beth and I, a couple of fools."

"You blaming him in the opening, getting it into all the papers, might just force his hand. And it certainly forced mine. We're twenty-four/sevening the search for the missing man."

"Maybe you should have twenty-four/sevened it before you swore in the jury."

"Oh, we'll find him and his alibi. The detectives pissed and moaned about the overtime, but they've already got leads."

"Speaking of the detectives, I saw Stone at the table, but not our good friend Breger."

"He took a jaunt."

"Anyplace interesting?"

"Vegas."

"Gambling?"

"No. But before he left, he told me he still had some questions about that night of the murder. Once again he asked if you would consent to allow us to examine your phone logs for that night."

"And once again I refuse," I said. "Attorney-client privilege. And I don't think the judge will set the precedent of allowing you to rummage around the phone records of the defense attorney after a trial starts."

"Maybe not, but not every defense lawyer is called just moments after a murder. I suppose we'll just have to see." He opened his briefcase, took out a blue-backed motion, tossed it onto the table before me. "I've been holding this for a while, but I think it's too hot to hold on to any longer. I'll be filing it before we leave the courthouse. I expect she'll rule tomorrow."

"Let me guess, Troy. You weren't the quiet type on the basketball court."

"I did my share of verbalizing," he said with his grin before he turned for the exit, followed by the two ADAs who were assisting him. Beth and I watched as the coterie departed.

I scanned the document he had given me: MOTION TO COMPEL THE DISCLOSURE OF CERTAIN TELEPHONE LOGS. "You'll have to answer this tonight," I said as I handed it off to Beth.

Beth snatched the motion with her good hand and quickly reviewed it. Her wrist had healed badly. The bones had needed to be rebroken, manipulated into proper alignment, and fastened together with metal pins inserted by a huge pneumatic device to keep them in place. For her it had been a summer of pain, but it looked as though the doctors had finally gotten it right and this would be the last of her casts. She continued reading the motion as she said, "He's right, you know."

"Who, Troy? Nah, he's just talking trash."

"No he's not. He seemed almost gleeful."

"Really? I thought he seemed a bit rattled."

"Not rattled, relieved. If you had been less specific, you would have kept your options open to the end. Any big surprises could have been accounted for. Now, if the other lover walks in, we're sunk. What if he shows up and matches the DNA and then gives himself a perfect alibi? What then?"

"He won't."

"Why not?"

"He has a reason to hide. Maybe he's married, maybe he's engaged to someone else, maybe his gay lover is a jealous fiend. Whatever, he hasn't come forward yet and won't in the future."

"But he might if he thinks the real killer is getting off because of his silence. He might suffer the embarrassment to stop a travesty of justice."

"He's not that noble."

"How can you be sure?"

"Trust me."

"I don't know, Victor," said Beth, staring now at the door out of which Troy Jefferson had just departed. "It's almost as if Jefferson already knew who the other lover was and was preparing to whisk him in as soon as you blundered into his trap."

"Wouldn't he have had to disclose that to us already?" I said, my voice betraying my sudden nervousness.

"Not if it was merely a suspicion that he can now send his detectives out to turn into a fact."

I wondered on that for a moment and then shook my head. "I had to do it. To win this thing I need the jury to see the missing lover behind every question, every possibility. If I just tried to offer him at the end, it would have looked like flummery. Now he's sitting right here at the defense table, ready to shoulder the blame when the evidence is equivocal. He's what the jury will see when that police technician testifies that she couldn't detect gunpowder residue on Guy's hands at the crime scene. She'll try to dismiss the result by claiming that the gunpowder washed off in the rain, but the jury will be wondering if maybe the police tested the wrong man. And when the DNA pattern of the semen gets put up on the chart, without my saying a word, they'll be wondering if they're looking at the DNA of a killer. By the time I get to closing, they'll have argued the case for themselves and found reasonable doubt."

Beth just stared at me, a faint amusement at my assurance in her eyes. "It sounds so easy."

"Genius always does. But in the end all our supposes don't matter." I rapped her cast gently with my knuckle, the sound sharp and hollow. "Hello. Anybody there? This is what our client wants us to argue, he has told us so repeatedly, so this is the way we go."

"I'm not used to seeing you so deferential to the client."

"He's a lawyer, and it's his life on the line."

"Let's just hope it doesn't blow up in his face," she said. "Have you decided if Guy is going to testify?"

"He wants to, but I won't let him. He'd have to say he knew about the other man and that he hit her on the night of her murder. Those two facts would kill us."

"But what about the open door, the sudden sound? How are you going to prove up the possibility that someone else could have slipped into that house the night of the murder?"

"That's why, dear Beth, they invented cross-examination."

CROSS-EXAMINATION IS a witch's brew. It most famously can be a truth serum for the untruthful, though that wasn't a problem yet in our trial. There were no liars here, no falsified testimonies being used to frame up our defendant. The case against Guy Forrest was powerfully circumstantial, and the circumstances, as presented by Troy Jefferson, were basically true. It was only the natural inferences flowing from those circumstances that we had quarrel with. But that just required a different recipe of cross, an alchemist's potion to turn the inconceivable conceivable, the unthinkable thinkable, the improbable into a stone-cold absolute possibility, to raise phantoms and conjure them into flesh and blood.

"NOW, MRS. Morgan," I said, "you stated in your direct testimony that you saw Mr. Forrest sitting outside his house about eleven o'clock on the night of the killing, is that right?"

"That's right," said Evelyn Morgan, a well-dressed matron with hair shellacked in place. She was a neighbor of Hailey's, across the street and a few numbers down.

"And Mr. Forrest wasn't wearing much, isn't that right?"

"Not from what I could see, though there were shadows, so I couldn't tell to the last inch."

"Good thing for the shadows, right, Mrs. Morgan? Were the upstairs lights on then, do you remember?"

"Yes, they were on. Or at least I think they were on. I noticed that because earlier I seemed to remember that the upstairs window was dark."

"And that window is to the master bedroom?"

"I was never invited inside, but I think so."

"Good enough. And then later, after you first spied Mr. Forrest, you saw a man in a raincoat go up the steps, talk with Mr. Forrest, take something off the cement step, and then go inside. And you said that man was me?"

"As best I could tell," she said.

"You've got good eyes, Mrs. Morgan," I said. "I notice you wear glasses. Were you wearing them that night?"

"Yes I was. I wear them until I go to sleep every night. And I don't sleep as much as I used to."

"Fine. Now, when you saw me go up those steps, was I holding an umbrella?"

"Not that I remember."

"A bag of some sort, any object I could have laid down beside the doorway when I went inside?"

"No, sir."

"And I wasn't inside long, was I, before I came out again?"

"Not that I remember."

"And the police came soon after."

"Yes, they did."

"It must have been quite a sight."

"Well, it is normally a very quiet neighborhood."

"You're married, aren't you, Mrs. Morgan?"

"Yes I am, for thirty-three years now."

"Thirty-three years. My, oh, my. And you have how many children?"

"Four, and two grandchildren, with two more on the way."

"That is something, yes. And with all that, and of course the volunteer work you testified about, you don't have much free time, do you?"

"I'm kept busy."

"I bet you are, Mrs. Morgan. I can see that you're not one of those sad, pathetic ladies who spend all their days sticking their noses out the window spying on their neighbors."

"I should say not."

"You've got too much going on in your own life to be like that."

"Yes I do, Mr. Carl."

"Which is why you say you saw Mr. Forrest sitting on the steps but you didn't see him actually leave the house, because you were busy living your life, not twitching curtains to see what the neighbors were up to."

"Yes, that's right."

"So if somebody had walked right up those steps and into the house, somebody, let's say, with an umbrella or a bag, you wouldn't have noticed, would you?"

"Maybe not, I don't know."

"In fact, a whole army could have gone in and out and you wouldn't have seen it, because you were living your life, not sitting by the window like a spy."

"I suppose."

"Thank you, Mrs. Morgan. That is all."

NOW, IT wasn't a sham defense I was presenting with my witch's brew, no, not at all. I'm never above presenting a sham defense, of course, poking holes in an airtight case just to create some doubt where none should exist is a defense attorney's job, but this wasn't that. Hailey had been murdered and if Guy was innocent, as I now believed, then some other person had come into that house, climbed those stairs, shot her dead. The man I was blaming hadn't done it, I knew that with perfect knowledge, since I was broadening the boundaries for the defense bar and, in effect, blaming myself, leaving my name out for propriety's sake. But someone had indeed killed her, someone, surely, and my job, as I perceived it, was to take the simple testimony that Jefferson presented and create a hole big enough for that murderer to walk through and do his dark deed.

"NOW, OFFICER Pepper, in your report you say when you made a quick examination of the house after finding the corpse, you noticed a small patch of carpet by the side of the door that was wet."

"That is correct."

"And it was about a foot square, isn't that right?"

"Approximately. I didn't take out the tape measure."

"Was the roof at that part of the house leaking?"

"Not that I noticed."

"The wall?"

"No."

"So this spot of carpet, it had been wetted by an umbrella, maybe, or a coat thrown to the ground, or a pair of boots."

"Yes, I suppose."

"Did you check it for fibers or debris?"

"It was checked, but I didn't do it. From what I understand, nothing unusual was found, other than some small stones which could have been there previously."

"Now, in that corner there was no umbrella stand or coatrack, was there?"

"No, sir."

"So this wasn't the place where Miss Prouix or Mr. Forrest usually dropped their wet things."

"Objection," said Troy Jefferson.

"Sustained," said Judge Tifaro.

"You're sustaining the objection just like that, Judge? No argument, no explanation given?"

"That's right"

"I'm just trying to show it was highly unlikely that either Miss Prouix or Mr. Forrest would have left anything there, that's all."

"Not with this witness. Objection sustained, move on."

"Wow, okay. I'll try. Now, Officer Pepper, isn't it possible, based on the size and location of that spot, that someone, anyone, came into that house that night and dropped something wet there, like a bag, or an umbrella, or their boots, on their way up the stairs?"

"Anything's possible."

"And if that possibility occurred, and that person left after whatever it was he did, then he would have taken the wet object, whether bag or umbrella or boots, with him, unlike Guy, who was still there and would have left it right in place."

"Anything's possible, like I said."

"Yes it is, Officer. No further questions."

I COULDN'T help thinking through the course of the trial about Roylynn Prouix and her little black book.

Troy Jefferson was laying out the smooth surface of his case, a simple explanation of time and space that made it impossible for anyone other than Guy Forrest to have killed Hailey Prouix. I, on the other hand, was trying to create a disruption in his continuum, attempting to distort time and space so that a gap appeared, a yawning hole big enough to allow someone other than Guy to step through and take the shot. It seemed a trick, what I was doing, a distortion, but as I worked, I realized it wasn't a trick at all. It was there, the gap, absolutely, and I was simply making its presence felt.

I thought of that primordial black hole of which Roylynn had spoken, the thing that had distorted her life and her sister's. She had said that Jesse Sterrett had been devoured by that same black hole. It had seemed at the time like the spinnings of a mind deranged by some great tragedy, but during the course of the trial I began to reassess. Each time in my cross-examinations that I bent the smooth surface of Troy Jefferson's case and allowed the hole to grow ever larger, it was as if the force of some massive body was becoming more evident. It was still shadowy, this body, still unidentifiable, but it was there, twisting time and space, opening its murderous gap.

The mass of a mountain, had said Roylynn Prouix, in a million millionth of an inch. With each cross, with each question, it seemed ever more present, ever more frightening, ever more true.

"**OFFICER JENKINS**, you testified that you found People's Exhibit Seven, which is a portable CD player with headphones, by the Jacuzzi in the master bathroom."

"That's right."

"Did this Jacuzzi have water jets built in?"

"Yes, there was a timer switch on the wall."

"Did you try the switch to see if the jets worked?"

"I did."

"Pretty loud, weren't they?"

"I suppose. In that small room, sure."

"Now, the headphones you found, are they the normal light-weight things that usually come with such players?"

"I don't know what usually comes with players, but these were pretty good headphones. If I can look at the exhibit, I could tell you more."

I brought People's Exhibit Seven to the witness stand. "Those are your initials on the bag, isn't that right?"

"My initials are first. The other initials are from the technicians who examined it in the lab."

"Fine. Now, if you could open the bag, take out the exhibit, and look at the headphones. Those are the same headphones you found by the tub, aren't they?"

"Yes. They are made by a company called Koss. They're the kind with padding that covers the ear."

"Pretty high quality?"

"I don't know for sure, but better than usual, I would suppose."

"And the disc inside was *Louis Armstrong's Greatest Hits*?"

"Yes, that's right."

"And it's still inside?"

The officer opened the case. "Yes."

"Now, Officer, did you happen to check the settings on the disc player before you put it into that evidence bag?"

"What do you mean?"

"The player has a little digital readout, doesn't it?"

"Yes, it does."

"And that readout gives all kinds of information. It tells the track number of the song being played. It tells the state of the battery. It tells the volume it is being played at."

"I suppose so."

"And did you determine those numbers when you found the disc player and put it into that nice plastic bag you wrote your initials on?"

"I didn't want smear any fingerprints, so, no, I didn't play around with it. Can I check my notes and see if I took down anything else?"

"Please," I said, having already reviewed the notes and knowing that he did not.

"No, I suppose not," he said finally. "I did make sure it played, though. I listened a bit to the disc."

"And it played pretty loudly, didn't it?"

"I suppose, with the headphones on."

"Now, I wonder if you might help us get a little more specific. May I approach the witness, Your Honor?"

Judge Tifaro gave me a skeptical look, which grew more strained when I smiled and waved two AA batteries at her. She glanced at Troy Jefferson, who stood and thought about it before sitting down again without raising an objection. "Go ahead, Mr. Carl," she said.

"I'm going to put in some fresh batteries and play the same CD that was in the player when you found it, and I'd like you to tell me whether or not it was this loud when you listened to it on the night of the murder."

When the new batteries were in and the player was set to a track called "Basin Street Blues," I asked Officer Jenkins to put on the headphones.

"Do you think it might have been louder than this?"

"Excuse me?" he said loudly.

I gestured for him to take off the headphones.

"How are those headphones, Officer? Comfortable?"

"Oh, yeah, sure."

"Do you think that the volume it was set at the night of the murder when you checked the sound might have been louder than this?"

"Yes, I think so. Yes, it was pretty loud."

"Okay, now, what I'd like to do is for you to put the headphones back on, and slowly I'll raise the volume. I'd like you to look at the little digital readout and when you're absolutely sure that it is at least as loud as or louder than it was that night, I'd like you to raise your hand to let us know. Is that clear?"

"Yes, sir."

"We're looking for the outer boundary of volume."

"I understand."

"All right, let's try it."

He put the headphones back on and stared down at the digital monitor, as did I. Slowly I pressed the volume button at the bottom of the player. I had started it very low, at two, and was raising it now to three, to three and a half, to four, to four and a half. I was watching not just the volume readout but also the time of the track. When it was at a volume of six and a half and the time into the track was 4:35, when Armstrong's brilliant horn is added to the mix in a roaring finale, I scratched my back.

A shot rang out, or something very much like a shot.

The whole courtroom jumped, the jury, the judge, the bailiff reached for his gun, all looked around crazily for the source of the shot, all but myself and Officer Jenkins, whose eyes were focused still on the little digital readout.

Beth, standing now, picked up the large legal volume she had dropped flat onto the defense table and apologized for the disturbance.

Troy Jefferson leaped to his feet and objected.

Judge Tifaro was starting to launch into a brutal admonishment aimed at Beth when Officer Jenkins raised his hand.

The judge stopped midsentence and, her mouth still open to speak, turned to stare at the witness.

Officer Jenkins took off his earphones. "It's hard to tell for certain, but my best guess," he said, still looking at the player, "is that the volume at the time was somewhere here between seven and eight, if that's helpful."

Officer Jenkins looked around at the quiet laughter, wondering what he had said that was so funny.

"Thank you, Officer," I said. "That's very helpful."

AND SO it continued, the trial of Guy Forrest, and so I continued with my witch's brew of cross-examination to bring to light a gap in time and space big enough for a murderer to walk through. And as I worked, as carefully and methodically as Troy Jefferson, and as that primordial black hole became a presence ever more real, something strange happened that made me wonder if indeed the entire space-time continuum had shifted.

A friend of Hailey's was testifying, which was strange, because I didn't know Hailey had any friends, and she was talking about the woman she knew. It wasn't such a flattering portrait, of a woman materialistic, casually cruel—I use the term "friend" broadly here—but as she spoke, I could detect something slight in the air about me, so slight I almost missed it, something shimmering in the courtroom. I had maybe noticed something before, some small distortion as, bit by bit, the testimony of the neighbors, of the crime-scene officers, of the witnesses who one by one linked together suspect and murderer, began to paint a portrait through their words. But in the testimony of this witness, this friend, it became clearer and clearer, word by word. I looked around to see if anyone else had spotted it, but, no, it had come only for me, with its sharp cheekbones and pursed lips and the sadness in its eyes.

The friend testified at one time to being in Hailey's office and hearing her speak, over the speakerphone, to a man she didn't recognize. She had met Guy before, this friend, and so she knew it wasn't he, but no names were used, and Hailey didn't tell her who it was. Something about the Stallone matter was all she could get, but she could tell, this friend, that there was something going on between Hailey and the man, something intimate and strong. And, no, they hadn't been fighting. And, no, there were no intimations of problems. And, no, she couldn't imagine that the man on the other side of that phone conversation, the way he spoke so sweetly to her, could have been her murderer.

Before she had finished her testimony, I leaned over to Beth and whispered, "Why don't you take this one."

Beth was lovely on cross, strong, clear, making it obvious that from the conversation the woman could have no real idea whether the relationship had any future or whether or not the man on the other side of that line might have turned murderous when rejected. In fact, the only thing we could really glean from the conversation was the strong link between the two, a link that could easily have turned wrong. Jefferson had thought the testimony would defuse my theory, when all it did was make the missing lover more mysterious, more threatening, a disembodied voice able to wreak any havoc.

I concentrated as much as I could on the testimony, but as the vision of the specter grew stronger, my mind wandered. It was Hailey, of course, conjured by my alchemy from some strange place to remind me. I had been struggling so hard to save Guy and protect my secret that I had forgotten what had driven me from the start, but here she was, Hailey Prouix, come to keep me to the decision that had been made.

Over the dead body of my lover I had pledged that I would discover the truth behind her murder and that the truth I discovered would be served, whatever the price to be later paid. And what was I doing to learn what had really happened, to learn who had really pulled the trigger and bring that killer to justice? Nothing. Absolutely nothing. That realization made me sick to my stomach as the testimony continued and the specter shimmered.

But just then a note was dropped in front of me as if out of the air. Without looking up, I opened it.

WE NEED TO TALK.

We need to talk. Are there four more frightening words in the English language? For a moment I suspected the message had come from my personal specter, but when I looked up from the note, the spell had been broken and she was gone.

So who was it, who needed to talk with me? I searched around until I found him, looking at me with that strange, bent gaze of his, and I knew without doubt that I was in serious trouble.

Detective Breger, back from Vegas and now in search of the missing lover, wanted to have a chat.

IF THIS had been a first date, there wouldn't have been a second.

Breger sat next to me at the bar, but he wouldn't look at me. He seemed uncomfortable, almost embarrassed to be meeting me without his partner, as if he were cheating. We talked a bit about the Eagles, we passed platitudes about politics. It was the kind of conversation bored strangers with real interest in nothing other than their booze suffer through. We were at the bar of a pizza chain out near the big suburban mall, a place that felt as empty of context as the huge shopping park in whose shadow it sat, a place that could have been anywhere in this great land, on the side of any highway, sandwiched between any two fast-food joints, a fine enough place to go only when there's no place else to be. Breger had suggested this place with its yawning emptiness, a place where no one knew us or cared about what we had to say to one another. Both of us were drinking out of politeness, but neither of us was really paying attention to the beers in our frosted franchise mugs. I was waiting for him to get down to business, he was waiting for something else, though I couldn't quite tell what.

"What's up, Detective?" I said finally, when we had talked of the weather about as much as I could stand.

"I'm just trying to figure out what's going on inside your head."

"Not too much."

"So it seems, but still I'm wondering," he said. "Why do you keep fighting our attempts to examine your phone logs?"

"Attorney-client privilege."

"I know how you keep us from looking, and the judge has backed you each time we've made the request, but I'm asking why."

"Privilege is like a muscle, Detective. If you don't exercise it, next time you turn around, it has become withered and weak."

He gave a quick and dismissive glance at my biceps. "We're still trying to figure out how Guy called you after he found his fiancée dead."

"Let's hope you get to the bottom of that mystery once and for all, save everybody a bit of worry."

He shook his head, took a sip of his beer. He didn't like my answer. I didn't like that he was still asking the question.

"Did you win in Vegas?" he said.

"Vegas?"

"Yeah, Vegas. Did you win or did you leave your money on the craps table?"

I waited a moment, tried to figure how to play it, and then decided to play it straight. Sooner or later the fact of our little trip was bound to come out, and sooner had just stepped through the door. "Some guy I was with thought he had a system."

"Did he?"

"Yes, but not a good system."

"Find anything of interest in the safe-deposit box?"

"Safe-deposit box?"

"Hailey Prouix's box at the Nevada One Bank, Paradise Road branch."

"Who exactly are you investigating, Detective?"

"And tell me, how did you find West Virginia?"

"Wild and wonderful, just as the ads say."

"Our office received a call that you were down there asking questions."

"Yes, well, that's what lawyers do. We ask questions."

"But why there?"

"I was getting a little history."

"And the man you were with down there, this Skink. It seems he also was in Las Vegas."

"Just an investigator I have working for me."

"We'd like to speak to him."

"That wouldn't be proper, considering he's covered by the attorney-client privilege, too."

"I am struggling here, Carl, struggling to figure out your side in all this. Stone doesn't like you. She thinks you want to ask her out but are afraid, and she's glad you're afraid. Saves her from breaking your heart. She says you're smarmy."

"Me?"

"Smarmy and weak and definitely hiding something. I don't like you much either, I've decided. I think you're whiny and manipulative and not half as clever as you think you are, but I don't really care about all that."

"Does that mean *you'd* go out with me?"

"Somehow I have the strange sense that you're looking for the right kind of outcome here. I have a sense, maybe, that you're as interested as me in finding out what the hell really happened to Hailey Prouix."

"You don't think Guy Forrest did it?"

"The evidence points right in his face. But I have to admit that some of what you said in your opening had been on my mind from the start. Like he really was in love with her. Like he never was in it for the money. Like he doesn't seem the type to end a fight with a bullet. But I've already told this to Jefferson, which is as far as my legal obligation goes. It is his decision whether or how to proceed. So it's not the doubts I'm struggling with. What I'm struggling with is you."

"You have unresolved feelings and you find them threatening. I understand. It's perfectly natural, really."

"You are in this deeper than you let on. You are in this up to your neck, though I can't quite figure out how. You are in this in ways that give me serious pause and leave me struggling to figure out what to do with something I found."

"Something exculpatory? If it's exculpatory, you have to turn it over. *Brady* v. *Maryland*."

"Now who's the jerk throwing out cites? But what I have is nothing right now, though I have a sense you might be able to tell me enough to make it more interesting."

"Tell you what?"

"Let's start with why you turned over the gun."

I paused for a moment, wondering what he had found, where he was going, whether or not I could trust him, even with a little bit of the truth. "I thought your possessing the gun," I said slowly, "might further the ends of justice."

"That sounds like bullshit."

"It does, doesn't it? That's the way it is with lawyers and politicians both, we can make even the truth sound like lies."

"What did you find in Vegas?"

"A story."

"Go ahead."

"A story about a boy who was killed a decade and a half ago in a little town in West Virginia."

"Hailey Prouix's hometown."

"That's right. He had fallen in love with Hailey, they had a stormy romance, and then he found out about something. He found out about something, and it made him mad as hell and put him at a crossroads. He was going to either run away with his love, Hailey Prouix, or hurt someone. And there he was, at the quarry on the south side of town, waiting to hear which way it was going to be, when the next thing he somehow falls off a ledge, cracks his head open, and dies in the water that had collected at the quarry's bottom. The natural suspect was a guy named Grady Pritchett, rich man's son, big man in high school who had been fighting with our dead boy just a few days before. All eyes turned to him, but he had an alibi, and a pretty convincing one at that. Hailey Prouix. Funny how it worked. And funny how after Hailey stood up for Grady Pritchett she got her college and law school all paid for so she could get the hell out of Pierce once and for all."

"How come I never heard any of this?"

"You haven't been asking the right questions."

"What kind of car does this Grady Pritchett drive?"

"Why?"

"Just asking."

"Doesn't drive a car, drives a truck. A big black pickup."

"Where does he live?"

"Just a few towns down the road from Pierce."

"And you think this Grady might have come up here and killed that girl?"

"Nope."

"You think he killed that boy fifteen years ago?"

"Nope."

"Then what the hell do you think?"

"I don't know. I haven't yet figured it out, but there's something connecting the two deaths. I met up with Hailey's sister. She's certifiable, in an actual asylum, treats some pop physics book as her Bible, but I took from her babbling that she, too, thinks the two are related. And if they are, I want to find out how. Believe this, Detective, all I want is for whoever killed Hailey Prouix to go straight to hell."

"Even if it's your client?"

"He didn't do it."

"What makes you so sure?"

"She seduced him for the Gonzalez money. She set him up for it, met him at a bar, let their knees bang accidentally, and seduced him completely and absolutely. He fell stupidly in love and lost his bearings and gave up everything for her. Like I said in my opening, for him it was never about the money, it was about a love that was transforming, or maybe more precisely the hope for a love that was transforming. She set him up for the money, yes, but his hope was real, and he never could have killed that hope. Even when it all turned bad, he closed his eyes and kept it alive, because it was the hope he was chasing more than even her."

"And obsession couldn't have turned to violence?"

"Not with him, not with her. See, no matter what happened, he'd always remember the way he felt when their knees banged accidentally at that bar."

Maybe there was something in my voice that betrayed me, because he turned to stare at me with that wandering gaze of his and he said, "And how did that feel exactly?"

"I'm telling you what I can."

"Maybe telling only what you can is not enough."

I didn't know what else to say. I couldn't explain the knocking of the knees and the way it had felt, the confusion and hope and lust all mixed together, I just couldn't. I would be betraying more than myself, more than Guy, I would be betraying her, too. So instead I decided to say something else, something that would resonate. It is always in times of maximum stress, when all alternatives fail, that lawyers tend to turn to that most unlikely tactic, the truth.

"I saw the body, Detective. I saw her on that mattress with a bullet through her chest. I saw the way her arms were crazily akimbo, I saw the way the blood contrasted with the pale of her skin. I've seen a few corpses, not as many as you, but a few, and they never fail to stun me with their abject lifelessness. It's not like you can just breathe life back into them, it's not like they're sleeping, it's something else, something distorted in a way that haunts the dreams. I can't just let that go, I can't just play my minor role and let the rest of you decide how it all gets sorted out. I saw the body, Detective."

He breathed in quickly through his nose, or was it a snort? I couldn't tell. He stared straight ahead for a long moment before downing his beer and swiveling away from me. He reached into his jacket and tossed something onto the bar, a dollar or two for the beer, I supposed, and without saying a further word he climbed off his stool and headed out the door, right out the door.

Gone.

A despair flitted over my shoulders in that instant, a despair that filled me with a shocking sense of hopelessness. There was something about Breger I found comforting, something solid. He had shown faith in me, kindness, too, in his way. I admired how fairly he had handled the case, and I wanted to tell him everything. I wanted him to understand and say that I had done right, that everything would be okay. For some reason, from him, it would sound like the real thing. But he had instead just snorted at me and climbed down and walked away, a gesture that let me know with utter clarity that I had not done right, that everything would not be okay.

I was sitting at the bar, feeling the despair, when I noticed a piece of paper in front of me. It looked like a bar tab. When I scanned the bar for the money Breger had left, there was nothing else, and I figured Breger had stuck me with the check. But then I looked at the paper more closely and saw that it wasn't a bill. It was something else.

A speeding ticket issued by the Philadelphia Police.

Left on the bar, for me, by my good friend Detective Breger.

I stared at it for a long moment, the name of the driver, Dwayne Joseph Bohannon, which I didn't recognize, the make and style of the automobile, the state and number of the license plate, the location of the violation, the date. The date. I stared at it for a moment and then a moment more, and then I took out my phone.

First I called Beth and told her that she would have to handle the next day of the trial all by herself.

"What should I do?" she asked.

"Vamp," I said. "With all your heart."

Then I called the airline and made a reservation for two on the first flight out the next morning headed for Charleston, West Virginia.

"Will you be needing a rental car at the airport?" asked the reservation man.

"Oh, yes," I said. "Yes indeed."

41

FALL HAD come to Pierce with a suddenness that stunned. How long had I been away, how long had the trial of Guy Forrest been going on? It seemed I had lost my temporal bearings. When I had driven into the little town before, it felt as though the promise of spring had just given way to the relentless summer. Now the dry colors of autumn had taken hold, the bright yellows and oranges heralding the death of a season. Right now it was a riotous bounty of color. In a few weeks all would be bare in Pierce.

We walked up the hill, through fallen leaves, their desiccated bodies crumbling beneath our feet as we made our way to the church.

Inside, our footfalls echoed about the plaster and wood of the main chapel. We knocked on the door of the rectory, and Reverend Henson bade us enter without asking first who we were. His face, when he recognized me, was distressed but not surprised, as if he had been expecting me to return all along. As if the only thing that surprised him was that I had waited so long and had brought with me someone new.

"Reverend Henson," I said, "I'd like to introduce Oliver Breger, a Montgomery County homicide detective. Hailey died in Montgomery County and he is investigating her death. I hope you don't mind, but I thought it important to bring him along."

The reverend smiled thinly at Breger. "A little out of your juris-diction, isn't it, Detective?"

"Mr. Carl said it might be interesting."

Breger wasn't looking at Henson as he spoke, his gaze instead was slipping around the small room with its cherry paneling and shelves filled with prayer books and theological texts. Behind the door hung the reverend's vestment, flat and black and surprisingly frail, pinned as it was, limp and small, to the wood. It was a com-fortable room, a place to read and prepare sermons, a place to have the pro forma talk with the bride and groom before the wedding or to hear stories from the family about the dear departed before the funeral, a comfortable room, but not lush. No, the Reverend Hen-son did not live a posh life in Pierce, it was clear. Whatever he had gained in the bargain he had brokered, it had not been his own ma-terial gain.

Henson shifted in his seat and asked us to sit. He wasn't happy having a homicide detective in his church, I was sure. I suppose he wasn't happy having me there either, but I hadn't come to make the good reverend happy. Something had happened in Pierce sixteen years ago, something rotten that the reverend was in the middle of, something that bore directly on the trial of Guy Forrest. The speed-ing ticket given me by the detective had shown with utter clarity that the deaths of Jesse Sterrett and Hailey Prouix were indeed re-lated. To demonstrate that to a jury, I was going to need the rev-erend's testimony. And I would need something else, something maybe Breger could help me get if I convinced him I was right. That something else was what had prompted me to ask Breger along. His own innate curiosity, so vital to the makeup of a first-rate detective, was what prompted him to agree.

"I've come again," I said, "to talk about Jesse Sterrett."

"Of course you have. But I've told you all I can, Mr. Carl. I have certain . . . responsibilities."

"You're talking about privilege, aren't you? Priest-penitent. Oh, I know about privilege. Detective Breger could tell you all about my reliance on privilege."

"I've thought about this ever since you left, I considered all my options, read what I could on the subject. It is a balancing act, to be sure, but I have done that balancing in my head, over and over, and I believe there is nothing I can do. I am truly sorry."

"You need to know, Reverend Henson, that it didn't end with Jesse Sterrett. It isn't over."

"There is nothing I can do."

"He killed Hailey."

"No, no, he didn't," he said. "I checked as soon as I heard the terrible news. He never left the state."

"He sent someone else to do it. And that's not all. He tried to kill me, too. An attempt on my life is something I take pretty personally, especially when it is my partner who ends up in the hospital, dazed with a concussion, her wrist snapped like a twig. The doctors are still trying to put it back together."

Henson startled behind the desk and then looked away. "I'm sorry."

"It isn't over, Reverend. No one paid the ultimate price sixteen years ago, no one was convicted of murder in his stead, Hailey saw to that, but if you ask Grady Pritchett, a price was paid nonetheless, a price almost more than he could bear. And now my client is on trial for his life. If he loses, they will kill him. I know you can't allow that. I know you can't allow a man to die for something he did not do."

"I'm sure it won't come to that. I'm sure you can pull it out with some dashing legal maneuver. I've heard about you Philadelphia lawyers."

"Oh, I have some tricks up my sleeve, yes I do. But so does the prosecutor, also a Philadelphia lawyer, with flashier moves than mine. And really, all I can tell you with certainty after a decade of practicing law is that no one knows what a jury will do. And here's the thing, Reverend. You coming in after the fact might not be enough. The appellate court might not believe you, or might decide you are speaking up too late. The court might let the verdict stand. You might end up in the prison parking lot, fists balled in frustration, as an innocent man dies for someone else's sins and for your silence."

"Maybe you're wrong. Maybe you're mistaken. What proof do you have?"

I stared at him for a moment. I could see the wavering in his eyes. Yes, he had been thinking about it for the weeks since I left, and they had not been easy weeks.

"I could sit here and try to prove it to you, Reverend. In my brief-case I have all manner of evidence, but, to be honest, none of it is conclusive. It is all wildly circumstantial. But you don't really need proof, do you? Your mind is asking for the evidence, but in your heart you know. In your heart you've known from the instant you learned of Hailey's death. You knew this moment was coming, and though you've been reading the texts and debating what to do, your heart's known what you needed to do all along."

He didn't answer.

"I'm responsible for accusing Guy Forrest of murder," said Breger, his words soft and comforting but his unsettling gaze now straight on the reverend. "In all my years I believe I've never been involved in the conviction of an innocent man. It would haunt me to the day I died if ever I was. If you have information that might convince me I am wrong about that man, I need to hear it."

"What happened to Jesse Sterrett sixteen years ago?" I said.

There was a long silence. The trees outside the window lost more of their leaves, a darkness came and passed as a cloud drifted over-head. There was a long silence, and then Reverend Henson said, "I don't know for sure. That's the thing, Mr. Carl, I've never known for sure."

"Then tell us what you do know."

"All I know is suspicion and surmise, and the anguished cries of a poet who died before either of the Prouix twins was born. That is all I know. But even so, Mr. Carl, even so, it remains a story to tear at your heart."

REVEREND HENSON

SHE CAME around shortly after I arrived to take over for the Reverend Johannson.

He had been a formidable figure in the community, the Reverend Johannson, with his great leonine head and deep voice. They said around town that listening to his uncompromising sermons was like listening to a prophet of God. As you can see, I was quite a change. I'm more squirrelish than leonine, and no one ever confused my squeak of a voice with the voice of God. Following the Reverend Johannson, I thought I'd be a great disappointment to the congregation, but that turned out not to be exactly so. I suppose some thought I wasn't up for the job, that I didn't project the image of stern righteousness they had come to expect in Pierce, but then again others greeted me with much warmth, as though I were a welcome antidote. 'Tis a hard thing, I suppose, to bring what seem to be our petty little problems to a prophet of God, even when sometimes they're not so petty.

When first I arrived, there was an initial period of greeting in the community and I was taken up in a gratifying whirl of activity. But then, of course, the invitations slowed appreciably, and I settled into the more peaceful rhythms of a small-town rectory, with much time on my hands. That was when Hailey came around to see me.

She was a lovely-looking girl, that was clear, with a sadness that was unmistakable and made her, somehow, intriguing to me. And she was provocative, too. She would dress a certain way and act a certain way and hold herself a certain way, all designed, I could tell, to get my heart to beating. And it did a bit, I admit, I'm only human, and I wasn't yet married. And she did keep wearing shirts the bottoms of which never seemed to reach the top of her pants. And her smile was truly a dazzling thing. She was fishing, almost desperately, daring me, it seemed, some of her comments were on the wrong side of salacious, but I steadfastly refused to take the lure, or even to much react beyond a disapproving rise of the eyebrow. I might not be as good a man as I could wish, but I saw before me a girl in some sort of trouble, and I knew exactly what she didn't need from the likes of me. So I didn't take the lure, and it was as if by not doing so I had passed her little test. Slowly I saw her manner ease and her provocative ways cease.

Her house was not far from here, on the same side of Main Street, and she seemed to be around more and more. We talked about things, nothing much at the first, the high school teams, some small-town gossip. It is amazing, I've found, how a little harmless gossip loosens the tongue. We spoke, and I felt echoes of problems deep beneath her veneer, but she didn't open up and I didn't push. Sometimes when you push you push away, and I sensed she was looking for something from me, though I couldn't yet figure out what. I tried to get her interested in some of the youth activities I had begun, a way to keep the young people out of the quarry and involved in a more wholesome setting. Her sister, Roylynn, serious and reserved, was one of the mainstays of our youth group, but Hailey would have none of it, and, to be honest, I could see she wasn't the type. But I maintained my warm welcome whenever I saw her, and we continued to talk, and slowly the talks turned from the coyly frivolous to the more serious.

"I don't believe in God," she told me one day in this very office. Her legs were slung over the armrests of a chair and she said it as if she meant to shock me, which I thought sweet, in its way. I mean, in our modern world, could anything be less shocking than that?

"What do you believe in, then?" I asked.

"Not much," she said.

"That's a problem, isn't it? If you don't believe the ground is solid beneath your feet, how do you dare to take a step? And if you don't believe the air itself won't poison you, how do you dare to take another breath?"

"That's stuff I can see," she said. "I believe in stuff like that."

"But can you, really? Scientists say the surface of the earth is continuing to shift every moment, not to mention the great uncertainties postulated in the quantum theories of physics." She gave me a blank look, but I continued on. "And how many in this very town have lungs black as tar from breathing air they thought was safe? No, Hailey, it seems the things in which you believe are not so worthy of belief. What does that tell you of that in which you do not believe? Maybe the only things worth belief are those we can't see with our eyes, but with our hearts. Maybe that's what makes belief at all special in the first place."

She stayed silent for a moment, thinking. You could see her trying to make some sense of the insensible.

"I suppose one thing I believe in," she said finally, "is love."

"There you are, Hailey," I said. "And what is love, after all, but the purest manifestation of God's presence on the surface of the earth."

I was pleased with myself at coming up with that. It seemed I had given some semblance of an answer in an area where there are truly only questions, and Hailey, well, she walked out with something like a smile. I felt pleased with myself. But I've learned since that self-satisfaction often blinds us to the fact that we are traversing the most treacherous of territories.

"REMEMBER BEFORE, when you said love is like a piece of God right here on earth?" she said to me a few afternoons later. I was working then in the cemetery, trying to keep it as best I could with what little horticultural talent I had, and she was helping me to yank out the more aggressive weeds.

"I don't think you can divide God into pieces like that, Hailey, but I might have said something to that effect, yes."

"Does that include any kind of love?"

A good question, that one, and she asked it with a kind of urgency, as if it had been troubling her over the past few days. I could see the problem right away, the dilemma I had blithely stepped into like a pile of horse dung, but I assumed I could wipe it off my shoes with little fancy blather.

"I suppose it does. All love is a great gift," I said carefully. "But how that love is expressed can turn it from something godly to something else."

"I don't understand."

"Well, Hailey, you might love your dog, the emotion might be stronger than you could ever expect and that would be a lovely, godlike thing. Jesus felt great love for all the animals in his kingdom. But you wouldn't marry your dog, you wouldn't take vows in a church with a dog, trying to be man and wife in the eyes of the Lord with a canine. That just wouldn't do. That would be worse than silly, don't you see?"

She looked at me for a moment and then said, "You're talking about sex."

"Am I?" I said disingenuously, because I was, absolutely, and Hailey was always too sharp to slip even the most clever bit by. "Well, maybe that's part of it. But whatever it is we're talking about, it's not the love that's the problem, it is the way it is expressed. Propriety is not just a matter of how to sip tea at some dowager's house. It is more, far more. It is how to live a life. And there are guides if you need them."

"Anne Landers?"

"Yes, or the Bible."

"Please."

"Hailey, you know full well where we are and what I am. I even suspect that is exactly why you are here."

She didn't respond, but the posture of her body showed she knew I was right about that.

"And sometimes," I continued, "there are things we know from experience, our own experience or that of others we trust enough to listen to. For example, I can tell you true that what might be a sun-dappled love to one might be something else to another."

"Excuse me?"

"It is sometimes hard to be sure what we are feeling, really, or what the other is feeling. What might feel like love might be something else, some urgent physical need that seemingly can't wait, although, of course, science and experience has proven that it can."

"You think it's just lust."

"It's always possible. And when you dress like you dress, it becomes all the more probable, don't you think?"

"No, it's not just that."

"Oh, don't be so sure, sweet Hailey. I'm not totally unaware of the world. I was once a boy myself, you know."

She tilted her head at me. "Boys?" she said. "Boys? Oh, no, Reverend, boys don't worry me." Then she smiled. "I eat boys like air."

I WAS troubled by that last comment, troubled by the whole conversation, to be sure, but that last comment most of all. I realized I had no idea what it was we had been speaking about, and I knew that to be a dangerous thing. Sometimes if you ask too many questions, you scare a child off, but then sometimes if you don't ask enough questions, you end up talking nonsense. I didn't know which it was with Hailey, but I felt an unease. "I eat boys like air," she had said. There was something about that line that tolled familiar. It was like a line from a horror movie, but I couldn't recall which. So I called a friend of mine, who taught English at a small college in Ohio and who, it seemed, knew every fact about every movie ever made.

"It's not from a movie," my friend told me. "It's the final line of a poem by Sylvia Plath, although in the original it is men she eats like air."

"Plath?" I said. "I don't think I ever read her."

"It's a girl thing," she said. "Like Nietzsche is a boy thing."

"I never cared much for Nietzsche."

"No, I suppose he's not big among the clergy. So who's quoting Plath?"

"Just a young girl who seems to be a bit troubled."

"Be careful there, Teddy. Plath is the patron saint of bewitched adolescent girls who find themselves overwhelmed by pain and disillusionment. We just hope they don't follow her career too closely."

"Really. Tell me about her, this Sylvia Plath."

"Oh, books have been written. The most important male critics think she's minor at best, but whole wings of women critics have clutched her to their breasts as an authentic feminine voice struggling free in a male-dominated society. And there's no doubt about the power in her work. Her father died when she was eight, and that seems to be the major impetus behind all her writing. She cracked up at eighteen, took pills to kill herself, and later wrote a famous book about it called *The Bell Jar*. Went to Smith, then to Cambridge. At a party she famously met a now famous British poet named Ted Hughes. They took one look at each other and they kissed hard—'bang smash on the mouth,' she wrote in her journal—and she bit his cheek until blood flowed, and that was it."

"Oh, my."

"Happiness for a time, they married, had children, wrote poetry, made names for themselves. But ultimately he cheated and left her poor with two kids, and she lashed out against him in her work. Many of the women critics blame what happened next on the husband."

"Tell me."

"Well, there's a disturbing strain of Holocaust imagery in her poems. She seemed to strongly identify with the Jews marched by the Nazis into the gas chambers. It might be because her father was a German, though certainly no Nazi, having emigrated to America at the century's turn. Anyway, one night, after her husband had left her, she put out bread and milk for her two children and then stuck her head in a gas oven and killed herself."

"My God," I said.

"She was thirty."

I felt a chill, just then. It wasn't only that Hailey had quoted a Plath poem, or even the shocking coincidence of both she and Sylvia Plath losing their fathers at age eight, it was something deeper. I sensed a desperation in Hailey, and a sadness, and an urgency, and I suddenly feared where that sad, desperate urgency might lead her. What was it that was eating at her, and would it drive her to some horrible mistake? I hoped she would come in again to talk, so I could maybe calm her or help her. Things would be different if she came in again. I would be more forthright. I would talk to her about Sylvia Plath. I would step in forcefully. I waited for her to come and see me. But she didn't, as if she was avoiding me, and, for whatever reason, I didn't go to her. And then I learned, through the normal channels of gossip, that something terrible had happened in the Prouix household.

IT IS a peculiar thing, sitting by the bedside, chatting amiably about this and that, nothing of any import, chatting oh, so amiably, all the while unsuccessfully trying not to stare at the white bandages that cover a young girl's wrists. You try to be cheery and funny, you tell stories and both of you laugh, you talk about the exciting events coming up in the near future, and still, all the time, there are those bandages. That's what it was like for me, sitting beside Roylynn Prouix's bedside after she was found in the bathtub up to her neck with red-stained water, horizontal gashes on her forearms.

The house the Prouixs lived in is now owned by the Liptons, and I have since been there many times, and it is pleasant and sunny, but I felt no sun in the house that day. There was a darkness, darker than the familiar black mood of a house visited by tragedy. Mrs. Prouix thanked me for coming and offered me a cup of tea, and I sat with her in mostly silence in the kitchen as she made it and I drank it. She smiled tightly and hugged herself as if she wanted to disappear, and I saw not a spark of life in her eyes. When she talked about her daughter, she spoke softly, in phrases so common they were devoid of meaning. "She's feeling better now." "Everything will be all right, I am sure." "It is so nice when friends come to visit." "More tea, Reverend, or a cookie?" Mrs. Prouix was unable to confront the fact that her daughter had stood on the precipice between her life and her death and had chosen to step through. Hailey came into the kitchen and joined us, subdued, as if her normal energy had been drawn out of her. I tried to start a conversation with her, but she let all my openings fall to the floor and flop there, like fish in the throes of death. It was awkward, more than that, it was unpleasant and frightening, the way she changed inside that house. And then we heard footsteps, coming up the stoop, heavy footsteps, and something strange occurred when we heard them. Mrs. Prouix seemed to shrink, if that was possible, and Hailey brightened as if a candle inside had been lit.

He came into the house with his overalls spattered with blood. And however dark the house had felt before he entered, it felt darker still with his presence. I stood, instinctively, pushed to my feet by a strange fear. He yelled something crude before he saw me, and when he did finally spy me, he quieted, as if daunted by my collar. Tall, gaunt, his broad shoulders leaning aggressively forward, his hands curled into near fists, his huge knuckles covered with thick black hairs. Lawrence Cutlip. When he saw me, he wiped his mouth with the back of his hand and stared for a moment before he smiled and called me by my honorific and thanked me for visiting his dear ill niece. There was a chilling warmth, chilling because it came too quickly and without effort and was only almost convincing. I felt the urge to leave, to run, to get away from that house, but I stilled my heart and fought my urges and sat down with him. When he offered a beer, I took it and drank, as did he, straight from the bottle. When, in the course of our conversation, he asked me if I played poker, I lied and said only a little, and he brightened even more and invited me into his game at the local Chrysler dealership, and I accepted with an expression of gratitude. When we talked, we agreed on important civic matters, even when I thought him dead wrong. I even laughed at his jokes, no matter how cruel. And all the time I sensed that the darkness I had felt in that house emanated straight from some black abscess in his heart.

Why did I stay in that house and let the likes of Larry Cutlip ply his charm on me? Guilt, pure and simple, a guilt that I felt as soon as I had heard the disastrous news about Roylynn and that I still believe was utterly deserved. I had missed what it was that was happening with her, missed it completely. I had been worried about Hailey, pretty, provocative Hailey, with her dazzling smile and suggestive questions, and the whole time I had assumed all was right with her quiet, dutiful sister. But that was blind of me, wasn't it? They were twins, after all, weren't they? And what it was that afflicted the one was sure to afflict the other. They expressed it differently, obviously, for reasons of their own, but they were both equally at risk, and I, feeling so proud of my forbearance, still had been seduced by the one to the point that I ignored the other. And so, I suppose you could say it was the guilt that sent me searching for an answer.

Roylynn was referred by the state to a county home for troubled girls, where she could be watched more closely, and I was glad to have convinced the welfare worker of such a move being necessary. She was well out of danger for the moment, I figured, though Hailey was still in that house, with that man, still in need of saving. And so I set my plan. I would identify the affliction and do all in my power to heal those children, that household, that family. The death of the father was part of it, I was sure, and there was precious little I could do about that. But this other, this Lawrence Cutlip, he was part of it, too, I sensed. Part of the darkness came straight from him, I sensed. And so I would do my scouting on his turf, drink with him, laugh at his jokes, play in his game, and all the time hope to gain a glimpse of what was afflicting those girls.

I lost in the card game. Larry Cutlip was a gambler, hard-core, who was in it, I could instantly tell, not for the conviviality or the conversation but for the money. He wanted me in the game only as long as I swam like a fish, and so as a fish I swam. But I didn't lose more than I could afford to lose, I hadn't put myself through college playing poker against private-school boys without learning my way around a deck of cards. So I played, and I lost, and I kept my eyes narrowed as I watched. And what I saw across the green felt table from me was a glimpse of something evil.

You look at me aghast, as if I am saying it was Satan sitting across from me, but I tell you a man can be evil without cleft feet and a tail. What is it to be evil in this world? It is to have an unsubmitted will, to swear allegiance to nothing but the inner demons of one's self,

and to use every possible means to bend others to those same
demons. Most of the people I see have given themselves over to
some other good, to their children, their spouses, their friends or
families, their business maybe, or their community or country, their
people, their God. You, Mr. Carl, as a lawyer, have submitted your
will to the workings of our country's legal system. You, Detective
Breger, have submitted your will to the pursuit of justice. Both of
you, I assume, have submitted your wills if not to God then to the
simple ideal of trying to do the right thing. The submission of will
is the start of goodness. Matthew five, verse three: "Blessed are the
poor in spirit: for theirs is the kingdom of heaven."

I spent three years ministering in prisons, I've seen bad people up
close, psychopaths with no conscience whatsoever, but still, in all my
life I think I've only met three people with a completely unsubmitted
will, three people whom I consider evil. One was the mother of a
childhood friend, whose evil I recognized only upon reflection long
after the friend had killed himself. One was in the clergy, believe it or
not. And one was Lawrence Cutlip. It took me a while to see it, they
all cleverly hide it behind a veneer of good intentions, but see it I did,
and it sent shivers. Nothing existed to temper his desire. Whatever he
wanted was right, whoever opposed him was wrong, everything he
did was justified and proper, everything in this universe existed for
the purpose of serving him. You could see it in the way he dealt with
people, the way he dealt with problems, the way, finally, he dealt the
cards. It was subtle, but not too subtle for someone trained to see the
flip of the finger and the distinct sound of cards slipped from the bottom of the deck at crucial points in the game.

Before the father of the twins died, Cutlip had been a worthless
drunk, surviving out of garbage cans and by petty thefts. Suddenly,
in one tragic accident, he gained a house, a family, a certain amount
of money, and still he talked about how he sacrificed his life to raise
his sister's family, how he suffered to raise them right. What he did
on the surface seemed righteous, but there is always, in evil people,
a desperate attempt to portray themselves as the souls of righteousness. And just as inevitably, whenever a portion of the evil
slips from that false cover of propriety, they are quick to angrily
blame someone else for the evil deed.

So I spent part of my time examining the inner demons of Lawrence Cutlip and being frightened by what I found. And I spent another part of my time reading a volume of the complete poems of a certain female author with whom at least one of the twins had identified. *"The world is blood-hot and personal,"* she wrote, and in every line there were expressions of anger, madness, despair. I am no scholar, and much of the poetry, I must admit, was indecipherable to me, but other of it was crystal clear. *"Dying is an art, like everything else,"* she wrote. *"I do it exceptionally well. I do it so it feels like hell."* And still other of it caused in me a deep alarm. *"The child's cry melts in the wall."* I couldn't stop myself from imagining the stifled cries of another young girl. There was one poem in particular that struck me. It was called "Daddy," and knowing of the similar timing of the father's death in the lives of Sylvia Plath and the Prouix twins, I seized on it immediately. The poem told of the author's attempt to come to grips with the choices she made in the wake of her father's absence, and when I read it as a clue into the mind of a fifteen-year-old girl, one line in particular seized me with terror. *"Every woman adores a fascist,"* wrote the poet, *"the boot in the face, the brute brute heart of a brute like you."*

HAILEY WOULDN'T much talk to me after my visit to her house. Oh, she still stopped by now and then, and we chatted, and she gave me updates on Roylynn's condition at the home and of the fine things Roylynn had written about it, but there seemed to be something diminished about her. Everything about Hailey seemed smaller, her energy, her smile, even her size, everything but her sadness. Whenever I tried to steer the conversation to God or love or any difficulties in her own life, she turned our discussion in some innocuous direction. And whenever I tried to bring up her uncle, she said something bland and then quickly left. She had shut me out, whether because of what had happened to Roylynn or because of my new seeming friendship with her uncle, I couldn't tell, but I could see that she still was troubled, and I understood that now more than ever she needed my help.

Then, suddenly, almost overnight, she changed completely. There was joy where there had been only sadness, and the dazzling smile was back. I commented on the transformation, and she smiled as young lovers smile, and I can't tell you how happy I was to see it. Yes, me, a man of God, happy to see a lover's smile on a young girl's face.

"Tell me about him," I said one afternoon.

"Who?" she said, though she knew whom I meant.

"The boy."

"Oh, Reverend, I eat boys like . . ."

"Just cut out the act and tell me about him," I said.

Her smile grew. "He plays baseball," she said, "and he's gorgeous, and I feel like, I don't know, like I can actually talk to him."

I had heard the rumors, and I assumed she was talking about Grady Pritchett. I didn't like Grady, thought there was nothing to him except arrogance and entitlement, but I welcomed anything that got her out of that house, away from that evil. I was still worried about Roylynn, of course, but suddenly I felt hope for Hailey, as if she had finally escaped from a nightmare.

And then they found the body of the Sterrett boy in the lake at the belly of the quarry.

I WASN'T a part of the official probe. I know you've already talked to the chief, and so I'll let stand whatever it was he says about what they found and how they investigated. That wing of the Sterrett family were buried in our cemetery, but they were not members of our congregation, and so, beyond the normal sadness I have upon learning of the death of any promising youth, I didn't think this much affected the Prouixs or me. But then I heard that maybe it was Grady Pritchett they were looking at as the killer. And then I heard that this Jesse Sterrett, whom I knew to be a good-looking boy, had been the best baseball prospect to come out of the county in fifty years. I knew then that Hailey was somehow at the heart of this tragedy, and I sought her out.

I looked for her at the house, the school, I asked her friends. No one knew where she was, no one had seen her. Up and down the valley I drove, searching to no avail while the bitter lines of the poetry I had been reading tied themselves into knots in my mind. *"And I am the arrow,"* wrote the poet, *"the dew that flies suicidal."* On the spur of the moment I thought to check the quarry.

There was yellow tape around the fence, but I ducked under it and through the rip in the fencing and clambered down the steep slope to the narrow ledge above the water. There, behind a large outcropping, curled like a lizard in hiding, I found her.

I stooped beside her on the ledge and said nothing for a long moment and waited for her to acknowledge my presence, which she failed to do.

"He was the one," I said finally.

She gave no answer.

"He was the one, Hailey, the one who brought a smile to your lips and a flush to your cheeks."

"Stop," she said quietly.

"What happened?"

"I don't know. I don't, don't know."

"No? They say it was Grady Pritchett that did it. The police are centering their investigation on him."

"It wasn't Grady."

"And how do you know that?"

"Because Grady is a coward."

"Maybe he is, but he's the one they're looking at. He's the one who will shoulder the blame even if it was someone else that did the deed."

"Maybe it was an accident."

"Yes, maybe. Wonderful athletes often are the clumsiest in their footing. But tell me, Hailey, who knew about you and the Sterrett boy?"

"No one, kids at school maybe."

"Did your uncle?"

She looked at me, her red-rimmed eyes.

" 'To do justice and judgment is more acceptable to the Lord than sacrifice.' Don't hide it, Hailey, tell me. Who did this to young Jesse? Who did this to you?"

"Stop. Please."

"I think I know."

"You don't know anything."

"I think I know. Let me read you something you might recognize." I took a paper out of my pocket. "It's from a poem I've been reading."

She turned her face to me, puzzled, but as I started to read from the Plath poem "Daddy," she curled her body defensively as if to ward off blows.

" *'I was ten when they buried you,' "* I recited. " *'At twenty I tried to die and get back, back, back to you. I thought even the bones would do. But they pulled me out of the sack, and they stuck me together with glue. And then I knew what to do. I made a model of you, a man in black with a Meinkampf look and a love of the rack and the screw. And I said I do, I do.' "*

"Shut up."

"I want to help," I said. "Let me help. But for me to help, you must step out of your hole and tell me what is happening. I can't do anything if you won't tell me. Save Grady, Hailey, and save yourself, too."

She didn't respond. She lay there, curled like a lizard, thinking, and I stayed beside her in silence. Waiting for her to speak, waiting for her to tell me something, everything.

"You want to help me and help Grady?" she said finally.

"Yes," I said. "I can and I will."

"Then, this is what you do. You play cards with Grady's father, he trusts you, I'm sure. You tell him I'll get Grady cleared of all charges in exchange for something."

"Yes," I said, hoping she was ready to tell me all.

"Tell him I want a college education for me and Roylynn, college and graduate school if that's what we want. Tell him in exchange for him financing our route out of this stinking little town, I'll make sure Grady is cleared. Do you got that, Reverend?"

"Yes."

"All right," she said. "Let me know when it is all agreed, and I'll talk to the police."

"Where will you be?"

"Here, I'll be right here. I've got no place else to go."

I MADE the deal. When I proposed it to Mr. Pritchett, he snarled at me, a Scotch in his hand, and nodded, and that was that. I ran back to the quarry and took Hailey with me to the police. I expected then that she would tell them what had happened, tell the truth, that the evil would be taken care of, I was certain of it. But, as always with Hailey, she betrayed my expectations. She insisted on seeing Grady first, and only then did she tell her story to the police, and a clever story it was. She saved Grady, financed her college and law degree, gave her sister a chance, everything she said she would do, but she did it all with a lie.

It wasn't enough, I couldn't just leave it at that. I had no evidence of what I thought had really happened, nothing more than the rantings of a suicidal poet, no witnesses who would back up my suspicions, but still I could not do nothing. I was compelled to do something. And so it was that I summoned Lawrence Cutlip to meet me in the chapel on a sunny Thursday afternoon.

He stood before me with his dangerous forward lean, a fresh wound on his cheek, his overalls spattered with the blood of slaughtered cattle. He held in his huge, hairy hands a rusted spade with a long wooden handle. We were in the center aisle of the chapel, the door to the outside world behind him, the cross behind me. He stared and smiled, and I felt a fear I had never known before and have never known since.

"I don't have much time," he said. "I've got some digging to do. So let's have it, then."

I didn't even want to know what he was digging or why, the possibilities that flitted through my mind were terrifying enough. I braced myself against the side of a pew to stop my shaking, and then, without pleasantries, I brought up the purpose of our conversation.

"You need to leave this town. This town, this county, this state, those girls. You need to leave, now, and never come back."

He tilted his head at me like a dog. "What are you saying there, Reverend?"

"I know what you are and what you've done. I know every-thing."

"You're kidding with me, right?"

"I am serious as my faith."

"Aw, you don't know what the hell you're talking about."

"I'm talking about you and those girls. You and that boy. Leave now, or I'll tell all."

He stared at me, a realization dawning in his eyes. "Who you been listening to? Hailey? Has she been blabbing? She's a lying bitch, always has been. You can't go around listening to a mongrel bitch like her."

"You need to leave."

"Leave, hell, that would be the best thing for me. Don't you think I want to leave? Don't you think I wanted to leave ever day of the past eight years? I done everything for those girls. They'd have nothing without me, nothing. They'd be on the street, starving or whoring, I wasn't taking care of them. I gave the best part of my life to them, sacrificed it straight up, spent my days butchering cows and my nights tending to their wants. But does anyone ever care about *my* wants? I've given up everything for them, and this is what I get in return, lies and accusations. They're both a couple of half-breed ingrates. Their father wasn't a hundred percent, I told my sis-ter that before she ever married that boy. Any wonder then at what is going on with his demon offspring? One slices her wrists because she wants to be the center of attention, the other's now telling lies about me. They's bad kids, that's just the way they is. Everything that's happened is their fault. There's something wrong with them, I've always knowed that, something sinister. But you, Reverend, be-lieving them lies. You should be ashamed."

"You leave now, right now, take your truck and go and never come back, or I'll make the calls."

"Aw hell, go ahead and make your calls. No one'll believe your ass anyways."

"Yes, they will. I'm a man of God. And Hailey will back me up. And Roylynn from the hospital will back me up. And your sister will back me up, you know she will, when you're in jail and she's no longer afraid of the back of your hand. And as for the boy?

Where was it you received that slice on the cheek? Did it bleed much? It's a wonder what they can do now in matching up blood."

He stared at me hard, and his eyes grew cold, he hefted the shovel in his hands. "I could kill you right now," he said. "Stick this shovel in your chicken neck and pop your head right off."

"I know you could, without a second's thought, kill me now in this house of God. But you know that someone's seen you come in, that someone knows you're here. If you kill me, they'd lock you up for sure, lock you up till they pull the switch. And you want to know something?" I took a step forward. "I hope you do. It would solve the problem for good. So don't just talk about it, do it. Do it or leave."

I stood face to face with evil for that moment, watched the shovel twitch as if it wanted to launch itself into my neck, watched as the anger played like a screeching chord across his face. He was ready to hit me, crush me, do anything to bend me to his will, but I stood as steady as my feverish fear would let me and held my ground.

And then a smile, a lean, cold smile. "I've been thinking of leaving anyway," he said. "Them girls is growed up enough. It's time to be on my way. I guess I will go, head out west, just as soon as I pick up my stake. Edmonds and Doc Robinson owe me enough to get a good start out there in Vegas."

"They don't owe you a thing. You've been cheating them for years, dealing from the bottom."

"Lies, lies, and more lies. You you're just a damn thief of lies."

"I've seen it, watched it happen over and over."

"They won't believe you. They know me. They're my friends."

"You have no friends, and I'm a man of the cloth. They'll believe every word of it. Who would they believe more? If you're not gone by tonight, I'm going to tell them about you dealing from the bottom of the deck. I'm going to tell them about you killing that boy. I'm going to tell them about you and the girls. I'm going to tell them everything."

There was a moment more of silence, where I could see a fire raging inside him. I fought the urge to back up, to back away, to run from his ungodly presence. I fought and won and held my ground, even as his body tensed, even as he brought the shovel back as if to land a great blow, even as that shovel rushed at me and past me and rang with a brutal clang on the steps of the altar behind me.

I turned around to glance at it lying there, at an oblique angle on the stairs, and when I turned back to Lawrence Cutlip, he was walking out the door.

And, all praises to God, I never saw him again.

"**SO THAT** is the story, gentlemen," said the Reverend Henson, sitting behind his desk, his forefinger sliding back and forth across the bevel on the desktop's edge. "That is all I know. No facts underlay my accusations, no secret confessions, just a series of my own surmises. I knew nothing for certain. Had I known anything for certain, I would have done all in my power to put him in jail where he truly belonged, but I guessed well enough and knew enough about bluffing to banish this evil from our lives."

"That was pretty damn brave," I said. "He might just as easily have killed you."

"What else was I to do? And in the end, I supposed it all worked out well. Hailey did go to college, as you know, and to law school, too. She never confided in me in any way after that, treated me like a business acquaintance, which I suppose I had become. She simply took her money and went off into her new life, God bless her. Roylynn took a few courses at the community college, but that was all. There were three more attempts at suicide which halted her formal education, but she seems to be fighting the urge successfully, for now. The money from Pritchett has been used to finance a continuing series of rest homes, like the one she's in now. I visit her when I can, I myself gave her the physics book she clutches so fiercely. I thought it would be a diversion, but it has become something to her like a Bible, and I don't suppose that is so bad a thing. We all need something to believe in."

"I met with Roylynn after I spoke to you," I said.

"Yes, I heard. I had hoped you would honor my request, but she said nice things about you."

"She told me that something called a primordial black hole killed Jesse Sterrett and her sister, something from the beginning of time with the power to obliterate anything that comes close."

"Yes, I've heard her say that. It's hard to understand, but I think I have an explanation. I believe that what she calls a black hole is simply her expression for the evil I saw in her uncle. He left that night and never returned, and I only knew of his whereabouts through the occasional references from Roylynn, who learned what she knew from her sister. It was she who told me of the nursing home in Henderson, a place I called as soon as I heard about Hailey. No, he had never left the property, I made sure of that before ever you came upon the scene, Mr. Carl."

"If I need you to testify, Reverend, would you come up to Philadelphia?"

"I would, yes, but what could I say? What do I have for you, really, except my suspicions, and from what I can glean from the lawyer shows on TV, my suspicions are not much use in a legal case."

"What exactly are your suspicions, Reverend Henson?" asked Breger. "Do you really think he killed the Sterrett boy?"

"Yes, I do. I saw it in his eyes as he held that shovel, but I own not an ounce of proof."

"Why did he do it?"

"Jealousy."

"Of Hailey?"

"Of course."

"But why? What exactly do you suspect was going on between Cutlip and his nieces?"

"You ask for a surmise when I gave you all the facts at my disposal. I don't think you have a right to anything more than that, and I won't put my darkest fears about those girls into words. But she was a young girl in bad circumstances and terribly confused. Whatever it was that had infected her and that she was trying, in her way, to tell me about, it had nothing to do with love. It was something else, something monstrous and ungodly. And if it survived his leaving this town, it did so in the dark recesses of a dark heart that never allowed itself to catch a glimpse of light."

OUTSIDE THE CHURCH, Breger I and took a slow walk in the graveyard. I weaved among the tombstones reading the now familiar names. Breger examined this stone, stared at this flower, this path, searched the cemetery as if it were a crime scene. While I stood among the graves, the harrowing lines of a dead poet rang in my ears.

"A white Camaro ran me down on a rocky road outside Henderson, Nevada," I said finally to Breger.

"I read the police report when I was out there."

"And it was a white Camaro with Las Vegas plates that was ticketed for speeding on the night before Hailey Prouix's murder."

"I thought you'd find the coincidence interesting."

"Who is he, this Dwayne Joseph Bohannon?"

"Just a guy from Henderson."

"Who works at the Desert Winds nursing home?"

"That's right."

"Let me guess. Long, scraggly blond hair, bad skin, worse teeth, scratching his arms like he's got the mange. A lovely young man in every respect. Bright, too. Goes by the name of Bobo."

"Cutlip's toady."

"That son of a bitch," I said. "That vampire."

"I met with Cutlip in Vegas. Bobo, too, standing behind the wheelchair. Followed some bank payments to the Desert Winds and found Cutlip. I asked the basic questions, showed him the picture of the corpse, had him identify his niece. He broke down when he saw it, and then his anger flared. A hard case for sure, but I didn't find him evil."

"Neither did I, actually, but my partner sensed something. What are you going to do?"

"I'll make a call to my contact in Nevada. Have him ask Cutlip some tougher questions."

"And what will that get you? You might shake him up a bit, but if he suspects he's a suspect, you won't get very far. He's a tough old bird. He'll clam up, shed crocodile tears over his niece, claim ill health, deny everything. I know, I've seen him do it. Better to leave him alone."

"Then maybe I'll ask my contact to give Bobo a roust."

"Bobo killed her. It seems clear now, doesn't it?"

Breger merely looked away.

"He killed her. And I'll tell you something else: He's the mystery man in black rushing out of the house. He was inside looking for something, and when the Forensic Unit technician showed up, he rushed out and beat her all to hell. With his hands scratched up like they were, you couldn't see the bruises from the beating. But he's the one."

"It's possible."

"So what are you going to do about it?"

"I told you."

"What about you convincing Jefferson to drop the case?"

He shook his head.

"You'll at least tell him what you heard."

"Jefferson wants evidence or nothing. What I heard is not evidence."

"What more do you need?"

"Facts, maybe. Proof. If my guy grabs a confession out of Bobo, I'll talk to Jefferson, but I can't without that. You've raised a lot of questions, but there still aren't many answers, including the big one. Cutlip may be a murderer, he may have killed Jesse Sterrett fifteen years ago out of jealousy or hate, but why would he send Bobo off to kill Hailey? Why would he want her dead?"

"I don't know," I said.

"Maybe when you find an answer we can do some business. But I'll tell you flat-out, Carl, without a confession Jefferson is going to stay on after your boy to the end, that's just the way he is. And the way the trial is going now, it looks like he's going to get him."

"I've been making some headway."

"Some," he said. "But not enough to overcome the fingerprints. Not enough to overcome the motive. Not enough to overcome the fact that only your client was in that house. And it doesn't help you blaming some mystery lover for the crime if you think Cutlip did it."

"A lawyer's got to lawyer."

"That's the problem with you guys. A surgeon's going to cut, a hunter's going to shoot, a lawyer's going to lie. I'll make the call to my contact. If Bobo says something interesting, I'll give it to Jefferson, who has to give it to you under *Brady*. That's all I can do."

"And if Bobo gives you nothing?"

"Then start gathering character witnesses for the sentencing phase, because you'll need them."

"You'll tell me what happens in Vegas?"

"I'll tell you."

I stood in the cemetery, thinking things through. I thought of the trial, what had happened already, what still needed to be proved. I was at a loss. What could I do? How I could raise the level of doubt?

"Detective," I said finally, "I might need a favor."

He didn't say anything, he just stood there with his shoulders hunched as if waiting for the weight of the world to drop down upon him.

"There might come a moment when Troy Jefferson gets sputteringly angry at something I do, and he's going to come to you for some additional proof."

"Same old same old."

"When he does, this time I want you to whisper something in his ear."

"Go ahead."

"Just one word."

"Go ahead."

"Will you do it?"

"I'll consider it, maybe, depending on the word. And in exchange."

"In exchange for what?"

"Your phone logs."

"Don't do that. Don't go there."

"That's the deal."

"I'm asking for one little thing, one word in his ear, just one word."

"I understand what you're asking. And it is not any little thing."

"The logs aren't even mine to give up. It's up to the client."

"Talk to him. Tell him that's the deal."

"You don't know what you're asking."

"Let's go, we've got ourselves a plane to catch."

"You have no idea what you are asking."

"Oh, I have an idea," he said. "I have plenty of an idea. Yes I do."

And I believed then that he did.

"**AND YOU** think this bastard, Hailey's Uncle Larry, actually killed her?" asked Guy as the two of us sat alone in the gray lawyer-client conference room in the county jail. I had just told him everything I'd learned in Pierce, the whole ugly story.

"I think he sent his lackey, Bobo, to kill her, yes."

"Why?"

"I don't know."

"Any idea?"

"Maybe she threatened to take away the money he needed for his luxury nursing home. Or maybe he was sick of his luxury nursing home and wanted the insurance money for a new stake. Who knows? It could be anything. But he did it."

"What can we do about it?"

"I don't know. There's a chance maybe this Bobo will turn against him. There's a cop in Nevada that's going to get him alone in a room and ask some tough questions."

"And if that gets us nothing?"

I didn't say anything. I kept perfectly still and waited.

"What do we do, Victor? What do I do?"

I waited some more, and then I said, "I have an idea, but it's risky."

"What is it? Tell me."

"If it doesn't work, it will blow up in our faces."

"Go ahead, Victor. What is it?"

I leaned forward and clasped my hands on the table and told him what I would have to do and then what Breger would have to do and then what Jefferson would have to do and then what I would have to do.

"Jesus. That's all you could think of, that risky Rube Goldberg contraption of a defense?"

"It is, yes. And the thing is, the trial's gone pretty well for us so far. Our gambit with the headphones worked out great. I think the possibility that someone else might have entered that house and killed Hailey has come alive for the jury. I think we have a pretty decent chance of winning this thing outright, without the risk. We've created a suspect, the other lover, and I think we've created enough of a hole in the prosecution's case for the jury to find both opportunity and motive. Our argument at the end of this case will be as strong as I could have hoped."

"Are you guaranteeing an acquittal?"

"No, I can't guarantee a thing, you know that, but we have a decent chance."

"I don't want to hear about chances. I need to get out of here."

"But there's something else. You know how they keep asking for my phone records and I keep refusing and the judge keeps upholding my refusal based on attorney-client privilege?"

"Yes."

"Well, the whole plan only works if Breger does his part, and Breger will only do his part if we offer up, in exchange, my phone records."

"So?"

I stood, walked to the narrow window to look upon another wall. This is why I had come alone, why I had left Beth at the office to work up some motions. "Guy, they want to know about the phone call you made to me on the night of the murder."

Guy stared at me for a moment, thinking of that night, that horrible night, thinking of what he had done when he stepped out of the tub. "Oh," he said.

"They have questions about that call that haven't been resolved by your own phone logs."

"Oh, I see."

"I haven't asked you this yet, but it's time. Why hasn't the phone call you made to me shown up on your phone records?"

"I was flustered. I was scared. I . . . I couldn't remember your number."

"So what did you do?"

"I used Hailey's phone. The red phone. It was right on the table by the bed."

"Why her phone?"

"Because . . . because I . . . because . . ."

"Guy?"

"Because your number was on the speed dial."

I didn't say anything, I didn't need to. Outside, it was a sunny fall day, one of those days that remind you of the summer that passed and foreshadow the end of the coming winter. It was a lovely day outside, but a brisk chill had descended into that hard gray room.

"You didn't think I would check it out?" he said. "You didn't think I would find out who it was, Victor? I gave myself over to her completely, sacrificed my family, my integrity, my very soul on her altar and yet she was sleeping with someone else. You didn't think I would do whatever I needed to learn who the bastard was? I spied on her, I followed her, I listened in to her conversations. She was wily, I got nowhere. But then the phone appeared and one night, when she was in the Jacuzzi, I checked out the speed dial, and there were the numbers, some totally foreign, but the first two, the first two strangely familiar. One was your office, Victor, one was your home. I think by then she wanted me to know, that was why she left out the phone. I think she was using you to tell me that it was over. You were her get-out boy, the excuse to break up with me, like she would have found a get-out boy for you when your time came. And you want to know something? By the time I found out, I wasn't even angry at you. I felt sorry for you instead, sorry that you had fallen into her web."

"Guy . . ."

"So who would I call when I found her dead? Who could understand even some of what I was feeling? Who could I trust? Only you. And in my panic I knew where to find your number with just the touch of a button."

"Guy . . ."

"So that's why I used her phone."

"I'm sorry . . ."

"No you're not."

He was right, I wasn't.

"And neither am I," he said.

"Then why did you keep me on as your lawyer?"

"First you were just there and I was desperate. Then I thought it through. There's nothing to do in here except think. I analyzed the case, the evidence, I put on my most dispassionate lawyer mind-set and came up with a strategy. The strategy I came up with, the one that made the most sense, was to blame the other lover. That's why I kept suggesting it. But I couldn't have that other lover just walk into the courtroom and take himself out of the case by providing an alibi, like being at home when I called. I needed to make sure that never happened, and as far as I could see, there was only one way."

"Keeping me on as your lawyer."

"That's right."

"You're a son of a bitch, aren't you?"

"I'd say we both are, Victor."

And what could I say to that? He was right, absolutely, we were both sons of bitches, and we had both been played for fools. We had each been made part of whatever strange journey was mapped out by Hailey Prouix and, truth be told, each of us was thrilled to our bones to be taken along on her ride.

"So what should I do?" I asked.

"About the uncle?"

"Yes."

"Maybe this Booboo guy will turn on him."

"Bobo. Maybe."

"But it won't be that easy, will it?"

"No."

"What's he like, the uncle? Have you met him?"

"Yes, I have. He's a hard man."

"And he killed Hailey."

"I think he did."

"But we don't want them looking at your records, do we?"

"No, we don't."

"It could ruin us both."

"That's right."

"It makes a lot of sense to play it out just like it is and let him get away with it."

"Yes, it does."

"He's old, dying, only a few pathetic years left in some nursing home. We should just let him be."

"All right."

"But we won't, will we?"

"It's your choice."

"We need to do something about him, if he killed her."

"It's your choice."

"She used us, she used us both. When I first saw her on the mattress, bloodied and gone, when I first saw her, I was devastated at my loss. My loss. But I've been thinking about her, what she lost. We just can't leave it like that. Whatever she did, she didn't deserve to die. Whoever was responsible for killing her should pay. That's what I think."

"All right."

"Do you think you can pull this off?"

"I'll try."

"You better do more than try, Victor. If all you do is try, I'll be here longer than I could bear. Don't just try it, Victor. Do it."

"You're sure?"

"Do it. And when that murderous bastard gets close, rip out his heart."

PART SIX

THE
GENTLE
DANCE

SO FAR it had been an ordinary sort of trial. Troy Jefferson was trying to make it seem a simple case of murder. I was complicating
things, flogging my theory that the unnamed, undiscovered, un-
scrupulous lover had done it on the sly. Jefferson and I were in
pitched battle, but we kept our interchanges formal, using the polite vernacular of the courtroom. The judge was refereeing with
dyspeptic fairness. The jury was relatively attentive. There had
been a few bold moments, a few comic interludes. The prosecution
felt confident, the defense felt hopeful. All expectations were that it
would play out as it had begun, one theory battling the other, decided by the jury as it mostly ignored the instructions of the judge
and reached its verdict. So far it had been an ordinary sort of trial,
but things were about to change.

Leila Forrest was in the courtroom that day, she was in the courtroom every day, standing by the man who had fled from her at first
opportunity. I would have liked to have seen a little spite out of her,
a little anger, but instead she sat behind Guy with concern etched
on her face. Yes, it is always useful to have the loyal wife sitting behind the defendant, and in other situations I would have designed
it just so, but not this time. I hadn't asked that she sit there, like an
ornament for the defense. I wasn't even sure it was helpful. But

there she sat, and in the breaks she and Guy talked quietly to themselves, maybe about the children, maybe about the past, maybe, God help her, about the future.

She had sat still with a stone face as her father testified, trying to bury the man who had married his only child and then deserted her. It was strong testimony, hard testimony, it made Guy look very bad, until I asked the question "How much did you make last year?" Such a rude question, and objected to, of course, but it was allowed, and the number was staggering, and the point was made: Guy was in line for a huge amount if he had stuck it out with his wife. Enough to make Guy look the fool for leaving, yes, a fool for love. But a man who killed for money?

The judge had not yet entered the courtroom on this day, so it wasn't only Leila who was waiting. Behind the prosecution table sat the stolid figure of Detective Breger, along with his partner, Stone. Stone sneered at me with her smile. I caught Breger's eye and signaled him I wanted to meet. He stood and left the courtroom. I followed.

"Any word on Bobo?" I asked when we had found a private nook in the hallway.

"He has disappeared. Flown. My coming out there was apparently enough to spook him."

"I'm not surprised."

"Have you spoken to your client?"

"Yes."

"What did he say?"

"He says you're being a hard-ass."

Breger didn't answer, he simply smiled.

"But he agreed. We'll let you look at the logs, but only after."

"After?"

"That's right."

"After what?"

"After it all plays out."

"You mean after the trial? What good is that for me?"

"No, before the end of the trial, but after what happens today plays out. When I tell you what I want, you'll understand."

"And if it doesn't play out like you expect?"

"We still have a deal."

Breger closed his eyes. "I can live with that. What's the word?"

"All you have to do is whisper it."

"So you said."

"In his ear, after the explosion."

"The explosion is coming?"

"Oh, yes it is."

"What's the word?"

" 'Uncle,' " I said. "The word of the day is 'uncle.' "

"ARE WE ready to proceed?" said Judge Tifaro from the bench. She was an efficient jurist, keeping the trial moving, witness after witness, brooking no delays as she pushed toward a verdict. No long, drawn-out, chatty proceedings for her, no months and months of keeping the jury in virtual lockup. She had set up a timetable and kept us to it. I liked that about her.

"Yes, Your Honor," said Troy Jefferson. "But before we bring in the jury, we have some housekeeping matters that have already been agreed upon by both sides."

"Excellent," said the judge. "It's gratifying to see you gentlemen working so smoothly together. What do we have, Mr. Jefferson?"

"A stipulation as to the admissibility of the ballistics report, People's Exhibit Twenty-three."

"Mr. Carl?"

"No objection."

"The report will be entered. What else?"

"A stipulation as the admissibility of People's Exhibits Six through Nine and Twelve through Twenty-two."

"Mr. Carl?"

"No objection. We retain the right to object to Exhibits Ten and Eleven on the grounds of relevance."

"People's Exhibits Six through Nine and Twelve through Twenty-two are entered into evidence. Anything else?"

"And we also, Your Honor, have certain technical, factual stipulations that have already been agreed upon and that will speed up the trial considerably."

"Let's have them, Mr. Jefferson. Put them in the record now, and I will read them to the jury with the appropriate instruction."

"Stipulation one: That the location of the killing subject to the indictment was 1027 Raven Hill Road in the Township of Lower Merion, Montgomery County, in the Commonwealth of Pennsylvania."

"Mr. Carl?"

"No objection."

"Stipulation two: that on the date of the alleged crime the owner of the said property of 1027 Raven Hill Road, according to the deed on file in the County Clerk's Office of Montgomery County, was Hailey Prouix."

"Mr. Carl?"

"No objection."

"Stipulation three: that the cause of death, as reported by the coroner, was a single gunshot wound in the chest portion of the body that pierced the victim's heart."

"Mr. Carl?"

"No objection."

"Stipulation four: that the gun in question, People's Exhibit One, is a King Cobra .357 Magnum, registered by the Commonwealth of Pennsylvania to Guy Forrest, with a Social Security number the same as the defendant's and an address given on the application as 1027 Raven Hill Road, Township of Lower Merion, Montgomery County."

"Mr. Carl?"

"No objection."

"Finally, Your Honor, stipulation five: that the murder victim found at 1027 Raven Hill Road, as stated in the indictment, was indeed Hailey Prouix."

"Mr. Carl?"

"Well, Judge," I said, "as to stipulation five, that the victim was Hailey Prouix, there we seem to have a problem."

The explosion wasn't loud, Jefferson had more control than that, but it was angry and sustained. Troy Jefferson did a classic double take, and then he let me have it.

"It was agreed to, Your Honor. We went over these stipulations carefully, word by word, Your Honor. Mr. Carl agreed, explicitly, and we relied on that agreement. He's backstabbing us now, backstabbing us. There is no doubt who was the victim. We have the birth certificate. We have the death certificate. Mr. Carl himself saw her lying there. I don't know what kind of crazy theory he is postulating here, but, Your Honor, he agreed, and he is bound by that agreement."

And the whole time I was standing calmly, smiling, and letting him roar, until Judge Tifaro put a stop to it. "Mr. Carl, is it the wording you are concerned about?"

"No, Judge, it is the fact."

"Did you agree?"

"Yes, Judge, but now I have questions that need answering, and so I am simply asking that the prosecution prove that the victim, as stated in the indictment, was Hailey Prouix and not just some woman who was going around using that name. It is a basic element of the case. He needs to prove it was her."

"Can you do that, Mr. Jefferson? Can you prove it was Hailey Prouix who was killed?"

"Of course, Your Honor. This is just a cheap delaying tactic, just another low blow from the defense team."

"Maybe it is, but don't get mad, Mr. Jefferson," she said with a note of sweetness in her voice, "get a witness. And preferably somebody who knew her well and long and who can link up the name on the birth certificate with the pictures of the corpse you've already admitted into evidence. Would that satisfy you, Mr. Carl?"

"Yes, Your Honor."

"Is there a parent?"

"Both dead," I volunteered.

"A sibling?"

"One sister," I said, "in a West Virginia insane asylum."

The judge stared at me when I told her that and then, without taking her eyes off my face, said, "Identifying the victim is a pretty crucial step, Mr. Jefferson. You couldn't have just expected the dead woman to identify herself. Can you get a witness?"

"Yes, of course."

"You were going to rest next week, isn't that right?"

"We planned to have the lab technician at the start of the week and a few other minor witnesses, and that was to be it."

"I guess that won't be it, will it? You'll be allowed to amend your witness list as you require, and I'll allow you additional time in your case due to the surprise, but I'll want the witness here next week, understand?"

"Yes, ma'am."

"Good. Get the name of the new witness to Mr. Carl as soon as possible. Any questions?"

"No, ma'am."

"Anything else? No? Excellent. Bailiff, let's bring in the jury."

I sat down as Jefferson gave me his "you'll pay for that one, you bastard" stare before he spun around to talk with his team. I'm no lip-reader, but it didn't take one to know what he was saying.

"Why the hell did he do that?" said Jefferson.

Only shrugs in response.

"Who can we get? Who's our witness?"

More shrugs, heads turning one to the other to see who had an answer, and then Breger leaned forward. Then Breger leaned forward and put his lips close to Troy Jefferson's ear and whispered. There were a lot of possibilities, a lot of names could have been pulled out of the hat to do what the prosecution needed to do, but it was Breger who leaned forward and whispered in Jefferson's ear.

Jefferson pulled back. "You sure he can do it?"

Breger nodded.

"Then get him, damn it. Get him now."

The jury was just starting to enter when Breger stood, straightened his jacket, gave me a quick wink before he headed out the door of the courtroom.

Good, that was done. Now for the hard part.

THAT NIGHT, back at my apartment, I gathered together my brain trust. I like the sound of that—brain trust—it connotes images of men and women in stark suits and tense poses, talking on cell phones and working on laptops as they draw on the entire breadth of their mighty resources to solve the seemingly unsolvable. Of course, I didn't have the resources or clout to have a brain trust that resembled a fashion ad in *GQ*, so I had to settle for Beth and Skink.

They hadn't yet formally met. I had told them each of the happenings in Pierce, related to each the whole brutal story of love, perjury, blackmail, the defiant priest, the suicidal poet, the crooked poker game, and, finally, the murder of a boy on the edge of his manhood. I had told them each what I had learned about Cutlip but had kept them apart for obvious reasons. I didn't want Skink spilling all he knew about Hailey and me to my partner, and I didn't want my partner wondering what I was doing with a creep like Skink. But now I had to come up with some possibilities, fast, and they were, well, my brain trust.

"Do I know you?" Beth said when she entered the apartment and I introduced her to Skink, sprawled out now on my couch, his shirtsleeves rolled up, his tie loose, his shoes off, leaning back with a proprietary casualness.

"Not in a personal way, missy, no," he said.

"What other way is there?"

Skink chuckled. "Let's say I had the pleasure of helping yourself out of a tight situation."

Beth stared at him bemusedly.

"Skink pulled you out of the car after the accident in Las Vegas."

"You were the one," said Beth to Skink. "I do know you. You were the one who saved my life."

"Glad to be of service to a lovely young lass such as yourself, I was. No reward necessary, though if you're considering buying me chocolates, think low-fat, please, as I gots myself a problem with cholesterol."

Beth pursed her lips first at Skink and then at me and then again at Skink. "So why are you here tonight?"

"I thought he could be of some help," I said.

"I am definitely confused."

"Skink wasn't in Las Vegas by chance. He was following us. At the time he was working for someone else."

"Who?" said Beth.

"Can't say, now, can I?" said Skink. "Disclosing that information would be a violation of my duties as a professional."

"A professional what?"

"Investigative services, ma'am, specializing in the brutal, the de-based, and the carnally depraved."

"What are you, the HBO of detectives?"

"And now he's working for us," I said.

"Oh, is he?"

"Once again, I am glad I can be of service."

"Victor," said Beth. "Can I see you for a moment?"

"Go ahead," said Skink. "Why don't you two young folk head off into the other room and discuss this among yourselves. Don't mind me."

"Don't worry," said Beth. "We won't."

I stoically withstood the harangue, being as it was absolutely jus-tified. We were partners, working together on the Guy Forrest trial, and all the time I'd had an investigator working on the sly. It made her wonder, she said. It made her wonder what the hell was going on. I could have tried to lie my way out of it, I could have squirmed like a worm to get free, but when you are dead wrong, it is not time to make excuses. When you are dead wrong, it is time to give a half smile and move right to the meat of it. So I let her blow up at me, get it out of her system, and then I tossed her that half smile and said simply, "He can help."

"How?"

"He knows things. Before he worked for us, he worked for Hailey Prouix. He knows things. He won't tell me all he knows, but he knows more than we do. He can help."

"That's good, Victor, because after what you pulled today in court, I think we could use all the help we can get."

"Exactly," I said.

"THE QUESTION," I said, when my brain trust was reassembled in the well of my living room, "is why. Let's assume that Cutlip sent Bobo out to do the killing. We still have to figure out why. Why? Why?" I turned to look at Skink. "Why? And how does it relate to what happened to Jesse Sterrett?"

"Maybe she was threatening to tell someone what had happened," said Beth. "Maybe he had crossed some line and she was about to tell the whole story."

"Not bad," I said, "except there's nothing to back that up. She was still taking care of him, was still apparently close to him. He was still the beneficiary on her insurance. There's no indication she was ready to do such a thing."

"Look at the money," said Skink. "It's usually about money, innit?"

"Yes, it usually is," I said. "The insurance money was pretty high, and he seemed pretty damned interested in it when we came to visit."

"But she was the goose laying his golden eggs," said Beth. "Why would he kill her for money when she was giving him everything he wanted as it was?"

"Maybe he was worried it was running out," I said. "Especially with Guy starting to raise questions about the missing funds. Or maybe he was sick of the place, Desert Winds, maybe he thought it was some sort of pre-morgue and he felt halfway already on the slab. Maybe she was using her support as a cudgel to keep him there, and he thought he could gain his freedom and a stake both with one fatal blow. He and Bobo would have themselves a hell of a time before the insurance money ran out and Cutlip's body fell apart."

"An interesting idea, that," said Skink. "A man used to freedom, as was our Larry Cutlip, it must chafe like a pair of iron knickers to be supervised, sanitized, and anesthetized in a place like that."

"You know him?" said Beth.

"Who, Cutlip? Yeah, I knows him. But the thing about your insurance theory there, Vic, is that he wasn't even sure he was the beneficiary before she died and he got a gander at the policy. He was just hoping."

"How do you know that?" said Beth.

"I just do, is all. I just do."

"What's he like?" she said. "I apparently met him, but after the accident I don't remember a thing about it."

"He's a saint," I said, "just ask him. Oh, he's done some tough things in his life, gone through some hard stretches, but everything he's done he's done for the right reasons. He sacrificed his best years to take care of his nieces, and he did the best he could, and he needs you to know it. Anything that went wrong, it was some other person's fault. The dead father, the meddling local minister, his sister, the girls themselves. But he provided a firm hand when a firm hand was needed. When he thinks tears will be effective, he'll break down and cry. When he thinks he can bully you, he'll get as vicious as a cornered rat. His surface is all ornery and hard, he doesn't like Jews much, or lawyers, or, really, anyone, but he likes to have someone around who will stroke his ego and tell him how good, how strong, how important he is, even as he sits in a wheelchair in a sad desert boomtown with a line feeding oxygen into his withered lungs."

"Sounds like you didn't like him much," said Beth.

"Actually, I was suckered. Before I knew the truth, I admired what he had done. I bought into his act. I guess he didn't spend fifteen years banging around Vegas without learning how to con gullible folk from back east. It was you who didn't like him, not at all."

"I didn't?"

"For some reason I couldn't fathom he terrified you, as if you had seen something in him that I completely missed. You said he reminded you of Murdstone."

"Murdstone?"

"From *David Copperfield*."

"The stepfather?"

"Yes, and you seemed particularly concerned with some of the things he said about Jesse Sterrett's death. He called it an accident, but you kept asking questions. He didn't like that, didn't like that at all. It was those questions, in fact, along with the letters, that started me digging in West Virginia."

"Wasn't I the perceptive little thing?"

"And then, while we were riding out of Henderson, you said you wouldn't be surprised if . . .'"

"If what?"

"I don't know. It was just before the accident. You never got a chance to finish."

"What I meant was that I wouldn't be surprised if it was Guy and not Hailey who was supposed to die."

Skink and I looked at each other for a moment and then back at Beth. "How do you remember that?"

Beth herself look stunned. "I don't know. I'm not sure. I was just listening to what you said about Cutlip and the beginning of the sentence and something slipped out of the recesses of my mind and became clear, and that was it."

"What a strange idea," I said.

"Is it, now?" said Skink. "Is it, now? Wouldn't that change everything? We're wondering here about motive, because why would Cutlip want to kill his loving niece? But Guy, now, that's a different story, ain't it? There are half a dozen blokes who wouldn't have minded seeing Guy Forrest bite the proverbial big one. And wouldn't Cutlip be one of them? Guy was starting to ask questions about where his money had gone. Guy was threatening his luxury existence. And the worst crime of all is that Guy was pumping it to Hailey—no offense, ma'am—pumping it to Hailey just like Jesse Sterrett was pumping it to Hailey. They was two men she was looking to marry. Maybe he killed them both."

"Out of some raw emotion," I said. "Something beyond him, something he couldn't control."

"Slow down," said Beth. "She was on the mattress right in the middle of the floor. You couldn't shoot her from outside the room, and you couldn't step into the room without seeing her there, clear as day."

"Really, now," said Skink. "Clear as day, you say. Vic, you was the first one to see her after Guy, right?"

"Yes," I said.

"Was the light on?"

"Of course, the overhead light."

"Not a lamp or anything else, just the overhead."

"As far as I remember, yes."

"Guy told us," said Beth, "that after he hit her, Hailey told him to turn out the light, and he did."

"Then, what about if it was Guy himself who turned it on, that overhead light, not the killer?" said Skink. "Think about that. Maybe it was off when she was killed."

"But still, even in the imperfect darkness," Beth said, "it would be hard to mistake petite Hailey Prouix for a lummox like Guy."

"Yeah, maybe, except our suspected shooter, Bobo, ain't no Einstein, is he? If you wanted a killing to be messed up to hell, I suppose he's the one you'd send to do it. And maybe there was another reason he made the mistake. You got the forensics reports hereabouts?"

"As a matter of fact," I said, "the lab technician is testifying Monday."

"Let me see it. And the autopsy report, too."

"What for?"

"Just haul them out and let me have a look-see."

The reports were in the trial bag I had brought with me from the office. Skink spread them out on the coffee table in front of the couch and riffled through them, one at a time, as he searched for the specific items he was interested in. It was a wonder to behold, Phil Skink in full calculating mode. His mouth twitched, his eyes blinked, he scratched his greased blue-black hair as if it were infested with lice—he looked like a deranged mainframe on the verge of a nervous breakdown. And the whole of the time he was letting out little verbal explosions. "Mmmmmbop," he said, or "Blip, blip, blip," or "Now, there's something, innit?" or, most strangely, "*Parlez-vous* to me, you frog bastard."

Beth and I stood back and let him at it, both of us afraid to get too close in case he blew up.

After a good twenty minutes he raised his head and said, "I think we got ourselves a G forty-eight."

"G forty-eight? Is that an exhibit or something?"

"Don't be daft. I'm talking those little balls what falls out of the cage. G forty-eight. G forty-eight. And you know what that gives us?"

"What?" said Beth.

Skink let a huge smile crease his battered face. "Bingo, mates. Bingo."

"THAT'S RIGHT," said the police technician from the stand, adjusting her glasses as she reviewed her report. "I determined that the gun was two to four feet away from the victim when it was fired." She took off her glasses and looked up at me. "But as I said in my direct testimony, that's only a rough estimate."

"Let's be as precise as possible about this, Officer Cantwell," I said. "You are estimating the distance from the victim to the end of the barrel, isn't that right?"

"Yes, of course."

"With the arm outstretched, the killer's eyes would have been considerably farther away. As much as two feet, isn't that right?"

"It's hard to tell how the gun was held, but that is certainly possible."

"So the killer, when he fired, could have been as much as six feet away from the victim?"

"Yes, or closer."

"Six feet. That's pretty far away with the light off, isn't it?"

"Objection."

"Sustained," said the judge.

"But, Your Honor," I said, "we have Mrs. Morgan's testimony that the lights were out at some point before she saw Mr. Forrest on the steps."

"Sustained."

"And there is absolutely no evidence that the light was on at the time of the killing."

"Argue what you want, Mr. Carl, at argument, but you haven't laid a foundation to allow this witness to testify what can or can't be seen in that room with the lights out. Continue, please."

"Officer Cantwell, were you ever in that room with the lights out?"

"No."

"With the lights on?"

"No."

"You've never been in that room?"

"I am a lab technician, Mr. Carl. I work in a lab. I of course consult the photographs and the police reports, but my job is a scientific analysis of the evidence."

"Then, Officer, let me ask you this. With any of your fancy lab equipment, your spectroscopes or infrared cameras, with your micron telescopes, with any of that stuff, is it possible for you to say whether the light was on or off at the time the shot was fired?"

"No."

"Good enough. Let's move on. Two to four feet from the end of the barrel to the victim, right?"

"That was my estimate."

"And you made that determination from the gunpowder residue on the comforter, isn't that right?"

"Yes, sir."

"Could you explain to the jury how the gunpowder residue ended up on the comforter?"

"A bullet is fired by the ignition of smokeless gunpowder, or nitrocellulose, in a cartridge. As the powder ignites, there is a violent expansion of gas, which propels the bullet through the barrel and then out into the world. In this case, through the comforter and into the heart of the victim. Under perfect circumstances all the gunpowder would be turned into the propelling gases during ignition, but as we all know, our world isn't perfect. Along with the bullet, the expanding gases discharge unburned powder, partially burned powder, and completely burned powder, or soot. If the barrel of the gun is close enough to the target, then some or all of these are deposited on the target's surface. An examination of the pattern of these discharges can allow for an approximation of distance."

"Were all three types of powder found on the comforter?"

"No, not on the relevant portion. Generally, if a shot is fired within a foot, there is what is called both fouling and stippling. Fouling, which can be wiped away easily, occurs when the completely burned powder is found on the surface. Stippling occurs from the unburned and incompletely burned particles of gunpowder. These particles become embedded in the surface or bounce off and abrade the surface, and their effects are not easily wiped off. From beyond a foot the soot generally is dispersed into the air and so no soot deposit is made. From the distance of a foot to maybe three or four feet, there will be stippling without fouling. When we examined the comforter, we found embedded unburned and partially burned powder, which gave us our approximate distance."

"How was this examination done?"

"Because of the color of the comforter, a dark blue, and the encrusted blood staining it, it was difficult to see the residue with the naked eye. We took an infrared photograph of the comforter, but that didn't prove very helpful, which isn't surprising, since infrared is better at revealing fouling than stippling. Then we made a search for nitrates using a Greiss test. We pressed a series of gelatin-coated photographic papers onto the comforter with a hot iron and then treated the papers to find the presence of nitrates, which would be found if there existed nitrocellulose on the comforter that had been incompletely burned. Nitrates were found in a wide, elliptical pattern, from which we concluded that the firing range was two to four feet."

"All very technical, Officer Cantwell."

"Most of our work is. That's why we're called technicians."

"Now, you found these nitrates over a large part of the comforter."

"Yes."

"And what you found would qualify as stippling."

"That's right."

"And this stippling would have been found not only over the comforter but also over the exposed surfaces of anything on the mattress."

"I would assume so, yes."

"Including the victim herself."

"Yes."

"And based on what you testified to earlier, this would have been clearly evident, as particles would be embedded in the skin or, in bouncing off, would have abraded the skin, isn't that right?"

"That is what you would expect, but I didn't examine the victim."

"You examined her clothes, correct?"

"She was wearing a short nightshirt, a teddy, it's sometimes called. We found blood and some nitrate residue around the bullet hole, what is known as bullet swipe."

"But no stippling."

"Yes, no stippling."

"Now, let's look at the autopsy report, shall we?"

"Objection. It is not her report."

"The autopsy report was introduced through stipulation. I'm not asking her to lay a foundation, I'm asking her to use the information she has already provided to help us analyze the actual report."

"Is this going somewhere, Counselor?"

"I hope so, Judge."

"Let's get there soon."

"In the autopsy report Dr. Regent analyzed many of the organs of the victim in this case, including the skin, isn't that right?"

"Yes."

"On the first paragraph on page four he mentions the bruise beneath her left eye, isn't that right?"

"Yes."

"In the second paragraph he mentions the general condition of the skin other than the bruise, doesn't he?"

"Yes."

"No other sign of insult to the skin, isn't that right?"

"Yes, that is what he wrote."

"Nothing about particles of gunpowder embedded in the skin, is there?"

"No."

"And nothing about abrasions from particles bouncing off the skin, is there?"

"Not from what I can see."

"So, in fact, in reading the autopsy, there is no evidence of stippling."

"That's right."

"No evidence that her skin was in any way exposed to the nitrates released by the handgun."

"Maybe not."

"Now, here is my question, Officer Cantwell. Based on the test you performed with the photographic paper and the comforter, and based upon the absence of stippling on the victim's clothes or skin, isn't it quite possible that all the stippling occurred on the comforter only because her entire body, including her face, was covered by the comforter?"

"That might be one explanation."

"So, to summarize your testimony, the shooter might have been as far from the victim as six feet, you can't in any way deny the possibility that it was dark in the room, and you maintain that it is quite possible that the victim was entirely hidden by her comforter."

"Yes, I suppose . . ."

"With all that, Officer, isn't it possible that the shooter didn't even know who it was beneath that comforter? With all that, Officer, isn't it possible the shooter murdered the absolute wrong person? Isn't that possible?"

There was to be no answer, of course. This was one of those obviously objectionable questions that lawyers throw in just so they can sneak in some argument in the midst of a cross-examination. But the point was made. It was the first time the jury had heard the possibility that maybe Hailey Prouix wasn't the intended victim, and they listened to the whole examination with admirable interest. And so, I could tell, did Troy Jefferson.

"I don't think they bought it," he said to me after Judge Tifaro had recessed for the day.

"They don't have to buy it, they just have to buy the possibility of it."

"So what are you going to argue, that the lover meant to kill Guy and killed his one true love instead?"

"A sad tale worthy of Shakespeare, don't you think?" I said. "The tragic story of one who loved not wisely but too well and threw it away by trying to kill off the competition and mistakenly murdering the woman he loved."

"Sounds like a movie of the week."

"Yes, it does. Maybe after this is over, I'll option the story to ABC."

"We have a new witness to add to our list."

"Someone interesting, I hope."

"Oh, yes, interesting as hell. You should never have tried to back-stab us like you did on that stipulation. We're calling the victim's uncle. He's known her all her life and he is thrilled as hell to testify against the man who killed his niece. He's going to identify her, and then he's got a few more things to say, and I'm going to let him say them."

"Really?"

"Count on it. He's going to bury your boy."

"I certainly hope not. I'd like to speak to him before he testifies, if that's all right. You know where he's staying?"

"He's at the DoubleTree."

"Nice."

"But don't waste your breath. He's not going to speak to you. He's not going to say a word until he's on the stand."

"It shook you a little, didn't it?" I said. "The wrong-victim theory."

"Not really. We had seen the possibility beforehand. We were just wondering what took you so long to figure it out."

As he walked out of the courtroom, I began to wonder the exact same thing. It must have always been a possibility, a close examination of the forensics reports would have shown it to me as clearly as they showed it to Skink. And if there was to be a parallel with the Jesse Sterrett murder, then it only made sense. The boy Hailey was planning to run away with, murdered. The man Hailey was planning to marry, an attempt on his life. It was so obvious. Why couldn't I see it?

Because of my obsession. I was obsessed with Hailey Prouix. Call it love, call it lust, call it what you will, but it was an obsession and it colored everything I had done in this case, for better or for worse. She was the focus of my interest, so I assumed she was the focus of the killer's interest, too. My obsession had been like a set of blinders, but the blinders were off.

Right from the courtroom I called Skink on my cell phone. "He's at the DoubleTree."

"All right," said Skink. "I'll get my man on it."

"Any luck?"

"Not yet."

"You better hurry. He'll probably go on tomorrow afternoon."

"It ain't so easy. It's a big desert."

"No excuses, Skink."

"I understand, mate."

And he did, we all did. It was no time for excuses, it was no time for sitting back and waiting, no time for mere hope. The blinders now were off and Roylynn had been right all along. There was indeed a primordial evil that had blown through Hailey Prouix's life and caused a swath of destruction. And now, in a court of law, it and I were coming face to face.

"**WE HAVE** time for one more witness this afternoon, Mr. Jefferson,"
said Judge Tifaro. "Are you ready?"

"Yes, Your Honor. The People call Lawrence Cutlip to the stand."

"Lawrence Cutlip? I don't see a Lawrence Cutlip on your witness
list, Counsel."

"It's a late addition, Judge, in light of Mr. Carl's decision to abro-
gate his agreement on the stipulation about the identity of the victim. Mr. Cutlip will identify her as Hailey Prouix."

"Ah, yes. Any objection, Mr. Carl?"

"No, Your Honor."

"I thought not. All right, then, Mr. Jefferson, but keep it short."

"I aim to, Your Honor, yes I do."

The doors in the rear of the courtroom swung open and a cold
breeze slipped in, followed by the decrepit remains of Lawrence
Cutlip.

Cutlip, in his wheelchair, was dressed in his good jeans, with a
fresh flannel shirt and clean white sneakers, all spiffed for the occasion. His thick grizzle was shaved close, and his wild ruff of white
hair was combed back and fastened to his skull with grease. Even
his dentures were in place, clean white pieces of plastic interspersed
among the brittle natural teeth to which his gums still hesitantly

clung. The oxygen tank was sympathetically hanging from the rear of the chair, its clear plastic line hooked around his ears and under his nose. Cutlip occasionally and noticeably wheezed as he was pushed forward by a large woman in short-sleeved nursing whites.

As the old man slid down the aisle between the benches and into the well of the court, he hunched in the chair, looking about himself suspiciously, not sure what to expect. When he saw Beth and me, he smiled awkwardly, as if we were old acquaintances of uncertain temper, and we smiled back warmly, as if we were old friends. We kept smiling even as the woman, biceps bulging, lifted Cutlip's chair to the witness box, even as Cutlip raised his hand, even as Cutlip gave and spelled his name, gave his address, swore his oath to tell the truth, the whole truth, and nothing nothing nothing, so help him God, but the truth.

"Mr. Cutlip," said Troy Jefferson, "how are you related to Hailey Prouix?"

"She was my niece, poor girl, the daughter of my sister."

"Does she have any other family?"

"Well, her daddy was a Cajun boy who died when she was young, and her mama left off this earth not ten years back. That leaves just me and her sister, Roylynn. But Roylynn ain't exactly all there, if you know what I mean, not even able to take care of herself. So that about leaves only me."

"Were you close to her?"

"Yes, sir. You know, my sister wasn't so disciplined, not really hard enough to get along in this world, so when her husband, he died in that lumber accident, she needed some help with them girls. I was living my life, minding my own business, but I saw that she and the girls needed me, and so I moved on in and supported them girls as best I could until they was old enough to take care of themselves."

"That was quite a thing, Mr. Cutlip."

"I couldn't let them pretty little girls just drift away like that. The way I saw it, I never had no choice. I only done what I had to do. Anyone with half a heart would have done the same."

"Did you stay close to Hailey through the years?"

"Yes, sir."

"Were you aware that she was engaged to Guy Forrest?"

"Yes, I was. She told me all about him."

"So you knew he was married."

"Yes, with them kids, too. I told her it was a mistake to get involved with the likes of him. He didn't seem the most stable, from what she told me, and from what he done to his wife and kids, not the most loyal neither. And then when she told me they was fighting over money, I got scared for her. I told her to get away from him, to get out before it was too late. There's no telling what a man like that could do. I told her, I did, but when it came to boys, she never did listen to me. She never listened to nobody."

Through the whole of this little speech Judge Tifaro was staring at me, giving me that look of hers, the stare that made you want to check your law license just to prove to yourself you didn't pick it up along with a screwdriver and a fifty-foot garden hose at Sears. She was wondering why I wasn't objecting from the first word, why I had done what I had done to let this man on the stand in the first place.

"No objection, Mr. Carl?" she said finally.

"No, Your Honor, but thank you for your concern."

She stared, I shrugged, Jefferson continued.

"And then what happened?"

"What the hell do you think happened? She ended up dead."

"I'd like to show you now a folder of photographs taken of the crime scene, People's Exhibit Six, already entered into evidence, and ask you to look at it, please. I want to warn you, Mr. Cutlip, the pictures are terribly disturbing."

Cutlip leaned forward in his chair as Jefferson brought him the folder. He opened the folder on the shelf in front of him and went through the photographs carefully, one by one by one. By the third his face was scrunched up as if against the cold and his upper lip was quivering. By the fifth he was in tears. By the ninth he was unable to look at them any longer and closed the folder. Only his soft sobs and wheezes could be heard in the courtroom.

"Mr. Cutlip . . ."

Cutlip wiped his eyes with the back of his big, slack-skinned hand.

"Mr. Cutlip. I have to ask you a question now. The pictures show a woman lying dead on a mattress. Do you recognize that woman?"

Cutlip gasped at the air and then said, "Yes."

"Who is it, Mr. Cutlip?"

"It is my niece. Hailey Prouix."

"Are you sure, Mr. Cutlip?"

"I knowed her all her life. I couldn't be surer about nothing in this world."

"I need to show you another set of photographs. People's Exhibit nineteen, photographs from the autopsy. If you could just look at the first two, please."

Cutlip nodded, the good soldier, and took the folder. He shuddered at the first photograph, winced at the second, closed the folder like it was a curse.

"Same," said Cutlip. "It's the same. It's Hailey."

"Hailey Prouix."

"Yes, sir."

"Do you miss her?"

"Mr. Carl," said Judge Tifaro, "are you awake?"

"Yes, ma'am, I am."

"Any objection to that question?"

"No, ma'am."

"Go ahead, Mr. Jefferson, ask it again."

"Do you miss her, Mr. Cutlip?"

"Yes, I surely do. I'm in line for the insurance money, but I'd just as soon as toss it for how I'm getting it. She was like a daughter to me, more. She was taking care of me still, she was taking care of her poor sister, and then that there man killed her. He done this to me, and now my heart weeps tears of blood. I got no choice but to miss her, to miss her ever day, ever damn day of the rest of my sorry life."

"Thank you, Mr. Cutlip," said Jefferson, trying unsuccessfully to hide his grin. "I pass the witness."

The judge's stare of inquest aimed right at my skull continued even as she asked for Troy Jefferson and myself to approach the bench. She waited for the court reporter to set up right by her side before she spoke.

"Mr. Carl," she said, "do you have any idea what you are doing in this trial?"

"Not really, ma'am, no."

"I didn't think so. You backed out of a stipulation which allowed this man and his tears onto the stand. I gave you opportunities to object at every step of his testimony, and still you ignored them. Is there anything you want to do now, any motion you want to make?"

"All I want, Your Honor, is the chance to pose a few questions to Mr. Cutlip myself."

"You want to cross-examine?"

"Yes, ma'am."

"You have questions for this witness?"

"Just a few."

"Are you sure? Don't you think it was bad enough already? Are you certain that it might not make more sense just to leave him be, hope the jury forgets what he said, and let the prosecution rest its case?"

"Just a few questions, Your Honor."

"Well, then, have at it, Mr. Carl. It's time to recess for the afternoon. So tomorrow, first thing, you'll get your chance. And do not say I didn't warn you."

ONCE BEFORE in my career, during its early, naïve stage, I had attempted to break a man on cross-examination. Carefully I prepared, laying out all my traps, hoping for the devastating blow. He was a city councilman, skilled in the use of language but hot of temper, and I believed I could make him blow. I was wrong. Oh, I brought forth flashes of anger and exposed to the jury with lovely clarity the brittle inconsistencies in his story, but that was all. He had murdered a man with his bare hands, proven later by a piece of physical evidence held closely by his wife, but on the stand I got none of that, and I felt my client's guilty verdict deep in my gut.

It taught me a fine lesson. Cross-examination is a lovely tool for highlighting inconsistencies and evident falsehoods, for painting a witness as a hapless prevaricator or even an outright liar, cross-examination can be the death of a thousand cuts for the credibility of that witness or an opponent's entire case, but it is not the place for the single crushing blow. There are too many formalities involved, too many safeguards. Compare the polite confines of a courtroom with a police interrogation room in the dank recesses of a precinct house, a place of intimidation, of psychological manipulation, of violence imagined or real. The interrogation room is the place to break a suspect. But Lawrence Cutlip would never submit to the interrogation room and, I suspected, in its confines, furry with sweat and fear, he would be comfortably at home, able to withstand all manner of the interrogator's tricks. He was not the type to be badgered into confession. So there would be no interrogation here. I would have to make do with cross-examination, which, despite its fearsome reputation, is a gentler dance.

So how was I to proceed? Advice was more then plentiful.

Phil Skink: "Go right at him. Fast and furious. Get him on the ropes and don't let up."

"It's not a boxing match, Phil."

"No? You're going in there to put him away, right?. It's no time for subtle mercy. You need be to Jack Dempsey—hook, hook, hook, and then step into the right what breaks his jaw."

"Have you found anything yet?"

"Don't you think I'd have told you?"

"I need it."

"I knows you need it, mate, and I'll be getting it, too. But you remember what I says. Jack Dempsey. Hook, hook, hook, and then the right to the jaw. Drop him like a sack of potatoes, you will."

Beth Derringer: "Be gentle, subtle. He can handle anger, he's used to it, it's all he's ever known, but the soft emotions will confuse him."

"Skink thinks I should be Jack Dempsey in there."

"Guys like Skink only know one way. But there is another. Dance around the truth so he doesn't realize what you're getting at until it is too late. A little bit here, a little bit there. He'll be expecting a masculine rush up the middle, a straight through line like a fullback off tackle. You should take a more circular tack."

"Virginia Woolf as opposed to Ernest Hemingway."

"Yes, yes. Exactly."

"It sounds nice, but I didn't know that the Bloomsbury group was a law firm. Woolf, Strachey, Forster, Keynes and Woolf."

"Let me tell you something, Victor. Be glad you never met up with Virginia Woolf in court. Be very glad."

Reverend Henson: "The thing with Cutlip," he said when I called him for his share of advice, "is that he wants to think he is a good man, despite all he has done. None believe they are evil, even the evil. And, more desperately, he wants the world to think he is a good man, too. So he'll deny everything, and deny it with a conviction that will be unassailable. But if he's trapped, then he'll change. He'll turn ugly, turn irrational, search desperately for someone who can't defend himself and lay the blame on him. As in the Bible, where Aaron was commanded to lay his hands upon the head of a live goat and confess over it all the sins of the Children of Israel. Leviticus sixteen, verse twenty-two: 'And the goat shall bear upon him all their iniquities unto a land not inhabited.' He'll try to do the same to some poor soul, someone not able to defend himself."

"I don't understand how that helps us."

"Because his efforts to hide his guilt through use of a scapegoat are necessarily futile. Hebrews ten, verse four: 'For it is not possible that the blood of bulls and of goats should take away sins.' You can only create a scapegoat by following the biblical command to confess. It is a necessary part of the process. When he tries to shift blame onto his scapegoat, then will his sins be evident for all to see."

To this counsel I added one piece more, lifted from the book I had been reading, *Crime and Punishment*. I often found literature of little use in the bare-knuckle world of the law, the psychological gap between the fictional and real is often so wide, but no one ever came as close to spanning that canyon as Dostoyevsky. In the book the investigating magistrate stalks Raskolnikov with an ingenious psychological method that I thought might be the only tactic to crack a hard nut like Cutlip. He patiently waits for Raskolnikov, guilty of ax-murdering two old women, to come to him. "He won't run away from me, even if he had some place to run to," says the investigator, "because of a law of nature. Ever watched a moth before a lighted candle? Well, he, too, will be circling round and round me like a moth round a candle. He'll get sick of his freedom. He'll start brooding. He'll get himself so thoroughly entangled that he won't be able to get out. He'll worry himself to death. And he'll keep on describing circles round me, smaller and smaller circles, till— flop!—he'll fly straight into my mouth and I'll swallow him!" And true to the method, 446 pages after the murders, Raskolnikov staggers into the St. Petersburg police station and exclaims, "It was I."

Cutlip seemed willing, almost desperate, to talk about his niece. He couldn't help himself. It would be my job to keep him talking, to keep him circling, to find a truth to which he felt compelled to get closer, closer, closer, until that truth, no matter how ugly, became bright enough to burn.

I took the schemes of all my advisers and swirled them together into a single desperate strategy. I would force Lawrence Cutlip to confront his crimes, edging him subtly when possible, shoving and badgering him like a boxer when necessary, spiraling him closer and closer to the flame of truth until the fire grew so hot upon his soul that he was forced, not to confess, because that was not his way, but instead to do as the Reverend Henson said he would do, find a scapegoat and shift the blame. Onto whom would he shift it, I had no idea. Bobo? Guy? Jesse Sterrett? It wouldn't matter, once it shifted, it would be apparent. And once it was apparent, the story would be over, Guy would be acquitted, and Cutlip would be under arrest. That was the upside. That was what I focused on as I prepared.

But there was a downside, too, a downside I couldn't ignore. If I failed, if my cross-examination proved to be too gentle a dance to dent Cutlip's armor, then consequences would befall my client and myself. Guy's defense would be exposed as a fraud. It would seem he was trying to foist blame on the grieving uncle, who had sacrificed his youth to care for his young nieces. And once the phone records were disclosed and Breger connected all the dots, the pointed finger aimed at the unknown lover would look just as fraudulent. A life sentence, no doubt, possibly death, or, at best, a mistrial, declared by Judge Tifaro, based on my behavior. And as for me, well, my legal career would be over for sure, a good thing, considering, but still. Thrust headfirst and unprepared into the cold black street of capitalism, I would be forced to find some other form of income, accounting maybe, or the wonderful world of retail. I heard that the Gap was hiring, which was a great comfort, let me tell you.

So it was strategy that I focused upon, but not only strategy. I brought to my apartment everything I had found about this case, from the forensic reports of the murder to the notes I had taken of my trips to Pierce, West Virginia, to the notes of testimony already collected, to the contents of Hailey Prouix's safe-deposit box. I examined everything, questioned every assumption, turned everything upside down and downside up, twisted back to front and vice versa. I reviewed my notes of Cutlip's direct testimony, and as I did so, and examined everything else, something seemed not right, something seemed out of order.

And then it came clear, in a sudden burst of insight, something I had badly mislabeled, something that was very much other than what I had thought it to be.

Now I had something, something definite, something to work with, something that might just force Cutlip to come face to face with his past, force him to describe smaller and smaller circles around the truth, until—flop!—and that would be the end of him.

And it had been there, the crucial piece of evidence, been there almost the entire time, right in front of my face.

"**MR. CUTLIP,** this is my client, Guy Forrest," I said, standing behind Guy with my hands on his shoulders. "Before this trial had you ever laid eyes on him?"

"No, I ain't."

"Ever spoken to him?"

"Nope, and can't say I'm sad about it neither."

"And yet it was your testimony that without ever meeting him or talking to him you were against your niece's marrying him, isn't that right?"

"After what he done to his family, walked out like a dog, yes, I was."

"You told Hailey Prouix she was making a mistake with him, isn't that what you said? You told her to get away from him while she could."

"And I was right about it, too, wasn't I?"

"Can I approach, Your Honor?"

The judge nodded.

"I'd like this marked Defense Exhibit Nine." I gave a copy to Troy Jefferson and took the original to the court reporter to be marked before dropping it in front of Cutlip. "You recognize the man in this picture?"

"I never seen this picture before."

"Just answer my question. Do you recognize the man in the picture?"

"Yeah, it's him."

"The record will indicate that the witness was pointing at the defendant, Guy Forrest. This, then, is a picture of the man who wanted to marry your niece and is accused by you and the state of murdering her. What do you feel about this man?"

"I hate his whole guts, what you expect? He killed my niece dead and stole my world like a thief."

"Good. Now, here I'm handing you a black Sharpie marker. Cross out the picture of this man you hate so."

"Why?"

"Indulge me."

"What for? I told you I never done seen this picture. I'm just here to say the dead woman, she was my niece. I don't understand."

"It's not up to you to understand, sir. It's only up to you to do it." I put a little juice into the "do it," just enough to get his back up about it, and it did. I saw that lovely serpentine flicker of hate in his eyes. "Don't be a coward, now, the picture's not going to jump up and bite you." That got a little laugh, which made him even angrier. "Just go ahead and do what I tell you to do. Cross it out."

He gave me a slow, insolent stare and then went at the picture with the marker.

"Fine, thank you."

I picked the photograph off the front rail of the witness stand and showed it first to Troy Jefferson and then to the jury, a fine color photograph of Guy Forrest with a ragged, violent zig-zag-zig running through it.

"So you never approved of Guy Forrest for your niece. Did you know she was seeing someone else at the time?"

"She said something or other like that, just to rile me."

"Rile you? Why would that rile you?"

"I didn't like her acting like no tramp."

"She never told you who he was, this other lover, did she?"

"No, not exactly. But I heard things. I heard he was some Puerto Rican or something."

"Puerto Rican?" I thought on that a moment, turned to Beth, who simply shrugged, and then I remembered. "You're referring to Juan Gonzalez, isn't that right?"

"Yeah, right. I heard she got mixed up with him somehow, and I hated to hear it."

"You rejected Guy Forrest as a suitable husband for your niece, without ever meeting or talking to him, and you were against her other Puerto Rican lover, so my question, Mr. Cutlip, is this: Of which of your niece's boyfriends did you ever approve?"

"Objection, Your Honor," said Troy Jefferson. "This is pretty far afield."

"It goes to bias, Your Honor. It goes to credibility. The People opened this door in direct, opened a lot of doors in direct. It is not for Mr. Jefferson now to object when I walk through them."

"I think that's right, Mr. Jefferson. You did open the door. Go ahead, Mr. Carl, but very carefully."

"I'll repeat the question, Mr. Cutlip: Of which of your niece's boyfriends did you ever approve?"

"None of your damn business."

"Oh, I think it is. Answer the question, please, or I'll ask the judge to compel you to answer it."

Cutlip turned to look at Judge Tifaro, who was peering down at him through her half glasses like a librarian from hell.

"There was some, I suppose," he answered.

"Who? Tell us."

"Well, there was the football player, that Ricky Bronson she was with her last years in high school. I didn't mind him so much."

"Is that because, as you so wittily told me, he was more interested in standing over the center than he was in being with her?"

"Maybe. And he wasn't even the quarterback." He slapped the rail and laughed, his little staccato laugh, and some joined in, which made him laugh even harder.

"What about Grady Pritchett? You didn't like him much, did you?"

"Oh, I didn't mind old Grady."

"You went after him with a shotgun, didn't you? Want me to bring him up here from West Virginia to tell the court how you went after him with a shotgun?"

"He was hanging around too damn much. He was older than her and arrogant and like the rest of them only interested in one damn thing."

"What was that, Mr. Cutlip?"

"Now you're being cute. You know damn well what boys want in a girl like that."

"And men, too."

"Hell yes."

"What about Jesse Sterrett? Did you approve of your niece's relationship with Jesse Sterrett?"

"They was just friends, not boyfriend-girlfriend or anything like that."

"Oh, they were more than just friends, weren't they, Mr. Cutlip? They were out-and-out lovers, weren't they?"

"No. You're wrong. He was, maybe, less than a man, from what I heard. From what I heard, I'd more expect him to be interested in that Bronson boy than in her." That same staccato laugh, but this time no one joined in.

"They were lovers and they wanted to spend their lives together and you hated that, didn't you, just like you hated the idea of Hailey's marrying Guy Forrest?"

"You're flat-assed wrong about that."

"I'd like this marked Defense Exhibit Ten," I said, dropping a photocopy before Troy Jefferson and taking the original up to be marked by the court reporter. When it was marked, I handed it to Cutlip. "You recognize what that is?"

"No, I sure as hell don't."

"It's a letter from Jesse Sterrett to your niece Hailey. Why don't you start reading it out loud to the jury?"

"Objection. There's no foundation for this letter to be entered into evidence or to be read to the jury. He said he couldn't identify it."

"I'll link it up, Judge."

"Will the purported author, this Jesse Sterrett, be testifying?"

"No, Your Honor."

"Then how will you link it up?"

"I ask for some leeway here, Judge. I believe I can lay the foundation for this document, but I'd like to do it in the order of my choosing. Remember, Your Honor, Mr. Jefferson chose to call this witness and have him point the finger of blame at my client."

"Let me see the letter." Judge Tifaro examined it and then examined my face to see if she could figure out what in the world I was trying to do. "How is this Jesse Sterrett relevant to this case?"

"You'll see, Your Honor, but he surely is."

"All right, Mr. Carl, pending a ruling later as to relevance and as to proper foundation, I'll allow your examination to continue for now."

"But, Judge—"

"That'll do, Mr. Jefferson. You took enough liberties with this witness, I think it only fair I give Mr. Carl the same opportunity."

"We take exception."

"Exception noted. Go ahead, Mr. Carl."

"Thank you, Judge. Mr. Cutlip, read the letter please."

"Let me put on my glasses, then." He fumbled in his shirt pocket and pulled out a set of reading glasses.

"Mr. Cutlip," said the judge, "you didn't put on your glasses when you were examining the photographs yesterday, did you?"

"Didn't need them for that."

"That's encouraging. Go ahead, Mr. Carl."

"Read the beginning of the letter out loud for the jury," I said.

" 'I am flying,' it says, 'I am floating through the air and I don't never want to come down. Never.' I told you he was like that, a sissy boy like that."

"Who?"

"The Sterrett boy who wrote this."

"Fine." I glanced up at the judge, who smiled slightly at the admission as to authorship. "Now, go to the end, Mr. Cutlip, and read the last sentence, read that one to the jury."

"Here it is: 'I can't wait to go to sleep tonight so I can wake up tomorrow and see your face and then after school and after practice run to the quarry so I can cover you in kisses till it's dark and we have to go home and then do it all again the day after and then again and then again.'"

"And it is signed 'J' for Jesse Sterrett, isn't it?"

"That's right."

"And the quarry in Pierce, where you lived, is where the teenagers go to neck, or spoon, or make out, or whatever the word is now, isn't that right?"

"Yeah, that's right."

"Is it still your testimony that Jesse Sterrett and your niece weren't lovers, that they weren't in love?"

"He might of been but she wasn't. I know for damn sure she wasn't."

"If she wasn't, why would she have kept this letter for fifteen years?"

"Objection."

"Sustained."

"All right, Mr. Cutlip. What happened to Jesse Sterrett?"

"I don't know."

"Yes you do," I said. "Tell the jury what happened to Jesse Sterrett, who loved your niece and couldn't wait to go to sleep because it meant he was closer to waking and seeing her again and covering her again with his kisses? Tell them what happened to Jesse Sterrett sixteen years ago."

Cutlip stretched his neck as if his collar were too tight. "He died."

"Objection, Your Honor. This is too much. Counsel is dredging up something that happened years ago in another state. There is no evidence of a connection and so no relevance to this testimony."

The judge peered down at Cutlip as he squirmed in the witness chair. "Where did this boy die?" asked the judge.

"In that there quarry."

"How?"

"He slipped and fell and died in the quarry, and that was all."

"His head was smashed in, wasn't it?" I said.

"From the fall." Cutlip stretched his neck again. "That's what the coroner, he said."

"Your poker buddy, Doc Robinson, your drinking and poker buddy, he was the coroner, right?"

"He said it was an accident."

"And a few days later you left Pierce, West Virginia."

"One had nothing to do with the other."

"A few days after your niece's lover Jesse Sterrett's head was smashed in at the quarry, you left Pierce, West Viriginia, didn't you? You left your home, your nieces, your sister, you left and never came back again, didn't you?"

"Yeah, I left."

"And you left because they found Jesse Sterrett dead. Isn't that why you left?"

"Your Honor, I still have my objection."

The judge continued to stare down at Lawrence Cutlip on the stand and said, "Mr. Carl, why should I not sustain Mr. Jefferson's objection?"

"This witness testified that my client killed his niece. I am permitted under the rules of evidence to inquire about specific instances of conduct that may weigh on his truthfulness and credibility as to that issue. What happened to Jesse Sterrett, I believe, is one of those instances."

"Objection overruled."

"I'm done," said Cutlip. "I got nothing more to say about that boy. I'm not feeling so well. I'm not a healthy man. I got problems. I got a weak constitution. I had beriberi. I been sick as a dog for the last seven years. I came here to tell you all that the dead girl, she was my niece and that this man kilt her, and now you're asking me all kinds of questions about something that happened too damn long ago. I'm a carcass already near dead and now you're trying to finish me off once and for all."

"Take a moment, Mr. Cutlip," said the judge, "to pull yourself together."

I turned my back on Cutlip's evil stare and leaned over the defense table to talk to Beth.

"How am I doing?" I whispered.

"Terrific," she said. "You have him on the run, and you've kept my red marker busy."

"What are we up to by now?"

"With his direct testimony, and with what you've done today, about a third."

"What do you think we need?"

"It's hard to say. Fifty percent would make it all pretty sure."

"Let me know when we reach it."

"You want me to signal you?"

"Yes."

"Some secret signal?"

"Not too secret. Just call something out."

"What, like Skink's bingo?"

"Yes, exactly. Bingo."

"Victor . . ."

"Just do it. Any word from Skink?"

"Not yet."

I shook my head, stood straight, turned around. "All right, Mr. Cutlip. Something different, something less trying. Ms. Derringer and I met with you before this trial at the Desert Winds retirement home, isn't that right? That's where you live, isn't it?"

"Sure do."

"That's out there in Henderson, Nevada, just a few miles from the Las Vegas Strip, isn't that right?"

"Sure is."

"It's a nice place, that Henderson, the fastest-growing city in America."

"So they say."

"And the Desert Winds retirement home is lovely, isn't it? The best of the best. The very lap of luxury."

"I suppose it's nice enough."

"Pretty expensive place?"

"Don't know."

"You don't pay the bills?"

"Was a lump sum deposited to take care of the bills."

"Who paid the lump sum?"

"Hailey."

"And you have your own personal attendant there at Desert Winds, don't you?"

"Yeah. My man Bobo."

"Bobo? Is that his real name?"

"That's what I call him."

"But his real name is Dwayne Joseph Bohannon, isn't it?"

"I don't know about the Joseph."

"But the Dwayne and the Bohannon are right."

"I suppose so."

"Who pays for Bobo?"

"Hailey, though not no more after that man killing her and all."

"Is Bobo in court today? Did he come to Philadelphia with you?"

"No."

"So he's still in Nevada?"

"Don't know. He could be anywhere. He comes when he wants and goes when he wants. Lately he's been a going."

"Now, Bobo does all that traveling in a pretty nice car, doesn't he? A white Camaro with Nevada plates."

"That's right."

"Bought with Hailey's money."

"What he earned taking care of me."

"How did Hailey afford the lump-sum payment for such an up-scale retirement place?"

"She was a lawyer."

"Yes, but so am I, and I couldn't afford it, and Ms. Derringer here couldn't afford it, and Mr. Jefferson here couldn't afford it. So I'm wondering, how did Hailey afford it?"

"I don't know. She said she had a case that came through, near drowned her in money."

"A case? And this case came through when?"

"Six months or so before she died."

"What kind of case, do you know?"

"Just a case. She said some guy went into a hospital for something minor and ended up like a stalk of celery."

I turned to look at the jury. They were nodding, they knew the case even if Cutlip didn't. "And after that money came in," I continued, "the money from that case, she moved you to Desert Winds?"

"Yep."

"And before that where were you living?"

"Around."

"Around where?"

"Motels here or there, around Vegas, whatever I could afford at the time."

"And Bobo?"

"He was in them motels, too."

"So you and Bobo knew each other before Desert Winds."

"That's right."

"Nice places, those motels?"

"Hardly. Some had bugs the size of rats, and then there was the rats. And for the prices we paid, they didn't have no HBO."

"Is there HBO in Desert Winds?"

"And Cinemax and Showtime."

"How nice for you that must be. Now, you mentioned in your direct testimony that your niece told you she and Guy Forrest were fighting over money, isn't that right?"

"That's what I said, yeah. That's when I knowed she was in trouble."

"Did she tell you that the fight was over the money from the case that near drowned her in money?"

"Yeah, something like that."

"The same money that had taken you out of motel land, with its bugs as big as rats and no HBO, and into the lovely, luxurious, Desert Winds."

"I suppose."

"And so the thought of Guy taking back that lump-sum payment and sending you and Bobo back down to motel land was pretty terrifying, wasn't it?"

"I could handle it."

"Really? Without HBO? Wasn't Guy Forrest, by complaining about the missing money, putting your whole luxurious existence at risk? Wouldn't you have done anything to keep from going back to those motels?"

"Mr. Carl, I'm a broken man. I'm stuck in this damn chair, this is my first time out of Nevada in six years, I haven't been able to keep down a drink in a year and a half. I got something in me that's chewing me up. It'll kill me, it will, and damn soon. I'm dying for damn sure, without nothing no one can do about it. My life is over already. What the hell do I care where I die? All I know is the only person in this whole damn world that ever did the least thing nice for me is dead, and I loved her pure, and to tell the truth I'm dying more of lost love than anything else. And nothing can happen to me from here on out, nothing you could ever dream do to me, could be any worse."

"How about Bobo, could he handle it?"

"Objection."

"Sustained."

"I'd like to mark this Defense Exhibit Eleven for identification. Do you know what that is?"

"It looks like a traffic ticket of some sort."

"Objection, Your Honor. Foundation. Relevance."

The judge took the ticket and examined it carefully for a long moment before frowning. "No, I'm going to allow this," she said. "I assume you'll lay the foundation for this in your case, Mr. Carl."

"The ticketing officer has already been subpoenaed to testify."

"Fine. Continue."

"Where is this ticket from, Mr. Cutlip?"

"It says here City of Philadelphia."

"What's it for?"

"Looks like speeding."

"On City Line Avenue, isn't that right? Could you tell the jury the make and license of the car?"

"A Camaro, white, Nevada plates."

"And who is it issued against?"

"It's hard to read the handwriting."

"Try."

"Looks like Dwayne Joseph Bohannon."

"Bobo."

"Suppose so."

"What was Bobo doing not six blocks from Hailey Prouix's house the night before the murder?"

"Don't know. Ask Bobo."

"Objection."

"I'd be delighted to ask him, Mr. Cutlip," I said over the objection, "but he seems to have disappeared, so I am forced to ask you."

"Objection, Your Honor."

"Sustained. The jury will disregard that question and please remember, questions are not evidence. Evidence can come only from the witnesses. Anything more, Mr. Carl?"

"Yes, Your Honor, I'd like to mark four photographs for identification, Defense Exhibits Twelve to Fifteen."

I gave the first to Cutlip to examine.

"Do you recognize the people in that picture?"

"Where'd you get this?"

"Just answer my question. Do you recognize the people in that photograph?"

"That's my sister and her husband and them two girls."

"They look pretty happy there don't they, a happy family?"

"Sure they was. Why not?"

"How old were the girls there?"

"Seven maybe. Tommy died when they was eight."

"Tommy Prouix?"

"That's right."

"Where was he from, this Tommy Prouix?"

"New Orleans. I met him down there in a bar. He was a wild-eyed Cajun looking for work. Told him there was lumber mills up West Virginia way that was hiring. He drove up, stayed with my sister till he settled, and then settled down with her."

"And this next picture, can you tell us what that is?"

"That's me and my sister and the girls."

"When was this taken?"

"After he was kilt, when I was forced to move in."

"You were forced to move in?"

"They needed something in that house, they needed a man. The girls had that Cajun blood in them and they was running wild, and Debra, my sister, she never really recovered from Tommy's dying."

"And she asked you to come back."

"I was traveling like before when I heard Tommy was dead. I came for the funeral, saw what was happening, and stayed. Them girls, they needed a firm hand, and so I did what I could. I found a job that paid decent in a local slaughterhouse and I cut down on my drinking so they'd have money for clothes and such."

"And you provided the discipline they needed."

"Yes I did."

"The firm hand."

"That's what they needed. I know I needed it, and my daddy

never flinched. Never once. Them girls needed it, too, especially Hailey."

"And like your daddy, you never flinched."

"No, sir."

"And so you laid your hands on them."

"When I had to. Never so it hurt, just so they'd know what they done was wrong."

"The girls, do they look happy in that picture?"

"It's hard to tell. I suppose they was happy enough. They was eating regularly, I know that."

"Let me show you another photograph."

"Where did you find these pictures? Where did you find that letter?"

"The same place, Mr. Cutlip, both in the same place. Do you recognize the two girls in that photograph?"

"It's Roylynn and Hailey."

"Your two nieces. How old are they there?"

"I don't know. Fifteen or so."

"They look very much alike in some respects. Can you tell them apart?"

"Well, it's not too hard. Hailey was always the one dressed like a slut."

"Was this picture taken before or after Roylynn tried to kill herself?"

"How the hell do I know?"

"Why did your niece, Roylynn, try to kill herself when you were in the house?"

"She ain't the one that was murdered."

"Please answer my question. What was going on in that house that caused Roylynn to want to die?"

"Nothing. She was crazy, is all. She still is. Was mental all her damn life."

"What was going on in that house, Mr. Cutlip?"

"They needed a firm hand, is all."

"What was the dark secret of that house, Mr. Cutlip?"

"There was no secret. We was just like everybody else."

"This last picture, Mr. Cutlip, who is that?"

"Where'd you get this?"

"It was with all the others."

"She kept all this crap?"

"Is that Jesse Sterrett?"

"I suppose."

I stepped up to the witness box. Cutlip flinched, but all I did was take the pictures. "I'd like Defense Exhibits Twelve to Fifteen placed in evidence."

"Objection, relevance."

"Overruled. Exhibits so entered."

One by one I showed them to the jury, the "before" and "after" pictures of the family, the pictures of the twins, and, finally, the picture of the sad, serious Jesse Sterrett. I handed this last to a woman in the front row, and as she examined it, I said,

"Another letter. I'll mark this Defense Exhibit Sixteen. Look it over closely, Mr. Cutlip. Do you recognize it?"

"No."

"You ever see it before?"

"No."

"You sure, Mr. Cutlip? It's got a jagged line through it, doesn't it, as if someone wanted to cross it out?"

"Yeah, so?"

"I want to show you the picture of Guy Forrest you crossed out this morning. I want you to compare the cross-out lines. Are they great large Xs, Mr. Cutlip?"

"No."

"They're like Zs, aren't they? Both of them."

"Yes."

"They look alike, these Zs, don't they, as if they were made by the same hand?"

"Maybe they do."

"Your hand."

"Maybe it is."

"Objection."

"This is a letter from Jesse Sterrett to your niece Hailey, written on the day of his death," I continued, over the objection. "Read the first paragraph of that letter, Mr. Cutlip."

"Objection, Your Honor. This has gone too far. There is no foundation for this or the other letter presented."

"I think there is, Mr. Jefferson," said the judge. "Mr. Cutlip earlier identified the author of the letters as Jesse Sterrett. He has now admitted that the zigzag mark on the letter is possibly his. The jurors can compare the mark on the picture of Mr. Forrest with the mark on the letter to see if they find a match. There is a sufficient foundation laid for Mr. Carl to continue with this line."

"Again we take exception."

"Exception noted. Continue, Mr. Carl."

"Read the first paragraph, Mr. Cutlip."

"I got nothing more to say."

"Read the first paragraph."

"I don't need to."

"Read it."

He glanced at the judge, who was staring down at him with no pity. He squirmed in his seat and began to read. "'I am so angry I could strangle a porcupine, and scared too, so scared, impossibly scared. I love you so much, want you so much, but now I have learned that secret you've been hiding, my anger burns least as bright as the love.'"

"What was the secret, Mr. Cutlip? What was Hailey's secret?"

"There was no secret."

"In the letter Jesse tells Hailey either he will run away with her or he will take out his anger on the man who inflamed it. He says there will be blood, no doubt about it. He tells Hailey it is up to her. That's right, isn't it?"

"I suppose."

"Now read the last paragraph."

"No."

"Tell the jury where he planned to meet Hailey to figure it out."

"No."

"The last paragraph."

"Read it, please, Mr. Cutlip," said the judge.

" 'I'll be at the quarry tonight, I'll be waiting for you. If you trust me enough to come I'll dedicate my every waking hour of the rest of my life to making you happy, I will. I swear. But if you don't come, if you won't run away with me, then I'll do it the other way. I'll do what I need to do to protect you and whatever consequences that come my way I'll bear gladly because I'll be bearing them for you. Tonight, I'll be waiting. Tonight.'"

"And he was at the quarry, wasn't he?"

"I don't know."

"He died there that night at the quarry, didn't he?"

"I don't know."

"And only two people knew he would be there, Hailey and the man who intercepted the letter, the man who tried to cross it out with a zig-zag-zig as clear as a signature."

"He was going to steal her away from her family."

"And that's why you killed him."

"I didn't."

"And that's why, just a few days later, you left Pierce for good."

"I told you, it just happened like that."

"No, it didn't, Mr. Cutlip. You told us an untruth. It was only after meeting with the Reverend Henson in the church that you left, wasn't it? After he threatened to disclose everything, wasn't it?"

"That's a lie."

"He's here, just outside the courtroom, the good reverend. He remembers everything."

"You're making that up. He's most likely dead by now."

"Should we bring him in and ask him?"

"You're bluffing."

"This isn't poker, Mr. Cutlip."

I turned around and nodded to Beth. She stood, left the courtroom for a moment, and then came through again, accompanied by the Very Reverend Theodore H. Henson.

Cutlip pushed himself to standing in the witness box when he saw the clergyman, and his face turned crimson, and I feared he would collapse right there with a heart attack. He raised his hand and pointed at the reverend and said,

"Ever thing he told you is a lie, ever damn thing."

"But still, it was after your confrontation with the reverend in the chapel of his church that you left Pierce forever."

He dropped down heavily into his chair. "I was ready to go anyways, and I didn't need him spreading his lies, getting ever one's tongues a wagging."

"Like the way you cheated at poker."

"Lies."

"The way you killed Jesse Sterrett."

"Lies."

"The things you did to Hailey."

"Lies, lies, and damn lies."

"Bingo," said Beth.

I stepped back as soon as I heard Beth relay our subtle signal. I stepped back and stopped and took a few breaths. This was it, now or never. I had made progress, strong progress, I had tied that bastard to a murder sixteen years ago, but still there was only accusation and denial, still there was no direct evidence relating to the death of Hailey Prouix. I had set the stage, and now was my chance, my one chance. I wanted to stop, take a break, I wanted to hold on to the hope for a little longer before it turned to hard reality, either way, but now was not the time for timidity. I faced the jury.

"I have one more letter," I said.

It was lying there, with my other papers, on the podium. Beth had two copies on transparencies, with certain of the phrases on one of them now underlined.

"Let's have this marked Defense Exhibit Seventeen," I said as I dropped still another copy before Troy Jefferson. "It's just a torn piece of envelope with a message on it, and I give it to you, Mr. Cutlip, and I ask you if you've ever seen it before?"

I stepped up to the witness box and placed the torn piece of envelope in front of him. He was startled to see it, I could tell. He read it slowly and shook his head as he read it and said nothing.

"Have you ever seen this before, Mr. Cutlip?"

"Where'd you get this?"

"It was with the others."

"She kept it?"

"All these years. Yes."

Cutlip put his hand on his chest and struggled for breath. "She kept it."

"Yes, she did, Mr. Cutlip. All those many years after you wrote it."

"I . . . I . . . No, this isn't . . ."

"This is your writing, isn't it?"

"I don't know."

"You wrote this to Hailey years ago, immediately after you left Pierce."

"I don't . . . I . . ."

"I originally thought this, too, was written by Jesse Sterrett. The other letters were typed, but this was handwritten, so I couldn't really compare. But now I know it was written by you. Everyone's voice is unique—word choice, expressions. I had Ms. Derringer underline all the expressions in this letter that matched the very expressions you used in your testimony. Should I have her put it up on the screen, Mr. Cutlip? Over half the words are parts of the same sentence constructions used in your answers yesterday and today. Should I have her put it up on the screen?"

"No."

"It's your letter, isn't it?"

"She kept it."

"You wrote this, didn't you? You wrote this to her."

He sat there staring at the torn piece of envelope, not moving, not moving, but all the while I could see him psychologically getting closer, closer, a moth circling a flame, getting closer, closer. And then, slowly, he nodded.

Flop.

"Let the record reflect," I said, "that the witness nodded yes."

"Record will so reflect," said the judge.

"Read your letter to the court, please."

"I can't."

"Read it, Mr. Cutlip, read your desperate note to your fifteen-year-old niece."

"I won't."

I took hold of a copy of what I had given Cutlip and read it out loud myself.

" 'It's killing me ever day, ever damn day, that we're not together. My heart weeps in the wanting. I'm less than a man without you, a carcass already near dead, dying of lost love. You done this to me, you stole my world like a thief. Don't listen to what they are saying, it's nothing but lies, lies and damn lies.' "

"Stop."

" 'I'm sorry for what I done but I never had no choice, I only done what I had to.' "

"Stop it, damn it."

" 'Never a love been so fierce or fearsome, never has it cost so high or been worth the entire world.' "

"She kept it, don't that prove nothing?" he said. "She kept it, don't that prove it all? You just a fool who don't understand."

"What don't I understand, Mr. Cutlip?"

"It wasn't like that, not something dirty. It was love, real and hard, the truest in the world. Fearsome and fierce, like I said, but also something alive, more alive than anything you'll ever see, like it had a mind of its own. And it wasn't my doing, it was her doing. It wasn't me that started it, it was her that started it. She seduced me. I had no choice in it. Whatever she wanted, she got. I had no choice. She seduced me."

There it was, the shift I was looking for, the shift of blame. I was wondering where it would fall, and I now I knew. The person he was scapegoating would be Hailey herself. I turned to look at Reverend Henson, who had prophesied what Cutlip would do. He stared back at me, his eyes glossy, but he was nodding. He had seen it, too. They all had seen it.

I turned back to that cur on the stand. I could barely stand to look at him, he disgusted me so, but still, along with the disgust I couldn't help feel a drop of empathic pity for the man. He was right, in his way, when he said that whatever Hailey wanted she seemed to have gotten. And what girl doesn't try to seduce her father, or the substitute that comes in to take his role? The poor fool, I almost believed it when he said he had no choice in it—almost—because there is always a choice. When you have the power, the responsibility, when you take hold of a child's hand, there is always a choice. And he made his. And in so doing he took from Hailey Prouix something she maybe didn't even know she had, but something she spent the rest of her life struggling again to find.

"How old was she?" I said in a voice so soft the jury leaned forward to hear. "How old was she when she seduced you, Mr. Cutlip?"

"I got nothing more to say."

In a voice still soft, weary with resignation, I laid out the charges. "You were jealous of Jesse Sterrett, weren't you, Mr. Cutlip? And you weren't going to let him take Hailey away from you, so you killed him."

"I want to go home."

"And you tried to kill Guy for the same reason, because he was taking Hailey away from you, and also to quiet his complaints about the money."

"I'm sick, I'm dying."

"And by accident, by tragic mistake, the killer you sent, your man Bobo, ended up murdering Hailey Prouix instead."

"Whatever Bobo done, I had nothing to do with," said Cutlip.

I stopped and turned to the jury. I watched their eyes as they watched him. It is often hard to read a jury, but I could read those eyes.

"Will the court reporter please read back that last answer?" I said.

As the reporter was reviewing the tape spit out by her stenographic machine, Cutlip spoke up.

"Maybe I want a lawyer," he said.

"One moment, Mr. Cutlip," said the judge as she waited for the court reporter.

The court reporter read from her tape in a halting monotone. "Question: 'And by accident by tragic mistake the killer you sent your man Bobo ended up murdering Hailey Prouix instead.' Answer: 'Whatever Bobo done I had nothing to do with.' "

"I ain't saying nothing no more without a lawyer," said Cutlip.

"You are refusing to answer any more questions?" said the judge.

"I want a lawyer. I got rights. I'm asking for a lawyer. I'm not saying nothing no more without a lawyer. Do I get a lawyer or not?"

"We'll see, Mr. Cutlip," said the judge. "We will see. This court is in recess. Bailiff, keep an eye on Mr. Cutlip and see that he does not leave the courtroom. Counsel, in my chambers. Now."

"**IMAGINE,**" **SAID** Judge Tifaro, leaning back in the chair behind her desk, sucking on the earpiece of her reading glasses, "all this from a failure to agree on a stipulation."

"We were set up," said Troy Jefferson.

"Yes, you were, Mr. Jefferson. And I must say, Mr. Carl, it was far easier to believe you were screwing up royally out of sheer incompetence than to believe you cleverly arranged everything so you could grill this Mr. Cutlip on the stand."

"Thank you," I said, "I think."

The judge shook her head with a disgusted admiration. The two sides had fully assembled in the judge's chambers, not a wood-paneled old-school type of place but, instead, a soft, pleasant room filled with country French furnishings. Beth sat with me. Along with Troy Jefferson and his other lawyers were the tag team of Breger and Stone. The court reporter had set up her machine just to the left of the judge and was taking down every word for posterity.

"Do you have any more questions for this witness?" said the judge.

"Yes, Your Honor."

"Do you think you'll get any more answers?"

"No."

"Neither do I. I am going to appoint a lawyer to represent Mr. Cutlip, and my expectation is that he will be advised to say nothing more and will follow that advice. So what do we do now?"

"Put him back on the stand," I said. "Let me ask the questions and let him plead the Fifth in front of the jury. That's what we ask."

"Of course you do. Mr. Jefferson?"

"We are asking instead," said Troy Jefferson, "on the record, that Cutlip's entire testimony be stricken."

"He was your witness, Mr. Jefferson."

Jefferson turned and frowned at Breger. "Yes, he was, but you repeatedly ignored our objections and allowed Mr. Carl to run roughshod over the rules of evidence while dredging up a death and unsavory happenings of fifteen years ago that have nothing, nothing to do with the present case. Reading letters into evidence without proper foundation; using the threat of extrinsic testimony to badger the witness into all manner of confession, even knowing such extrinsic testimony to be not admissible; using a comparison of scrawl marks sixteen years apart to authenticate documents—all of this is contrary to the spirit and letter of the rules of evidence. With all due respect, you were wrong to permit it over our objections, Judge. Allowing in this inflammatory and irrelevant testimony was hugely prejudicial to our case. The testimony should be stricken and the jury instructed to ignore everything they heard."

"I don't think that would be possible, do you, Mr. Jefferson?"

"Then we ask for a mistrial. A mistrial based on misconduct on the part of the defense so that jeopardy does not attach and we can try this sucker again."

The judge turned to me. "Mr. Carl?"

"If the question of the trial is who killed Hailey Prouix, then I could hardly imagine any testimony more relevant, Your Honor."

"Testimony about abuse of the victim a decade and a half ago at the hands of this witness?" said Jefferson.

"Yes."

"Testimony about the death of that boy in that quarry?" said Jefferson.

"Absolutely."

"It all seems rather distant, Mr. Carl," said the judge.

"Exactly, Your Honor," said Jefferson.

"Still, Mr. Jefferson, the question of relevancy is solely a question of whether the evidence makes some fact of consequence more or less likely to have occurred. Do you think that the testimony of Mr. Cutlip has no bearing on the question of whether it was the defendant who killed Miss Prouix?"

"No, Your Honor."

"Really. The testimony raised no doubts?"

"Not reasonable doubts, Judge. And as to the question of prejudice—"

"The question is not prejudice, Mr. Jefferson, but unfair prejudice. My guess, Mr. Carl, is that your new theory is that Mr. Cutlip, out of fear of Mr. Forrest's complaints regarding the money, and with the added spur of jealousy, sent . . . Bobo, is it?"

"Yes, Judge."

"Sent Bobo to kill Guy Forrest and that Bobo, by mistake, because of the low light and the comforter covering the whole of the victim's body, killed Hailey Prouix instead. Will that be your theory in closing?"

"Yes, Judge."

"What about the mysterious lover?" sneered Jefferson.

"A minor detail wrong," I said.

"I find there is sufficient evidence to support that argument," said the judge. "I also find the testimony of Mr. Cutlip relevant to the new defense theory and, though certainly prejudicial to your case against the defendant, not unfairly prejudicial in any way. I also find that a sufficient foundation was laid for the introduction of the letters read into testimony, foundation based on the testimony of the prosecution's own witness. My only question, Mr. Jefferson, is why aren't you bringing this Bobo in for questioning right now?"

"We're looking for him, Judge," said Detective Breger. "He has apparently disappeared from his home in Henderson. The Nevada police have put an APB out on his car."

"The white Camaro."

"Yes, Judge. The white Camaro."

"If you want a warrant to bring him in, I'll sign it."

Just then there was a knock on the door, and the judge's secretary poked her head into the office. "There's a phone call for Miss Derringer."

"Excuse me," said Beth as she stood. We all watched as she left the office.

"Telemarketers," I said. A soft spurt of nervous laughter died at the judge's impatience.

"Mr. Jefferson, my expectation is that you will immediately put this witness into police custody and inform the proper officials from the state of West Virginia of what happened in court today. At the same time I will have an attorney appointed for his benefit. I will not, however, put this witness back on the stand simply to plead his Fifth Amendment privilege. *That* would be unfairly prejudicial. I suppose we'll have to wait to see exactly what his new lawyer advises before continuing. Now, Mr. Jefferson, one more question."

"Yes, Your Honor."

"Do you really think, after hearing what they heard, the jury will convict Mr. Forrest of murder?"

"The evidence against Mr. Forrest remains very strong."

"You think so, do you?"

"He was the only one in the house, it was his gun, his fingerprints are on the gun, there is a strong monetary motive—"

"Yes, yes, yes, but what about Mr. Cutlip's admissions?"

"I believe that Mr. Carl is a skilled attorney, practiced in the arts of deception and trickery, who was able to badger and twist an old man to say pretty much anything he wanted the man to say."

"Thank you," I said, "I think."

"Maybe your opinion of Mr. Carl's skills is higher than mine," said the judge, "but I don't think that old man said anything he didn't want to say. You haven't yet closed, your case is still not complete, and Mr. Carl here can always screw things up, I have no doubt, but you understand that a certain threshold has to be met before I can even allow a case to go to the jury."

"I understand the law, Your Honor. We believe we have already met that threshold."

"I suppose you'll find out for certain when the defense makes its motion at the close of your case."

The door opened, and Beth came back into the chambers, but instead of returning to her chair, she stood at the door. "Can I see you for a moment, Victor?" she said.

Judge Tifaro nodded. I stood and walked to her and leaned over, letting her whisper in my ear as all watched.

"Judge," I said, "could you excuse us? Something has turned up to which we need to immediately attend. Mr. Jefferson and the detectives will want to come along, too. It might be better if we just recess everything until tomorrow morning."

"What is it, Counselor? What have you found?"

"Bobo."

THE SEABRIGHT Motel squatted on a desolate commercial section of Route 1 leading to the Delaware shore, surrounded by outlet centers and strip malls. The exhaust and sound from six lanes of traffic covered the two-story cement block like a fulsome blanket. The only sign of the bright sea still twenty miles away was the aqua painting above the lit neon VACANCY. It was a weekday and summer was over and most of the spaces in front of the building were empty. Those cars still parked were battered and old, their shocks sagging from the weight of sad, rambling stories. Except for the white Camaro in the corner, the white Camaro with the silver Nevada plates and the right side dented in all to hell.

Bobo had fallen back into motel land, and he had fallen back hard.

We came down in a caravan: a black unmarked van, carrying Beth and me, Jefferson, one of his assistants, Breger and Stone, followed by two Delaware State Police cars we had teamed up with in Dover, their lights off and their sirens silent.

Slowly we passed the motel and then parked in the lot of a huge discount store next door to the SeaBright. The six of us, along with four uniformed state troopers, congregated at the edge of the high chain-link fence separating the two properties. Two of the troopers held shotguns at the ready.

"So what do we do now?" said Troy Jefferson. "Has the Delaware judge signed that warrant?"

"Not yet," said one of the troopers. "They'll radio us when he does."

"You want us to go in anyway?" said another of the troopers. "We can knock and ask if he wants to talk."

"He's probably jumpy as it is," said Breger. "I don't think the sight of four uniforms is going to calm him any."

"Let me wander over and see if he's still there," I said. "He spots me, I'm just a guy in a suit. My man's waiting for me on the other side of the fence. Once we know the situation, we'll be better able to figure something out."

"Just find out where he is," said Jefferson, "and where we can all stand unobserved, and then come right back."

"Fine."

"Don't be a cowboy," said Stone.

"No threat of that," I said. "I'm too smarmy to try anything brave." I winked at her before I skulked around the fence to the corner of the motel's lot.

In the shadow of a large sign advertising a mini-golf just a bit farther down the strip, I found Skink waiting for me. He was wearing his brown suit and fedora, leaning against the sign pole, tossing something up and down in his hand, looking every inch the insouciant private dick out of a different era.

"I finally figured out where you find your wardrobe tips," I said as I eyed his getup. "From the colorized versions of old detective movies on TNT."

"You took your time showing up."

"Just a little distraction called a murder trial. He still here?"

"Yes he is."

"We're lucky he didn't leave."

"Yes we are," he said. And then I noticed that the thing he was tossing up and down in his hand was a spark plug.

"How'd you find him?"

"Outgoing call from the DoubleTree this morning."

"Did he make you?"

"Nah. He wasn't here when I first showed up, gave me a fright, it did. But then he came roaring back into the lot with a bag of McDonald's and a bag of booze. He's up on the second floor, two-oh-nine, emptying them both. I don't know which bag will kill him first."

"Why is he here of all places?"

"Had to go somewheres, didn't he? But he grew up only a few miles down the road. Might still have pals around to help him out while he waits for it all to blow over."

"Two-oh-nine?"

"The room above the car."

The door was closed, the window was curtained, the room looked dead. And inside was the man who had murdered Hailey Prouix.

"Cutlip almost confessed to everything on the stand today," I told Skink while I stared up at the room. "Killing Jesse Sterrett, his abuse of Hailey, even her murder. Almost."

"Who'd he blame?" said Skink.

"He said the Sterrett boy asked for it and Hailey seduced him."

"Bugger all. We ought to tell Mr. Sterrett when we gets a chance."

"I'll drive you back down if you want, let you meet up with your old pals Fire and Brimstone."

"Maybe we'll call."

"You know what his last words were before he finally took the Fifth and refused to answer anything more? He said, 'Whatever Bobo done, I had nothing to do with.' "

"Loyal bastard, isn't he?"

"How'd you ever get hooked up with him in the first place?"

"He found me," said Skink. "Hailey left him my name in case of trouble."

"There are four cops with shotguns behind that fence. I want you to hold on here while I head up to Bobo's room. As soon as I get to the door, go over and tell everyone waiting on the other side where I am."

"Are you sure you want to go alone? You don't want me along, or one of the cops?"

"I don't know how he'll react to a crowd, and I don't need anybody reading him his rights either. I see trouble, I see a gun, I'll disappear and let our cops shoot the bastard to bits. But right now it's better all around if it's just me that goes up. Tell those clowns in the uniforms that they can bring their cars into this lot and put on the lights and cock their shotguns if they want. It won't hurt if Bobo sees them out there once I'm inside. But under no circumstances are they to rush the stairs and start firing. If they spook him, there's no figuring what he'll do. Can you manage all that?"

"I'll try."

I patted Skink on the shoulder. "You did great."

"I always does great."

I returned his gap-toothed smile. We had a moment, one of those touching no-touch male moments, a glance, a nod, an urge to hug stifled. Who would ever have expected that I'd have to stifle an urge to hug Skink? To strangle his ropy neck maybe, but not to hug him. We had our moment, and then I headed off for Bobo.

The stairs were outside the building, at the end opposite Bobo's room. I strode quickly through the lot and around the tiny fenced-in swimming pool to reach them. I must have looked a sight, a man in a blue suit hurrying across the asphalt, his gaze steady on a second-floor window as he moved, but I reached the steps without so much as a twitch of that curtain. Slowly I climbed, stepping softly so that my footfalls barely registered on the metal stairway, and then, carefully, my back to the brick, I made my way along the portico to the corner room.

I stooped down below the level of the peephole as I passed the door to Room 209. His door. Something tickled my neck as I passed it. I reached out a hand and brushed the door with my fingertips. It was hot, sizzling, as if there was a strange, evil fire raging inside.

Past the door, I squatted at the window. Between the curtain and the sill closest to the door was a slight opening. Carefully I placed an eye at the opening and gazed inside.

It was a small, filthy room. My view was tightly constricted, but still I could see the bed unmade, the floor littered with fast-food wrappers, emptied beer cans, the crumpled cellophane of cookie packs and potato chip bags. A flickering blue light filled the room with an uneven glow, a television light, but I heard no sound over the incessant roar of the highway. And strangely, even as I could see the action of the screen play on the scuffed block walls, there was something else, some other change in the light, as if something was moving, circling, spinning between the light source and the wall.

And then that thing moved, circled, spun into view, and my breath caught in my throat like flesh on barbed wire.

Bobo, ghostly thin, pale, in jeans but shirtless, one hand gripping the neck of a bottle, the other the butt of a gun, his lank blond hair spinning around his face as he slowly danced in loose circles to a music I couldn't hear. Bobo. Circling 'round and 'round. Like a moth 'round a flame. Circling. But it wasn't the mere sight of him circling like a moth that caught my breath, or the sight of his gun either.

When I had seen him in Nevada, his hands and arms had been scratched and scabbed as if infested with colonies of vile insects, but now it was as if the infestation had moved in marauding armies beneath his skin to cover the whole of his body. The entirety of his arms, his shoulders, his neck, his back as far as could be reached with his nails, on all of it the skin was ripped and flayed, raw, the wounds open and wet, oozing, the blood and pus running in narrow streaks from wound to wound.

It was as if Bobo, for some reason, for some reason that I could very well imagine, Bobo was trying to tear himself apart.

There is always a moment of shock when we catch a raw glimpse of another's utter humanity. We don't want to see it, we don't want to gaze beyond the surface of this clerk, of that cop, of that acquaintance, of that murderer, we don't want to be confronted with the deeper truth. But when we are, when against all our best efforts it is pressed into our consciousness, it never fails to shock us or to change us. And the shock is even greater when in our arrogance we believed that our understanding had reached beyond the mysteries of the other's soul. Here, now, peering through that crack between the curtain and the sill, seeing the wet wounds of Dwayne Joseph Bohannon's self-flayed skin, his suppurating hair shirt of septic gouges, I received such a shock. He was a cruel tool, stupid and violent, someone who had found his level with Lawrence Cutlip, that was what I knew for sure before I climbed those motel stairs, and there was an undeniable truth in all of it. But having made that climb, I saw a side I had never before considered. All the failures of his life, the disappointments, the desertions, everything he ever wanted and had been refused, everything he had never wanted but had gotten stuffed down his throat, the boy he had been and the man he had become, the entire breadth of his sorrow was written there on his flesh as if in a script of blood. I read it all, and like some great biblical passage it reached into my soul, and something changed, something changed, something dark went out of me.

I turned from the window. It was too much to bear, but the change had happened just that quickly.

The police cars were already in the parking lot, the officers crouched behind them, shotguns at the ready. Breger and Stone and Troy Jefferson were standing in a clot of law enforcement behind the crouching uniforms. And standing together, still farther behind, was my brain trust, Beth and Skink. And each of them, every one of them, was staring at me, wondering what the hell I was doing up there. I had planned on retreating if I saw a gun, I had planned on running and letting it play out as I knew it would. There would be a knock, an order, a demand. There would a shot fired and then another and then a fusillade that would rip Dwayne Joseph Bohannon apart. He would be ripped apart and would disappear from the earth as surely as if he had fallen into one of Roylynn's black holes, another of Cutlip's victims. It would play out just like that, except I couldn't let it play out just like that anymore, not after the glimpse I had caught of that boy's inner torment. The inevitable gunplay at the end was not inevitable.

I glanced back at the force arrayed in the parking lot and then knocked on the door.

"Dwayne," I said through the metal door, hot, I now knew, not from his evil but from the sun. I was standing in the gap between the window and the door, protected, I hoped, from anything fired from the room. "It's Victor Carl. We met in Henderson. You ran me off the road, tried to kill me. We need to talk."

No answer.

I knocked again. "Dwayne. It's no use. The police are already here. But I can help. I forgive you for what you tried to do to me. I'm here to help you."

I pressed myself against the wall and waited for the curtain to be pulled aside. It was.

A voice came muffled from behind the door. "I have a gun. Tell them I have a gun."

"They have bazookas, Dwayne."

"Really?"

"Let me in. I'm a lawyer. I can help you. I want to help you."

There was a long moment when I heard nothing, nothing, before, slowly, the door opened a sliver and then a sliver more, until the chain was taut. Dwayne Joseph Bohannon stood in the doorway, the gun in his hand, his face in shadow, a dirty tee shirt, stained with his blood, hiding the most hideous of his wounds.

"Thank you," I said.

He leaned forward. The light hit his face. I had to look away.

"Will you let me in?" I said.

"I don't know what to do."

"Let me in and we'll figure it out together."

There was a hesitation, and then the door closed for an moment before opening wider. I reached into my pocket, turned off the tape recorder, stepped inside.

Ninety minutes later I walked out that door with Dwayne Joseph Bohannon by my side. He was wearing a clean shirt, a jacket, his arms were outstretched in front of him, palms up, fingers open.

He followed me along the portico, down the stairs, past the police cars and the uniforms, all the way to Troy Jefferson, standing between Breger and Stone.

Dwayne glanced at me. His face was hideous, scabbed and scratched, infected and bleeding, but still I smiled and nodded him on. He wiped his nose with the sleeve of his jacket.

"I want to tell what happened," he said in a slow, stuttering voice. "Everything. I want to tell. I do. I want to. But first, Mr. Carl here, he told me I need a doctor. A skin doctor. To stop this itching. I'm itching like crazy. I need a doctor. Then I need a lawyer. A different lawyer than him. He told me I have the right and that I ain't gonna say nothing until I do."

Troy Jefferson just stared at him.

"Oh, yeah," said Dwayne, pulling a piece of paper out of his pocket and handing it to Jefferson. "Mr. Carl, he also gave me this."

"**YOU WERE** in there for an hour and a half," said Troy Jefferson as he looked over the subpoena I had served on Dwayne Joseph Bohannon. Bohannon himself had been cuffed and placed, into the back of one of the patrol cars while the cops searched the motel room. "Have a nice conversation?"

"It was hard to go deep, you calling up to the room every ten minutes or so, though I was touched at your concern for my welfare."

"The Delaware cops were nervous. They didn't know you could sleaze yourself out of tighter spots than that."

"Practiced as I am in the arts of deception and trickery."

"There you go. Did he tell you anything?"

"No, not really."

"You mean he didn't fall down on his knees and confess to the Hailey Prouix murder?"

"I wouldn't let him."

Jefferson's head jerked up. "You wouldn't let him? What the hell do you mean, you wouldn't let him?"

"You know how it is, Troy. Defense attorneys never want to know for sure."

"But you're not his defense attorney."

"Old habits die hard."

"If he had actually confessed, it would have saved your client."

"My client is already saved."

"Don't be so damn sure."

"You heard the judge. After Cutlip's testimony she has doubts whether the case should even go to the jury. What happens now if I put Bobo on the stand during the defense case and ask him if he killed Hailey Prouix? He'll plead the Fifth in front of the jury and kill your case."

"The judge won't allow that."

"Oh, yes she will. It's an acquittal, probably before the case goes to the jury. And rightly so, considering you have the wrong guy. Cutlip sent Bobo east to kill Guy Forrest and the kid screwed up. My client was the intended victim, not a perpetrator. You have the wrong man, Troy."

"You set me up."

"Maybe I did, and if I did, I must admit, it felt fine."

"Son of a bitch."

"But, Troy, no one else has to know about it. The press is going to want a statement from both of us after this. Either you can go in front of the massed media and admit to being played for the rube, or you can stand side by side with Detectives Breger and Stone and announce that your office had broken the case wide open and found the two actual killers of Hailey Prouix."

He turned his head and stared at me without saying a word.

"If your office wanted to take credit for continuing the investigation even after the indictment," I said, "for unearthing the crucial speeding ticket, for bringing Lawrence Cutlip into the jurisdiction and effecting the arrest of Dwayne Joseph Bohannon in cooperation with the Delaware State Police, I wouldn't contradict a single word."

"You'd sit back and let us bask in the glory?"

"Absolutely."

"Why?"

" 'Cause I'm a sweetheart, and because all I want is for it to be over. But you have to decide quickly. Guy shouldn't spend another day in jail."

"What about the Juan Gonzalez fraud?"

"Time served, no more. He's through as a lawyer, and he's paid enough penance for burying that file, trust me. Time served, no probation, he's free to start his life over again."

Jefferson twisted his mouth into thought. "I'll run it by the DA. He agrees, we'll do it all tomorrow morning in court. Your boy will be out by noon."

"Good. And you ought to give Breger a commendation for his work in this case. In fact, the old man's probably close to retirement. A raise in grade might raise his pension, too, make those golden years a little more golden."

"He doesn't like to be called the old man."

"Best as I can tell, he doesn't like a lot of things."

"I'll see what I can do."

"But for everything to go down like we've agreed, you have to promise me one more favor."

"Aw, now, here it comes, here's the payoff. All right, Carl, let me hear it. What's your price?"

"You need to show pity on Bohannon."

"Come again?"

"He's a screwed-up kid who fell in with someone truly evil and lost himself in the process. Cutlip bent him to his will and, in so doing, destroyed him. I'm not saying he shouldn't pay for what he did, but he was just a tool that Cutlip used and tossed away without a backward glance. Bohannon was going to scratch himself to death out of guilt if we hadn't shown up when we did. Give him a deal and take your venom out on Cutlip."

The cops came out of the room waving a plastic bag with the gun inside. It had been sitting atop the bed, just where Dwayne and I had left it for them to find.

"I'll think on it," Jefferson said before leaving me to talk it over with the ranking uniform. It wasn't hard to figure what would happen next. They would take Dwayne now to Dover and charge him with a firearms violation. They would take him to Dover, but he wouldn't be in Dover long. Jefferson would extradite him to Pennsylvania, where he would be assigned a lawyer who would make a deal in exchange for his testimony against Lawrence Cutlip. I didn't know how long he'd get, it would be a lot, and all of it deserved, but he would get some kind of a deal, and the Delaware firearms charge would undoubtedly run concurrently. He'd spend part of his life outside the prison walls, and that didn't bother me one bit. It was funny how at the start of the case I had wanted nothing but the harshest vengeance visited upon the man who shot Hailey Prouix through the heart, and now I had done what I could to make sure the law went as easy as possible on her killer. But I had seen the writing on his skin.

"You don't look very happy," said Detective Breger, coming up from behind me. "You should be dancing."

"I'm jitterbugging. Doesn't it show?"

"It looks like you ate one fried oyster too many. But you had quite the day, finding Bobo and, before that, breaking Cutlip like you did."

"I didn't break Cutlip."

"Sure you did."

"No, Detective. He wanted us to know about him and Hailey. He was proud of it. As soon as he found out she had been keeping his letter with the others, that she never stopped loving him for some twisted reason, he wanted us to know. All I did was let him. The hemming and hawing, the tears, the hesitancy, it was an act, and I was his straight man, but he wanted to crow."

"He pretty much confessed to murder on the stand."

"That was the price for his bragging rights. I'll bet right now that bastard is smiling. I'll bet right now he's talking about her to his fellow inmates. How supple she was, how fine she was. How she was the sweetest twelve-year-old ever to sashay down a junior high corridor."

"Stop it. You're beating yourself up over something you weren't even in the same state to stop. All you did was clean up the resulting mess. You have nothing to be sick over, you did swell."

"I don't feel swell, I feel dirty."

"Guys like that, even locking them up makes you want to take a shower."

I kicked at the cement.

"You did well, son," said Breger.

"Are you turning sweet on me, Detective?"

"No. In my book you're still an obnoxious punk. By the way, we need you to sign off and let us examine those phone logs."

"What?"

"The phone logs. To your home phone. We still want them."

"No you don't."

"Really, we do."

"No you don't."

"Yes, yes we do. We need to tie up all the loose ends. That was the deal."

"You don't want those phone logs, trust me. Jefferson will make an offer, Bobo will confess, both he and Cutlip will end up in prison. Put them away, swallow the key to Cutlip's cell, and end it."

"I was right, wasn't I?"

"No phone logs."

"All along I've been right."

"The case is over, our deal is null and void."

"The thing that puzzles me, Victor, is how in the hell you thought you'd get away with it."

"But I did, didn't I."

He stared at me for a moment, his strange gaze playing across my face, and then he burst out in laughter, a deep, bellowing laughter, the first I'd ever heard from him. He burst out in laughter and slammed me in the back. "Maybe you did at that," he said, walking away, and then he burst into laughter again.

I walked over to Beth and Skink, who were standing together in a corner of the lot.

"What went on in there?" said Beth. "We were scared out of our skulls for you."

"It's over. The case is over. Jefferson has to okay it with his boss, but it looks like Guy's getting out tomorrow."

"You were up there for an hour and a half."

"It seemed longer," I said.

"Did he do it?" said Skink.

"I wouldn't let him tell me, but, yeah. He did it."

"What went on in that room for an hour and a half?" said Beth.

"I had some questions, and he answered them, and that was it."

"You don't want to talk about it."

"No I don't. Ever. Never. But I'll tell you this: What he told me will haunt my dreams to the day I die. Let's get the hell out of here."

We turned away from the scene at the motel, the three of us turned away and started heading down the road, our shadows marching before us like soldiers.

"There's a crab shack on the bay what I know of," said Skink, "where they gots them fat and covered with spice. You interested?"

I looked at Beth. She shrugged.

"They serve beer?" I said.

"Longnecks, mate."

"Music?"

"A jukebox from heaven. Nothing from after 1967. Five plays a buck."

"Sounds about right," I said.

So that's what we did, the three of us. Skink drove us down to some red-painted shack on the bay with brown paper on the tables, where we pounded on the hard shells with our hammers and ate till our fingers bled. Skink lit a cigar and told us stories, Beth cracked jokes, I drank beer enough so the sea shifted and the land heaved and the sun dropped low over the water. It was a night of celebration and camaraderie, of noisy arguments with the blowhards at the next table, of sadness and hilarity, of Skink baring his teeth in laughter. Elvis was on the jukebox, and so was Louis Armstrong, blowing the blues, and by the end the brown paper was covered with bits of red shell and long-necked bottles, cobs shorn of corn, a cigar butt, all in an evocative pattern that would have made Joseph Cornell proud. It was a lovely evening, proof that life could be more than the sordid adventure we had just passed through, a lovely evening, perfect enough to almost make me forget.

Almost.

I AWOKE with a start from my sleep. I sat up on the living room couch, scratched, looked around. In the dim city light slipping through the slats of my shade, the apartment looked old and hard, lonely. I had been there too long to be objective enough to figure what it said about my life, but somehow, now, it seemed lonelier than it should.

Then I noticed that the chain latch of my front door, the chain I fastened each night out of habit, was hanging loose.

Guy had done it again, left me like a thief in the middle of the night. This time I didn't scour the apartment frantically for him, this time I didn't desperately work out where he was headed. This time I knew. I rinsed my face in cold water, I put on a pair of jeans and a white tee shirt, my raincoat, took a six of Rolling Rock out of my fridge, and headed out after him.

He had just been released and didn't know yet where he wanted to go, so I had volunteered my place for a few nights while he decided. He was through as a lawyer, his felony conviction on fraud would see to that, and his marriage was broken, though not irretrievably, as Leila remained forever stalwart. There were more questions than answers in his future, which might have been the best thing he had going for him. But he seemed dazed when he stepped out of the prison, justifiably confused and angry, having been accused of murdering his lover and forced to defend himself without ever yet having been given the opportunity to mourn. He just needed time, he told Leila, who was standing outside the prison yard with me, and I assumed that after having spent six months sleeping on a prison cot, he needed a full-size bed, too. Which is why I was sleeping on the couch when I awoke with a start to discover him gone.

The houses all along the fine suburban street where I found him were well lit, all but one. Their outside lamps were shining, and within the ambit of those lights families were sleeping, parents were holding one another, kids were snug in their beds, all asleep, all preparing for the next day of their lovely lives. Work, school, friends, family, good food, fast food, noisy triumphs, quiet defeats, hope, hope. Life was waiting for those asleep in the confines of those houses, all but one.

Hailey Prouix's house was dark as death.

Guy Forrest sat on the steps in front of her house, the same step, in fact, on which I found him the night of Hailey Prouix's murder. I didn't say a word as I walked up, sat down beside him, twisted a beer free from its plastic noose. He didn't say a word when he took it, just gave me a glance like he had been expecting me. I took a beer for myself. Two soft exhalations as we popped the tops. We sat there together on the steps and quietly drank.

Her house had been scrubbed of blood, and scrubbed again, and still it lay fallow. But not for long. With the trial now over, a sign would soon sprout on its lawn and a lockbox with a key would blossom from the knob of its front door. Realtors would drive their Lexuses to the curb and bring their clients in for a look. The first few might come with a morbid interest, getting a glimpse for themselves of where the mattress lay on the floor, where the woman lay on the mattress, from where the shots were fired. But then the curiosity seekers would disappear and the young couples would arrive. They'd hear the whispers and smile, knowing that an unsavory past would lower the price. One of those couples would discuss it long and hard and then make a lowball offer that would be quickly accepted. After closing, the couple would scrub it down for the umpteenth time, strip the floors, paint, lay wall-to-wall and buy a big sleigh bed for the master bedroom where they'd make love with the wild freedom allowed young marrieds with no children to knock late at night on their bedroom door. Later they'd paint the second bedroom a sweet powder blue, buy a crib, set up a black-and-white mobile to catch their new baby's attention. They'd bring the bundle home and spend their nights pacing the upstairs hall-way in a vain attempt to get the baby to sleep, and in their love and exhaustion the warmth of family would fill the house and scrub away the blood far more efficiently than the toughest wire brush or harshest chemical cleanser.

But all that awaited still in the future. Now, as Guy and I sat on the steps, Hailey Prouix's house was dark, dark as death, and for that I think we both were grateful.

"I dream about her," he said softly, finally, after a long silence. "I dream I'm holding her, I'm kissing her, I'm making love to her. Sometimes in the middle of the night I smell her in the air, and my heart leaps."

"I know."

"You do, don't you, you son of a bitch?"

I didn't say anything. What could I say?

"Let me have another."

The scrape of his nail on the metal top, the quick exhalation of the gas. The desperate gulping, as if there were something more than beer in the can.

"What am I going to do?" he said.

"You can stay with me for as long as you need to."

"And then what?"

"Anything."

"Or nothing."

"Guy. You have to move forward."

"Forward to where?"

"It's up to you. Remember the old proverb, 'In crisis there is op-portunity.' "

"That's what you have for me, some old Chinese proverb?"

"I think it was Kennedy who said it, actually."

"Shut up."

"But he was indeed speaking of the Chinese word."

"Just shut up."

"All right."

"I thought she would save me, Victor. I thought it would save me. I sacrificed everything I had for love, absolutely everything, my family, my future. It demanded everything, and that's what I gave it, and I thought then it would save me."

"Well, there was your problem right there."

"You don't believe in love?"

"I suppose I do, like I believe in television, or the interstate highway system, but neither of them is going to save me, and I don't expect love to either."

"You're just being a hard-ass."

"You abdicated your life to love because that meant you didn't have to take responsibility for your own failures. You thought this thing you craved would swoop down and save you."

"It wasn't a thing."

"There's no difference. A big TV. An SUV. Someone new to love. It's still something outside yourself, so it will never be enough. There is always more to crave, and more and more. That's the secret, Guy, the terrifying secret. There is nothing big enough to fill the gap. Nothing is coming along to save you. Your only chance is to save yourself."

"How?"

"Figure it out. Your whole life has been a series of blind reactions. The Wild West life leading to the strictures of law, and marriage leading to abandonment of everything for love. Maybe it's time to quit reacting. Maybe it's time to sit down and stop running from where you are and decide instead where it is exactly you want to go."

"Simple as that, is it?"

"Sure. But whatever it is, I have a pretty good idea it starts with your kids."

"I love my kids."

"Then show it. Show them."

"But that means going back to Leila."

"It doesn't have to."

"I don't know if I can go back to her, back to that life."

"Make it new."

"If you have all the answers, why are you so damn miserable?"

"Faulty execution."

We both laughed and then sat quietly for a long moment.

"God, but I was happy with her," he said, his sigh coming like an explosion. "There was a time with Hailey when my happiness was perfect. That's what I miss, that feeling, still young, free, in love. It was like a drug. How do I get it back? I need to get it back."

"You don't listen, do you?"

"Tell me about the sister."

"Who? Roylynn?"

"Where is she now?"

"West Virginia."

"Does she look like Hailey?"

"The spitting image."

"What was it like, seeing her?"

"Strange. Affecting. Sad. False."

"Maybe I should meet her, talk to her."

"Why?"

"Just to be considerate. I mean, she lost something, too. I think I should pay my respects. I think I ought to. What do you think?"

"I think you're pathetic."

"Maybe. But still, I don't know. Just to see her. Just to talk. I think I should."

"She's in another world, Guy. That bastard damaged them both, and I don't know who was damaged more, Roylynn in her asylum or Hailey. You have to move forward, you have to find a new life."

"I want what I had."

"You forget quickly, don't you? What you had was dead already."

"You don't know that. I've been thinking about it. We had problems, yes, but I think we could have worked them through."

"Your love was a con from the start."

"Shut up."

"She seduced you for the money. She seduced you because she knew all along that Juan Gonzalez had a preexisting condition that would have destroyed her case."

"Shut up, you bastard."

"Don't you understand what Cutlip did to her? He hurt her so badly, took something so precious from her, that she never recovered. He put a flaw in her heart. She couldn't love, not the way you thought she could. It was never there for her, only for you. It was all in your emotions, not hers."

"You don't know a damn thing. It was real, and it would have lasted. I wouldn't have allowed it to disappear. We would have worked it out."

"Let it go."

"I don't want to let it go."

"Move on."

"I don't know how."

He was right, he didn't know how. But I knew how for him.

I don't know if I would have done it without Roylynn. I remembered her, so heartbreakingly beautiful, sitting in the golden glow at her asylum, and I remembered how I felt when I saw her. He would feel it, too, I was certain. If he found her, which wouldn't be so difficult and which he seemed inclined to do, he would feel it, too. *She's in me*, she had said about her sister, *she always has been. I can feel her breath in my breath, her touch in my touch. When I look into a mirror, I see two faces. When I speak, I hear two voices.* What would happen if he went to Roylynn? What would it draw out of him? Whatever he felt would have nothing to do with the lovely woman with her slim black physics book, but it would be real to Guy, and the damage it could cause was hard to predict. Reverend Henson had told me to leave her be, and though I had ignored him, he was right. She didn't need to be further haunted by the ghosts of her sister's past. And neither did Guy.

"Remember our theory, the other-lover theory?" I said.

"Sure."

"Remember how neatly it worked? The other lover had been given a key for assignations. The other lover had been shown your gun so he knew where it was. It explained all the facts in evidence, how the killer could do what he did."

"I remember. It was my theory. I almost had to throttle you to get you to argue it. So?"

"So, since we know that Bobo was trying to kill you and instead killed Hailey, how do we explain those facts now?"

"Who cares?"

"There was no break-in, so how did Bobo get a key? There was no evidence of a mad search of the closets, so how did Bobo know where to find the gun? How did Bobo know to climb the stairs in the dark and turn to the left in the dark and find the mattress right there, on the floor, in the dark, the mattress where you would have been sleeping if you had been sleeping? How did Bobo even know where you lived?"

"Cutlip must have known."

"How? He'd never been to Philly."

"What are you trying to tell me here, Victor?"

"I'm trying to tell you to think it through."

"I don't want to think it through."

"You want to live your life turned around, wallowing in the past. Fine. Wallow. Think it through."

"Stop it."

"Think it through, Guy, and then tell me how true and perfect was the love you had with Hailey Prouix."

"I don't believe you. I don't believe a word."

"Don't take my word on it," I said. "Just think it through."

The questions I had just asked him were the same questions I had climbed the stairs of the SeaBright Motel to put to Dwayne Joseph Bohannon, and why I had wanted to go in there alone. At first I intended to trick him into a confession. That was why I had brought the tape recorder. But the sight of his gentle circling and self-flayed flesh had changed my plans. It wasn't a confession anymore I was seeking when I entered that room, but still I had questions that needed answers. I was hoping for some explanation other than the one I had developed, desperate for some innocuous answer that had been eluding me. Instead he showed me a scene different from what I imagined, more painful, more pathetic, more heartbreaking. It chokes me now to even conjure it.

Henderson, Nevada. A private room at the Desert Winds. Cutlip sits in his chair, sitting as tall as his withered frame will allow, staring down. Dwayne stands beside him. And curled on the floor, like a little girl lost, in tears, like a girl facing punishment, curled on the floor is Hailey Prouix. I remember her always so strong, in control, always the master of the situation, so I find this tableau incomprehensible. I had expected to find Hailey the manipulator, the plotter, the Hailey that I knew, but I believed Bobo, every word, and so she is on the floor, in tears, begging. Begging? Begging that he not demand this of her. Begging him to leave her finally alone. But Cutlip isn't listening, like he's never listened. *You been a bad girl*, he tells her, like he's told her before, hundreds of times before. *You done let it climb out of control. And now there's trouble, and someone need clean up the mess. He'll take ever thing we have, ever damn thing. But I know how to handle peckerheads like that. You've been a bad girl, and once again I need clean up your mess. Like before. For twenty-five years that's all I done. But this is it, no more after this, I'm too tired, too sick. My love can only stretch so far. No, don't be going on like that. I always know'd what you needed before, and I know this time, too. Now, you tell Bobo here where he hides that gun you told me about. You tell Bobo what we need know and your daddy'll take care of it, just like I always done before.*

Hailey Prouix.

Even before Bobo confirmed it, I knew in my heart that Hailey was part of the plot to kill Guy. A final sacrifice, a final offering to the destructive love, the Shiva of her emotions, that incomprehensible thing between her and her uncle that warped her and defined her at the same time, one final unspeakable act to end it once and for all.

She was so happy that last day of her life, so relieved. The night before, I was to be her alibi. She had expected to return home and find Guy dead on the mattress. Guy had said she was startled to see him at home, and I'm sure she was, having braced herself for the sight of her bloodied and dead fiancé. And then, assuming that Bobo had backed out of the killing, relief fell upon her like a prayer. Then and there she decided to leave Guy, to do the right way what she was letting Cutlip do the worst way—the troubles, the money, the scandal be damned. That was why she was so happy that last day, why our lovemaking was so joyful and expectant, why the possibilities seemed suddenly so verdant.

And so she had ended it with Guy, that very night, and was lying in bed with a fresh bruise and a fresher future, when she heard the front door of the house open, and she knew, immediately, who it was. Bobo. He hadn't given up, he had simply gotten the day wrong or, scared off by the traffic ticket, had delayed a day, not thinking it mattered. And now here he was searching for the gun. And now here he was coming toward her step by step. And now the past that she had thought she had shucked forever just the night before was climbing up the stairs.

It is impossible to know what was darting through her mind at that very moment. Sadness, fear, disgust, despair, relief? Was she thinking of her father and the way he deserted her those many years ago by his death? Was she thinking of the dark nights when her uncle crept into her room? Was she thinking of Jesse Sterrett and the way he was murdered and how she protected her uncle while she used her lover's death to get herself out of Pierce? Was she thinking of me? It is impossible to know what was darting through her mind, but we do know what she did as Bobo approached. She didn't shout, she didn't rise and send him away, she didn't pull Guy from the bathtub to protect her, she didn't call for the police. What she did instead was lift the comforter high over her head so that Bobo wouldn't know for sure who was beneath, so that Bobo would think it was the original target, so that Bobo would take the gun and fire into the mattress and end it all.

She wasn't the first Prouix sister to try to kill herself, but she was the one who succeeded.

There were moments when I had imagined I understood Hailey Prouix, and, to be fair, not all of those moments were in the depths of sex when understanding flows like cheap champagne through the overheated synapses of the brain. There were moments when I felt a deep connection with her, moments when I believed I caught a glimpse of the interiors beneath her lovely shell. There were moments, God help me, when I thought the solution to Hailey's sadness might just be me.

And now, sitting in the dark on the steps of the house in which she died, sitting beside another of her lovers, all I knew with certainty was how little of her I understood. What is love when it is based on myth, on a false image, on the lies we tell ourselves? What is love when the imagined object of the emotion bears no relation to actuality? Can that even be love at all?

I didn't have any answers, but by believing I loved her I had convinced myself I understood her, and in so doing I had failed her. If I had the least inkling of what she'd been through, maybe I could have done something, said something, forced something, maybe I could have changed everything. But of course I did not. I had deluded myself that I understood, when in reality I understood nothing.

Nothing.

"Oh, my God," said Guy in a moan of recognition. He was thinking it through, we were thinking it through, and it would take us both a very long time.